John Bainbridge is the author of over thirty books, including several crime novels and thrillers, as well as non-fiction and topographical books about Britain. He has also written widely for newspapers and magazines. John read literature and history at the University of East Anglia. In his spare time John likes to wander on foot through the countryside. In the past he has gained experience of fighting with swords and traditional archery. He once spent a year living wild in an English woodland - which he says gave him a better understanding of how medieval outlaws survived. *Loxley* - complete in itself - is the first in a four-part sequence *The Chronicles of Robin Hood.*

By the same author

Fiction
The Shadow of William Quest
A Seaside Mourning
A Christmas Malice
Balmoral Kill

Non-Fiction
The Compleat Trespasser
Footloose with George Borrow
Rambling – The Beginner's Bible
Easy British Bakes and Cakes

Loxley – The Chronicles of Robin Hood was first published in Great Britain in 2015 by Giles and Bentley.

ISBN-13:978-1511774376

ISBN-10:1511774371

LOXLEY

The Chronicles of Robin Hood

John Bainbridge

Giles & Bentley

CHRONICLE THE FIRST

One

It was the noise of an arrow.

That was for sure. Somewhere ahead and in the distance, like a sudden echo of wind at the tail end of a gust. Where it came from and where it went was unclear. But it was there. Unmistakable to a man who had spent all of his life using a longbow.

He reined in the horse and glanced all around. The trees bore the delicious early leaves of the first day of May. He could scarce see the blue of the sky above the canopy of branches and boughs that overhung the rough track heading south and east towards Nottingham. It was, he thought, the best time of the year to be riding through Sherwood.

And then the sound came again. Closer now, ahead and to the left. He dismounted and led the horse away from the track, down a winding side path leading into the oaks and beeches. The ground beyond rose sharply into a wooded hillside. He tethered the horse and took off the bow and quiver of arrows that had been fastened at the back of the saddle.

Then he sat on a grassy mound and waited. For a few moments the forest was quiet. The birdsong resumed and there was the sharp rattle of a woodpecker attacking a tree.

And then there were other noises, somewhere along the track beneath him, shouts and then an anguished cry. Not far ahead on the old track to Nottingham, not more than a few hundred yards. Angry voices. And then the whining pitch of someone pleading for mercy. The horseman was familiar with the tone of a desperate man. It was one of the more common sounds of King Richard's England.

He untethered the horse and turned its head back towards the main track, holding the bow and an arrow on the saddle in front of him. As he reached the road to Nottingham the sounds came again. A man laughed and jeered. Then the hurried pleading came again. A man frantic beyond measure begging in a voice that got louder and louder. A voice on the edge of screaming.

He turned a corner of the road and saw the little party ahead of him. Four men standing on the track. A fifth sitting against the bole of a battered oak, his hands clasped together, almost as though in prayer. A small fire was burning opposite the prisoner. Nearby, on the ground, was a bow and a handful of arrows.

The four foresters looked up as they heard the beat of the horse's hooves on the hard ground of the track. The horseman saw the men glance at each other and then string themselves out across his path. He stopped a few yards in front of them.

One of the men stepped forward and touched his forehead, looking admiringly at the horse.

'A fine mount, my lord...' he began. He grinned a wide smile of brown teeth, little different in colour from the scraggly beard surrounding his mouth. The horseman noticed that the man's hand was playing with the hilt of his sword. 'But the bow, my lord? Not the weapon of a gentleman, surely?'

'It suits me...' was the reply.

'I'm sure you're aware my lord that only nobility and sworn foresters may carry a bow in a royal forest?'

'I might be King Richard,' said the horseman.

The man laughed and turned to the others, 'A gentleman of good humour, fellows...' he said.

He turned back to look up at the man on the horse. 'But not I think the King. For one thing he's fighting those upstart bastards in Normandy and for another, well, I've seen Lionheart. An older man than you and stockier. I stood not a yard away from Richard when he came to Nottingham, before he set out on his great journey to take Jerusalem.'

'You mix in exalted circles...'

'I do indeed,' said the man. 'And why should I not? My lord the Sheriff made me the head forester of Sherwood some eight years gone.' He stuck out his chest. 'A position of great and royal responsibility.'

'It is indeed,' the horseman replied. 'And may I know your name?'

'William a' Trent, my lord. And your own?'

The horseman didn't reply, but raised himself in the saddle to look over the heads of the foresters at the man crouched by the tree.

'Who's that?' he asked.

'A poacher of the king's deer,' one of the foresters replied, turning to give the prisoner a kick.

'You ill-use him,' said the horseman. 'Where's the deer he poached?'

The foresters laughed.

'His arrows missed,' said Trent. 'He was ever a bad poacher.'

'Then he's known to you?'

'The weaselly little bastard's name is Much, son of the miller at Grimston. He lives in a hovel not a mile away.'

'Why is he not working in his father's mill? Grimston's a good twelve-mile off?'

'The mill no longer stands,' said Trent. 'The Sheriff had it burned to the ground...'

'And the miller?'

'Hanged, my lord. I swung him myself from the Grimston Oak. The man was a rebel, always urging the villagers to fight the lawful taxes. And a better poacher than his son, forever at the royal deer...'

'Do you intend to hang the son?'

Trent pointed an arm in the direction of the fire.

'We're not heathens, my lord,' he protested. 'Poaching alone doesn't bring about a hanging. The penalty is mutilation. We're heating an iron in the fire so that we might burn out his eyes. We'll castrate him then and set him loose to wander in the forest.'

The other foresters grinned as they looked down at their prisoner.

'And who has decreed such a punishment?'

Trent looked up at him as though the horseman was simple.

'My lord the Sheriff,' he said. 'It's the only punishment that curbs the poaching in Sherwood. And it's the law as decreed by the late King Henry.'

'Then I'm sure you are aware that King Richard relaxed the forest laws at the time of his coronation, at the express request of his mother, Queen Eleanor? This man should be taken to Nottingham and put on trial.'

Trent gave a hearty burst of laughter. 'What's the merit in that, my lord? It'll only delay matters. My lord the Sheriff will only give the same ruling. Besides, we take no notice here of the yearnings of a senile old hag like Eleanor – the Sheriff's very words...'

'I bet he wouldn't dare utter them in the presence of Lionheart?'

'Richard's a long way away. And given his folly in battle he may never return.'

The horseman sprang lightly from his horse.

'I think I may have a rest from my riding,' he said, 'and a drink of water.' He looked across at Trent. 'Those words you just said... You know that contemplating the King's death is treason?'

'At the court, maybe. But we're not at the court. These are the depths of Sherwood.'

'Treason is treason,' said the horseman. 'But then I'm no admirer of Lionheart myself, so your words, as far as I'm concerned, are lost on the trees.'

Trent gave a slight bow.

'Your lordship is gracious,' he said. 'But I'd be honoured to know your name?'

The horseman ignored the question

'You say this Much missed the deer?'

'There are better archers in the shire...'

'Then he has committed no offence of poaching?'

'Ah, but the intent was there. That's all we need. The bow and arrows lying by the track show that he intended to kill the King's deer. And he was carrying them unlawfully into Sherwood.'

The horseman held up his own bow and an arrow.

'As am I?' he said.

'But from the way you speak I can tell you are nobility and not a villein and peasant, my lord.'

The man let out a deep sigh. 'Not a villein,' he replied, 'though my grandfather was, freed from his bondage for saving the life of his lord. But I'm no noble either. Just a freeman. And, by your rules, I am breaking the forest laws...'

Trent shifted uneasily from one foot to another.

'It is so,' he said at last. 'Perhaps you should return to Nottingham with us and let my lord the Sheriff decree the right or the wrong of it.' He nodded in the direction of Much. 'But first we'll blind and castrate this villein...'

'I think not,' said the horseman.

'What?'

'I think you should let him go,' said the horseman. 'He's learned a lesson. That's enough.'

'If you interfere, we may do the same to you...'

The horseman smiled, grasping again the animal's reins.

'I'm going to ride on my journey now,' he said. 'And when I go I intend to take the miller's son with me.'

'You intend to...' Trent turned to one of his men. 'Oswald, put out the prisoner's eyes. I'll castrate him myself.' He turned to the other two. 'You men, take and bind this upstart. The Sheriff can deal with him. If he resists shoot him down.'

One of the men raised his crossbow in the direction of the horseman. But he had hardly brought it to bear before the horseman's arrow thudded into his chest. In little more than a breath, a second arrow cut into the throat of another of the foresters. The horseman threw down the bow and drew his sword in time to ward off a blow towards his head from Trent's sword. He parried the blade and brought the hilt of his own crashing down on Trent's head, sending the man sprawling to the ground.

As he turned he became aware that the forester Oswald had reached down and taken up the fallen crossbow. He charged towards the man who was raising the weapon to fire. But in a second the man began to gasp, dropping the crossbow back on to the ground, his arms flailing in all directions as he struggled to breathe. Much stood behind him putting all his slight weight into pulling the rope that had bound his wrists against the forester's throat.

It was soon over.

The horseman turned again on hearing Trent swear, as he tried to reach out for his sword. He stepped over to his fallen opponent, bringing his foot down on to Trent's hand, his sword pressing firmly against the man's throat. As he looked down he could see fear in the cold grey eyes of the forester.

'Are you going to kill me?' Trent whispered.

The horseman nodded, pulling the brown hood up over the back of his head.

'Yes, but not yet,' he said. 'I want you to take a message for me. To the Sheriff. Tell him that the day is near.'

'What does that mean?'

'He'll know...'

'Who are you?'

The horseman regarded Trent for a while before replying.

'Loxley,' he said at last.

~

'This is a wretched place to live,' said Loxley, looking around the thatched hovel that Much called home. 'Your roof leaks and it stinks like a pig died.'

After the encounter with William a' Trent they had galloped off further down the track to Nottingham, halting briefly at the hut so that the miller's son might gather up a few possessions.

'Best I could do,' Much replied. 'Where else could I live? The Sheriff forbade me a return to Grimston. My father's mill's no more. I live here and work my lord Gisborne's land as a serf. This is common land apart from the forest or I'd not have this...'

'Gisborne?'

'Sir Guy of Gisborne.'

'A Gisborne that used to dwell near Bowland Forest?'

'You know him then?'

'I've... heard of him,' Loxley replied. 'He was in the Holy Land and then Normandy with the King.'

'He's been back now from Normandy a six-month. Broke and in disgrace, they say. King Richard would have no more of him. But the Sheriff will take any turd into his employ. The Sheriff waves a hand and Gisborne enforces his will.'

'Broke but has land?'

'It's how the Sheriff pays him, with a bit of ground here, a village there, and ownership of all the poverty that lives and works the place.'

'So Gisborne's in Nottingham...' Loxley stood in the doorway of the hut, looking across the heath to the edge of the forest. 'Gisborne...'

He turned at last and looked at Much. Trent had been right, the miller's son did look like a weasel with his long nose and pointed pock-marked face.

'And what of you?' he asked. 'Where will you go?'

Much pushed his dirty black hair away from his brow.

'Into the forest,' he said. 'Where else is there for me now? The cry will be out by dusk. Trent will have me outlawed. Made wolfshead. There to be taken by any man for the Sheriff's reward. To live on my wits and the forest game until my luck runs out. Not just mutilation then, but swinging by the neck. Or dead by the quarrel bolt of a crossbow if I put up a fight.'

The little man had wrapped a cloak around him, taken up a longbow and a quiver of arrows and was putting a crust of bread into a sack. He looked around his home for the last time and shrugged.

'Not that I'll miss this. You might as well sleep in the forest for all the shelter this roof gives. I'll not be alone. I've friends in Sherwood. Many a two-legged wolf is there already. These have been hard times. The harvest's failed these five years. What are people to do but poach and steal?'

'I'll go with you to the edge of the forest,' said Loxley.

'The edge of the forest? Don't you see, you'll need to come with me. As sure as hell you'll be wolfshead too by dark. There's foresters dead in Sherwood. Trent attacked and himself another favourite turd of the Sheriff of Nottingham. You must lose the horse and take to foot like me.'

They walked on for a while, Loxley leading the horse. Already the first signs of darkness were making the ground between the trees look dim. It was a long time since Loxley had been in this part of Sherwood, but even as he looked along the track his memory brought back the routes taken by the many tracks and paths. And he recalled the secret ways that led to the forest's far depths, to the hidden places where men seldom went. To the mysterious glades where, it was said, all the devils of hell rode loose.

'Who leads the outlaws in Sherwood?' he asked.

Much laughed for a moment and then looked solemn.

'Nobody *leads* them,' he said. 'They're wolfsheads. They might band together for protection but they go out alone to look for food or someone to rob. Who should lead them? They're outlaws, not men at arms.'

'And one by one they're captured, mutilated, hanged. Made to betray each other in the hope of a mercy that doesn't come. It was ever the way.'

Much nodded. 'And what do you expect of starving and desperate men? The wise ones of the shire went to Normandy with Lionheart, where at least they get food and plunder.'

'Fighting another man's war and not their own!'

Much turned and grabbed Loxley's arms. 'Look, you're a young man. A freeman, not a villein. Even a freeman don't understand how it is for a serf. We're no more than cattle to them who run the land. It's always been so. It'll always be so. It's the way God ordained it. Don't the priests tell us that?'

Loxley laughed.

'I know one that wouldn't. A kirtled brother who'd rip the bellies of the overlords if they said such a thing to him.'

'He must be a rare priest?'

'He is indeed.'

'I know of one like him.'

They had come to a crossroads, the track ahead leading towards Nottingham, the narrower paths on either side soon losing themselves beneath the trees of the forest.

'This is where we part company,' said Loxley. He thought for a moment. 'Much, where can I find you if I need you again?'

'I've a sister. She's married to the man who has the Blue Boar tavern on the highway to Linby. She's safe enough if you want to leave word. Or do you know the great glade in Sherwood, with the great oak? I'll seek shelter there for a few nights. But be wary if you go that way, lest you get an outlaw's arrow in your back. They've a signal for wayfarers they don't know. Put your hood way up over your head and sling your bow over your right shoulder. They may just challenge you then afore they shoot.'

Loxley grasped the older man's hand.

'Take care then, Much. We may meet again...'

'You'd be wiser coming with me.'

'Wiser doesn't change the world.'

'No, but it keeps you alive a tad longer.'

~

A mile further on a side track, marked by a stout oaken cross, led off the Nottingham road, plunging down into a wooded vale. A good path, which was as well for the last of the Mayday light was vanishing above the trees. As the path narrowed, Loxley could hear the sound of running water and could almost smell the freshness of a river.

It was a small building of ancient yellow sandstone, there between the water and the press of oak trees. A chapel of sorts, given the cross carved above the door and the Norman-arched window in the side wall through which candlelight spilled. A donkey grazed in a small paddock outside, looking up at him as he approached before resuming his task of chomping the grass.

Loxley tied the horse to a birch tree and, taking his bow, crept down to the stout wooden door of the chapel. It creaked open, though the noise was almost drowned under the sound of the river. There was the scent of incense but almost darkness beyond. He could make out two smoking candles in the light coming through the doorway. They had been recently extinguished.

Someone had heard him approach.

He rested his bow against the wall, reaching with his right hand across his chest to touch the hilt of his sword. He leaned into the cold stone on one side of the arch before stepping forward a pace. It was all so quiet, the cry of the river hushed by the thickness of the old walls.

Loxley eased the sword from the scabbard and held the weapon out in front of him. He walked away from the door allowing the last of the evening light to penetrate the gloom.

A step forward.

And then...

A great arm encircled him from the rear, trapping the sword against his chest, and he felt a man's hot breath against the nape of his neck. Loxley instinctively raised his head as he felt the cold blade of a dagger pressing against his throat.

Two

Robert de Lisle felt uneasy.

Mayday should have been a time for joy but his mind wandered, even as his eyes took in the boisterous revelry of the May evening. The platter of meat lay untouched on the long table in front of him, the flagon of ale, a particular favourite, scarcely tasted. To both sides of him his fellows laughed and jeered as the tumblers finished their performance with a sprawling fall across the hard stone floor of the great hall, sending a burst of noisy jollity echoing through the corridors and right out on to the battlements of Nottingham Castle.

He hardly looked up as the master of the revels stood before him and announced the next entertainment. A wrestling match between a red-haired giant, newly arrived from Hathersage, and his own champion Arthur a' Bland, an over-muscular tanner from the town. The crowds in the great hall gathered around to watch the contest on three sides only, leaving a clear view for their betters who were sitting and feasting at the table beyond the great fireplace.

There was silence then and he couldn't understand why. Robert de Lisle looked up to see a great crew of faces gazing expectantly up at him. So deep was he in his own thoughts that he looked back at them almost in puzzlement. And then he realised that he was expected to give permission for the bout to commence.

He waved an arm. There was a great cheer and the two half-naked wrestlers went at each other like charging stags, chests crashing, arms enfolding and each trying to gain a purchase on the other's shoulder so that there might be a throw to the floor.

The noise from the crowd almost deafened him and took away the concerns that plagued his mind. He was obliged to watch the wrestling, a favourite entertainment of his, even though this night his heart wasn't in it. It was an exciting tournament, for the two big men were well matched, though there was more brawn than skill to the fight.

But de Lisle thought that the result was predictable. Arthur a' Bland was the champion of the shire and had never been defeated. And that was the way the wagers were going. He glanced sideways along the table and watched in distaste as coins were slid along the planks from one end to the other. Robert de Lisle favoured wrestling as a skill and not just an entertainment on which money might be gambled.

As he watched he saw the giant from Hathersage thrown half across the room. The Nottingham tanner seemed to be on his usual good form. Robert de Lisle nodded appreciatively in his direction. The tanner nodded back and then launched himself in a dashing leap at his opponent.

And it was at that point that his fortunes changed. The Hathersage giant stepped swiftly to one side, grasping the tanner's right arm and swinging him round so that he crashed against the wall. And then, taking in a mighty breath, he grasped the tanner, one massive arm over the man's shoulder and the other under his thighs. With a great bellow he raised the tanner high above his head and, after what seemed to be an age to the moaning onlookers, sent him crashing to the floor. The man from Hathersage gave a wild cry as he launched himself through the air, crashing down on the tanner's chest. The Nottingham wrestler's arms splayed out as he gave a terrific groan, his head falling back to slap against the ground.

The crowd began to moan and mutter at the defeat of their champion. Robert de Lisle heard the man next to him, a landowner from Newark, moaning that the wrestling move had been unfair, firstly to the men seated the other side of him along the table, and then to him directly.

'A foul and craven move!' He breathed his rancid breath into de Lisle's face. 'Don't you agree, my lord Sheriff? A foul and craven move?'

The Sheriff turned his head away.

'No, I do not agree. There are no rules in our wrestling. Every man fights in the best way he knows. I'm sorry you've lost your wager, but the contest stands.'

'But my lord...'

'It stands...'

The Sheriff of Nottingham got up from the bench and made his way around the table, summoning the wrestlers to him with a gesture of his hand. The Hathersage giant had helped Arthur a' Bland to his feet and aided him the few yards to where de Lisle stood.

Robert de Lisle looked up into the stranger's face.

'Your name?' he asked.

'John Little of Hathersage, my lord Sheriff.'

'Little? What a name, my lords,' he said, with a gesture to the top table. His words were greeted with a burst of laughter.

'They told me I was to fight *Little* John,' Arthur a' Bland grunted. 'I thought it might be an easy match. But this *Little John* beats me by half a foot...'

'You bear no grudges?' asked de Lisle.

'My lord Sheriff, if I could have lifted this giant in the same way then I would have done so. I'm a strong man, but this man is a Hercules. I salute him and look forward to the day when I might wrestle with him again.'

'Good words,' said the Sheriff. 'And for those generous words I'll give you the same purse.' He turned to the tanner. 'Go and get your cuts and bruises dressed. Then help yourself to some ale and venison.'

Arthur a' Bland bowed and walked away. John Little turned to follow him, but the Sheriff raised a hand, cautioning him to stay.

'Are you a free man or a villein?' he asked.

'A villein, my lord, in the service of Sir Hugh Courtenay of Hathersage. But my master allows me to wander for wrestling matches, at the cost of half my purse on each triumph.'

'Rather an unfair agreement. I know your master. He's a spindly little wretch who'd faint at the sight of a bloody fist or a sword. Don't look embarrassed, John Little. Heed my words.'

'I know not what to say, my lord.'

'Then say nothing. But listen to me further. I hold Nottingham for the King's brother, Count John of Mortain. I have his ear. I can grant you your freedom at any moment. If you consent to work for me.'

'My lord?'

'You are too great a man to remain a villein all your life. I need men, strong men, in my employ. Men who are able to mix with the poverty out in the Sherwood villages. Someone like themselves. Only *not* like themselves, if you see what I mean...'

'I think I do...'

'And there's not just freedom in it but gold too. Far in excess of the purse I've given you tonight.' The sheriff pulled at his neat beard. 'I can send word to Sir Hugh right now... if you agree?'

The great man considered for a moment.

'I think I might...' he said at last.

'Then come to see me first thing in the morning. I'll tell my clerk to expect you.'

John Little gave a bow and turned to walk away.

'Little!'

The Sheriff called him back.

'My lord.'

'Tell nobody of our discussion.'

'No, my lord.'

The Sheriff watched as the huge man walked out of the hall. A promising development, he thought. Even better than...

'My lord Gisborne...'

A voice had whispered into his ear the very words he had been thinking. He turned to find the captain of the guard at his elbow.

'What was that?'

'My lord Gisborne has returned,' said the captain.

'And not before time,' the Sheriff grunted.

~

'Easy to slice open your throat,' said the voice, with as much humour as threat in the tone. 'What sort of man comes into my chapel so late in the evening?'

The blade rubbed menacingly up and down against Loxley's skin.

'I've come to murder the priest and lay the place bare,' Loxley muttered. 'I'm a ravager from the north.'

'I had to kill the last ravager that came this way...' The knife was taken away and the grip of the mighty arm loosened. 'A skulking rogue like you once tipped me into that river out there.'

'And as I recall you threw the rogue over your shoulder and half-drowned him in its weeds...'

'I expected you sooner, Robin...'

Loxley turned and looked into the merry face of the fat monk.

'You've been dining well on the King's deer, Tuck.'

'Not just his deer,' muttered Tuck. 'His coneys too. And his fish. Blast me if Lionheart can't spare a few offerings for a humble brother...'

'They'll still hang you. Benefit of clergy or not. And I hear tales of a monk who goes up Barnsdale way and robs travellers?'

'The villain!'

'It's no wonder the abbot threw you out of Fountains Abbey.'

'He had no sense of humour...'

'I'm told he caught you out whoring?'

'A blasted lie!'

'Gluttony then?'

'Well... that can't be denied.'

'And you ignored the Rule and lay abed all through the services...'

The monk drew a hand over his tonsured head.

'Eating does make you very sleepy.'

Loxley looked around the tiny stone chapel.

'So now you guard the bones of Saint Withburga?'

'Martyred at this very place,' said Tuck, 'her bones lie in the altar yonder. Put your hands in those hollows and the touch of her will heal the leprosy and any other ill that happens to plague you.'

'I'm told she was martyred elsewhere and that those are the bones of a dead sheep!'

'Pilgrims bring a certain amount of faith with them to my lonely cell...' said Tuck, scratching his head.

'And do all of their offerings make their way into the coffers of the mother church?'

'Some... after a deduction of expenses. I do have to fund my work amongst the poor...'

Loxley sat down at a table against the wall and poured two flagons of ale from a large earthenware jug. The monk relit the candles.

'And have there been any other travellers passing through Sherwood?' he asked.

The monk sank down the ale in one great gulp before he replied.

'The Abbot of St. Mary's was robbed by outlaws on the Newark road only this morning. And an hour or two ago Gisborne was to be seen riding fast to Nottingham with fifty men. How are matters in Loxley?'

There was a long silence.

'My village has gone,' Loxley said at last. 'Gisborne had a busy time burning down every last home. Many were killed and the rest pursued into Loxley Chase. The rebellion didn't last very long.'

'Bastard!' said Tuck as he crossed himself. 'You would have been wiser to ride in another direction, Robin. Sherwood is alive with gossip. Much of it about you. It would be unwise to ride on to Nottingham.'

'I have business there...'

Tuck reached out to fling a log into the tiny fireplace.

'The Sheriff knows you are coming. The thought of your arrival plagues his mind. You may as well let me kill you now...'

'Is Alan at Nottingham yet?'

'Our minstrel warbles in the great hall of the castle. A favourite of the Sheriff, they say. Such a soothing voice, there in the background. I've never known a man who could sing and listen so well at the same time.'

'They've no suspicion of him?'

Tuck laughed. 'Blast me, why should they? Minstrels are ten a penny and my lord the Sheriff is fond of his entertainment and can hum a good tune himself. It's from Alan that I know they talk of you being in Sherwood. But these are just rumours. There are always tales of a hooded man riding through the forest. The Sheriff's soldiers see a thousand phantoms behind every oak.'

Loxley drained his flagon and stood in the doorway of the monk's cell. Darkness had come to Sherwood and he could hardly see the trees on the far side of the little river. His horse whinnied companionably at the monk's little donkey.

'I believe they know without a shadow of a doubt that I've come to Sherwood.'

Tuck frowned.

'What are you not telling me?' he asked.

Loxley recounted his adventure of the day.

'Much, the son of the miller? Aye, I know the poxy little rascal. Not worth the saving, Robin. He's a man born to hang. Better to get it over with than find yourself dancing in the air alongside him.'

Robin of Loxley poured more ale into the flagons.

'Tell me about the outlaws?' he said.

Tuck raised despairing hands to the roof.

'What is there to tell? Outlaws are outlaws. They skulk for a month or two in Sherwood. Then they're caught to hang or put against a tree to meet the bolt from a crossbow. They band together for warmth. Poach the deer, rob travellers, some of whom deserve to be robbed, many who don't. Being made wolfshead just postpones the inevitable death, which is the fate of them all.'

'Sherwood has a foul reputation for being lawless,' said Robin. 'Well, that was the tale in Loxley.'

'Five years of poor harvests have sent many a villein into the forest. Gisborne would outlaw every villager if he had his way. Only the better sanity of the Sheriff prevails. He sees the need to have his poverty actually working the land.'

'And they don't rebel?' asked Robin.

'Hard to think of rebellion with an empty belly and nowhere to hide. But the Sheriff fears revolt. It's the one reason he reins in Gisborne. It's why he has the terrors at the thought of you coming back to Sherwood.'

Robin gazed into the fire making pictures in the flames. It had been a long day and a great weariness had come upon him with great suddenness. The monk had lowered his head and was starting to snore. Outside the donkey brayed in the darkness and an owl called. The candles guttered into extinction.

An hour later Robin of Loxley watched the fire die as well. He pulled the hood over his head for warmth. The movement of the bench awakened Tuck.

His eyes searched the darkness, coming to rest at last upon his visitor.

'Ah, so a hooded man has come to the forest. You've killed three of the King's foresters and humiliated William a' Trent. The Sheriff fears you and Gisborne craves your blood. There's not a wolf in Sherwood will be sought with the ferocity that they'll have in mind for you, Loxley.'

~

'Loxley is dead, my lord Sheriff.'

'Is that so?' said de Lisle, looking up across the table at the tall, dark soldier in chain mail who stood before him. 'And when exactly did he die, Gisborne?'

'At Loxley, my lord. He died as we burned the village. Sent tumbling backwards into one of their foul huts. A crossbow bolt in his breast. And his rebellion has been put down entirely.'

'Go on...'

'There's not a house left in the place. All gone. The ringleaders of the revolt are dead. And Loxley was seen falling back through one of the doorways before the place was consumed by flames.'

'You saw Loxley die yourself?'

'Yes, my lord...'

De Lisle stood and walked across to the fireplace. He gazed down into the night ashes for a moment before replying.

'You're a fool, Gisborne!'

'My lord?'

'A bloody fool!'

'I don't understand?'

'Do you believe in phantoms, Gisborne?'

'Well, I...'

'I do not, Gisborne.' De Lisle almost spat the other man's name. 'I believe that the dead are safely ensconced in heaven or hell. I don't accept that they walk the earth.'

'But...'

The Sheriff walked over and leaned forward on to the table, his face no more than a few inches from Gisborne's own.

22

'Watch my lips, Gisborne. And listen to my words very carefully,' he said. 'If Loxley is dead how could it be that he was in Sherwood this very day? How did it happen that he set free a poacher, humiliated Trent and killed three of my men? How is it that a dead man can wield a sword and shoot a longbow?'

'I'm at a loss, my lord...'

'You usually are, Gisborne, you usually are.'

'I saw him fall...'

'Don't lie to me!'

The sudden raging shout echoed up into the rafters of the great hall.

'Did you hope that he would slink into the greenwood and be heard of no more? Did you imagine that you could come back to Nottingham with such a ridiculous tale and be rewarded with yet more of my gold? Is it any wonder that Lionheart banished you from Normandy?'

'My lord!'

'You are trying my patience, Gisborne. I let you come to Nottingham and gave you employment, aye, and against my better judgement. Count John suggested that I show you some favour, despite the fact that his brother Lionheart held you in such contempt. I heeded his recommendation. To my cost.'

Gisborne drew a hand across his brow. 'I've been charged with a very great task, my lord. This is a lawless shire. I need more time. I need more men.'

De Lisle let out a great breath.

'We do not have time,' he said. 'Every day there are more outlaws in Sherwood. The King's absence in Normandy encourages rebellion and the very lawlessness you talk of. And when I give you men you have an unpleasant habit of getting them killed.'

'These are violent times...'

De Lisle gave him a dangerous smile.

'They are indeed, Gisborne,' he said. 'But isn't it strange that while your men fall like ninepins at a village fair, you always come safely home?'

Gisborne crashed a fist on to the table.

'You have no right to question my courage, my lord.'

'I have every right,' the Sheriff said. 'You are in my pay, Gisborne. You are my servant. I gave you work when no other lord would.' He waved an arm. 'Let's admit it, Gisborne. You are a broken knight. Nobody wants you. You've gambled all your Bowland lands away with a few throws of the dice. The King came close to taking off your head. Without me you have nothing.'

Gisborne was silent for a moment before he replied.

'I've been unfortunate,' he said at last. 'It's not easy for a poor knight to prosper in these times. I went on the crusade at my own expense. And I fought hard, yes, almost to the gates of Jerusalem. And I would have got inside the gates if King Richard's nerve had held. Lionheart always despised my courage. He wanted no one to be braver than himself. That was the reason for our falling out in Normandy.'

'What a warrior you are, Gisborne!'

'I'll deal with Loxley. And with the outlaws in Sherwood. I'll rid the shire of these vermin...'

'See that you do, Gisborne,' said de Lisle, 'though I confess I've heard these vows before. Oft times you promise me mountains and deliver but molehills. I brought you here to hunt down my enemies. Now go and do it.'

The knight stood for a moment as though he wanted to say more, but seeing the implacable look in the Sheriff's eyes turned and marched away. De Lisle went back to the last of the fire and held out his hands for warmth. It was a while before he noticed William a' Trent cowering in the corner by the oak door.

'Ah, Trent,' said the Sheriff. 'I'll not trouble to ask how one villain could overpower you and slay three foresters. I'll give you the opportunity for vengeance.'

Trent knuckled his forehead.

'I want you to go down to the kitchens, Trent,' de Lisle continued. 'You'll find a giant feasting there. A villein named John Little. Bring him before me right now. Tell him... tell him I have a task for him to undertake.'

Three

They came fast.

Three horsemen, two swinging swords at their side, the third low in the saddle and bearing a lance.

Fast and deadly.

Fast and deadly from three different directions

It had been an hour since Loxley had left the monk's cell to continue his journey to Nottingham. He had left the horse in Tuck's care. He was afoot and vulnerable, for there were no trees in this part of Sherwood in which a man could seek shelter from charging horsemen. He was halfway across a vast open stretch of heathland when he saw them approach. They had ridden together on the road out of Nottingham. But even as he watched they separated. Riding away from Loxley.

And for a moment he thought they might have no business with him. Then they had turned the heads of their mounts to face him. One in front and the others on either side. There was a pause as though they were simply enjoying the fresh morning air.

And then they had charged, yelling to spur on their horses. Loxley fancied he could feel the vibration of the hooves across the soft ground. They were so close he could see every detail of their faces and clothing. And the look of triumph in their eyes.

He swung the longbow off his shoulder and thanked God that he had not unbent it as he often did when making a long journey. He pulled three arrows from the quiver, jamming two into the soft earth in front of him. He put the third into the bow, raised the weapon very slightly and sent the arrow into flight towards the soldier in front. He didn't pause to see it thud into the man's chest, though he was aware, out of the corner of his eye, of the lance flying through the air. But even as he noted the success of that first shot he had loaded and fired a second arrow at the soldier to his left.

The shot was too speedily done. He saw the arrow tear into the man's right shoulder and heard the soldier give a great cry. A noise which brought the charging horse to a sudden halt.

Even as he turned Loxley knew there would be no time to swing round and fire a third arrow. Instinct made him throw himself to the ground, just as the man's swinging sword, powered by the speed of the horse as well as the practised turn of the sword-arm, cut through the air where his throat had been a second before.

As the horse brushed against his side, Loxley rolled once on the ground and regained his feet. Before the horseman could bring his mount about he had fired the third arrow, square into the soldier's back. The horse came to a halt, its rider dangling down on one side.

Loxley dropped the bow and drew out his sword, for the wounded man was still mounted, head bent forward, walking the horse very slowly towards him. At a glance he could see the other two soldiers dead on the ground.

The stricken soldier came to within a few yards before he dropped his sword and slid down the side of the horse. He tried to stand and made a couple of staggering steps towards Loxley. And then he fell back to the ground, head raised and grasping the arrow in his shoulder. There was a look of desperation on his face as Loxley approached, his eyes never wavering from the sword in the outlaw's hand.

'Who sent you?' Loxley asked.

'Gisborne,' the man gasped, his eyes watering with the pain of his wound.

Loxley nodded towards the distant edge of the heath.

'Is Gisborne out there?' he asked.

'Whoring in Nottingham... he prefers others to do his dirty work.'

'Are there more of you?'

'Gisborne thought three would be enough.'

Loxley examined the man's wound.

'The arrow is not in very deep,' he said. 'I need to pull it out and it will be painful.'

The soldier looked astonished.

'You are not going to finish me off?'

'What would be the point?'

And without giving any warning he yanked the arrow free. The man cried out at the sudden pain, sweat on his brow and blood from a bitten lip streaming down his chin.

'You may yet live,' Loxley continued. 'What is your name?'

'Walter of Thirsk.'

'You're a fair way from home.'

'I haven't seen Thirsk since I was pressed into service when I was thirteen. I was a villein then and I'm a villein now. But soldiers at least have a chance to plunder and add to their wealth.'

'Maybe, though you could seek a better master than Gisborne. I'll dress your wound and put you on your horse. Do you think you can ride back to Nottingham?'

'I feel weak, but that is a good horse. It'll see me home yet.'

Loxley tore some cloth off the soldier's jerkin and bandaged the wound as best he could.

'It's not neat but it should stem the bleeding,' he said. 'Try not to ride against me again. I usually aim my arrows a sight better than that.' A sudden thought occurred. 'Did Gisborne say who I was?'

Walter nodded.

'Aye, he said you were Robin of Loxley.'

'Were you at Loxley village when Gisborne razed the place?'

'God have mercy, but I was spared that. It would've been like putting Thirsk to the torch. Gisborne's a murderous bastard at the best of times. A madman when he's in one of his black moods.'

Loxley helped the soldier on to his horse.

'I'm going into the forest now,' he said. 'You take the road into Nottingham. And may Gisborne and the Sheriff have mercy on you.'

'Amen to that,' Walter replied.

As he brought the horse's head round in the direction of the town, he looked sideways at the outlaw as his sometime enemy picked up his bow and quiver and strode towards the far trees. Loxley pulled up the brown cloth hood as though to shield his head from the increasing glare of the morning sun.

'Robin of Loxley,' Walter muttered as he urged the horse forwards. 'Robin... Robin i' the hood.'

~

Much was drunk and the long and low room of the Blue Boar Tavern seemed to swirl round in a great haze of oblivion as he tried to stand up. The others looked on and laughed at the state of the little man. His sister, married to the landlord, threw up her arms in despair.

'This is folly,' she said at last. She reached down for a bucket of water and emptied it on to Much's head. The tatterdemalion figure poured out a great stream of blasphemous words and fell back on to the bench.

'This is stupidity,' she yelled at the packed room. 'Here you all are, carousing and drunk, and every one of you a wolfshead with money promised to anyone who'll take you to the Sheriff. A hundred men at arms could be outside for all you know. The villages are thronged with treacherous scum who'd betray you. And then where would I be and my good husband. Out in the woods, hiding with you and our thatch fired and that'd be the end of us!'

Much grinned up at her.

'Ah, Moll... Moll,' he said, 'Will Stutely's outside a-keeping watch and a more sober man you... not a drop of ale's touched his lips since his poor wife died. We're safe enough.'

'Aye, and I've heard that so often before. There's many a villager danced on the gallows, convinced they were safe!'

'Sherwood's a big place, Moll. There aren't the men at arms and foresters in the shire to be everywhere. They'll not catch me...'

The room erupted with a great burst of laughter.

'They already have Much,' said a tall red-haired man, more sober than the others, who was sprawled across a bench by the fireplace. 'I hear Trent had you tied like a hog and was heating the irons in the fire.' He brushed back one of his long locks to reveal a vivid red mark on one side of his forehead.

The little man turned to face him.

'You mind your business, Scarlock,' he spluttered. 'I'd a been out of there in a flash even if the stranger hadn't come along.'

'Not what I heard. I heard tell you were trussed proper and just awaiting the moment that Trent would cut your balls off. Perhaps he did! Your voice has been a bit high of late.'

This brought more laughter and a disapproving look from Much's sister.

'Leave him be, Scathlock, or whatever your name is,' she protested. 'And you knows I can't abide coarseness. Save your lewd comments for the forest.'

The man walked across to her, gave a low bow and kissed her hand. 'My apologies, madam. Sometimes I forget I was raised a freeman and a gentleman in the King's service. As for the name, well, I deplore the Scarlock.' His hand strayed upwards to the old wound just below his hairline. 'This scar I got in Normandy and was lucky to live. The mark itself's hard to bear for a man of my vanity. I scare need a baptism from it.'

He smiled, took her hand and kissed it once more.

'My born name is Scadlock, Will Scadlock of Derby, though I accept Scathlock from the drunkards who congregate in this place. But of late I favour Scarlet, particularly when I hear the name on the lips of beautiful women, such as yourself, madam....'

Much's sister, who looked almost as weaselly as her brother, tittered and blushed as Scarlet kissed her hand once more.

'You're a caution...' she simpered. 'You'll have my husband taking you outside for a leathering with all these advances.'

The landlord looked askance at the suggestion, shaking his head and struggling to lift another barrel of ale on to the great serving table which took up much of the room.

'You, Madam, may therefore call me Will Scarlet. Not to be confused with Will Stutely who sits mournfully under an oak tree outside.'

Much fell back on to the bench, his mouth open and his eyes trying to discern the roof through the great cloud of smoke issuing from the fireplace.

'Will this and Will that,' he muttered. 'Isn't a Will a private part? Isn't that a name for it? A man's prick or a woman's...'

'Much!' barked his sister.

Her brother yawned instead of saying the word.

'Just saying...' he added a moment later. 'I've heard Brother Tuck recite from the old ballads where such a thing is mentioned. "Will this and Will that..." He sang the words. "And Will to Will for pleasure..."

Scarlet looked across at the other outlaws.

'Get him out of here and throw him in the pond,' he said.

'Put one Will in another Will and then she'll get your measure...'

He continued the song as two of the men picked him up and hastened him through the door.

'My deepest regrets, madam,' said Scarlet, as the door slammed shut. 'Sherwood Forest makes savages of the best of men.'

'He always had a coarse mouth, Master Scarlet. Even as a boy our father used to wash it out twice a day in the mill pond. Much was for ever blaspheming and oathing and whoring. I think it comes from being born an ugly little turd in an ugly world. Handsome men like you don't need to curse, Master Scarlet. I can see you're every inch a gentleman. You're welcome here anytime. Unlike some!'

Scarlet smiled as he followed the other men out of the tavern. 'If only you knew,' he said quietly to himself. Then he gave a great burst of laughter. The outlaws had taken him at his word and flung Much into the stagnant looking pond on the edge of the nearby green. The little man was coughing and gasping for air, arms flailing as he fought his way up the muddy banks and out on to the grass.

'Don't you fear that the miller's son might stab you in the back?' said a man with long fair hair who was leaning against the tavern wall. 'You bait him too much, Scarlet?'

'It would do you no harm to come into the tavern and get merry on the ale, Will Stutely,' he replied. He turned and rested a hand on Stutely's arm. 'Grief is a terrible thing, my old friend, as I know to my cost. It does no harm to shade its pain with drink... though perhaps not as much as the miller's son puts away.'

'It's not drink I need, Scarlet,' Stutely replied. 'It's vengeance.'

'Your Meg was my sister,' said Scarlet. 'She wouldn't have wanted you to burn inside over her death. Or to risk your life seeking revenge. Haven't you killed enough soldiers?'

'Not the right ones. Not the four men who held her down and took her before they cut her beautiful throat. Norman bastards! I know the four. I know them well. When they're in hell I'll go in the tavern and drink myself into oblivion.'

Scarlet was silent for a moment, remembering the day that Stutely had ran into the village with the news. He recalled how he had clutched the hilt of his own dagger until his palm bled.

He turned to Stutely.

'The afternoon's wearing on, Will. It's time to make our way back into the forest.'

Stutely nodded.

'Hard to think we were gentlemen once,' he said.

'And we'll be gentlemen again, one day,' Scarlet replied. 'You'll get your vengeance, Will. But it's better we do it together.'

They wandered over towards the green.

'Scarlet...'

'Yes...'

'What Much was saying. About his rescuer. There was something in your expression when Much said the word. Loxley. As though it was familiar to you?'

Scarlet looked up to where the moon was rising over the trees.

'It is familiar to me,' he replied. 'And if it's the man I'm thinking of then all hell may have come to Sherwood Forest.'

~

The minstrel strummed the strings of the lute with a peculiar gentleness, a fine and quiet playing that was not commonly heard in the great hall of Nottingham Castle. He had stopped his singing an hour before at the request of the Sheriff, who said that he could not appreciate the lyrics and conduct official business at the same time. But as a lover of good music he had positioned the minstrel in a corner and instructed him to play on.

The afternoon was over. In the hours before the evening feast a mood of lethargy had spread over the servants and entertainers in Nottingham Castle. The tumblers, favourite performers of my lord Gisborne, were asleep in front of the fire. Men at arms leaned harder on to their spears and crossbows as the boredom of the long day overtook them. The captain of the guard stifled a yawn as he gazed from the battlements towards the dark and sinister fringe of Sherwood Forest.

The minstrel looked out through a window of painted glass and concluded that it was going to be a long fine evening. The light was drawing out now that spring had arrived. His fingers thrummed the strings from habit, for his mind was elsewhere. Alan a' Dale could almost play and sleep at the same time, so long had he been at the minstrel's trade.

It had ever been so, since his boyhood on Stainmore when the pedlar had given him the instrument and taught him the rudiments of its use. From the first time his fingers produced a note he knew that he would not graze sheep as his father had done. After a few years of playing he had wandered down to the great fair at Brough and performed for the crowds for the first time. A lady of the castle had heard him, brought him into the hall of her husband, and had him taught letters so that he might appreciate all the better the words of the songs. Minstrels and balladeers had come that way and helped him enlarge his repertoire. Then he had roamed himself, from castle to castle and town to town, always welcome to a night's lodging and a purse of pennies, for none sang or played sweeter than Alan of the Dale.

Robert de Lisle, Sheriff of Nottingham, had had such a pleasant afternoon, sitting in the ante-room adjacent to the great hall, looking over a table full of deeds delineating newly-acquired lands. The ownership of land not only increased his purse but also his power. His father had been a very minor landowner and was often sneered at by more powerful overlords. De Lisle had always been quite certain that nobody would sneer at him. Ambition and a calculated ruthlessness had got him where he was. At first he had been prepared to use his own dagger. He had oft reddened the blade with the blood of his enemies. Now he had lackeys to do the work for him. And there were still a great many rivals to remove from the scene.

How beautifully that minstrel played!

De Lisle appreciated talent and was prepared to pay to keep it near. The minstrel would be well rewarded. The Sheriff found his tunes to be particularly relaxing. A labourer worthy of the hire indeed.

If only Gisborne and those other hangers-on could fight with such commitment and zeal. How swiftly all of his foes might be vanquished. His thoughts seemed to conjure up Gisborne out of thin air. A moment before the Sheriff had been alone. And now Sir Guy stood before him, looking awkward, as he always did when he had bad news. A soldier stood closer to the doorway, clutching a wound in his shoulder.

'Gisborne?'

'My lord Sheriff...'

De Lisle gestured a hand in the direction of the injured man.

'Walter of Thirsk?' he inquired, speaking very quietly. 'One of your creatures, Gisborne.'

'A very brave soldier who fought for me in the Holy Land, my lord Sheriff.'

'That wound looks fresh?' said the Sheriff, his voice quieter than ever.

'An injury from an arrow, my lord.'

'Really?'

Gisborne recognised the danger in the tone of that one word. He looked down at his feet.

'It was Loxley, my lord Sheriff,' he said very quietly.

De Lisle stood and walked across to the window. The people selling goods in the market square were packing up to go home. A man at arms was very obviously asleep down by the gate. A soldier that needed a flogging to wake him up.

'So your brilliant idea to ambush Loxley didn't work, Gisborne?'

'You know Loxley's reputation, my lord. He's quite deadly with a longbow.'

A pause.

'Yesterday, Gisborne. You remember yesterday?'

'My lord?'

'Yesterday, Gisborne, you informed me that Loxley was dead. Now he is merely deadly.'

Sir Guy remained silent.

'And what happened to the other two soldiers you sent out?'

Gisborne took in another deep breath.

'They are... killed.'

The Sheriff paced the floor.

'Killed...' de Lisle said the word so quietly that Gisborne could scarce hear it.

'And you, Walter of Thirsk,' de Lisle continued, speaking to the injured soldier, who looked as though he was trying to ease himself round the doorway. 'How is it that you are alive?'

'The outlaw Loxley was merciful, my lord.'

'Merciful,' de Lisle's lips moved the word so silently that Gisborne was unsure whether he had spoken at all. Then louder. 'Loxley is not known for being merciful.'

Louder still.

'Isn't the truth of it that you ran away?'

'No, my lord.'

'You are a coward, Thirsk!'

The words echoed around the castle.

'A bloody coward!'

'I am not a coward. I...'

'Don't tell me what you are not!' de Lisle roared. 'If I say you are a coward, you are a coward. If I say day is night then day is night. I am your lord, and I say what you are.'

'Lord Sheriff...' Gisborne intervened.

De Lisle swept a hand across the table knocking the many parchments on to the floor.

'Get your creature out of my sight, Gisborne, lest I send him to the dungeons and have him racked. And you alongside him, Gisborne!'

Gisborne waved an arm and Walter of Thirsk slunk away.

'And you can get out as well Gisborne,' said the Sheriff, calmer now. 'But before you go I'll tell you something. I anticipated the failure of your plan. And this morning I sent someone into Sherwood to do the task properly. One man might yet succeed where your blundering cowards have failed.'

'One man?' Gisborne looked puzzled.

'A man worth any three of yours...' he waved an arm in dismissal.

As Gisborne left the ante-chamber de Lisle followed him to the doorway and watched him hurry across the hall and out into a distant corridor. 'What a creature you are, Gisborne,' he muttered. And then he became aware of the minstrel sitting almost at his feet.

'I am sorry that my words interrupted your music. Play on...'

As the Sheriff turned away Alan a' Dale thought back on the words he had heard and wondered how best to end his duty so that he might send a message into Sherwood Forest.

Four

Loxley loved the soft light of May evenings and the freshness of the leaves upon the trees. It was going to be a warm and dry night and he intended to take his sleep in the greenwood. Somewhere off the track where he would not be disturbed or threatened by late night travellers.

It had been an uneventful day's journey since his battle with the three soldiers. A delightful walk through some of the thickest woodlands of Sherwood, a safe passage towards Nottingham where you could head into cover at the slightest sight or sound of anyone on the road. Not that he had encountered anyone. The old road was deserted. Loxley had heard rumours that few used it these days, lest they be robbed by the outlaws in the forest. That in itself made the road particularly safe. Outlaws would soon abandon any track where people with fat purses no longer travelled.

He heard the sounds of the little river long before he saw it. For a while the undergrowth denied him a glimpse of it. He knew from memory that the great road from the north into Nottingham was scarce a mile away. He hadn't been to this part of the forest for several years and he recalled that the path he was on crossed the river at a ford before heading towards the busier route into the town. A good place to spend the night, where he could drink fresh water and wash off the dust of the day. He paused for a moment to listen, but could hear no sounds except the almost deafening exhilaration of the woodland birds.

The path swerved to the left and a dozen yards away was the ford. It was as he remembered it, except that on the upstream side of the wading place someone had placed half a tree trunk to serve as a footbridge across the slow-flowing water.

He had scarce stepped on to it before he became aware of the man on the far side. At first glance a veritable giant, as muscular as he was tall with a ruddy and untidy beard concealing much of his face. All except the very green eyes that were looking, challengingly, in his direction.

Loxley paused and looked again.

It was not a giant. The far bank was several inches higher than the side he stood upon and this made the figure seem larger than he really was. But even so, he was taller by half a foot than Loxley himself and was wielding a quarter staff even longer than himself.

Both men stepped further on to the bridge until there was hardly a yard between them. The stranger held his head slightly to one side, regarding Loxley almost as he might consider a passing water rat. The giant took one hand off the staff and flicked it in Loxley's direction as though summoning him to retreat.

'This is my bridge and you trespass upon it!' he growled, in a deep voice that echoed around the glade.

Loxley looked down at the tree-trunk and then cast a glance around the edges of the forest before looking into the man's eyes. After a moment's consideration he gave a slight bow.

'My apologies, your grace. I had no idea I was confronting the King of England,' he said.

The giant looked puzzled.

'What do you mean by that?'

'Well, as I understand it this glade is a part of Sherwood. A royal hunting forest and the demesne of King Richard. Therefore the river and the bridge must be his also.'

'They're mine...' the man said, very quietly.

'I've seen Lionheart,' said Loxley. 'A tall man but not a giant like you. He'd a more handsome look upon him. And the stench wasn't quite as bad. Not the most pleasant of men, but certainly not the oaf I see before me now.'

'I'll drown you with those words on your lips...' the man muttered, holding out the quarter staff.

Loxley let out a great sigh.

'This will be the second fight I've had today,' he said. 'But we have each other at a disadvantage. We both carry daggers, but I have a sword and a bow. I can't use either against that mighty tree you carry.'

'There's many a good plant growing on your side of the river. I'm prepared to give you time to cut one. Though don't delay, for I grow impatient to cross. Unless you would care to wrestle for the right of passage?'

'I'm no wrestler and could certainly not match your weight and strength,' he replied. 'Tell me, stranger, what's your name?'

'I am John Little of Hathersage.'

'Little?'

'Spare me the humour. I've heard the jests a thousand times before... Now either make way, give me your apologies, and throw yourself into the water. Or cut a bough to fight with.'

Loxley retreated to the bank and spent a few moments selecting a piece of wood, cutting and pruning something almost as considerable as the weapon John Little carried.

He stepped back on to the bridge, holding the wood in both hands.

'I confess I'm no artist with the quarter staff,' he said. 'If you would just get out of my way and let me pass there need be no conflict between us.'

John Little gave a humourless laugh. 'I take it you were braver in the fight you said you had earlier in the day?'

'I used my longbow,' said Loxley. 'And the men had the disadvantage of being mounted.'

'Men?' said the giant, looking curiously at Loxley. 'How many men?'

'There were three of them. Two slain and one wounded.'

'Is that true? Or are you as much a braggart as you are ugly?'

'I can't prove it to you,' said Loxley. 'They were three soldiers from Nottingham.'

John Little rubbed his beard as he considered the information.

'The Sheriff's men?' he asked.

'I believe they served Sir Guy of Gisborne.'

Little spat into the river.

'And why should that nob Gisborne want you dead?' he asked.

'It's a long tale and would best be told when we're not balancing on such a narrow bridge...'

'Then we come back to the purpose of our combat... fight me or step away...'

Loxley was considering what else to say when John Little charged, his staff held out so that the thinnest end shot towards Loxley's face at such a force that had it landed it might have penetrated the front of his skull.

Instinct more than intention brought up his own staff to parry the blow. But within a second of that move he swung the weapon round and crashed the thickest portion against Little's thigh.

The giant took a step backwards and held out his staff defensively.

'I've felt worse from the bite of a gnat,' he said. 'A girl could handle a staff better than you...'

He had hardly uttered the words before Loxley advanced along the bridge, the point of his own staff aimed at Little's face. The giant fell for the feint, bringing his own weapon up to protect his head. But at the last moment Loxley fell into a crouch bringing the point into the pit of the giant's stomach. The move took Little's breath away, causing him to lean forward and lower his guard. Loxley swung his staff around with all the force he could muster against his opponent's head.

John Little staggered and fell down on to his knees, managing somehow to hang on to the bridge.

'Damn you, Loxley,' he yelled, looking up at his enemy, 'that was a cheating blow...'

Loxley shook his head.

'A fair blow with a quarter staff. Or so I was taught.' He paused for a moment, resting on his staff. 'And how do you know my name?'

Little clambered to his feet.

'I need to know your name so that I might carve it on your grave,' he answered. 'Come on you bastard, fight...'

Even before he was completely upright he swept the staff at low level towards Loxley's legs. Loxley tried to counter by putting his own staff upright on the bridge in front of him to block the blow, but too late. The heavy piece of wood caught him a stinging blow to the side of his lower leg and with a cry of pain he tumbled sideways into the river.

Grasping his staff John Little jumped in after him, crashing another blow on to Loxley's shoulder even before he reached the water. Little landed upright, his chest and head out of the depths. But of Loxley there was no sign.

He reached out, using the weapon to brush through the pool leading down towards the ford. He turned back towards the bridge, sweeping the staff across the surface of the river on the expectation that he might catch Loxley's head as he emerged to catch breath. But even after passing under the tree trunk bridge there was still no sign.

And then there came a great blow to the head which knocked all the sense out of him, followed by a crushing pressure against his throat. His eyes caught the flowing water and then the tree branches overhead outlined against a darkening sky. Suddenly, the whole of nature seemed to reel, accompanied by a thundering ache in his brain.

The pressure on his throat eased momentarily, giving him a chance to gasp out a few words.

'For the mercy of God!'

And then Loxley's staff was withdrawn and he felt himself being dragged across the river and up out of the water. His head felt like it was being torn in two. It was several minutes before he realised the terrible sound he could hear was the heavy breathing of both Loxley and himself as they both lay floundering on the bank like marooned and dying fish.

'So what's this jest about your name?' asked Loxley as the both finally recovered their ability to breathe. 'I see nothing amusing about John Little.'

The giant rolled over on to his side to face him.

'And a good job too!' he said. 'For if you did I'd hold your head under that water and let you swim your way to hell!'

'But what is the jest?'

'They call me *Little* John...'

'Little John? I can't say such a thought would ever have crossed my mind,' Loxley replied, quite earnestly.

'Just as well! There's nothing little about any part of me.'

'I assume not... I shall never call you anything but John and just that.'

John nodded his head, 'Well, that's all right then.'

'How did you know my name is Loxley?'

John gave a great burst of laughter.

'You were... described to me. By the Sheriff in Nottingham Castle. I fought in a wrestling match there. Afterwards that bastard de Lisle approached me. He offered me a good purse if I'd come into the forest and kill you.'

'So do you intend to finish the work?' asked Loxley.

'You have a smug face, Loxley. And I'd like to wipe that grin from it. But no. Selling out our own kind isn't what we do in Hathersage.'

'You hail from Hathersage? Does Sir Hugh Courtenay live?'

'Aye, the bastard still breathes. I'm a villein in his service, though I am allowed to roam so that I might increase his reputation with my wrestling. That was the other deal. The Sheriff said that he'd ask Count John to intervene with Sir Hugh for my freedom.'

'You know, that's a good bargain for a villein. Aren't you tempted?'

John considered for a moment.

'You know what these scum are like? Say I went back to Nottingham Castle, carrying your head. For he demanded that as proof. Do you really imagine I'd get my purse of gold or my freedom? I'd finish my days rotting in de Lisle's dungeon. If I was spared to live so long. I'll not go back to Nottingham.'

Loxley sat up.

'Then why fight me at all?'

'I've heard of you, Loxley. Heard of the rebellion in Loxley Chase. I'm curious as to just why you've returned to Sherwood? If you've come looking for trouble... well, that's something I might be able to help you with. I'm not going back to Hathersage. I'm in the mood for a fight if you have need of a wrestler?'

Loxley stood and paced up and down. At last he returned to John.

'What I have in mind... it'll be bloody dangerous.'

'Better danger than the life of a peasant,' John replied. 'What *do* you have in mind?'

Loxley sat down again and then lay back, looking up at the darkening sky. He was silent for a while. And then he turned to John.

'I can't overturn the injustices that beset England,' he said. 'That's too big a task. But I intend to light a flame in Sherwood Forest. A flame that might one day turn into a great fire of freedom that'll engulf this land. I'm going to show the people of Sherwood how to get back their self-respect. How to bring these bastard overlords to account. I want every man and woman in this forest to be at liberty and to be able to hold their heads up. No more villeins... only the freeborn.'

'You tried in Loxley,' said John. 'From what I hear villages were fired, and men put to the sword...'

'Loxley Chase was too small. There were few places to hide, no concealments to strike from. But here...' Loxley waved an arm towards the trees. 'Here in Sherwood, and Barnsdale beyond. A great forest. Places to hide thousands of men. Hidden dells and caves. Great areas where the Sheriff and his soldiers are terrified to go. And we'll not fight them like we did in Loxley, as though we were an army. We'll hit them when they least expect it. And then be away in the trees a moment later. Then strike again miles away, the same day.'

John let out a great breath.

'It sounds good,' he admitted, 'but it's been tried before. Why should it work this time?'

'It'll work,' said Loxley, 'if I have to die in Sherwood to prove it, I'll make it work!'

John walked down to the river to drink and splash water on his face. He said nothing for several minutes. Once he looked in Loxley's direction for quite a while before sipping some more water. He came over at last, kneeling down beside him.

'You talk of thousands of men,' he said. 'How many have you?'

Loxley smiled. 'Well, you must be worth a dozen. And I have a minstrel who is as skilled with a sword and dagger as he is with a lute. And a fat monk who could probably best the both of us with a quarter staff.'

'Well, that's four...'

'And there are the ones I haven't recruited yet..'

'And they are?'

'The outlaws skulking in Sherwood.'

John stared open-mouthed at him.

'You're mad!' he said. 'They're a bunch of minging hedge-thieves. They'd rob you and cut your throat sooner than fight alongside you. They'd be useless in any sort of battle! They might be skilled with a longbow but they wouldn't know one end of a sword from another.'

'Then I'll teach them how to fight.'

'But don't you see, Loxley, they don't want to fight at all! They're a cowardly and drunken lot. A bit of poaching is all they're prepared to risk.'

'You could still go back to Hathersage...'

John hit the sides of his head with the palms of his hands.

'I'll stay in Sherwood, despite your madness. And I'll tell you why I'll fight at your side. Because the Sheriff and Gisborne are so anxious to have you killed. You must have something about you if those two bastards are having nightmares.'

Loxley patted him on the shoulder.

'It's getting dark,' he said, 'and I'm aching all over from your blows. I know a farm near here where we can get something to eat and a safe night's sleep. Tomorrow I must meet with that minstrel I mentioned. He might have news for us. He gathers a great deal of information while he's warbling in Nottingham Castle.'

'And then?'

'Back to Sherwood to root out these outlaws. And it might be safer, John, if you don't let the word Loxley appear on your lips. The Sheriff has informants everywhere.'

He pulled up the brown hood and walked back across the footbridge to retrieve his weapons.

'So what shall I call you?' John shouted across the river.

'My given name is Robin.'

'Robin then,' said John. 'Robin i' the hood.' He chortled. 'A good name for a forest rogue that,' he considered. 'Robin Hood!'

Five

Robert de Lisle looked out from the top of the great tower of Nottingham Castle. He usually slept badly and would often come to this vantage point to watch the dawn rise. The town, so far below, was already busy as merchants entered through the open gates to set up their wares for the market.

Market days always made de Lisle uneasy. They brought an atmosphere of carnival and chaos to a place that was already hard to control. He looked down at the streaming crowd. Anyone of them could be Loxley or a thousand other threats to his control of the king's peace. Most of them were his poverty, the villeins and peasants who had some excuse to leave their work on the land and come in to the town. Market days were a necessary if despicable part of his week. Scarce one went by when he didn't find it necessary to have one of the scum hanged, or mutilated, or thrown in a dungeon to be forgotten.

With a great groan the castle gate was pushed open. He watched as a hundred men at arms poured down towards the market place. His new tactic to keep the peace was to flood the town with troops.

He doubted it would really work.

'My lord Sheriff...'

Gisborne was at his elbow.

'Gisborne...' he almost purred the name. 'My dear Gisborne, you are unwell?'

'My lord?'

'We don't usually see you up so early. Couldn't you sleep? Or did your whore awaken you as she crept out of your bed?'

'My lord!'

The Sheriff waved a hand towards the gathering crowds below.

'Just look at that reeking mob, Gisborne. Hundreds of them, strong and dangerous. And so few of us. How easy it would be for them to overthrow us if they had the courage and full bellies. It never happens because they lack our ability to work together. They may outnumber us, but they always fail to unite.'

Gisborne leaned against an upright in the crenellations and looked down towards the market place. A smile crossed his face as he turned back to face de Lisle.

'They are but carthorses, my lord Sheriff. Whip them as you will, they lack the courage to kick out.' He laughed. 'No, even carthorses have more spirit! These peasants are but sheep. Even their bleating is silenced if you go to their villages and string a few from the surrounding trees.'

De Lisle looked the soldier up and down.

'What a warrior you are, Gisborne,' he muttered. 'How easy it is to wage war on unarmed villeins. You've almost cleared out some of my villages. Half the men hanged, the others driven into Sherwood.'

He looked into the distance at the dark and menacing fringe of the forest.

Why did he always feel uneasy at the mention of the word... Sherwood?

'And the consequences of that, Gisborne, are severe. Empty the villages and who can we tax? Who can we have to drive the oxen on the plough? You don't murder the poor, Gisborne. You work them to death. That's what they're for.'

'I'm a soldier, my lord. If I see a threat I seek a solution... the soldier's way.'

'The soldier's way didn't work very well with Loxley did it? He still roams Sherwood... perhaps...'

Gisborne wiped the sleep from his eyes as he considered de Lisle's words. Then the memory of the day before came into his head.

'Perhaps, my lord? Of course, you had a plan?'

'More than a plan, Gisborne. A certainty, I hope. You recall that wrestler from Hathersage, John Little?'

'Little the giant?' Gisborne grinned at the contrasting words.

'The very one,' de Lisle replied. 'I've sent him into Sherwood to seek out and kill Loxley. I expect him back very soon with the good news that all our troubles in that direction are over.' He patted Gisborne's arm. 'You may deal with the wrestler on his return.'

'Deal with him?'

'I promised him a purse and his freedom.' The Sheriff shook his head. 'I think that was a tad too generous. If John Little returns you are to throw him into the dungeon. He's to speak to nobody. I don't want Loxley's name mentioned or rumour of his demise to get out into the town or the forest villages. I want Loxley expunged from the face of the earth.'

'And John Little?'

The Sheriff considered for a moment.

'Keep him in the dungeon until he's told you all. And then Gisborne, and then... you may deal with him the soldier's way.'

Gisborne smiled, bowing his head to acknowledge the order.

~

'One day they'll sing ballads of you,' said Alan a' Dale. 'I may well compose a few myself.'

He and Loxley stood at the edge of the forest. Beyond were a few worked fields leading to the great walls of Nottingham town. They watched as more villagers made their way on foot and in carts along the north road on their way to the great market held in the shadow of the castle walls.

'Oh, that I should live so long!' the other man replied. 'Whatever you write set it to a good tune, so that people might hum that long after they've forgotten the words. What news have you for me?'

The minstrel looked serious.

'Bad news, Robin,' he said. 'All of Nottingham is stirred up with your deeds at Loxley. And many are thrilled at your besting of those three soldiers in Sherwood the other day.'

'News travels fast!'

'Not all good news,' said Alan. 'There's a wrestler, a giant of a man called John Little. The Sheriff has sent him into Sherwood to hunt you down, promising him a gold purse and his freedom. I've watched him fight, Robin. He's a formidable opponent.'

Loxley smiled and gave a whistle. John came out of the trees towards them.

'My God,' said Alan, reaching for his knife.

'Hold fast with your dagger,' said Loxley. 'John Little and I've had a discussion on these matters. He's decided he favours me more than he does de Lisle.' He turned to the wrestler. 'John, this is my friend Alan of the Dale. He hails from Stainmore, close to where the Viking Erik Bloodaxe met his doom. Which he'll sing you an account of if you throw him a penny.'

'I'm intrigued, Robin,' said the minstrel.

'John and I discovered each other when we succumbed to the temptation to bathe in the river. He's decided not to return to Hathersage at the moment but to throw in his lot with us. Now we seek the outlaws of Sherwood together.'

'I hope they'll listen to what you have to say before they cut your throats,' said Alan. 'They should be working the road on a market day. They're usually either thieving or drunk.'

'We've roamed the north road for much of the morning,' Loxley replied. 'As we've not been robbed we must assume they are sleeping out the morning on an alehouse floor.'

'If de Lisle find you are so close to Nottingham...'

'How fares the Sheriff?'

Alan considered for a moment before replying.

'He is a tormented man in so many ways. But I give him the credit for liking my tunes,' he said. 'De Lisle has so many concerns that he scarce sleeps at night. Lionheart screams at him to tear more taxes from the pockets of the poor. Count John of Mortain badgers him to acknowledge and help him expand his power. De Lisle fancies that he is being stretched like the rope in a village tug o' war.'

'By God, you almost tempt me to weep a tear for the bastard,' said John. 'I could put him out of his misery. Wander in to the castle and break his neck.'

'Perhaps one day, John,' said Loxley. 'And how is friend Gisborne?'

'Ah, now there is a dangerous man,' Alan considered. 'A black-hearted bastard with little left to lose, yet desperate to win back favour with the King. Well, with any king, for he has little loyalty to King Richard. He's been crawling around Count John, though at the moment the rival court has little room for him amongst all the other sycophants.'

'Another one to put out of his misery then?' said John Little.

Alan nodded.

'And more dangerous than de Lisle in his way,' he agreed. 'His one saving grace is that he fills the forest with outlaws. With men we might need. But at a high price. He's to ride tomorrow to take taxes from the villagers at Oakden, in the company of his usual armed rabble. No doubt he'll do it to excess, despite the Sheriff's concerns that he's stripping the countryside of serfs.'

'Oakden,' said Loxley, 'is but a few miles from here. We could be there tomorrow. It might be the occasion we need to launch our war.'

'What, with three of us?' said John.

'Only two, for I need Alan to return to Nottingham,' said Loxley. 'If we could find the outlaws it would make the fight easier.'

Alan shook his head. 'I do wonder who'll kill you first, Loxley? Gisborne, the Sheriff, or the outlaws in Sherwood? I'd not wager on it, for it's too close to call. And another matter, my friend. I know you're white hot to seek revenge for Loxley. But do remember that there are villagers in Oakden who don't want their homes burned and their beasts taken. Don't let your passion run away with you. Not every villein and freeman can cope with being made wolfshead.'

With a wave he headed back towards the town.

'Wise words, Robin,' said John. 'So how are we to do it?'

Loxley thought for a moment or two.

'I can only think of one way, John,' he said at last. 'And that's to stand aside and let Gisborne collect the Sheriff's taxes.'

~

Sir Henry Fitzwalter liked to call his home a castle, though many smiled at the description. True, it had begun its existence in that way, the original Saxon hall being replaced with a fortified tower by King William as he harried the mid-lands and north of England in the brutal years that followed his victory on Senlac Hill. But in the hundred and more years since, much of the tower had crumbled, and a stout-walled manor had been built along the lines of the original hall, with outbuildings and a farm nearby.

It was by no means defensible. It had fallen thrice during the nineteen long winters of King Stephen's miserable reign. Three times it had been repaired. Three times Henry Fitzwalter's family had crept back out of the forest to find their home fired and plundered.

Sometime during the Anarchy his family had decided to stop fighting and try and live in peace with all sides. Their neutrality had mostly worked. As they had hoped they had been left alone. Walter was smiled upon by his mightier neighbours as a genial old man, who was not worth bothering with very much.

As a family the Fitzwalters were mostly Saxon. But during the civil war the solitary daughter of the house, the last in an ancient and royal Mercian line, had allowed herself to be tupped by one of the Empress Maud's Norman knights, the strikingly handsome Walter of Evesham.

Henry Fitzwalter had been the son of that brief romance, though he had never known his father. A week before his son had been born, Walter of Evesham had fallen at some minor siege, a crossbow bolt through his throat.

And now Henry Fitzwalter knew that his own death could not be far away. He felt old and just walking around the house left him tired. But for one matter he was ready to seek the eternal life that he continually prayed for. His wife had died many years before. His two sons had died in infancy. His outstanding worry was his daughter Marian. A child that had come like a gift from God in his middle years.

For much of her life she had been a wild creature, spending more time in the forest than at home. He had watched with concern as she scrambled up trees. Noted with pride her skill with a bow and frowned at her desire to use a sword and a quarter staff. It was as though she was somehow absorbing the expected talents of his dead sons.

And then there had been a transformation. The young girl with burrs in her dark hair and the forest dirt smeared across her face had turned into something of a beauty. The transformation had occurred as his own health had declined, when she seemed to want to spend more time at home, caring for him and handling the affairs of the manor to spare him the bother.

That very day she had journeyed to Rufford on estate business. She was late back and he was concerned that she might have encountered an ill-fortune. Women were so vulnerable in these disputed lands. They were considered property in the way that houses and livestock might be. Henry Fitzwalter had few men to give strength to his household. And he was aware that men of power were looking at his daughter in a new light. His few acres were not much but they were enough to inspire greed and lust in others.

The week before the corpulent Abbot of St Mary's had called, eyeing up Marian with an expression that went a long way past piety.

'And of course, my dear Fitzwalter, you may rest assured that the church will take the greatest care of Marian when the time comes for you to make your peace with God,' he had said, tapping his fat and beringed fingers on the table in the great hall.

'In what way?' Fitzwalter had asked. 'My daughter has her lands and wealth enough. She has the capability to administer this estate.'

The Abbot had opened his mouth in surprise at the words, before his thick lips assumed a humourless smile.

'But Marian's a woman and will be alone in the world. The Holy Church will always have her best interests at heart.' He had leaned forward, waving a warning finger. 'We must beware, my dear Fitzwalter. This shire is filled with covetous... no, rapacious young men. No woman of means is safe. They will court your daughter and then cast her aside once they have your lands.'

'I think not...' Fitzwalter had replied. 'She'll not be so easily taken. She is, after all, a royal ward of the king. Lionheart spent a night here on his return from the Crusade. He took a shine to Marian in the best of ways. They drew a bow together. He decreed that in the event of my death Marian would become a royal ward, not to be married without his personal consent. And her agreement. I've a warrant to that effect bearing the Great Seal of England.'

The Abbot tightened his lips in a gesture of annoyance.

'I wasn't aware of that,' he said.

'There's no reason why you should be.'

The Abbot drank the dregs of a flagon of wine. He looked thoughtful before he spoke again.

'King Richard is far away. Normandy. France. Well, they're dangerous places. And Lionheart has given his brother Count John stewardship of this shire?' He glanced into the darkest shadows of the empty hall. 'In confidence, my dear Fitzwalter, Count John seeks the support of those who have power in this place. He may well consider that he has control over royal wards in the King's absence. He might give Marian to anyone he chooses.'

'I think not,' Fitzwalter protested. 'She is a great favourite with Count John.'

The Abbot put down the flagon with a bang. And then smiled unctuously.

'Fitzwalter, these are dangerous times. There are hotheads around Nottingham. Du Bois of Newark has an eye for a pretty face. And he'd welcome your lands and not be very bothered as to the fate of Marian once he had acquired them.'

'Du Bois is a fool...'

'He may be,' said the Abbot, 'though I would urge you not to express such sentiments outside these walls. But Sir Guy of Gisborne is anything but a fool. He knows your daughter. The way he moons over her looks is the amusement of all in Nottingham Castle.'

'He is a penniless knight!'

'Gisborne's the Sheriff's pet dog,' the Abbot replied. 'And every now and again de Lisle feels obliged to throw the dog a bone...'

'I will not have my daughter discussed in such a manner!'

The Abbot held up his hands in appeasement.

'My dear Fitzwalter, I didn't mean to cause offence.'

There had been a long silence.

'My dear Fitzwalter...' the abbot began again. 'I have perhaps put these matters to you in an unpleasant way. But it's out of my very real concern for Marian's fortunes...'

Fitzwalter put his palm to his forehead, trying to rub away a tightness that had appeared above his eyes. The Abbot of St Mary's visited too often and usually left him with a headache.

'You have another solution?' he asked.

'A very sound and proper answer to this dilemma,' the Abbot gave a broader smile, resting a hand on Fitzwalter's shoulder.

'Which is?'

'My belief is that Marian should be married to God.'

'Married to God?'

'I've already discussed the matter with the Prioress of Kirklees.'

'*You think I would allow my daughter to become a nun?*'

'Marriage to God would ensure Marian's well-being. Take her out of the clutches of the dreadful young men who rampage across the shire...'

'Then these lands of mine would become the property of your Abbey!'

'I would have the stewardship of them. That's true. But they would be administered in the best interests of all concerned. Your peasants well treated, the land properly farmed.'

Fitzwalter got to his feet so quickly that the pain in the head nearly took him back down.

'My lord abbot,' he said at last, 'Marian will never be married to God. Or to anyone else who isn't her choice.' He strode away, across the hall, pausing for a moment at the door. 'My steward will guide you safely to my boundary. I bid you good day.'

As Fitzwalter left the hall he caught a glimpse of the abbot biting at his knuckles. He looked out again across the fields and towards the forest and the road from Rufford. He really wished that Marian would hurry back.

~

'My dear Robin, what you are proposing is exceedingly dangerous,' said Tuck, pouring more wine for Loxley and John Little. 'If you have to take on Gisborne and his men then it would be better to do so in Oakden. At least you *might* have the support of the villagers. Though they had little fight in them the last time I was there.'

The three men sat by the fireside in the room alongside the chapel of Saint Withburga, where Tuck lived and ate and slept.

'It was my first thought,' Loxley replied, 'but Alan suggested that such an open rebellion might not be in the best interests of the villagers. Better to rob Gisborne and his men on the way back to Nottingham.'

'The three of us?'

'We'll have the cover of the Sherwood trees. And our bows can send off six arrows in the time it takes Gisborne's men to load a single quarrel in a crossbow.'

'We need the advantage of height,' said John. 'We must find a place where we can keep Gisborne and his men penned in. If we give any of them a chance to scatter into the forest then we'll be lost... there'll be no chance of getting away.'

Loxley dipped his finger into the wine and drew a map on to the table.

'I've considered that,' he said. 'Halfway between Oakden and Nottingham the old road enters a hollow way, where the feet of travellers have worn down the level of the ground. The road is twenty feet lower than the surrounding forest. If we can keep them from breaking out of there then we may have a chance. If we can catch them by surprise we can be away into the forest before they know what's happening.'

John shook his head. 'I don't see how that helps. One of us would still have to descend into the hollow to grab the taxes.'

'But if we can pen them in well and make it impossible to get out of the hollow we may be able to force them to send someone out with the money.'

'We need more men, more bowmen,' said Tuck. 'This really is the best plan?'

'What else can we do?' asked Loxley. 'If we attack them at Oakden then all the villagers will be made wolfshead. If we attack them at the hollow we have a chance of taking the money and returning it to the villagers so they don't starve next winter. Or are you suggesting we let the Sheriff have the money?'

Oakden was a mean village of thatched and timbered houses, surrounded on three sides by the fields where the inhabitants slaved to make money for their lord. On the fourth side the trees of Sherwood dipped down to a rough stockade that was meant to keep wolves from raiding the enclosures where the sheep were held. It was the end of the day. Only with the approaching dark was the labour of the peasants coming to a conclusion. As the villagers stumbled exhausted towards their homes they looked with disapproval at the dozen men who had wandered into Oakden from the direction of Sherwood.

'Not pleased to see us,' Much muttered. 'Look at the way they glower!' He turned to Will Scarlet. 'Might be better to move on, Will. I wouldn't put it past this lot to sell us to the Sheriff.'

'We're safe enough for one night,' said Ralph Gammon, an outlaw with untidy dark hair. 'This is my village and I'm well thought of in this place.'

'Who's this?' asked Stutely, nodding at an old man who was coming up towards them.

'Cedric usually speaks for the villagers,' said Ralph. 'He hates the Sheriff as much as we do, but favours a quiet life.'

Cedric stood in their path, his arms folded. He looked at Ralph and gave a nod.

'Good day, Ralph,' he said at last. 'I trust you haven't brought trouble to this village.' He looked at the outlaws. 'These are wolfsheads. Every man.'

'And so we are, and one day so might you be,' said Will Stutely. 'These are perilous times...'

'Perilous enough, without bringing yet more peril to Oakden,' said Cedric. 'Just having you here could put a rope around all our necks.' He turned to Ralph. 'You must be a madman coming back here!'

'I came to see my wife,' said Ralph. He looked at the gathering crowd of villagers. 'Where is she?' he asked. 'Where is Joan?'

The villagers looked at each other, their feet shuffling with embarrassment. Some of them drifted away to their homes. Cedric came a pace closer to Ralph.

'She's gone, boy.'

'Gone? Gone where?'

Cedric gave a great sigh and patted the youth on the shoulder.

'A week or more ago she went,' he said. 'William a' Trent came here with a dozen men, seeking to press women into service at Nottingham Castle. They took Joan and three others. My daughter was taken as well. There was nothing we could do.'

'You didn't protest?' asked Ralph.

Cedric looked angry. 'Protest? Of course we protested. They took my brother Geoffrey's wife! He protested and they hanged him from that oak over there. They threatened to burn the village and have all here made wolfshead. It's because we protested that they've increased the taxes we have to pay.' There were tears running down his face. 'My daughter's a pretty darling... how safe do you think she'll be in Nottingham Castle? That bastard Gisborne was leering at her the last time he was here. How is any woman safe in Nottingham Castle?'

Ralph turned to Scarlet. 'We've got to get into that castle and get them out of there!'

'We're a few ragged outlaws,' Scarlet replied. 'It would take an army, hundreds of men, siege engines... I pity you and your lady, Ralph, but how can we?'

'Will Stutely,' Ralph turned to the man next to him. 'You're quiet, Will. And we all know why, don't we? We know what happened to your wife. If you had the knowledge that she was alive and in Nottingham Castle wouldn't you go there? Whatever the odds?'

Stutely put an arm around Ralph's shoulders.

'Aye, I would, whatever the consequences.' He looked across at the other Will. 'You're wrong Scarlet. We don't need an army or siege engines. Only guile. Cunning can defeat a thousand men at arms. We should help Ralph get his wife back. And the other women if we can. But if we rush in without preparation we will be throwing our own lives away in vain. We need to think this matter through.'

'You may stay one night in Oakden,' said Cedric, 'but not a moment longer. We all have families that we're not prepared to risk. And you're to use the shelter by the sheep pens, away from our homes. Then at least we can say that we knew not of your presence here.'

Six

They came to Oakden just after dawn.

Gisborne and six horsemen, with twenty men at arms, and a donkey cart to carry the money and goods confiscated from each village lying on their route.

Gisborne, who hated early mornings, was in a foul mood, grunting at the comments made by William a' Trent who rode alongside him.

His thoughts were of a hearty breakfast in Nottingham Castle, a blazing fire of logs, and the warm flesh of that pretty slut Clorinda, who had groaned and clung to him as he rolled out of bed in the middle of the night. For a few moments, as he dressed and put on his chain mail, he had seriously contemplated wandering to the far side of the castle and slitting de Lisle's throat. Visualising the Sheriff squawking like a butchered pig as he tumbled away into eternity.

Now there could be profit in that!

Nottingham would need a new sheriff and who better qualified than a gallant knight who had fought in the Crusades. Sir Guy of Gisborne, Sheriff of Nottingham. Yes, it did have a certain ring to it. And there were a great deal of riches available to any man who held that office and managed the shire with an eye to a fortune. Certainly enough profit to restore the Gisborne castle and estates in distant Bowland.

Clorinda, of course, would have to go. That obliging little whore could have no part in the life of a gentleman knight on the way to prosperity and influence. But would Lionheart sanction such an appointment? Gisborne sighed - probably not. The rift between himself and the king was too deep. Count John then? More of a possibility there, for the king's brother had control of the shire.

And with de Lisle gone matters would be handled very differently. Gisborne would root out every last bit of rebellion and disaffection in Sherwood Forest. Every outlaw would be hanged or put to the sword. Villages that resisted the lawful rule of their lord would be burned out of existence. Villeins would be forced to labour until they dropped. And he would roll back the power of the church. The ghastly Abbot of St Mary's could crawl to a hermit's cell. There would be no more land grabbing to line his pockets. There...

'My lord,' Trent said insistently. 'We're riding by Oakden. The track veers to the left just here. This is the road to Newark.'

Gisborne reined in his horse and looked about him. He and Trent were a dozen yards in front of the men at arms, who had halted at the junction of paths. The dense trees of the forest pressed in on them, the fresh May leaves swaying in the slight breeze.

'Very well,' he said, turning to ride back. 'And Trent, when we get to the village I want the place searched thoroughly. These bastards always plead poverty. But you can be assured that they'll always have something hidden away somewhere.'

'Yes, my lord Gisborne.'

A smile crossed Gisborne's face.

'Concealment of lawful taxes is a felony,' he said. 'If we should find anything hidden away in any of their hovels, well... I want that particular hovel torched. And all who live there to be summarily hanged, whether they be man, woman or child. You understand?'

'Yes, my lord Gisborne.'

'Then let's get these idle bastards out of their beds.'

The track from the forest and down into Oakden was less than a half mile. Despite the early hour some of the villagers were already working in the more distant fields. Gisborne could see them looking across at the road and sensed the alarm that his presence had brought to them. They rested on their tools for just a moment and then began to labour furiously.

The smoke of morning fires clung to the still air over the miserable collection of huts that comprised the village. A few women were carrying water from the village well. A number of children were preparing to go to the fields to undertake a day's toil.

Only the sheep made a noisy protest as Gisborne and his men rode on. Trent looked in their direction and noted the half dozen men pouring out of the shepherd's shelter near to where the enclosures met the forest. Not labourers, nor villagers, for he knew them all. A few of these strangers carried swords and daggers. All of them had a bow in their hands and a quiver of arrows slung across their bodies.

'My lord Gisborne!' He pointed. 'Wolfsheads!'

Gisborne swung round in his saddle. There was no doubt about it, they were outlaws and armed outlaws at that. He drew out his sword and waved it in their direction.

'Wolfsheads,' he yelled to his men, who were struggling with swords and crossbows. 'Get them, you fools! Before they can string their bows! Faster! Faster!'

He slapped his horse on the flank with the flat of his sword and led his men into a charge, scattering the sheep in all directions as they tore across the enclosure towards the men. Three of the outlaws were struggling to string their bows. The remainder drew swords and sped uphill towards the shelter of the Sherwood trees.

But it was too late.

Gisborne and his mounted men were on them before they could reach safety. One of the wolfsheads turned in a attempt to hold back Gisborne with a sword, but could not stand against the momentum of the charging horse and the skilled warrior upon it.

Gisborne used his own weapon to sweep the sword out of the outlaw's hand. Then he turned his horse round in its own length, sweeping his blade at the man's face. Its weight took off the top of the outlaw's head, sending fragments of skull and brain across the grass. Despite the blow the outlaw staggered a good yard before crashing backwards to the earth. Gisborne experienced a terrific feeling of exhilaration as he turned to face the rest of the fugitives.

But there was little left for him to do. Two more of the outlaws lay dazed upon the ground, having been ridden down by his men. The three remaining had thrown down their weapons and held their arms out wide as his men aimed their crossbows in their direction. Gisborne spat at the ground. They had yielded just when he was in the mood for more killing. And yet...

'Tie their hands behind their backs and guard them well,' he shouted at the foot soldiers. Then to Trent and the other mounted men. 'Come with me to the village.'

God, why did these Sherwood villages have to give off such a stench! The stink of the pigsty smelt sweeter than any one of these hovels. He looked down at the filthy villagers. Ah, there was Cedric, the old man who always seemed to have enough lip to address his superiors. The one these wretches always put forward to speak for them.

'You know the penalty for sheltering wolfsheads?' Gisborne began.

'We didn't know they were here,' Cedric replied, gazing at the ground.

'I didn't ask that,' said Gisborne, very quietly. 'I asked if you knew what the penalty was for sheltering wolfsheads?'

Cedric mumbled something that Gisborne pretended not to hear.

'I can't hear you, villein! Speak up!'

'The penalty is death...'

'The penalty is death, *my lord Gisborne*! Show some respect for your betters!'

'It is death, my lord Gisborne...'

'Exactly, yet I come to Oakden and find six wolfsheads living in your village. I'm going to take them back with me to Nottingham Castle to have their necks stretched.' He leaned forward. 'Can you give me a good reason why I shouldn't take you to swing alongside them?'

'I swear before God that we didn't know they were here.'

'He lies, my lord,' said Trent.

Gisborne smiled.

'I believe he does lie, Trent. Not only to me, but before God. Cedric is a maker of false vows. A blasphemer who takes the name of Our Lord in vain.'

Cedric looked in despair at the other villagers, waving a hand towards them.

'Ask anyone here, my lord Gisborne, and they'll tell you that we knew nothing of their presence in our village.'

Gisborne glanced around the place, seeming to be deep in thought.

'I ought to burn Oakden to the ground and turn you all out into the forest. But for some reason the Sheriff believes that you should continue to exist to work the land. Do you have the taxes ready, Cedric?'

The villager nodded and pointed to a pile of bags on a table in front of his own home.

'Everything we have, my lord,' he said.

'Good!' Gisborne replied. 'And you are sure that it's everything, Cedric?'

'I swear to it, my lord.'

'You *swear* to it,' Gisborne mocked. 'Well! Just as you swore that there were no wolfsheads in Oakden? Just to be sure that you're not cheating the Sheriff I think I'll have my men search these dung pits you live in.'

Gisborne sat impatiently on his horse as some of the men at arms searched the huts. At last Trent appeared before him.

'I believe the old fool is telling the truth, my lord. There's nothing hidden in their homes.'

'Of course there isn't, Trent. They've buried it somewhere in the forest.' He looked at the villagers. 'I will spare your homes today,' he said. 'But I will return in thirty days to collect exactly the same amount in taxes as I have taken today.'

'My lord, I beg of you...' Cedric began.

'I don't like beggars, Cedric, so be silent.'

He leaned over to Trent and whispered something into his ear. Trent rode away towards the foot soldiers, leaning over to give them an instruction, followed by a broad grin.

'The Sheriff will be most displeased with you all,' Gisborne addressed the villagers. 'Yet he won't allow me to put you all to the sword... Nevertheless, you must be taught a lesson...'

He nodded towards Trent and the men at arms.

The first crossbow bolt caught Cedric in the shoulder, spinning him round, then the second took him in the broad of the back. A third swept right through the side of his throat, sending him into a crazed dance that persisted as three more bolts tore into his chest. He threw out his arms as though trying to balance himself and staggered towards the villagers. He had covered barely half the distance before he pitched forward on to his face.

The archer was dressed in green and brown, melding in with the trees of Sherwood, which crept within an arrow's distance of the road between Oakden and Nottingham. It was good to get out into the forest and practice with the longbow. An arrow was taken from the quiver at the archer's side and put to the bow. The elm was a good fifty yards away and the knot on its trunk perhaps six inches across.

The secret of firing a longbow was to always believe that you would hit the target. There had to be no doubt about the ability to strike home. Those had been the wise words of the master bowman in the castle who had taught the archer how to shoot. You simply had to believe that there was not the slightest question of missing what you aimed at.

On the downturn of breath the arrow was let loose. A smile crossed the archer's face as the arrow shaft was seen to shudder as it thudded into the very centre of the knot. The archer walked forward and retrieved it.

Then the archer heard the crash through the bracken. A stag burst through the clearing away from the road. Someone was about. More than one person, for the archer heard the mumble of several voices, somewhere in the trees. Above the hollow way through which the broad track passed. And there they were. Three men all carrying bows and with swords at their sides. The archer looked askance, for one of them was clearly a monk. A very familiar monk.

The archer pulled up a brown hood and shrank back into the forest.

~

'I can hear the bastards coming,' said John. 'We're only just in time.'

Somewhere along the road the three men could hear the chatter of men and the whinnying of horses.

'Sounds like there's quite a few to contend with,' muttered Tuck, as he strung his bow. 'I fear we're going to have a busy morning.'

'All the more reason for you to stay out of sight, Tuck,' said Loxley. 'John and I are known to them as outlaws, but you are not. Your presence at Saint Withburga's shrine, with travellers bringing gossip, is useful to our cause. Better that you're not forced to flee into the forest just yet.'

Tuck nodded.

'And here they come,' he said, pointing a finger as Gisborne and three mounted horseman entered the hollow way, sinking down into its depths so that they seemed a long way below the three ambushers. Men at arms on foot followed, guarding a donkey cart in their midst.

'They've got prisoners,' said John. 'Outlaws by the look of them.'

Loxley looked to where five men were being dragged by ropes behind the three horsemen who rode at the rear of the column.

'Aye, wolfsheads,' said Tuck. 'Will Scarlock or whatever his name is. And the other Will. Stutely, I believe. The weaselly little runt is Much. I don't know the others.'

Loxley looked along the length of the hollow way at the miller's son. 'Much is the one I rescued from Trent and the foresters the other day. It seems as though justice has caught up with him.'

'His brains are in his arse,' said Tuck. 'He's overdue for a hanging.'

Loxley considered the situation.

'This might just solve our problem of getting the tax money up here. There are the extra men we needed.' He turned to John. 'See how quickly you can get to the rear of the column. Those outlaws are unguarded from behind. Slip them a dagger to cut themselves free.'

In a moment John had vanished into the trees lining the rim of the hollow way.

'Let's see if we can distract them while John does his work,' said Loxley. 'Keep an arrow aimed at those horsemen, Tuck.'

He loaded an arrow himself and half-drew the bowstring. Then he stepped out on to a bare patch on the top of the steep earthen bank. He saw Gisborne look up at him, a questioning look on the face under the helmet.

'That's far enough, Gisborne,' Loxley shouted. 'My men are all around you.' And then in a louder voice. 'Drop your weapons! There's an arrow in the gut for any man who moves.'

'Loxley!'

'Yes, my lord Gisborne,' he replied. 'Back from the dead. You did tell de Lisle I was dead, I believe?'

'I merely anticipated this present event,' said Gisborne. He whispered something to the horseman on his right. In a second the soldier had drawn his sword and was spurring his horse towards the narrower end of the hollow way. He had scarce moved two yards before Tuck's arrow pierced his heart, flinging him back to the ground.

A foot-soldier who happened to have a loaded crossbow stepped out from one side of the column and raised the weapon towards Loxley. He didn't have time to sight it before Loxley's arrow flew into his open mouth, its head protruding from the back of the soldier's neck. Loxley reloaded the bow, aiming it in Gisborne's direction. Gisborne, who had half drawn his sword eased it back into the scabbard.

'You're braver than you used to be, Gisborne,' said Loxley. 'I thought that burning villages and murdering the old was more your mark. For a moment there you showed a tad more courage.'

'You'll hang for this, wolfshead!'

Loxley nodded.

'Undoubtedly, but not I think today.'

Gisborne heard the noise of a scuffle behind him and turned his head. The three soldiers at the rear of the column had been unhorsed by the once-captive outlaws and were being tied with the very ropes that had once held their prisoners. He saw John Little, the wrestler from Nottingham Castle, aiming an arrow towards the men at arms who had turned round.

He looked up again at Loxley.

'I see you've taken up with the very assassin the Sheriff sent into Sherwood to kill you,' Gisborne said. 'You should tell your giant that de Lisle will cut his bowels open when he catches up with him.'

Loxley gave a bitter laugh. 'There'll be many a day passes before I let that happen. I may just slit open de Lisle's bowels first.' He shouted towards John and the freed outlaws. 'Get the money off that cart and get back into the forest.'

'This is an outrage!' Gisborne blustered. 'Robbing the King of his lawful taxes is treason! You'll have your bowels cut out as well, Loxley. And fired in front of your eyes while you still live!'

Loxley drew back his bowstring a little further.

'You may not survive to see it, Gisborne,' he replied. 'And I suspect that very little of that money would ever find its way into the coffers of Lionheart.'

He saw the outlaws vanish into the forest. A few moments later John Little was at his side.

'What are we to do with them, Robin?' he asked, very loudly. 'We could cut them all down. Save the weakest man. Send him back to de Lisle to tell him what we've done!'

'Not this time, John.' He looked towards the men at arms. 'If you follow Gisborne into Sherwood again I'll not let you escape alive. Speak that message to your fellows in Nottingham Castle.'

'Damn you, Loxley!' Gisborne crashed a hand down on to his saddle, startling the horse who careered a trifle until its rider brought him to rest.

'Not Loxley anymore,' said John. 'Loxley's gone. Robin Hood fights for Sherwood now.'

'Robin Hood?' said Gisborne. 'What nonsense is this?'

'A nonsense that'll plague your nightmares, my lord Gisborne,' shouted John. 'Keep out of this forest or I'll slay you with my bare hands.'

'What's a name, after all?' asked Robin. 'Nothing to the baptism of slaughter you'll experience if you ride this way again.' He whispered to John who nodded and stepped back into the trees. 'I regret we must take our leave of you, Sir Guy. Think well of what happened today and reflect on my words. We hold Sherwood and everyone in it. Touch our holdings at your peril.'

'*Wolfshead!*'

'You're the wolfshead now, Gisborne! There isn't a law in England that'll protect you if you ride into Sherwood again.' He gestured towards the trees. 'I'll leave some men here to guard this hollow way for one hour. Leave before that time is up and you will die.'

He stepped back into the trees.

~

'Who are you?' asked Scarlet as they marched across the clearing towards the denser undergrowth of Sherwood Forest. 'Are you really Loxley? I know of you! You brought death and destruction to Loxley Chase. Villages burned, villeins put to the sword. Do you intend to bring all of that to Sherwood?'

'I didn't bring the death and destruction,' said Robin. 'The bastard overlords did that. We fought back. We didn't skulk in the greenwood like the outlaws of Sherwood...'

'What do you expect us to do? Throw our lives away? There's no way of defeating de Lisle and Gisborne. They hold all the castles that ring the forest. They outnumber us. They come and go as they please. And will always do so, whatever your fine words. Robin Hood! What sort of name is that?'

'Loxley village has gone,' Robin replied very quietly. 'And I'll not use its name again until I've dealt with the people who destroyed it.'

He stopped walking and turned to face Scarlet. 'You saw what we did today? The tactics we used? You are right! We're not an army, trained to fight the armies of the Sheriff and the overlords. We need to combat them in our own way. The way we fought today.'

Much stepped between them. 'We should listen to him, Will. He saved our lives. That's twice he's saved mine. I'd rather die fighting than flee like a tormented deer. Everything we've tried before has failed. Maybe we should fight in the way that Robin suggests.'

'I've little left to live for,' said Stutely. 'I think Robin is right! Loxley or Hood, his name makes no difference to me. Better to die fighting than be butchered like a sheep. I...'

They heard the beat of the horse's hooves on the hard path just as they were reaching the trees. William a' Trent has been ordered by Gisborne to take a chance and ride out of the hollow way before the hour was up, in the hope of bringing more soldiers out of Nottingham Castle to scour the forest. He hadn't travelled far before he encountered the fugitives, noting that they had unstrung their bows. He drew his sword and charged towards the wolfshead Robin Hood. Flinging his bow aside Robin tried to get out his own blade, waving the outlaws away as he turned to meet Trent's charge.

But the clash was not to be.

Trent was only three yards away when an arrow took him in the chest. The horseman dropped his sword and reins as he grasped its shaft, screaming with a mixture of fear and agony. The animal came to a sudden halt as Trent died in its saddle.

Robin glanced around to see the origin of the shot. For several moments he couldn't see where it had come from, so hidden was the archer in brown and green attire on the edge of the trees.

The figure in the shadows waved an arm in greeting and then was gone, lost in the darkness of the undergrowth.

Seven

'Let me understand you, Gisborne,' the Sheriff said very quietly. 'You collected the taxes from Oakden. Killed Cedric the head man. Captured several outlaws. And then in turn you were ambushed and robbed by Loxley?'

'Yes, my lord Sheriff. Only the wolfshead has taken to calling himself Robin Hood. God knows why!'

The Sheriff patted the table for a moment, then poured the remnants of a flagon of wine down his throat. He looked around the hall, finding some satisfaction in the fact that the guard at the door trembled as his eyes came to rest upon him. He held the man's frightened gaze for several moments more before turning back to Gisborne.

'And your men, Gisborne? What were they all doing when this ambush took place? Those men at arms you took with you? Did they make no resistance at all?'

Gisborne shuffled nearer to the table.

'They were pinned down in the hollow, my lord,' he replied. 'I lost two of my best soldiers in the fight...'

'Fight, Gisborne? What was this fight? You mentioned no fight?' De Lisle stood, his voice louder. 'This wasn't a fight, Gisborne! This was a woodland murder was it not?'

'It was...'

'Where is William a' Trent? I want to hear his report.' De Lisle looked curiously at Gisborne. He had watched through the window as Trent's empty horse was led into the castle courtyard. He had already guessed the answer to his question. 'Bring me Trent, Gisborne...'

Gisborne looked even more uncomfortable.

'I regret...' he began.

'Tell me?' De Lisle's voice was scarcely audible.

'William a' Trent died very bravely, my lord. He said to me that he thought the outlaw's claim that they'd left men to guard the hollow was a monstrous bluff. He charged out some moments later.'

Gisborne looked down to avoid the Sheriff's questioning eyes. 'He was correct, my lord. There was no guard. We found his body on the way back to Nottingham. He had obviously come across the outlaws as they were trying to escape. They shot him down with an arrow.'

'I see...' De Lisle paced up and down. 'A good man, Trent. Always loyal. A good soldier who knew the ways of the forest. I would rather have lost any man but Trent.' He looked across at the knight. 'I would much rather have lost you, Gisborne!'

'My lord!'

'*My lord*!' De Lisle imitated the unctuous tones. 'What a creep you are, Gisborne!'

The guard at the door trembled as the Sheriff's sudden shout seemed to shake the room. 'You're a fool! All Sherwood will be laughing at us by tomorrow. If you had followed Trent's example and charged out of that hollow you could have cut down all of those bastard wolfsheads! You could have brought me back Loxley's head!'

His arm swept the flagon from the table with such force that it crashed into the wall. The Sheriff breathed deeply and then, reaching down, grasped the edge of the table and sent it rolling over towards Gisborne.

The knight took a step backwards.

'My lord Sheriff...' he said.

'Get out of my sight, Gisborne,' de Lisle yelled. 'I want you back out into that forest at first light. Take an army if you have to. Fight those mutinous scum in Sherwood. If anyone resists put them to the sword. Burn their hovels. Do whatever it takes until they scream betrayal to those wolfsheads. And if you fail me, Gisborne. If you fail me again. Better that you die in Sherwood.'

~

'You live here?'

John Little looked at the narrow clearing in the trees. A couple of shelters, not unlike sheep pens, had been built against an earth bank. The ashes of a great fire lay alongside the broad path that wound past the bones of dismembered animals.

John shook his head and looked into the resentful faces of the rescued outlaws.

'Pigs live better in the mud of a village sty!' he said. 'I'd rather rot in the dungeons of Nottingham than live like this, Robin. And all these stinking bones? A butcher's shambles stinks sweeter!'

'We're wolfsheads,' said Ralph Gammon. 'It's how we're forced to live. Like animals driven into the forest.'

Robin Hood walked the length of the little valley and then returned to the outlaws.

'If you stay here you'll be caught,' he said.

'Of course we'll be caught, Robin,' said Much. 'We're hunted creatures. Only a matter of time before they take us.'

'Maybe,' said Robin. 'But you don't have to make it easy for them. This lurk of yours is much too near Nottingham. I'll wager they can see the smoke of your fires from the castle walls. If you stay here you'll die.'

Will Scarlet sat down on a fallen tree and looked up at them all.

'And what does our new and gallant leader suggest?' he asked. 'I mind well what happened in Loxley Chase. You've some nerve to come here and preach to us...'

Robin look down at him and nodded.

'I do have some nerve,' he said. Then to the other outlaws. 'Will is right. Terrible mistakes were made at Loxley. Good men died. I shoulder the blame for every drop of blood spilled. But we learned lessons there. We'll not make those mistakes again.'

'You have to trust Robin,' Tuck intervened. 'Or do you want to spend all your days living like pigs?'

'What choice is there?' said Much. 'It's the order of things, God's will that some are powerful and many more poor. Perhaps when the King comes back from Normandy. Lionheart will see how de Lisle and Gisborne are breaking his own laws and bring 'em to heel.'

Robin sat down next to Scarlet. He thought for a while before speaking.

'Did King Henry care for you when he extended the forest laws?' he said at last. 'Do you think his son Lionheart loses sleep worrying about you? I've seen him. Heard him speak.

Lionheart's an arrogant bastard who cares nothing for you and very little for England.'

'But he's our king!' said Much.

'A king who's never in England! Except when he wants to loot it and rob the poorest villein to pay for his glorious expeditions, first to the Holy Land and now Normandy.'

'But God appointed him...' said Ralph. 'Appointed him to reign and rule and keep order...'

'They appoint themselves,' Robin replied. 'These Plantagenets are the devil's brood. From hell they came and to hell they'll return. God had nothing to do with it.'

'And what does Brother Tuck say to that?' asked Scarlet. 'Treason and heresy in one speech, brother?'

'To me there is but one King,' said the monk. 'And I don't think He's a Plantagenet.'

'You'll have us hanged and drawn for our treachery,' said Scarlet. 'Our friend here, this Robin Hood would have us wage war on Lionheart as well as those scum Gisborne and the Sheriff.'

'Not yet, Scarlet,' Robin said. 'I'm content to see off the Sheriff first. The rest may not come in my life. But why should any man or woman bow his knee to someone who has appointed *himself* their superior? Much there and Ralph. They matter to me far more than Lionheart or Count John of Mortain.'

Scarlet turned to face him.

'Your words frighten me, Loxley,' he said. 'They've the curse of death on them.' He held his head in his hands. After a long minute of silence he looked up. 'But I can't deny that such thoughts are strangers to me. I've considered these arguments myself in the dead of night.' He looked around the clearing. 'What should we do with this midden?'

'We should leave it before first light,' Robin replied. 'I know a place deep in Sherwood. A secret valley with fresh water and good dry caves. There are no tracks to it, only hidden paths where one man with a bow could hold back an army.'

'Do you mean Thripper's Drumble?' asked Tuck. 'The place we sheltered in for a week when Brian du Bois pursued us?'

'The very place,' said Robin. 'It's been used before. Sherwood folk hid there over a hundred years ago, when William the Bastard and his Norman army wasted the shire after the Conquest.'

'I didn't know it really existed,' said Stutely. 'I thought it a place of legend.'

'I know of it, though I've never been,' said Much. 'A place of ghosts and demons. Nobody goes near that part of Sherwood. They say it's the gateway to hell.'

~

'The Abbot of St. Mary's thinks you should become a nun, my dear.'

Henry Fitzwalter sat in a great chair by his fireside and looked across at his daughter. 'He believes that you should be married to God, so that on my death all of my lands go to the church.'

Marian remained silent for a long while, warming her hands close by the blazing logs. How pretty she looked, her father thought, with those long locks of dark hair against a face that looked pale even in the heat.

'I can't imagine it, father,' she replied. 'Being confined and never able to wander in the forest.' She looked around the room. 'I'm sure I'd be better employed tending to the estate. And I can't really think of life without you, anyway.'

Fitzwalter reached down for the long metal poker and prodded back a log that looked as though it might tumble forwards into the hall.

'I can't live for ever, Marian,' he said at last. 'And these are troublous times. Is there nobody you'd think of taking as a husband?'

She laughed heartily.

'I saw the way the abbot was looking at me when he was here. I think he'd be thrilled to take me himself!'

'Marian!'

'It's true! You must have noticed. The vow of chastity is the last thing on that awful man's mind. I've heard the tales, father. And not just about girls...'

'Now you go too far. You spend too much time in Sherwood, listening to the village gossips. And what nature teaches young people isn't wisdom. A dose of the Bible might do you a power of good.'

'I'd rather be out under the trees...'

'Sometimes I think you're a changeling,' said Fitzwalter. 'A forest spirit swapped you for my real daughter. Your dear mother was so quiet and modest. Never wanted to leave the castle. Content to just sit by the window and embroider. But you... if I had had a son I doubt he would have been so rowdy.'

Marian reached forward and heaved a log on to the fire.

'It feels so good out in Sherwood,' she said. 'I feel... free.'

'But all women must wed in the end. It's the only way they can remain safe. How about Brian du Bois?'

She looked shocked.

'Brian has women all over the shire. At least three mistresses within an arrow shot of Newark Castle. You are jesting?'

He chuckled. 'Just a little! There is Sir Guy of Gisborne, of course. I saw the way he looked at you when he was here.'

'There might be some merit in that suggestion,' she said. 'I could stab him with my dagger on our wedding night and do the people of Sherwood quite a favour. At first I used to think that Guy was quite mad. But he's not. He's just evil. In fact I'm surprised he's still alive. I shouldn't think there's a villein in Sherwood who wouldn't wish to kill him.'

'These are sinful thoughts, my pet,' Fitzwalter replied. 'We should not contemplate any man's death in our humour. My own father was slain during the Anarchy. Murder isn't a matter for levity!'

She smiled across at him.

'I stand reproached,' she said. 'But if you heard half the things I do about what happens out in the forest...'

'We live in dangerous times, Marian. And that's why I worry about you being out in Sherwood so much. It isn't safe for any woman. I'm never at ease until you come home.'

She stood and rested a hand on his shoulder.

'I do take great care,' she said. 'And I always keep a knife at hand!'

He looked up into her dark brown eyes.

'*Changeling*!' he said.

~

Gisborne found it hard to sleep.

Whole scenes went through his mind where he murdered de Lisle in so many different ways. The Sheriff was an upstart. De Lisle's ancestor might have come over from Normandy with King William, but only as a man at arms, not as a knight and a gentleman like Gisborne's forebear Gilles de Falaise.

Falaise had fought magnificently on Senlac Hill. His courage had been noted by the Conqueror, who in time had rewarded him with all those great lands of Bowland. Family tradition told how Gilles had loved those wild moorlands so much that he had taken his name and title from one of the moorland streams – the *Gisburn*.

And now, thanks to the duplicity of others, Sir Guy had been cheated out of those lands. The die had been cast. Much of the estate had fallen into the clutches of Sir Brian du Bois. Not that the custodian of Newark Castle had ever bothered to visit them. They were just another acquisition won by one of his very successful wagers. The man had the devil's own luck. Worse still in that he had been Gisborne's oldest friend. Such a betrayal! How could a friend do that to you?

For a few moments Gisborne had a convoluted dream where he killed de Lisle and somehow had the blame put firmly on du Bois's shoulders. The Sheriff dead and the master of Newark swinging from a rope on Nottingham's walls.

'Why can't you sleep?' said the tired voice next to him.

In his ire he had almost forgotten that she was there. Clorinda of the ripe breasts and tempting face. The whore he had snatched as a trophy from the burning hovels of Loxley.

She reached across and snuggled into his shoulder, her hand working its way down his chest and across his stomach.

'Haven't I satisfied you enough?' she asked. 'You seem so distracted.'

'I've matters of great importance to consider.'

'More important than that?'

Her palm and fingers began to work upon him. He felt a delicious warmth spread through his body. And then de Lisle's face seemed to loom out of the darkness. He reached down and cast her hand aside.

'Don't you want me, my lord?' she almost whimpered.

'Yes, but not tonight. I've too much to consider.'

'Robin Hood?'

He sat up and held her shoulders down on to the pillow.

'Where did you hear that name?'

'Robin Hood's the talk of Nottingham. You can't stop the gossip, my lord. Your men had the tale round the castle the moment they came home. It was told with advantages round the market by even time. The minstrels are already singing ballads.'

'He's just an outlaw,' Gisborne said, 'a wolfshead like all the rest.'

'That's not what the soldiers are saying, my lord. They're saying that he's Loxley the rebel. Come to Sherwood to take vengeance for what happened to his village.'

'He's not a rebel, he's a wolfshead. And I'll have him hanging before the week is out.'

She pulled off the blanket so that he might see her breasts in the moonlight which flooded in through the windows. She felt annoyance when he seemed not to notice.

'You should take care, my lord!' she said petulantly. 'We all know who Loxley is, don't we?'

'I know he's your cousin, Clorinda. That you grew up together in Loxley. That you yourself played a part in their pointless rebellion. If I wasn't so fond of you I'd have you at a rope's end for the rebellious little bitch you are!'

'Guy...' she said very softly, stroking his face. 'You don't need to be angry with me. Loxley means nothing. A village burned. A fugitive in the forest. Hunt him down for all I care. Cut him to ribbons with your sword. Hang him from a tree. Rack him, quarter him, I don't care. It's not my fault that Loxley and I share blood.'

He regarded her for a moment and then asked the question that had often been on his mind.

'And is that all you've shared?'
'Yes,' she lied.

~

Alan a' Dale stretched out on top of the wall surrounding the market place in Nottingham. The watch called midnight and moved on towards the castle gate. He had had a most pleasant evening in the taverns of the town, singing the new ballad of Robin Hood and Gisborne. The drunken audience had yelled approval at the deeds of the new outlaw.

The hooded man come to the forest.

There had been raucous laughter at the misfortunes of Gisborne and cheers at news of the death of William a' Trent. And they had liked his song. He had paid for no ale that night. Even a tavern whore had done him a favour for no consideration, in gratitude for his amusing lines.

Alan had a talent for composing swiftly. And he always kept the lines and the tune simple so that men might learn the songs and pass them on as they journeyed around the shire. He wondered how accurate his account of the skirmish had been. The story had been given to him by one of the men at arms who had been there. An amiable fellow who was the source of much castle gossip.

Sometime tomorrow he would journey into the forest. He had made an arrangement with Loxley that a message would be left in the hollow of a tree. Saying where the outlaw might be and how to make further contact. Giving orders as to just what a minstrel in Nottingham might be expected to do next.

It was a dry and warm night and soon the effects of the ale overtook him and he fell asleep on the wall. He heard the taverns turn out their drunken multitudes as he drifted away.

He seemed to have slept only minutes before he woke with a start. Even before he was properly awake he heard the mutterings of men. And then the whinnying of horses and the barking of orders.

Soldiers were on the march.

Alan eased himself to the ground and wandered along to the castle gate. A strong force was assembling. At least thirty horsemen and a hundred foot soldiers and crossbowmen. Gisborne himself, clad in chain, wearing a blue cloak and with a helmet on his head, was trotting his horse up and down, as though impatient to be off.

At last the column was assembled and, with a wave of his arm, the little army set out in the direction of Sherwood Forest.

Alan rubbed the sleep from his eyes and trotted after them.

Eight

It was a small village situated deep in the forest.

A few thatched houses surrounded by a similar number of hard-won ploughed fields. The trees of Sherwood pressed hard against the wooden boundary fences, as though desiring to claim back the land that had been taken from them. A few pigs had torn up the turf of the tiniest enclosure. Cattle for milking had been brought down into the yard of the largest farmhouse. The smoke from the house-fires hung over the glade. The clattering of a blacksmith's hammer came from the forge situated hard by the road to Nottingham. Nearby a donkey attached to a cart brayed at their approach.

'And this place is?' said Gisborne to the Sheriff's clerk who was riding alongside him.

The clerk scratched his nose.

'The hamlet of Breevedon, my lord Gisborne,' he replied. 'A holding of my lord the Sheriff.'

Gisborne leaned back on his horse and considered the buildings before him.

'A profitable village?' he asked.

The clerk laughed. 'They barely survive, my lord. They send to Nottingham little in the way of taxes. They pay their way mostly in rabbits.'

'Rabbits?'

'Rabbits, my lord. They say their land is too poor to work. Mostly they send rabbits to the castle in lieu of taxes.'

Gisborne grunted and then yawned. Another early morning start and he was not in the best frame of mind. He looked across at the trees and wondered if they concealed outlaws.

'Is this an obedient village?' he asked.

'Obedient, my lord?'

'Do they obey the laws of the forest?'

The clerk snuffled.

'There has been poaching in the district...' he began.

'Poaching?'

'My lord the Sheriff couldn't prove that the poachers came from Breevedon. There was just... poaching in the district.'

Gisborne looked again towards the trees.

'Are there any other villages near?'

'No, my lord,' said the clerk, 'the forest is too thick hereabouts and the ground dry and hard to work. It's why my lord the Sheriff tolerates the failures of the Breevedon villagers to... provide.'

'Does he?'

'There are many such villages elsewhere in Sherwood, my lord. Villages that can but subsist.'

Gisborne considered the little man's words. He wished the trees weren't so damned close.

'And the blacksmith? Is the forge of use to the district?'

'A man named Gilbert is the blacksmith, my lord. Gilbert of the White Hand they call him.'

'The white hand?'

'His hands are scarred thus, my lord. From the sparks from the fire or the constant beating of the hammer against metal. I forget which. The forge is of use, being on the road to Nottingham. It is much used by travellers.'

'And does this Gilbert pay his taxes?'

'He always has, my lord. He usually pays in arrowheads and bolts for crossbows.'

'Good.'

A breeze sighed through the Sherwood trees, bending the boughs and sending a creaking sound across the hamlet. Gisborne looked back at his men. They were looking in all directions. He knew that the thought of outlaws and the other day's ambush was on their minds. Some of the soldiers with him today had seen their two comrades fall in the hollow way. He knew that they were all thinking of William a' Trent with the arrow plunged deep into his chest.

They looked nervous, like soldiers in any army that has suffered a setback or a defeat. One or two were muttering and had scared looks on their faces. Gisborne knew from his years of campaigning that such terrors could spread. And on reflection the outlaws were probably far away. They mustn't be perceived as deadly phantoms hiding in ambush behind every tree.

The soldiers stood to attention as they noticed Gisborne's roving eye. That was more like it. Discipline, that was what soldiers needed. The defining quality that turned a rabble back into an army. It was time to set an example. It was time to strike back at these peasants.

He saw a movement out of the corner of his eye. The blacksmith had emerged from the forge, a sack over his shoulder which he heaved into the cart.

'You there!' Gisborne called.

The man came over. Black-bearded and burly with a look of arrogance in his eyes. He stood before Gisborne and looked him straight in the eye.

'What's in the sack?' said Gisborne.

'Arrowheads, my lord. I'm taking them to Nottingham Castle.'

Gisborne nodded.

'You're going there now?'

'Straight away, my lord.'

'You are Gilbert?'

'I am, my lord.'

Gisborne looked down at the blacksmith's hands. He couldn't see anything particularly white about them. They just looked like the rough and worn hands of any peasant. He raised his glance to the man's face. The blacksmith was still looking up at him in that insulting manner. The kind of behaviour that would usually get a villein whipped – or worse.

For a moment Gisborne considered cutting off those battered hands as a sharp lesson to the other villagers, who were now gathering close by the track. But no. There was always a shortage of arrowheads in Nottingham. And men to make them. De Lisle would be peeved.

Not the lesson to be served out that day.

'Very well,' he said at last. 'You may go.'

The blacksmith knuckled his forehead in a salute that was almost an insult in itself. Then he turned and walked back to the cart. Gisborne turned his horse and watched as the man drove away. The blacksmith and cart were soon absorbed into the forest trees as though they had never been.

Insolent bastard!

Gisborne noted that he was breathing very heavily. He opened his mouth and took in one deep breath before turning the horse to face the rest of the villagers.

There were not many of them. A couple of old people stood in the doorway of the nearest hovel. The rest were younger. Half a dozen of them, men and women, who looked as though they laboured on the land. Two small children were looking at Gisborne's men with great curiosity. A boy of about fourteen stood halfway between Gisborne and the others.

'Who is the head man?' Gisborne said to the clerk.

'There really isn't one. It's a mere hamlet. There aren't enough people here to have appointed anyone in charge. I suppose we should have questioned the blacksmith about the affairs of the place. That's if you have any questions?'

Gisborne sighed impatiently. He looked around as though suddenly bored with the whole enterprise. For a moment the villagers breathed easier, thinking that their visitor might be considering riding away. Gisborne turned the head of his horse and trotted forwards a few yards. His men stood to attention as though ready to march.

But then Gisborne turned again to face the boy.

'Come here!'

The boy took a step closer to Gisborne, bowed his head and touched his forehead.

'What's your name, boy?'

'Matthew, my lord.'

'What do you do here?'

'I help with the ploughing and tend to the pigs and cattle.'

'Do your father and mother live?'

The boy pointed at the couple standing by the doorway of one of the houses. Gisborne thought they looked too old to be the parents of a youth his age. Hard usage had a way of ageing people before their time in these Sherwood villages.

'Do you know who I am, boy?'

'No, my lord.'

It gave Gisborne some satisfaction to see that the youth was terrified of him. Matthew of Breevedon hardly looked up and when he did it was with a face pale with fear. He stuttered over his words, wiping his mouth with the back of a hand to remove the spittle that was dribbling down his chin.

'I am Sir Guy of Gisborne. Your lord. Your master.'

'My lord... lord... Gisborne,' Matthew stuttered.

'Correct,' said Gisborne. 'Look up at me, boy.'

William obeyed, his lips trembling, one hand waving up and down in front of his chest.

'Do you ever poach in the forest, Matthew?'

The boy looked affronted.

'No, my lord, I swear I do not!'

Gisborne gave a nod of approval.

'That's good, Matthew!' he gave the boy an icy smile. 'You know, of course, what the penalties are for poaching?'

The boy nodded.

'And that is why you would never do such a thing?'

'No... my lord!'

'Why do the people of Breevedon not pay taxes?' Gisborne asked, as though he had just thought of it. 'Why do they assume that rabbits will do instead of money?'

'The land provides no money, my lord Gisborne,' Matthew answered. 'My lord the Sheriff understands that. That's why we send rabbits to Nottingham Castle.'

Gisborne put on an expression of thoughtfulness.

'Ah, so you provide rabbits as an alternative to paying the King's lawful dues?'

'Yes, my lord Gisborne.'

Matthew of Breevedon looked bewildered, glancing sideways in the hope that one of the other villagers might come over to answer all of these confusing questions.

'It must take an awful lot of rabbits to match the royal taxes?' Gisborne continued. 'Do you catch the rabbits yourself?'

'Sometimes, my lord,' Matthew answered. 'I catch a great many, though all the men in Breevedon catch some.'

Gisborne looked carefully around the village and the tiny fields beyond.

'I see no warren here,' he said. 'Where do you catch all these rabbits?'

'In... in Sherwood, my lord,' the boy stammered. 'There are many rabbits to be found in the forest clearings.'

'So you catch the rabbits in Sherwood Forest?'

Matthew nodded, wishing that the man would ride away.

'Then you *poach* the rabbits in Sherwood Forest?'

'My lord...?'

The clerk leaned forward towards Gisborne.

'With respect, my lord Gisborne,' he said, 'it's not poaching if it's sanctioned by my lord the Sheriff...'

'Has the Sheriff sealed a document sanctioning the villagers of Breevedon to take rabbits in such a way?' Gisborne asked. 'Do you have such a charter?'

The clerk looked flustered.

'Well, no, my lord,' he said. 'It's just a custom of Breevedon.'

'Poaching is not a custom, master clerk,' said Gisborne. 'It's a crime against forest law. If there's no charter then there's no sanction. These are the laws enforced by command of the late King Henry of beloved memory, are they not?'

'My lord,' the clerk whispered, his mouth and foul breath inches from Gisborne's face. 'You'll recall that Lionheart relaxed many of the forest laws on his coronation. At the express request of his mother, Queen Eleanor.'

'Lionheart is not here,' said Gisborne, loudly, so that his men might hear. 'Nor Queen Eleanor. But I am, master clerk, and I am charged by the Sheriff to bring law to this wretched forest of Sherwood.' He looked down again at Matthew of Breevedon. 'You realise, boy, that I could have you mutilated for poaching rabbits in Sherwood? Your balls cut off and your eyes taken out?'

The boy whimpered. Tears ran down his cheek. He turned away and vomited on to the grass by the side of the track. He looked back at the horseman with terror in his eyes.

'However...' Gisborne began.

Matthew of Breevedon caught on to the very slight note of hope in the way Gisborne said the word. He flung himself down on to his knees and held his hands in front of him as though in prayer.

'Have mercy on me, my lord... I didn't know I was doing wrong. I didn't know...'

'Shut up!' said Gisborne.

The boy snapped into tearful silence.

'I am prepared on this occasion to overlook your offence,' Gisborne continued, aware of the surprise on the clerk's face as he uttered the words. 'I am prepared, Matthew of Breevedon, to be merciful.'

'Thank you, my lord,' the boy grovelled. 'Thank you for your mercy...'

'Be silent!' Gisborne snapped. 'And listen to me, boy. Mercy has a price. And the price you pay is information.'

'My lord?' The boy looked puzzled. He glanced towards his parents and then the other villagers. Then he looked up again at Gisborne. 'My lord?'

'There are a great many outlaws in Sherwood,' said Gisborne. 'Have you seen anything of these wolfsheads? Tell me the truth now for my mercy depends on your honesty.'

'No wolfsheads ever come to Breevedon, my lord.'

'That isn't what I asked. I want you to tell me if you've seen any wolfsheads in the forest?'

Matthew seemed even more confused.

'I see a great many men in the forest, my lord,' he replied. 'Many of them aren't known to me. They could be outlaws.'

There was a truthfulness in the answer, Gisborne thought. And besides, the boy was too terrified to lie.

'My lord Gisborne...' the clerk began.

'What is it?' said Gisborne, annoyed at the interruption.

'I know these villages well, my lord. No wolfsheads would seek shelter in Breevedon. The place is too poor. These villeins have scarce enough food for their own bellies...'

Gisborne looked across at the villagers. They certainly looked half-starved, thin and raddled. He wondered how they had the strength to work the land at all. The holdings of land they worked could not possibly provide enough food to give them nourishment to live. There were not enough acres. There were not enough beasts. The boy might not poach anything but rabbits in Sherwood but the rest of the men must be getting meat from somewhere. And given their physical state none of them could be very skilled at the poaching.

He made up his mind what he had to do.

'Matthew of Breevedon,' he said. 'I shall spare you and you may continue to provide rabbits for Nottingham Castle.'

The boy muttered thanks that Gisborne could scarcely hear.

'But for the rest of you,' Gisborne shouted across at the villagers, 'there will be no mercy. I believe that this village is a poaching village. And it's clear that you do not pay your lawful taxes.'

'Do you wish me to record a judgement for my lord the Sheriff?' asked the clerk. 'So that they might have to pay a penalty?'

'Don't be a fool!' Gisborne replied. 'How would they ever pay it? No, this village contributes nothing to the common good. In time many of these men could join the outlaws in the forest. We need to set an example, master clerk.'

'An example?'

'Something to teach the rebels in Sherwood how to obey.'

He turned the horse around in its own length and faced his men.

'Three of you,' he waved a finger at the soldiers. 'Round up the animals and take them back to Nottingham Castle.'

'My lord,' Matthew's father stepped forward, his wife still clutching at his elbow. 'Without our beasts we'll starve!'

'Oh, I promise you won't starve!' Gisborne yelled.

He turned back to his men. 'You six at the front,' he ordered. 'Take torches from those fires and burn down these hovels! Go on, fire the thatches! I want every last one of these dung pits destroyed! Except the forge.'

Matthew's father came near and clutched at Gisborne's foot.

'For the love of Jesus, my lord. Spare our homes, I beg you!'

'Take your hands off me, villein! To touch me is to assault the King's representative. Such assault is punishable by death!'

He turned to the captain of the troops. 'I want this villein hanged from that tree. And this whore by his side!'

'My lord...' the clerk protested.

'Silence!' shouted Gisborne. Then to the soldier. 'Get on with it!'

Matthew of Breevedon ran forward towards Gisborne, only to be intercepted and dragged to the ground by two of the soldiers. He raised his face and Gisborne was thrilled to see the expression of pure hatred there.

As Matthew's parents were dragged away, the other villagers massed and began to edge forward towards Gisborne.

'There you see, master clerk? They do have rebellion in them after all! Well, we'll settle this insurgence.' He looked again at the soldiers. 'Hang every last one of them. Cut down any that resist.' He glanced across at Matthew. One of the soldiers held a dagger by the boy's throat. Gisborne held up a hand.

'No,' he ordered. 'Spare the boy. I gave him my mercy. Just hold him down until these peasants are swinging from the trees. Besides...' he said quietly, turning to the clerk, 'I want him to wander off into Sherwood and tell the rest of the scum who live in the forest just what they might expect if they question their position in life ever again.'

As they rode out of Breevedon Gisborne turned just once, a smile of satisfaction on his face. The mean huts were nearly burned to the ground. The men of Breevedon, their women, and two young children, were dancing from the branches of the great oak that stood in the middle of one of the fields.

Matthew lay on the ground nearby. Crying out as though his mind had gone.

Nine

It seemed a particularly dense stretch of Sherwood Forest. The trees were packed close together and the undergrowth at the edge of the narrow path seemed to consist only of impenetrable brambles. The great oaks curved over the line of the track, the full May leaves almost hiding the sky.

'No one could wander much off this path,' Much muttered, bashing the dense bushes with his quarter staff. 'You sure this is the right place?'

Robin turned and smiled.

'You'd think there was nothing here, wouldn't you?' he said. 'And with good fortune that's what the Sheriff's men will believe as well. I was shown the secret when I was a boy. By an old forester who'd found sanctuary here when Empress Maud's troops were rampaging through the shire.'

'And what is this great secret, Loxley?' Scarlet could hardly keep a tone of hostility out of his voice. 'Are we supposed to bed down by the path?'

'Watch this,' said Robin.

And as they stood they looked askance at him as he walked a few feet more to where the trunk of a particularly large oak barricaded several feet of the path, its trunk meeting a collection of huge sandstone boulders which breasted a small hillock.

'I can quite believe there are demons,' said Ralph Gammon. 'It feels like the ends of the earth. I doubt anything lives here except the beasts of the forest.'

'Not really demons are there?' asked Much.

'Only me!' said Gammon, pulling a horrible face at the little man.

The outlaws looked and laughed.

'Gammon's a demon, Robin,' said John Little, looking up again. 'Well, bugger me!'

They all looked along the path but Robin Hood was nowhere in sight.

They jumped up and rushed along to where he had been standing but there was no sign.

'It's as though he's vanished into thin air...' said Stutely.

Much looked all around. 'Mebbe the demons *have* took him!'

They searched around for several minutes but could find no trace of Loxley. Nor any way off the path. Scarlet, suspecting a ruse, looked up into the trees, thinking that the outlaw had shinned up a tree when they were distracted by Ralph Gammon's face-pulling.

'Robin!' John called out.

There was no answer, just a slight breeze through the boughs and the distant drumming of a woodpecker.

Tuck watched them all with amusement and then got up from where he had been resting on the far side of the path.

'We can keep this game up all afternoon,' he said, 'but I'm hungry and we need to light a fire so that we might feast. Come. I'll show you the trick.'

He strode to where the oak met the boulders and put his hands on to the rock nearest the tree.

'Not even John Little could move that!' said Stutely.

'No more can I,' Tuck replied. 'At least not if you just press against it.'

He slid his hands between the rock and the tree.

'Watch,' he said.

And with almost no effort he slid the long and narrow boulder sideways, leaving an opening of some four feet.

'How is it possible?' said Much, with a look of amazement. 'Why doesn't it just tumble down?'

'Our ancestors were wise men,' Tuck replied. 'Cleverer than us in so many ways. Look down here,' he pointed at several stone rollers, all neatly carved at some distant time in history. 'Who made this door into Thripper's Drumble, nobody knows? It may have been the people who hid here when King William the Bastard was attacking the shire. Or even older than that.'

'I've heard the tales of Thripper's Drumble,' Will Stutely considered. 'Though I thought it a legend. The old folk of the forest said it was a sacred place, used by pagan priests at the time of the Romans.'

'Whatever,' said Tuck, 'do come inside, and see the rest. My stomach is growling for food.'

They all passed through the gap in the forest's barricade and Tuck slid the rock closed behind them. Robin Hood was lying on an earthen bank beyond, head resting on a mattress of thick green moss.

'Took you longer than I thought,' he remarked. 'Well, what do you think of the secret door?'

Even Scarlet was impressed.

'It'll more than do'. He pointed along a path leading into the trees. 'This leads to the Drumble itself?'

'Follow me,' said Robin. 'Just a few hundred yards now. And look up there...' he pointed to some high ground to their right. 'You keep a man posted up there and you can watch all the paths around in case of trouble. You can see for a couple of miles. Plenty of time to put out any fires if the Sheriff or Gisborne dare to enter this end of Sherwood.'

They walked down the track in his footsteps as it wound down into a hollow, a narrow glade amongst the trees with a tiny brook running to one side. On the other was a sandstone bank some twelve feet high lined with ash and birch trees. There were four dark hollows leading into the stone between the bushes.

'Are those caves dry?' asked John.

'They are indeed,' said Robin. 'We lived there for weeks when du Bois was pursuing us. In winter too, with rain and snow. They were as snug as you could wish. And the largest cave has a mystery from the old times. There's a chimney where you can keep a blaze going. But we could never discover where the smoke went. Somewhere deep into the earth, maybe. Certainly not out into the forest. A boon if you have to lie low.'

Scarlet looked all around.

'And is there a back way out?' he asked. 'Some way to escape if we were discovered?'

'That's the joy of the place,' said Tuck. 'The largest of the caves has a tiny tunnel that emerges into the thick of the forest a good half mile away. And the Drumble itself narrows into a tiny path leading to a gorge with a river running through it. Wade down its waters and you'll find yourself well clear of this part of Sherwood. Now please may we eat?'

Even from a mile away Gilbert of the White Hand could see the smoke rising high above the trees of Sherwood. And he knew in his heart what had happened.

'Bastards!'

He swung the little cart around and headed back towards his village. The thought occurred to him that he might meet Gisborne and his men as he returned. Well, so be it! He reached under the sack behind him and drew out a bow and a quiver of arrows. He would at least try to kill Gisborne before he was overwhelmed by the men at arms. But as he approached Breevedon only a solitary figure emerged on to the track before him. He pulled the donkey to a halt.

'Alan, what are you doing here?'

'I followed Gisborne from Nottingham,' Alan a' Dale replied. 'When it became clear he was heading for Breevedon I took the short cut across the hill. I got there just as... as...'

'How many?' asked Gilbert.

'All of them. Every man, woman and child. Hanged. They only spared the boy, Matthew. Gisborne usually leaves one alive so that he might spread the word of fear.'

Gilbert was silent for a long while. Then he climbed down from the cart and led the donkey towards the village.

'Where is Matthew now?'

'I don't know,' said Alan. 'He ran off into the forest. I think he's lost his mind. They burned all the homes. Everything but the forge.'

'Why did they leave the forge?'

'They're short of arrowheads in Nottingham Castle?'

'The only arrowhead I'll make now is the one that'll tear into Gisborne's black heart.'

'Loxley's come back to the forest,' said Alan. 'He'll be in need of arrowheads. I picked up a message from him secreted in the hollow tree. He's gone to Thripper's Drumble.'

'Then we must join Loxley. And seek a vengeance in blood. Like the old days when we battled du Bois...'

'You'll come then?'

Gilbert didn't reply at once. They had turned the last corner and come out at Breevedon. He left the cart and walked across to the great oak from which the bodies hung. He looked at the bulging dead eyes of a dozen faces. Several of the villagers had soiled themselves as they perished.

'Terrible! Terrible!' he said. 'Hanging like crows on a forester's gibbet.'

He staggered forwards and for a second Alan thought that the blacksmith might fall. He reached out and took him by the shoulder. Gilbert breathed deeply and then seemed to compose himself.

'I'll come with you to Loxley,' Gilbert said. 'Better to die as men in Sherwood than come to this.' He turned to Alan. 'But first I need to bury these poor folk. You will help?'

Alan gave a nod.

'It's safe enough,' he said. 'Gisborne must have gone back to Nottingham by the Lambley road. He might have thought that Robin Hood could have got word of his journey here and be waiting to ambush him if he returned the way he came?'

'Who's Robin Hood?'

~

The three men appointed by Gisborne to drive the animals of Breevedon back to Nottingham were not having a happy time. Soon after leaving the village they had taken a wrong turning, losing the route by which they had arrived. None of them were adept at marshalling such a mixed collection of beasts. They had been born in the town and been soldiers since they were boys. At last they had found a track they recognised.

'God aid us, but this is a dreadful place,' one said. 'I'll be glad to be whorin' in Nottingham this night.'

'That bastard Gisborne should've let us journey with him,' said another. 'And what he did in that village... I don't hold with it. They're folk like us. And you notice he didn't get his own hands dirty. Not one of 'em did he string up. It's our souls he puts at peril.'

The third nodded agreement.

'Always the little folk who pays the price,' he said. 'Look at William a' Trent. He started out as a man of arms and thought himself mightier than he was. Always seeking preferment. And now he's food for worms. Food for worms.'

'Trent deserved it,' said the first. 'Always lickin' round the Sheriff's arse. He should've accepted his place. Keep your face down. Knuckle your head as they pass. And don't go lookin' for trouble in Sherwood Forest. Better to be in Normandy with Lionheart than at the beck and call of de Lisle and Gisborne. At least Lionheart loves his soldiers.'

'Nay, you're wrong there,' said the second soldier. 'Lionheart's no better than Gisborne. Just another who'd get yer slain for their glory. Better not to be a soldier at all. I'd rather be a villein ploughing in a field.'

'All very well till Gisborne arrives in yer village and strings yer from a tree. Yer'd soon wish yerself back freezing on the battlements of Nottingham Castle.'

'You two gossip like old women,' said the first soldier. 'You know what they say? God's ordained our position in this life. And we're burdened with it till we die!'

'*They* say it's what God decrees. But have you ever heard God himself say it? Convenient for our lords ain't it, coming out with such rot. If we all comes down from Adam and Eve then shouldn't we be equal. Take Lionheart. He might be king but he's a man like I am. He shits and scratches his arse. Belches at the table. Bleeds if you cut him. It's just his fortune that he rules over us. And the same goes for the lot of 'em.'

'Don't talk like that in Nottingham. They'll have yer stretched!'

'I ain't such a bloody fool!' the other replied. 'But one day there'll be a reck'ning, you see!'

'You're all wind! If there's a reck'ning it won't come from the likes of you. Just look at the way you... who the bloody hell's that?'

A figure had stepped out into the shadows beneath the trees which lined the road. A bowman clad in green with a brown hood. The animals had started at the sudden appearance of the archer and scattered to one side of the track.

'It's Robin Hood!'

'Don't be a bloody fool! It's just some peasant on his way home...'

'What, with a longbow? In the forest? If it ain't Robin Hood it's some other wolfshead.'

'A wolfshead on his own! Let's take him! You know what the reward is?'

'I value my life more than gold...'

He had scarce uttered the word before an arrow hit a tree just inches away from his head. A second arrow sank into the ground just by the feet of one of the soldiers. A third clipped the mail on the shoulder of another.

'Bugger this!' said the first soldier. As he turned to flee he saw that his two companions were ahead of him speeding back the way they had come.

The archer watched them until they were out of sight, smiling at their cowardice. A fourth arrow was removed from the bow and put back into the quiver. Then the archer walked along the track and began to drive the animals towards the nearest village.

What an exciting day it had been.

~

'And you thought it necessary to wipe out my village of Breevedon, Gisborne?'

De Lisle had placed himself in a great seat, almost a throne, at one end of the great hall of Nottingham Castle. He looked down at the knight, who stood awkwardly at the foot of the flight of five steps. 'Breevedon?'

'I took my orders from you, lord Sheriff. Your exact words. Put them to the sword, you said. Burn their hovels. Wipe out the rebelliousness that flows in the very blood of these Sherwood villagers. And I was merciful. I spared the village of Lambley.'

'How generous of you!'

'The people of Lambley pay their taxes... and on time. Those who obey are not punished. Those that fail are. What did Breevedon contribute? Rabbits!'

'I happen to be very fond of eating rabbit.'

'There is no shortage of rabbits in the shire, my lord. And I did spare the forge and the life of the blacksmith... Gilbert of the something. In view of the fact that he provides arrowheads for our soldiers.'

'And do you imagine Gilbert the smith will still feel inclined to make arrowheads, knowing that you've wiped out everyone in his village? His relations, probably, knowing the way these vermin breed?'

'He has no choice, my lord. If he refuses to work for us I'll burn his forge and hang him as well.'

De Lisle gestured towards the window.

'Why not burn down the whole of Sherwood, Gisborne, and hang all my poverty? The way you're going we'll have nobody left to serve us and pay the taxes?'

'I did what I did on your own instructions...'

'I said rebellious villages, Gisborne. Outlaw villages.'

'Breevedon was a hotbed of poachers...'

'Rabbits, Gisborne, rabbits.'

'It's the principle of the thing, lord Sheriff. And word of Breevedon's fate will be all round Sherwood by now. An example's been set. Perhaps now we'll see some deference to our laws.'

The Sheriff gave a great sigh and waved him away.

'Oh, Gisborne! Get back to your little whore. I've seen enough of you for one day!'

~

'This is your fault, Loxley! Their deaths are on your conscience!' said Will Scarlet, fingering the dagger in his belt. 'This is what comes of rebellion,' he muttered to the others.

The two men stood facing each other in the glade of Thripper's Drumble. The last light of the long May evening was fading away. The other outlaws sat around, the despair showing in their faces. Alan and Gilbert, having brought the news, rested with their backs to the sandstone bank.

'It's what comes of the reasons for rebellion, Scarlet,' said Robin. 'Gisborne was sacking villages in Sherwood long before I came back.'

'Aye, and he got the taste for it in Loxley! Another of your ill-judged adventures.'

'And what would you do, Scarlet? Do the right thing, like these bastards are always telling you? Slave away and work yourself into the grave? Dare to want to get food for yourself? Have no freedom? Kiss the Sheriff's arse?'

Scarlet pulled out the dagger and waved it in Robin's face. The scar on his face seemed redder in the dying sunlight.

'Easy for you to say, Loxley! You're not a villein like those villagers. You were born a freeman. You don't understand what it's like to be chained to a place...'

'My father was a small farmer. Freeman or not, the bastards burned it over his head and put him to the sword. And talking of free men, Scarlet, aren't you one yourself? And you fought for Lionheart in Normandy? Didn't you sell your freedom for the king's gold? You weren't pressed to fight. You battled for advantage.'

'Take out your dagger, Loxley,' Scarlet spat the words. 'Come on... come on... or do you only fight at a distance with the longbow?'

Robin took out his own dagger. He held it by the blade for a moment, and then threw it to the ground, the hilt quivering as it buried itself into the earth.

'No, Scarlet, I'll not waste my blade,' he said. 'I don't need to prove anything to you. At least I've never fought on their side. I've never taken their gold.'

'I'll kill you for that, you bastard,' Scarlet retaliated. 'And I'll make you eat those words before you perish.'

He walked towards Robin with the dagger. But as he held it out further, the sweep of a sword knocked it from his hand. He turned to find Stutely standing beside him.

'It's not the way, Will. Think of Meg. My wife and your sister. Gisborne's men murdered her long before Robin came to the forest. I want to fight back. I want vengeance. It seems to me that if we follow Robin we have the best chance of achieving something. Even if we die in the attempt.'

'I've been a soldier,' said Scarlet. 'I've no fear of death. But those villagers out there. What if thousands die just so that we can prove a point? We can skulk here in the forest. They can't.'

Gilbert walked across to him, putting an arm on his.

'No, they can't, Scarlet. I lost most of my family in Breevedon and I'll tell you this. There's not one that wouldn't have been prepared to make that sacrifice if they thought that life might get better for the folk of Sherwood. I've heard tales of you, Will. I know you're a bold warrior. Sherwood needs men like you to fight back. I've known Loxley for many years. He's made mistakes. We all have. But we learn from them and fight cleverer the next day.'

'I weep for you, Gilbert,' said Scarlet. 'It's just what they did at Breevedon...'

Robin stepped forward and looked Scarlet in the face.

'I can't make you stay, Will,' he said. 'If you feel you must go, then go with my respect. I'm sorry for what I said. But if you stay and fight with us then perhaps we can learn from each other?'

Will Scarlet looked across at him and then wandered over to the edge of the trees. He stood there alone for several minutes before returning to the other outlaws. He reached down, picked up his dagger and put it into his belt. He came over to Robin.

'So how do we start?' he asked.

~

'Why don't you kill the Sheriff?' asked Clorinda, as she and Gisborne stretched out on the bed. 'He's an old fool! Far better out of the world than in it.'

'You think I should kill de Lisle?'

'Why not? You'd make a better Sheriff than him.' She turned and nuzzled into Gisborne's shoulder. 'But do it quickly. They say that Count John's coming to Nottingham very soon. Wouldn't it be good if he arrives just as there's an urgent need to fill the role of Sheriff?'

Gisborne stared up at the ceiling and considered the matter.

'It's certainly true that John doesn't like de Lisle. He only supports him because he's efficient. And there's no other candidate in Nottingham but me.'

'There you are then!'

Gisborne imagined scenes where de Lisle died in different ways.

'It's no good,' he said at last. 'The Sheriff is the King's representative in the shire. To kill de Lisle would be tantamount to treason.'

She drew her lips across his and for a moment her tongue explored his mouth.

'I'm not saying you should strike him down with your sword,' she said, drawing her head away and resting it on the pillow. Her mind projected pictures on to the ceiling. 'But just imagine... just imagine that the Sheriff should die on the eve of Count John's visit. That he perished naturally in his sleep. No one would question your part in that.'

Gisborne gave a mirthless laugh.

'I can hardly smother him in his bed!' he said. 'He has guards on the door.'

Clorinda made a temple roof of her hands, almost as though she was praying for divine guidance. After a little thought she clapped them together.

'I said perish naturally, my lord,' she said. 'He goes to bed feeling unwell. He dies in the night. The way people in Nottingham die all the time.'

'And how's that to be achieved?'

'My granny taught me all you need to know about the plants of Sherwood. The ones that cure. The ones that kill. You feast with the Sheriff. I prepare something for you to slip into his food. How simple it would be.'

He turned to face her. The moonlight lit up her face. He was almost shocked at the look of malevolence that he found there.

'What a deadly little harlot you are!' he said, as he turned to take her.

Ten

'At last! Someone's coming,' said Much. 'Four riders and a cart.'

He was positioned halfway up an oak tree, watching the road that cut through the depths of the forest a few miles from Nottingham. The other outlaws, who had been resting on the ground around the tree roots, sprang to their feet.

'How far away?' asked Robin.

'A bowshot,' Much replied. 'Bit less, mayhap.'

'Then we'll take a toll for their passage through Sherwood. John, take Ralph and Gilbert and work your way behind them. Scarlet, you come down with me. Much and Will Stutely, you cover them from here, but stay hidden in the trees. Shout at once if you see anyone else coming.'

'You'll forgive me if I disappear back to my chapel,' said Tuck. 'Best if I'm not seen as one of your wretches too soon.'

Robin nodded.

'And you, Alan,' he said. 'You serve our cause better as a minstrel than a wolfshead. You go with Tuck. You can part at the Blue Boar and take the great road into Nottingham.'

The monk and the minstrel departed, taking a narrow side-path into the trees.

'You ready, Scarlet?' Robin asked.

The outlaw gave a nod and together they slid down a bank towards the road. Both men fitted arrows to their bows and stepped out in front of the travellers.

The little party comprised of an old man and a girl, accompanied by two servants on horseback and a third driving a pony cart. They came to a halt as the outlaws emerged from the greenwood. Robin watched the old man's hand wander down to the hilt of his sword. He eased back the bowstring a trifle and shook his head.

'Best to keep your fingers away from that sword, sir,' he said. 'We mean you no violence. We are simply collectors...'

'Collectors?' said the old man. 'You look like wolfsheads to me.'

'We collect not for our own profit,' Robin replied. 'We're gatherers of alms for the poor people of Sherwood. After taking out a modest deduction we distribute all we acquire.'

'So you rob the poor to give to the poor?'

'Not at all,' Robin protested. 'Honest poor folk pay no tribute to us. Even the rich needn't pay anything, if they are truthful about the money they carry and are of good reputation. What's your name, sir?'

'I am Henry Fitzwalter of Edwinstowe.'

'And I'm his daughter, Marian,' the girl intervened, looking curiously at Robin. 'By what right do you rob us on the King's highway? We are honest travellers on our way to Nottingham. I'll not have my father disturbed in this way!'

'And why are you travelling to Nottingham?' asked Scarlet.

'We're summoned by the Sheriff,' Marian replied. 'On the King's business. And not yours!'

'What? Honest travellers but going to meet de Lisle? A likely tale! Let's search their cart, Robin.'

'Robin?' Fitzwalter looked quizzically at the man before him. 'Then you are Robin Hood? Loxley as was? Your deeds go before you. Though I was expecting a bolder man. Not a hedge-robber!'

'Watch your words, old man!' said Scarlet. 'A week or more ago we'd have robbed you without mercy. It's thanks to Robin Hood that we now take but a tithe.'

'My father's elderly and not well,' said Marian. 'I won't have him bothered in this way.' She took out the dagger at her belt. 'I'll fight any one of you...'

'I'm quite capable of defending myself, Marian,' said Fitzwalter. 'Leave this to me.' He drew his sword. 'I challenge you to combat, Loxley. Man to man!'

'Put up your weapons,' Robin said. 'Nobody's going to harm you. The good name of Henry Fitzwalter is well renowned in Sherwood.' He took the arrow out of his bow and replace it in the quiver. 'Your deeds go before *you*, sir.'

'You're a strange wolfshead, Loxley. Proposing to give away what you take,' said Fitzwalter. 'As it happens I've twelve gold pieces in my cart. You are welcome to search. But you have my oath that nothing else is concealed.'

'Your word is good enough,' replied Robin. 'There's no more honest man in the shire than Henry Fitzwalter.'

The old man bowed his head at the compliment.

'Tell me, Lox... Robin Hood, what would you do if you searched my cart now and found a hundred gold pieces... or a thousand.'

'Our rule is simple,' said Robin. 'If we're lied to, well, then we take all. If we know that the traveller we intercept is honest and poor than we take nothing. If the person's a stranger to us, then we invite them to make an offering for the deprived of the shire.'

Fitzwalter laughed.

'Well, that seems honest to me. If only the Sheriff and Gisborne gathered taxes with such compassion! You've heard of the dreadful business at Breevedon?'

'Gisborne'll pay for that day's work!' said Scarlet.

'He will indeed, either here or in a better world,' said Fitzwalter. 'It's a sin that these killings are undertaken in the King's name. But what do you hope to do, Robin?' He glanced back at the three outlaws on the track behind him. 'You have very few men to defeat the forces of de Lisle? Hard to bring him to battle with such a number.'

'We have few men,' said Robin, 'but we do have Sherwood. It's hard for de Lisle to deploy his army in this forest. We're fighting a new kind of war.'

'And I wish you well...'

'Are you to be long in Nottingham?'

'I'm not sure,' said Fitzwalter. 'The Sheriff requested our company. He sent a message to say that he'd matters he wished to discuss with me. And particularly requested that I bring my daughter. Not a wise request. It'll be all I can do to stop Marian cutting Gisborne's throat!'

'With relish, father,' the girl said.

'Hopefully, we'll journey home tomorrow. That's if Marian isn't in the castle dungeon by then. It'll be poor company. The Sheriff says the Abbot of St Mary's is a fellow guest.'

'You have my sympathy,' said Robin. 'There's another man destined for hell!'

'Indeed.'

'If you should find yourself at this spot tomorrow, then call out. We'll be in the vicinity. Perhaps you'd be our guests and dine in Sherwood? Much, who's hiding up there in the trees, has acquired some venison.'

Fitzwalter reached down and took the outlaw's hand.

'I'll shake upon that, Robin. It may be I'll have some castle gossip for you.' He smiled as he rode on. 'Come, Marian, we have a way to go.'

The girl hung behind as the servants and the cart trundled onwards. She reined in her horse, looking down at Robin. The expression on her face was as dark as her hair.

'You're lucky I didn't slit your throat!' she said, before turning her horse and cantering up to her father.

'They say that Fitzwalter was a dangerous fighter in his day,' said Scarlet. 'But I'd be more afeared of the daughter!'

~

Robert de Lisle stood by the window that looked down into the courtyard of Nottingham Castle, feeling the draught that blew in from Sherwood Forest. A dozen monks were gathered below, heaving sighs of relief that their long journey on foot was over. Two reached up to help the Abbot of St Mary's off a white pony that was quite as fat as its rider.

Odious bag of wind!

One of the great puzzles of life was how the Abbot had gained so much influence. Personally approved by the Pope, who had threatened excommunication when the late King Henry, of blessed memory, had tried to remove the fat priest from office. But even Henry, who was no stranger to being excommunicated, had failed to topple this particular abbot. The late King had died cursing the man's very name.

It was not that the Abbot was particularly pious.

He had a foul reputation. For ever grasping away other people's lands. Coveting youths of both sexes. But principally, they said, a buggerer of boys, though nobody had dared make such an accusation public in the Abbot's hearing. Count John liked to have the man fawning nearby. Having sycophants around was John's greatest flaw. De Lisle had sat close by on so many occasions, listening to the fat Abbot dripping poison into the ear of the King's brother.

And Lionheart hadn't been immune to the priest's flattering comments. The Abbot always arrived at court loaded with gold as a contribution to the King's foreign adventures.

And now he was back in Nottingham, for at least a night. Come to undertake business of a personal nature, he had said, in the document that had preceded him. He had had the nerve to inform de Lisle that he wanted the Sheriff to request the presence of that old fool Henry Fitzwalter and his daughter. Well, Marian Fitzwalter he could understand. The girl was an adornment on the face of the shire. And she was the heiress to a deal of land. It must be about that! The Abbot was motivated by little beyond avarice and lust. And he surely couldn't be imagining that Marian might be persuaded to succumb to his physical charms.

His thoughts were disturbed by his clerk.

'My lord... Sir Brian du Bois seeks an audience with you.'

Goddammit, what in hell did he want?

'On what matter?' he asked.

'He wouldn't say, my lord Sheriff.'

De Lisle sighed.

'You'd better bring him up. Oh, and keep the Abbot out of the way while du Bois is with me. Give the wretched monk some food. That should distract him.'

The little man bowed and left the room. A few moments later he returned and ushered in du Bois.

'You're a long way from Newark, Sir Brian?'

The knight gave a nod and sank unbidden into a chair.

'A damned dangerous journey too,' he said. 'Sherwood being full of wolves... most of them two-legged, I hear.'

He drew a hand through his exceptionally fair hair and looked up at de Lisle. The Sheriff always pictured the eyes of a snake whenever he fell into the range of the man's gaze. Sir Brian had a reputation for being the most handsome man in the shire. De Lisle couldn't see it. There was something overblown about the good looks, they were a tad *too* perfect. Looks that might have been purchased for this life from the Devil. The Sheriff was wont to think of du Bois as Lucifer. A fallen angel, made handsome to explore the world's vices.

'You've heard?' de Lisle said.

'A wolf I've hunted before,' du Bois almost purred. 'Loxley...' His mouth almost ate the word. 'Time to mount the head of that particular wolf on my wall.'

'Is that why you're here?'

Du Bois stretched out his legs.

'Not entirely,' he replied. 'That old fool the Abbot was at Newark the other day, scrounging on my hospitality. He happened to mention that Fitzwalter's daughter had been summoned to Nottingham. I thought I might drop in to renew an old acquaintance.'

'How are your women, Sir Brian?'

'I'm bored with them, de Lisle, every last raddled hag of them. I need a new adventure where women are concerned. I've decided to take Marian Fitzwalter as a bride.'

The Sheriff almost exploded with laughter.

'My dear Sir Brian, sometimes your humour overwhelms me.'

Du Bois looked up at him, a flash of anger across his face.

'Where is the amusement in that? I've tasted every other woman of quality in the shire. It's Marian's turn!'

The Sheriff poured out two flagons of wine and offered one to the knight.

'But marriage? Where women are concerned you usually taste but don't purchase. Why's Marian so different? She's a foul-tempered little bitch at the best of times. She battered your face with her fist the last time you made advances to her.'

'That's just her spirit, de Lisle. I find women with a bit of fight in them, particularly entertaining when you bed them. It all adds to the excitement. And leaving that aside it'd be a dynastic match. Henry Fitzwalter is an old man and his lands at Edwinstowe border my own.'

'Ah, so you want his estates.'

'They have to come to someone. I have the power and the money to administer them properly.'

The Sheriff wandered over to the window and looked down again at the Abbot's fat pony, which was now lying down after the exhaustion of its journey.

'Our friend the Abbot covets those very lands,' he said. 'I understand he intends to wed Marian to God. He told me he's reserved a place for her at Kirklees Priory.'

Du Bois looked up with a devilish smile.

'It'll never happen,' he said. 'Marian's a wild creature. I doubt she's even a virgin, for I'm told she spends most of her time cuckolding the wives of Sherwood peasants.'

'I've heard that rumour,' the Sheriff replied. 'It may be true. She certainly does roam the forest, but with that intent? She's just a tomboy who hates the thought of sitting around all day embroidering.'

'I'll find her some amusing activities after our marriage.'

'If she does take you, it'll break Gisborne's heart. He's quite set on Marian and her land himself.'

Du Bois looked up at the ceiling and chuckled.

'And how is Gisborne? Still a failure?'

'I wouldn't turn my back on him if I were you, Sir Brian. He has a dagger kept sharp in your honour. He won't forgive you for snatching his lands at Bowland.'

Du Bois reached into his pouch and produced a pair of dice.

'Not snatched, but won,' he said, tossing and catching them. 'And won fairly. If I could find enough fools to play against, these little friends would gain me all England.'

'Gisborne says you've weighted them!'

'How I'd love him to say that to my face!'

De Lisle refilled the knight's flagon.

'If you promise not to kill Gisborne, you may stay for supper, Sir Brian. Perhaps you can entertain us with your proposals to bring me the head of Robin Hood?'

~

Robin could see the walls of Nottingham castle from the woodland glade on the edge of Sherwood. Why he was so near to the town, he wasn't quite sure. The rest of the outlaws were camping in the greenwood not far from where they had met with Henry Fitzwalter, in the expectation of meeting that gentleman and his daughter on the following day.

And so he had wandered along the track that Fitzwalter had taken earlier, noting the hoofmarks of the horses and the indentations made by the cart's wheels. He had seen only a pedlar coming the other way, a sorry looking man carrying his wares in a great pack upon his back. Robin had dodged into the undergrowth to avoid a conversation, resisting an opportunity to halt and gather gossip from someone who'd been so recently at Nottingham market.

And there they were, the walls of the town and the towers of the castle. He knew them well from earlier days. Somewhere behind those great stones were the women of Oakden, including Ralph Gammon's wife. Probably ill-used as servants by now, or worse. As he watched, Robin toyed with a few plans on how they might be liberated. None made any sort of practical sense. The chances of freeing women scattered around the castle without the loss of most of his men were beyond hope. Yet something had to be done or the headstrong Gammon would throw away his life in an attempt.

Then he saw her and he smiled.

She was working her way along the hedge of a field just beyond the forest. Looking around and bending now and again to pick some plant. He knew her at once. How often he'd run his hands through that long brown hair, chased after her lithe figure in woodland games in Loxley Chase.

He waited until she came nearer to the trees before saying her name.

'Clorinda!'

She started, almost dropping her basket.

'You mad bastard! I thought there was no one near.'

'What are you doing here, Clorinda?'

'Gathering plants. What does it look like?'

Robin came nearer and looked in the basket.

'Plants that kill,' he said. 'Who's offended you now?'

'My business! Not yours.'

'Gisborne, perhaps?'

She shook her head.

'Not him.'

'I remember your skill at poisoning. I'd never want to eat in your company.'

'I don't recall us doing a lot of eating,' she smirked. She looked back towards the town. 'You're mad to come here, Robin. The Sheriff has patrols in these fields close to the castle. He'll hang and draw you if you're taken.'

'Are you still being humped by Gisborne?'

'You've heard?'

'The Sherwood villagers make jests of it.'

She frowned.

'I'm not interested in the tittle-tattle of peasants.'

'You should be,' Robin replied. 'Gisborne is the most hated man in the forest. And you're his whore. There's many a man of Sherwood who'd slit your throat if he found you here alone.'

'I fear no one,' she said. 'They know what Gisborne would do if anything happened to me.'

'You really imagine he thinks so much of you?'

'I know he does. And I shan't always be his whore.'

Robin laughed and raised his hands to the sky.

'So you fancy yourself as Lady Gisborne? You were ever a girl who had wild fantasies! Trust me, Clorinda. It'll never happen. There would be no advantage in it for Gisborne. What land would you bring? Where's your chest of gold?'

She put down the basket.

'It could've been you, Robin. We might have had a quiet life in Loxley together.' She came nearer, resting her hands on his shoulders. 'If you'd cared for me as much as you cared for the other peasants, we might have made our way up in the world.' She raised her right hand and then slapped him across the face. 'But, no, you had all of me that you wanted and threw me aside. Gisborne's not like that. He always brings me to his bed.'

He grasped her hand and took it to his lips.

'Ah, so the lust is still there?' she said, looking into his eyes. 'What a shame that Gisborne'll have to kill you. And sometimes, Robin, when he's taking me, I'll fancy it's you.'

She reached up and brushed her lips against his. And there was something in the gesture that triggered so many memories of long winter nights in Loxley and summer afternoons in forest glades. His hands brushed against her breasts and then reached down the firm side of her hips. They fell back on to the grass, Robin looking up at the moving flashes of her brown face as it intermingled with the blue of the sky.

And then it was all over and she was adjusting her clothing, a dark silhouette against the light.

'You know that Gisborne would give me gold just for saying I've seen you,' she said. 'He knows I'm your cousin and would reward me particularly for my loyalty to him.'

'And what would he say if I told him what we'd just done?'

She gave a merry laugh.

'He'd never believe I'd be so stupid. And I shan't be again, Robin. That was for old times' sake. Something to remember you by when they've hanged you.'

'You could come into the forest with me?' he said.

'I find a bed in the castle so much more comfortable,' she replied. 'And I intend to have a longer life than you, not scrabbling to death like a hunted beast.'

'Will I see you again?'

She laughed and picked up her basket.

'Not like this,' she said, 'though I may come along to see them hang you from the castle walls. It'll be a dainty sight! And when your body writhes at the end of the rope, well, then I'll recall how you writhed just now.'

~

'Why are we here?' Fitzwalter asked.

They all sat around the long table in the great hall of Nottingham Castle; Robert de Lisle, Gisborne and the Abbot of St Mary's on one side; Henry Fitzwalter and his daughter on the other. Brian du Bois lounged on the great stone shelf beneath the nearest window.

'I've summoned you all at the request of my lord Abbot,' said de Lisle. 'He wishes to discuss a personal matter with you and the Lady Marian. Having heard his views it seems to me that what he wishes to discuss raises wider matters, relating to the peace of the district.'

'What kind of waffle is that, de Lisle?' said Fitzwalter. 'The peace of Sherwood has nothing to do with me. Keeping the peace is your mission.'

De Lisle gave him an icy smile.

'Naturally,' he replied. 'And that's why I've summoned you here. As gentry in this district I've a right to count on your support, have I not?'

Fitzwalter shrugged. 'I suppose so!' he grunted, turning to face the Abbot. 'And just what is this personal matter?'

'Well...' the Abbot began, 'I...'

But the Sheriff held up the palm of his hand to silence him.

'Perhaps we might come to that in due course, lord Abbot? My main concern is with the increase in lawlessness in Sherwood. Villages refuse to pay taxes, wolfsheads abound in the forest and now a spirit of rebellion in the air.'

'Yes, my lord,' Gisborne intervened, 'and we've the rebel Loxley, or Robin Hood or whatever he calls himself, out there fermenting the overthrow of ordered society.'

Fitzwalter drew a finger across the table, following a crack in the wood.

'I trust we aren't boring you, Fitzwalter?' said the Sheriff.

'No... no, I'm fascinated by the discussion, even though it's pointless.'

'Pointless!' Gisborne spluttered.

'Pointless,' Fitzwalter said. 'You treat the people of Sherwood worse than you do the beasts of the field. Then you wonder why they protest?'

'They have no right to protest!' thundered Gisborne.

'I always thought you were a fool, Gisborne...' said Fitzwalter.

'If you were a young man I'd challenge you for that...' said Gisborne. 'But I'll ignore it.' He turned to Marian. 'You should persuade your father to see reason, milady.' He added.

'It seems to me that my father's the only one here showing any reason,' she said, looking along the faces on the opposite side of the table. 'You hammer the people of Sherwood into the ground. You impose taxes they've no chance of paying. Then when they can't you hang them and burn their villages. Where is the reason in that?'

'Lessons have to be learned, my dear Marian,' said the Abbot.

'And tell me, my lord Abbot, do you think that Christ would've hanged the people of Breevedon and burned their homes, as Gisborne did the other day? Isn't Christianity supposed to protect the poor and the vulnerable?'

The Abbot turned red. 'You are young, Marian, so I'll ignore that blasphemy. But I urge you to restrain yourself. Women have been burned for less!'

'And wasn't Christ nailed to the cross for saying much the same?' said Marian. 'Or do you interpret the word of God only to suit yourself?'

'I really see no reason why the lady Marian should be here at all,' interrupted Gisborne. 'These aren't matters that should be discussed in front of women.'

Marian stood. 'Very well, I'll leave.'

Her father stood beside her. 'And I'll return home as well.'

The Sheriff held out his arms, waving them back down into their chairs. 'Please... please sit. These are contentious matters and it's understandable that people might get agitated.'

He turned to Marian. 'We are reasonable people, lady Marian. But you have to understand my difficulties. I've been appointed by the King to administer his laws in this shire. Our King, as we all know, has been appointed by Almighty God to rule us. His word... his laws are... therefore... the word of God and must be obeyed.'

'Exactly!' said the Abbot. 'Through the King's laws we are all subject to the will of God!'

'And what if Harold had triumphed at Senlac?' asked Marian. 'We might have a king of his line and not a Plantagenet at all.

Such a king might have decreed quite different laws. Aren't these laws made by man and not God? Would God want us to obey Lionheart even if he were wrong?'

'That is treason!' said the Abbot. 'I do urge you, Fitzwalter, to have a care of your daughter. Her outspoken words demonstrate just why she needs the guidance of the Church.'

Fitzwalter was silent for a moment.

'I wondered when we would come round to that,' he said. He turned to the Sheriff. 'Is this old thorn still pricking away at my lord the Abbot?' he asked.

'I've said it before and I'll say it again, I believe that Marian should enter Kirklees as a nun. For her own safety,' said the Abbot. 'These are perilous times and we've seen today the kind of correction the girl needs.'

'We've seen how the church covets the lands of Edwinstowe,' Sir Brian du Bois said, walking across from the window. He sat on the table next to Marian and looked down at her. 'A nun? That'd be a terrible waste!' He turned to Fitzwalter. 'I'm prepared to offer my hand in marriage to your daughter. It's good common sense. Our lands adjoin and I can look after them and Marian...'

Gisborne sprang to his feet, but de Lisle waved him down before he could speak.

'My daughter isn't available for marriage,' said Fitzwalter. 'And certainly not to anyone in this room. Not even to God!' he added, turning to the Abbot.

'I think we should all calm down,' said de Lisle. 'You may care for some food?'

He clapped his hands and six women entered the hall, each bearing a platter of meat and vegetables, which were placed in front of the guests at the table. Gisborne watched as Clorinda placed food in front of the Sheriff, her eyes glinting at him as she turned away.

'There are practical reasons why we should consider the future of your estate,' de Lisle said to Fitzwalter. 'Edwinstowe lies at the heart of Sherwood. The villages around are some of the most lawless in the district. If we are to shackle this... Robin Hood, well, then we need to impose an iron hand on the forest. Particularly in your vicinity, my dear Fitzwalter.'

'So you want my daughter to marry or to take orders? You want me put out to grass? And the Edwinstowe estates to pass out of the hands of my family?'

They all looked up as the Abbot chomped away, very noisily, at his food.

'My God, de Lisle, I've journeyed a good way and you serve up but a sample,' he said, through a mouth still full of food. 'My monks eat better than this!'

The Sheriff pushed his own platter along the table to him. 'Take mine, lord Abbot. I haven't an appetite today.' He hadn't finished the words before the Abbot started on the offering in front of him.

He looked back at Fitzwalter.

'Marian... has to wed sometime...' he began.

'No doubt, but in her own time,' said Fitzwalter. 'Is this the only reason why we were summoned to Nottingham?'

'It's important to chase these rebels and wolfsheads out of Sherwood,' said Gisborne. 'If we were only able to fortify your house. Station men at arms there under my command. I'd be happy to take up residence at Edwinstowe. It would give us greater control of Sherwood.'

'And to the lady Marian, eh Gisborne?' said Brian du Bois. 'You might as well argue, my lord Sheriff, that I fortify Edwinstowe as an outlier of my own castle at Newark. I'd be very happy to spend more time at your castle, Fitzwalter.'

Henry Fitzwalter got to his feet.

'We've had a wasted journey,' he said to his daughter. 'Come Marian!' He turned to de Lisle. 'And next time, lord Sheriff, I'd be grateful if I were only to be summoned to Nottingham on really urgent matters.'

They both strode out of the hall at great speed.

De Lisle turned to the others.

'You bungling fools!' he said. 'I asked you to leave the conversation to me. But no, you all had to wade in like idiots at a village wooing. I'd be grateful if you'd all leave Nottingham. I'll approach Fitzwalter on my own in a week or so, without the aid of any of you!'

'Oh my God!'

'What is it, my lord Abbot?' the Sheriff asked testily.

'I think I'm dying!' the Abbot groaned. 'My very guts are ablaze!' He clutched at his chest and folded over the table, a trickle of vomit joining the food stains that had dribbled down his chin. 'I'm poisoned, de Lisle!'

He pointed at Gisborne and du Bois. 'One of these bastards has done for me!'

Eleven

'I take it you don't actually live here?' asked Marian.

The venison had been eaten and the great fire had burned low. The outlaws sat in quiet conversation with Henry Fitzwalter, drinking the last of the wine that he and his daughter had brought in their cart from Nottingham.

'We live deeper in the forest,' said Robin. 'This is but one of our lurks. Convenient for keeping an eye on the north road.' He looked sideways at the girl. 'So the Sheriff thinks you should be wedded and the fat abbot thinks he can get you into Kirklees Priory?'

'Over my corpse!'

'You're not tempted by Gisborne or du Bois?'

She laughed.

'Who would be? I'd rather be a wolfshead in Sherwood Forest.'

'Not so bad on a fine day like today, but you should see the place when the rain falls for a week on end. And being made wolfshead, well? Every man's hand turned against you and no protection from the law. Any passing stranger can slay you.'

'Even with all that,' Marian said. 'I've always loved the forest. I'd rather be out amongst the trees than in any room at Edwinstowe. I envy Lionheart out there fighting his battles in Normandy. At least he's filling his days with a purpose.'

Her dark eyes flashed in the glow of the afternoon sun.

'And what of you, Robin? I heard what happened at Loxley. Didn't you think of journeying to another part of England? Coming to Sherwood must be dangerous for you?'

'Even as a freeman it's hard to explain your presence in some other shire of the realm. The lord in any district would want to know your business. They'd assume you're an escaped villein or a wolfshead. No, better to live in Sherwood and try to change the world from here.'

'Live in Sherwood or die here? They'll hunt you down like any other rogue wolf. Or are you hoping for a miracle when Lionheart comes home?'

'I put no faith in kings,' he said. 'They're all as bad as each other. King Richard cares nothing for England. And if Count John becomes king, well, will anything really change? Show me a Plantagenet and I'll show you the spawn of the devil. From hell they came and to hell they'll return!'

They walked into the trees for a while.

'Can you imagine an England without a king?' she asked at last.

He turned to face her.

'Why not? What have they ever done for the people of England, except extort money from them? Lionheart only takes an interest in Englishmen when he needs soldiers for his mad adventures.'

'But who would rule?'

'The people of England,' he said. 'And one day it'll happen. Villeins, peasants, slaves. Who thought up such terms? The kings and their sycophants. Let's sweep them all away; the lords, the sheriffs, the likes of Gisborne and du Bois... who needs them?'

'My father's a lord...'

'And a good man,' said Robin. 'He utters more words of wisdom and fairness than I've heard in a lifetime. But de Lisle and Gisborne and du Bois? They're a corruption on the face of England.'

They walked until they could see the track to Nottingham in the distance. The town itself was hidden by the trees and a rise in the ground, but the smoke of its fires filled the afternoon sky.

'Who taught you to use a bow?' she asked.

'An archer who'd come to end his days in Loxley. He'd fought in King Henry's wars in France. Even in his old age he never missed a target. He taught me how to kill with a sword and dagger as well. His name was Adam. He died of a sickness just before the revolt at Loxley.'

'Marian!'

The distant shout came from her father.

'He's anxious to continue our journey. It's a long way to Edwinstowe.'

'I'll send some of my men to escort you,' said Robin. 'There are other wolves in the forest who're hungrier than we are. Not every Sherwood outlaw shares my views.'

She turned to him.

'Robin... you've given me a lot to consider. I wish you well in your adventures.'

She took his hand for a moment.

'Don't let them win!'

~

'How fares the Abbot?'

De Lisle walked the battlements of the castle with Gisborne and du Bois. The sun was setting over the trees of Sherwood. The Sheriff's minstrel was nearby, thrumming a tune on his lute. A new melody that pleased de Lisle. One that he had requested again and again through the afternoon and evening.

'He'll live!' said Gisborne, a note of disappointment in his voice. 'Though he still insists that we poisoned him.'

'He would,' de Lisle replied. 'There's a man who must for ever have a grievance.'

He leaned on the top of the castle wall.

'Did you poison him, Gisborne?'

'Certainly not, my lord!'

'Only you see how it is, Gisborne? When the Abbot was eating from his own platter, well, he exhibited no symptoms at all. But then I gave him my food. And almost instantly he clutched his fat gut and began to moan.'

'The man's a glutton, lord Sheriff. This wasn't poison, merely overeating.'

De Lisle turned to face him.

'I do hope so, Gisborne. Because if it was poison then the presumption must be that someone was attempting to poison me? What do you think, du Bois?'

Brian du Bois smirked.

'Well I'm absolved. I've no connections with your kitchen,' he said. 'Gisborne, doesn't your harlot work there?'

115

'Anyone can creep into that kitchen...' Gisborne said. 'And many labour there who resent our authority. You should let me hang a few of them, my lord.'

The Sheriff made a gesture of despair to du Bois.

'You see how he is, Sir Brian?' He nodded towards Gisborne. 'Gisborne rampages through Sherwood hanging my peasants and now he wants to put the rope around the throats of my servants. Before long I'll need to take the plough to the fields myself and make my own feasts. There'll be nobody left to labour for me.'

'The destruction of Breevedon was a necessity,' said Gisborne. 'And my actions are bringing the Sherwood rebels to their heels. One more example, that's all that's needed. One more village brought to order.'

'Do you have a village in mind, Gisborne?'

'Reynworth, my lord. The peasants there haven't paid any taxes this year and they are due by the end of this week. I intend to take a considerable number of men and claim what is rightfully ours.'

'It's a long way from Nottingham...' said de Lisle.

'Exactly, lord Sheriff,' Gisborne continued, 'the peasants of Reynworth probably feel that they're out of our sight and mind. They need to feel the stamp of authority. I'll set out tomorrow and collect the taxes the day after that...'

'And lose them all to Robin Hood on the way home,' du Bois sniggered. 'My lord Sheriff, Reynworth is a considerable village. There's a spirit of resistance there. They're well known for harbouring wolfsheads. The foresters tell me that the poaching in that part of Sherwood is out of control. I very much doubt they'd take much notice of Gisborne.'

'Your humour's lost on me, du Bois,' said Gisborne. 'I'm as experienced in battle as you. And if the villagers of Reynworth resist, then so much the better. I'll put them all to the sword and wipe their hovels from the face of the earth.'

'Here we go again, Gisborne,' said de Lisle. 'Yet more of my poverty despatched to hell.'

'There's an alternative, lord Sheriff,' said du Bois. 'By all means let Gisborne go to Reynworth, but let me take my soldiers as well. I can approach Reynworth from the north and Gisborne from the south. When they see our force of arms they'll almost certainly pay up their taxes – if they can. And we'll leave the men and women of the village alive to work your lands for you.'

'Gisborne?'

'I've no objection,' said Gisborne. 'Though du Bois's presence is unnecessary. And I don't believe you'll see a penny of any tax money. They don't have any.'

'Nevertheless, I believe that Sir Brian's plan is excellent. And Sir Brian, you'll be in charge of this expedition.'

'My lord!' said Gisborne.

'Just this once, Gisborne. Please oblige me.'

'Very well!'

De Lisle waved them away.

'Now both of you go and make preparations and leave me to enjoy the sunset.'

When the two knights had stamped away, de Lisle said to Alan a' Dale, 'Give me that tune again, minstrel.'

He sighed with pleasure as its notes swept from the battlements and out across the Nottingham market place where the townsfolk gathered to share the beautiful music.

~

The abbot had been in a foul mood as he had set out from Nottingham Castle the next morning, riding his fat pony with his small procession of monks in his wake. His guts still trembled and his bowels felt in constant need of an evacuation. He had looked up from the courtyard at the windows of the Sheriff's apartments.

Someone had tried to poison him, that was certain sure.

But who?

De Lisle resented the authority of the Church. He made no bones about that. How pleasant it would be to have him excommunicated. And Gisborne and du Bois? They both had ambitions with the Maid of Edwinstowe. They loathed the idea of seeing Marian vanish behind the high walls of Kirklees Priory. Oh, a wicked thing to put carnal ambitions before the needs of the Church.

Carnal thoughts.

The Abbot was no stranger to them. From his boyhood, when he had been sent to York to become a monk, the Abbot had been a slave to them. Sometimes he succumbed. Even now. And then there had to be the inevitable days of being scourged and wearing a hair-shirt. For in his way my lord the Abbot took the sanctions of his religion most seriously.

As he rode he thought of young Marian. How he would like to enjoy her. What pleasure it would give to hear her squeal beneath his fat bulk. He sighed and clutched his gut again. The ache was still almost overwhelming. Marian was not likely to yield to such a temptation.

He turned his head and frowned at the little party of monks now lagging behind.

'Keep up! Keep up!' he shouted. 'This is Sherwood Forest. You know what can happen to you here!'

The youngest monk, new to the Abbey, looked worried, glancing here and there into the trees. A handsome boy, thought the Abbot. He wondered just how compliant and discreet he might be. He wondered... A shaft of pain thrust through his stomach. He took his hands from the reins and clutched and rubbed the mound of flesh surrounding his belly. Ah, that made it easier...

Damn de Lisle!

And yet... And yet?

It couldn't have been de Lisle. It simply couldn't have been. The Sheriff had given him his own platter when he complained about there not being enough to eat. He hadn't felt ill until he took the meat and the vegetables prepared for the Sheriff.

A smile creased the Abbot's round face for a moment, removing the expression of pain that had dominated his features so much since leaving Nottingham.

The poison was intended for Robert de Lisle.

What a delicious thought.

But who?

Some aggrieved peasant in the castle kitchens? Maybe. Maybe. Perhaps an act of vengeance for the slaying of so many villagers in Sherwood? Perhaps on the direct instructions of this Robin

Hood? That was a possibility, for the Abbot knew well the reputation of this Loxley. But was it not more likely that the poisoning was a method of removing the Sheriff for political reasons?

Yes!

Who then?

Gisborne or du Bois?

Both had political ambitions. Both of them would stoop to such nefarious methods if they thought it might improve their positions. They both had the ear of Count John. Du Bois was liked by Lionheart himself, and had been offered preferment at the first opportunity. No hope for Gisborne with the King, though. Richard was wont to say shocking words at the very mention of Sir Guy's name. And Gisborne clearly hated the Sheriff. Not surprising, for he was treated like a disobedient hound every time he was in de Lisle's presence. And didn't Gisborne's whore slave in the castle kitchen?

Gisborne then.

If only he hadn't been in such pain the Abbot would have enjoyed this reckoning of events, this inspired trail of deduction. But another pang took all such thoughts from his mind. His bowels grumbled and he had to pull his sphincter muscles closer together to prevent soiling his beautifully crafted saddle.

He held up an arm and halted his pony.

'We will pause here for a few moments,' he said to the monks. 'Well! Help me down someone!'

The pretty young monk ran forward and acted as a dismounting block for the Abbot. But his master was now in such dire straits that he scarcely noticed his presence. Muttering 'Hold my pony,' the Abbot ran into the trees.

He only just made it in time to secrete himself behind an oak and pull up his robe. The evacuation came with such power that it made every muscle of his body heave while sweat soaked his brow. For the love of Christ what had the poisoner used? The abbot determined that if he ever found out who was responsible he would seek a terrible vengeance. If it was Gisborne... at the very least, excommunication and exile from the land.

He was sure that Lionheart would grant that.

And if it was just a kitchen peasant, Gisborne's tumble perhaps, well, then he'd have her flayed alive, or maybe burned in the market place in Nottingham. A sure but slow death. And he would watch her die. And it would give him great pleasure.

Ah, there was an end to it! His bowels seemed to have nothing more to give.

And then the knife pressed against his throat and he managed some more.

'Here's a stench!' someone muttered.

'Course it is,' said a weaselly little voice to the other side of him. 'It's me lord the Abbot of St Mary's. What d'you expect?'

'Get him down with the others,' said someone else.

The Abbot was jerked to his feet, his robe flopping down, and with one man on either side he was rushed back to the road. A glance showed that his monks were gathered around the cart, surrounded by several armed wolfsheads in brown and green.

A dark-haired outlaw stood in the middle of the track, watching as he approached, a bow held in one hand and a sword in the other. He came nearer and gave a quick bow of the head.

'My lord Abbot,' he said.

'This is an outrage...' the Abbot began.

'Well, that stink certainly is, eh Robin?' said the little man with the ugly face of a fitch.

'Robin Hood!' said the Abbot.

The outlaw gave another bow.

'Your servant, my lord Abbot.'

'You intend to rob us? This is an insult to God and his Church, wolfshead!'

Robin Hood held out his arms as if in appeasement.

'We intend to do no such thing!' he protested. 'We never steal money given to God. But we do ask for a toll from anyone travelling through Sherwood, most of which is given to the poor of the shire. What's in your cart, lord Abbot?'

'Nothing. Nothing at all. Well, some ten pieces of gold donated by my patrons in Nottingham for the restoration of the shrine of Saint Edberga. And six sacks of wheat for the Abbey.' The Abbot waved a hand. 'See for yourself...'

'Look in the cart, John,' Robin said. 'If there's nothing but that you may go on your way.'

John Little rummaged around in the cart, moving the sacks of wheat to one side to find the little bag of coins concealed underneath. He undid the cord and looked inside.

'Exactly what he says, Robin,' John said at last. 'Ten pieces of gold, nothing more but the sacks of wheat.'

'You are poorer than your reputation allows, my lord Abbot?' said Robin. 'The gossips have maligned you...'

'These are hard times, wolfshead,' said the Abbot. 'The Church has to thrive despite its poverty.'

'Shall we let him on his way, Robin?' asked Scarlet.

'Perhaps we might...'

Robin had scarce said the words before he noticed the look of relief cross the Abbot's face. And more than that. In his eyes was a quick flash of triumph.

'But on the other hand...'

He saw the Abbot hood his eyes.

'I'm told you were gathering up debts while you were in Nottingham, my lord Abbot? Foreclosing on honest traders who owe money on properties you own in the town. Is that so?'

The Abbot gave a slight nod.

'My abbey cannot function as a charity,' he said. 'In order to fund our great and Christian undertakings we need to collect any monies owing to us. You see in that little bag the modest remuneration we have received.'

Robin walked over to the cart, noting the look of concern on the Abbot's face.

'You went all the way to Nottingham for ten pieces of gold?'

'It's a great deal of wealth!' said the Abbot. 'And will be put to good and proper uses.'

'Will it?'

'And I travelled with my monks on this occasion because I had other business in Nottingham.'

'With the Sheriff?'

'Indeed. With the Sheriff.'

Robin rested his hand on the side of the cart.

'Where did you get this wheat?' he asked suddenly.

'Get the wheat? At the town mill, of course.'

Robin ran a hand over one of the sacks. He saw out of the corner of his eye how agitated the Abbot appeared to be. The man of the church walked closer.

'If that's all we'll be on our way,' said the Abbot. 'We have a long journey ahead of us.'

Robin shook his head.

'Not just yet,' he said. 'John, cut open the sacks.'

'I protest...' the Abbot roared.

'Scarlet, if the Abbot makes another sound then cut him open as well.'

'With pleasure,' said the outlaw, drawing out his dagger.

'Well, look at this, Robin,' said John. Out of the first sack he drew out a heavy smaller bag. He opened the other five sacks and found five more.

'Count them,' Robin ordered.

John emptied the bags on to the floor of the cart.

'Three hundred gold pieces,' he said at last. 'Enough to keep the whole of Sherwood warm and fed for the winter.'

'We have to protect the Church's money from thieves,' the Abbot blustered. 'That's the only reason it was concealed. It is intended for the poor.'

'And we'll make sure they get it, lord Abbot,' said Robin. 'We'll save you the hard labour of distribution.'

'You'll hang for this, wolfshead!'

'Undoubtedly, but we still intend to take the coins. And bless you for your charity from the good folk of the shire. Put the coins back in the bags, John.'

'Will you leave our church with nothing?' asked the Abbot. 'For the shrine of Saint Edberga?'

'You may keep the ten gold pieces you declared,' said Robin. 'Had you informed us about the rest we might only have taken a tithe. But as you lied to me we'll now take all but the ten. Now get out of my sight!'

The Abbot and his monks went swiftly away.

'Did you see his face? Like a Sherwood thunderstorm,' said Will Stutely. 'But by God, Robin, I hope you never find yourself at that man's mercy.'

'I never expected any charity from the Church, anyway,' said Robin. 'Let's get back to Thripper's Drumble.'

~

'So let's understand each other,' said Gisborne, as the two little armies marched north. 'Tomorrow morning, I'll halt a few miles this side of Reynworth. That'll give you time to circle round to the other side of the village. Then we'll close in from north and south. The peasants will be contained. Any that resist will be put to the sword or hanged. And we'll burn Reynworth to the ground.'

'I don't need instruction on how to conduct a campaign, Gisborne,' said du Bois. 'I've slaughtered more peasants than you've had whores...'

'With respect, my lords,' the Sheriff's little clerk intervened, 'that was not what my lord the Sheriff said. I heard his words clearly. He said that you were to simply ride to Reynworth to collect the taxes. The villagers are not yet overdue with their payment. The time allowed has not quite expired.'

'But they will be late, master clerk!' Gisborne said testily. 'When does any Sherwood village pay on time? This is to be a punitive raid. To set one final example to these rebellious villeins.'

'My lord the Sheriff said...' the clerk persisted.

'My lord the Sheriff is not here,' replied Gisborne.

'Oh yes he is, Gisborne,' a silky voice came from behind the three riders. Gisborne and du Bois whirled round. The Sheriff, on horseback, had overtaken the long line of men and had been listening to the conversation of the two knights for several minutes. 'Speechless, Gisborne? How unusual for you!'

'You came alone through Sherwood?' said Gisborne.

'Don't be a fool! Of course I didn't. I came with fifty men at arms. They're at the back of this... procession.'

'Even so, my lord Sheriff, you took a great risk. Robin Hood and his rebels might have seized you. It's not safe for you to ride in Sherwood.'

The Sheriff rode in front of them, turning his horse and bringing the expedition to a halt.

'I have command of this shire, Gisborne. I'll not let some wolfshead dictate to me where or where not I might ride. There are no forbidden corners of Sherwood for me. That's a message for every wolfshead and villein in the forest.'

'But why should they heed your message?' asked Gisborne.

'Because I am the Sheriff of Nottingham!' shouted de Lisle.

The thunderous words made every soldier in the column look up.

'Robin Hood has scant regard for such titles, my lord.'

'Then I'll teach him some respect, Gisborne,' said the Sheriff. 'Don't you see that this is what he wants? He craves a Sherwood where we daren't go unless we have a guard of hundreds. He longs for us to keep out of his domain. Well, I shan't oblige him, Gisborne. Once we accept such terms our authority is lost.'

'There's little authority in having an arrow in your back!' said Gisborne. 'And that's why I favour the fierce action I've proposed. These wolfsheads are nothing without the tacit support of the Sherwood villagers. If the villeins see that backing Robin Hood leads to their homes being burned and their families hanged then they'll turn on him.'

'There's some truth in what Gisborne says, lord Sheriff,' du Bois intervened, looking pained at having to agree with his rival. 'No wolfshead has lasted long in Sherwood in the past. Like all wolves they are eventually forced to thieve and scavenge. The villagers get tired of it and bring them in to us, bound and gagged often... more usually dead.'

'Maybe so, but I don't intend to underestimate this Robin Hood,' said the Sheriff. 'He came close to a victory in Loxley Chase. I don't propose to give him so much rope in Sherwood.'

'Give him rope and he'll hang himself,' said du Bois.

'Perhaps, but do remember that I'm appointed as Sheriff to keep the peace in this shire. Not to see Sherwood turned into a battlefield. And remember, Gisborne, we need villagers and villeins to provide food and goods. To pay taxes to support the administration of the King and his servants. Slaughter them all, as you would wish to do, and who'll labour in the fields? Who'll provide the gold?'

'You want me to spare Reynworth?' Gisborne looked aghast.

'No, Gisborne. I've every expectation that you'll put the Reynworth peasants to the sword. I fully expect to see their houses burning like funeral pyres by tomorrow's sunset. But if anyone asks... if at some point in the future we're questioned on these events, by Count John or Lionheart or whoever... well... we went to collect taxes. But I need to see wolfsheads there, or at least some resistance before you draw your blade.'

~

'I'm concerned about Ralph Gammon,' Will Scarlet whispered to Robin, as they took the secret path towards Thripper's Drumble. Loxley was surprised at the intimate tone of the conversation. He was more used to Scarlet berating him or threatening to disobey orders.

'He seems jolly enough.' Robin looked round and noticed Ralph lingering behind on the path. 'Considering his worries about his wife, he's surprisingly happy most of the time.'

Scarlet shook his head. 'Ah, you haven't known him as long as me. He puts on a brave performance, but it's all show. He likes to cheer up the others. Kindliness is in his nature. But I've been watching him in his quiet moments. I've seen how restless he is in his sleep. He's near to despair.'

Robin glanced back again. Ralph Gammon had fallen even further behind, his right hand occasionally beating back the overhanging twigs as though they were irritating summer flies.

'I'm considering how to get the women out of Nottingham Castle, but it's not an easy proposition,' he said. 'We must watch out for...' He pointed ahead. 'Here's Alan and there's trouble in his face.'

Alan a Dale was stood at the edge of the Drumble. A horse was tethered nearby.

'Where did you get the horse, Alan?' asked Scarlet.

'The castle stables,' the minstrel replied. 'And hard riding I've had of it. I'm not used to horses. Very different from the little ponies we used on Stainmore.'

Robin waited for the outlaws to gather around him.

'And the trouble?'

'I sang and played for the Sheriff last night. On the castle battlements. Not an easy performance for he had Gisborne and du Bois with him. They were discussing matters of interest. That's why I'm here.'

'Another raid on Sherwood then?'

'Reynworth is the place,' said Alan. 'Gisborne and du Bois set out this morning. They intend to camp at some village on the way and collect taxes at Reynworth tomorrow morning.'

'How many men?' asked John Little.

'At least two hundred with the forces of Gisborne and du Bois. They intend to surround Reynworth, Gisborne to the south and du Bois in the north. They'll let nobody in and nobody out. If the people of Reynworth can't produce the taxes they owe, they intend to put the villagers to the sword and raze the place to the ground. Du Bois is to take anything they loot to Newark to save having to journey back through our part of Sherwood.'

'Two 'undred,' said Much. 'We can't take on that many. And I happen to know they won't be able to stump up their taxes. There's not a gold piece in the place.'

'We could try and defend the village,' said Stutely.

'We can't match their numbers,' said John. 'It'd be throwing our lives away. And Reynworth would get burned and everyone murdered just the same.'

Robin looked deep in thought. The others knew the signs and were silent.

'Perhaps we won't need to defend Reynworth,' he said at last. 'I think I've a better idea. Alan, we need to borrow your horse.'

~

It was getting near to dusk when the archer approached the chapel of the shrine of Saint Withburga. Tuck was sitting on a bench outside. He watched the trout feeding in the stream and ate the last portions of a chicken that a pious villager had brought along as an offering.

'You would do well not to travel in Sherwood so late at night,' Tuck said, looking up. 'It'll be black midnight before you get home.'

'I was returning home when I saw something that I thought you should know about. A matter that might concern Robin Hood. I'd have dealt with it myself but there were too many of them.'

Tuck threw the last chicken bone into the water. He always believed that such a measure encouraged the fish to linger, so that he might catch them on his line.

'Too many of what?'

'Soldiers,' the archer replied. 'Men at arms marching through Sherwood with a purpose. Led by Gisborne and du Bois. I left them as they prepared to camp for the night at Blidworth. The Sheriff was there as well.'

'How many men at arms?'

'At least two hundred and fifty. Perhaps more.'

'Are we at war?'

The archer sat next to him on the bench, fingers playing on the fine yew wood of the longbow. 'A war on the villagers of Sherwood, anyway. They attack Reynworth tomorrow morning. The old excuse. They haven't paid their taxes.'

Tuck looked grave.

'But the Reynworth taxes aren't due for a few days yet,' he said. 'I was there only last week and the matter was discussed.'

'Can they pay their taxes?' asked the archer.

Tuck shook his head.

'They haven't any way of paying.'

'Then it's an excuse for a slaughter.'

'I must leave at once. To see if I can find Robin.' He turned to the archer. 'You mustn't go there. You really mustn't. There's danger in it. I doubt that even Robin Hood and his outlaws could deal with such a force. If you intervene you'll throw your life away.'

'I've no intention of doing that. But I'll not stand by and watch this murder take place.'

Tuck stood up, buckling on his sword and taking up a quarter staff that was leaning against the wall.

'I hope I'm not too late,' he said.

The archer held up a hand to wave farewell.

'I wish you'd let me tell Robin about your mission?' Tuck said, taking the archer by the arm.

'You made a solemn vow, Tuck!'

'I know... I know. But if it leads to your death? Well, there'll be no peace for me.'

Twelve

They were expected of course.

De Lisle always knew they would be. Some villein from Blidworth would have crept through his circle of guards in the night, to warn the people of the neighbouring village. In the distance a few men worked in the fields surrounding the hovels of Reynworth. But it seemed every other inhabitant of the wretched little place was gathered there to watch the soldiers of Nottingham arrive.

'I thought they might have fled into the forest by now,' du Bois remarked.

He had left his own troops stationed around the northern perimeter of the village, closing off the road on that side. He had cantered across to join de Lisle and Gisborne who had ridden into the middle of the houses with their own men.

'Someone must have told them we were coming,' said Gisborne.

The Sheriff gave him a look of despair.

'You amaze me, Gisborne!' he said.

'This is Sherwood Forest, Gisborne,' explained du Bois. 'A whisper travels swiftly through the trees.'

'They're too clever to live!' said Gisborne. He scanned the crowd of some fifty villagers who were walking towards them.

'Do you see any wolfsheads?' he asked the Sheriff's clerk.

'None that I recognise, my lord,' the clerk replied, searching the faces as the villagers approached.

'Of course there are no wolfsheads, Gisborne,' said the Sheriff, looking in even greater despair up at the sky. 'Are your wits in your arse? They've had word of our coming. Did you imagine they'd be standing here awaiting a rope round their necks?'

'Then we'll hang them for not paying their taxes,' Gisborne replied. 'There's some good dry thatch on those houses. I'll have the place blazing in no time at all. Look at the impudence on their faces.'

The Sheriff held up a hand to silence him.

'Who speaks for Reynworth?' he shouted at the villagers who were now gathered in front of his horse.

A tall man with a great yellow beard stepped forward.

'I speak for the people here, my lord Sheriff,' he said.

'And you are?'

'Aelrig the Saxon, my lord.'

'Saxon!' muttered Gisborne.

'Are you a villein, Aelrig?'

Aelrig held his head back with pride.

'I'm a freeman now, my lord. The last Sheriff released me from my bonds for aiding him when he tumbled from his horse.'

'Drunk was he?' asked de Lisle.

'He was a trifle merry, my lord. With respect.'

'Are there any wolfsheads here?' asked Gisborne, looking again at the crowd.

'No, my lord Gisborne. Certainly not. This is an honest village.'

'He protests too much,' Gisborne said to the Sheriff. 'Look at the arrogance in his eyes. Let's start our work.'

The Sheriff turned to him.

'Not yet, Gisborne,' he said. 'They're bound to offer something towards what they owe. Let's see their offering. Then you can destroy the place.'

He turned to the villager.

'You know why we're here, Aelrig?'

Aelrig looked down at his feet.

'Look at me, man!' shouted de Lisle. 'Do you know why we're here?'

'You've come for the King's taxes, my lord.'

'Correct.'

'Not due till the end of the week, my lord Sheriff,' said Aelrig.

'They're due whenever the Sheriff says they're due,' said Gisborne. 'Let me hang this wretch, my lord. Let him be the first.'

De Lisle held up a hand to silence him. He looked down at Aelrig.

'Do you have *any* contribution to the taxes?' he asked.

'Yes, my lord Sheriff.'

'What portion of what is owed?'

Aelrig signalled to two men in the crowd who came forward with four cloth bags. They held them out towards the Sheriff's clerk.

'All of it, my lord Sheriff.'

'All of it?'

'We were about to set out for Nottingham this very morn, my lord. Only the cattle broke out and we were delayed. Then you came riding up. We'd have been at the castle by tonight. Here's the taxes, my lord, and a good blessing on King Richard.'

'How can they have paid?' protested Gisborne to the Sheriff. 'Only last week we had word they had no money in Reynworth. Now they can pay in full. Let me make this peasant talk. We'll soon find out where this money came from!'

'Silence, Gisborne!'

The Sheriff looked down at Aelrig. 'I have to say that I'm surprised that you've found the money. I understood this to be a poor village.'

Aelrig knuckled his forehead and smiled. 'We spread that rumour, my lord. There are so many outlaws in Sherwood it's best to seem to have no wealth.'

De Lisle didn't like that smile. He glared down at the villager and Aelrig bowed his head.

'Count the taxes, master clerk,' he said.

It took some time, but eventually the little clerk looked up at the Sheriff.

'All here, my lord,' he said.

'Du Bois, you will take this money to Newark. I'll have it collected from there.' Then to Gisborne. 'Turn your men around. It's a long journey back to Nottingham and I'd like to do it before nightfall.'

'We're *leaving*?'

'What do you want me to do, Gisborne? They've paid their taxes. Oh, I know you'd burn the place regardless. But we can't be seen to punish peasants who obey our rules. Let's just get out of this filthy hole.'

The soldiers were at least a mile away before the villagers erupted into a great burst of laughter.

'Light the signal fire,' ordered Aelrig.

~

'There's the signal,' said Will Stutely, pointing to the plume of black smoke climbing towards the blue of the sky. 'Do you see anything, Ralph?'

Ralph Gammon was in the tallest branches of an elm, looking across at the village.

'Alan was right,' he shouted down, 'they're splitting their forces. Gisborne and the Sheriff are riding towards Nottingham. And du Bois and his men are coming towards us.'

'How many?'

'Hard to tell. Forty or fifty perhaps. Some have crossbows, other spears. About a dozen men on horseback. And there's du Bois at the front.'

Robin looked around. There was no deep hollow on this road to Newark, which might have made the ambush easier. Just open heathland, pressed in on two sides by the trees of Sherwood Forest.

'Our only hope is to take them down here. There's no better ground.' He turned to John Little. 'I'll take Scarlet and Stutely and we'll hide ourselves out on the heath. You take the rest of the men and stay on the edge of the trees. Post someone along the road where it disappears into the forest. We don't want them to get away with our money. Don't shoot your arrows till you see my first one strike home.'

John nodded. 'The ploy must have worked. Reynworth remains unburnt. Gisborne won't be pleased. I expect he came all prepared for a massacre.'

'Du Bois might enjoy the slaughter for him if our surprise doesn't work. It pains me to take down those men at arms without warning. But we've no chance if we step out and challenge them.'

'It was a clever idea of yours to give the villagers the Abbot's money,' said Scarlet to Robin. 'Let's hope we don't have to let them ride off with it.'

'We must let some of them get away,' said Robin. 'I want du Bois alive. It's important that word gets back to Nottingham that we seized the money. I don't want any blame to fall on the villagers of Reynworth.'

'They're getting closer, Robin,' Gammon yelled down from the tree.

'Come down, Ralph. Let's get on with this business. Stutely, Scarlet, with me!'

He tore off at a great pace across the heath, while John ordered the disposition of the rest of the outlaws among the trees. For a few minutes all was quiet. As the outlaws settled, the birds began to sing again. Somewhere deep in the forest a vixen yelped. A slight breeze stirred the topmost boughs of the Sherwood oaks. 'Spread out,' he said to the two Wills, 'half a bowshot apart. I'll get closest to where they'll appear where the road winds over the heath. Take your lead from me.'

Robin had scarcely got into position to one side of a bramble bush before he saw them coming. Du Bois and the horsemen at the head of the column. And there were the men at arms, pressed soldiers mostly, who probably didn't want to be there at all. Men who just wanted a life without danger. He looked across the heath at Scarlet, who'd himself been pressed into military service. Robin wondered what thoughts were crowding into Will's mind at the sight of marching men, some of whom he might have served with. Yet it was near impossible to spare any lives in such an encounter.

The horsemen were riding by now and the first of the foot soldiers were just a few yards behind. One horseman had bags of money tied to his saddle. He had to be the first to be brought down.

Robin levelled the arrow in his bow and took aim at the man's back. Not a difficult shot, normally. And no great distance. But the slight breeze of the morning was turning gustier. He took a step sideways into the direction of the wind to compensate, pulling the bowstring as he manoeuvred. Aware that he was now in full view of the first of the foot soldiers.

He heard one of the men at arms yell a warning even as he loosed the arrow. He saw the horseman fall sideways down the horse. The animal bucked in panic, before galloping at speed down the road towards the edge of the open ground. He caught a glimpse of Much running out of the trees and throwing himself forward to grab the reins.

'Wolfsheads!' someone yelled. 'Take him! Take him!'

Du Bois and the other horsemen had turned in line and were facing Robin. They looked all set to charge. Robin placed another arrow on to his bow.

'Loxley! Down you bloody fool!'

It was Scarlet's voice.

Robin didn't wait to look for the threat. He just fell to the ground on one side of the bramble bush. Three crossbow quarrels tore through the place where he'd been standing a second before.

He risked a glance up.

Four of the horsemen were charging straight at him, three with drawn swords and the fourth waving a mace. They were coming so close that he could see the hatred in their eyes. The earth seemed to shake under the drumming of the hooves.

Robin pulled back and without even aiming loosed the arrow. It took the horseman with the mace in the shoulder, sending the weapon flying into the bushes. A moment later arrows from Scarlet and Stutely brought down two more of the horsemen.

The surviving rider was closing on Robin now, sword held back ready to take a killing swing at the outlaw. Robin threw down his bow and drew his own sword, preparing to parry the blow – a nearly impossible task as the soldier's sword came arching in with the terrific speed of the galloping horse to give it momentum.

At the last second, Robin threw himself to the ground and rolled sideways out of range with great speed. The horseman tried to turn the animal to counter the move, but the velocity of his charge made it impossible. He galloped past and it was some twenty yards before he could slow his mount sufficiently to change direction.

Even as he turned, two arrows tore into him, one catching him in the chest and the other in the face. His arms flew outwards and he tumbled backwards from the horse.

Robin glanced to his side and saw Scarlet and Stutely reloading their bows. He saw the reason why. Du Bois and the three other horsemen had begun their attack. He picked up his own longbow and fitted an arrow to the string.

The bolt from a crossbow broke through the air a few inches from Robin's face. He risked a glance. The foot soldiers had assembled into a line and had begun their own advance across the open ground. A man with a crossbow stood in front of them and was aiming again. The situation was becoming perilous.

And then a volley of arrows from the trees tore into the ranks of the men at arms, sending them into a wild panic as they recognised their exposed position. Several turned in time to see the rest of the outlaws step out from the trees. They scarcely got the glimpse of Robin's men before another flight of arrows came flying towards them.

It was too much to endure.

The panic spread as four of the soldiers fell to the ground. The rest fled back in the direction of Reynworth, casting aside their weapons in their desperation to get out of range of that murderous hail of arrows. For a moment the remaining horsemen circled. The thought must have come into their minds that they were surrounded by a greater force of arms. They could only imagine what might be in the trees.

And then du Bois tried to instil some order into his demoralised men. Robin could see him wave in the direction of the three outlaws out on the heath. And then du Bois charged along the track after the fleeing soldiers, shouting at them to rally. He seemed oblivious to the outlaws who were running out from the edge of the forest. He probably never saw John rush towards him at an angle, swinging a quarter staff the size of a small tree.

It caught du Bois full in the chest, sending him flying backwards from his horse, the breath crushed from his lungs. In a second, John had thrown himself down on to his victim's chest and had a knife at his throat.

And then Robin became aware of three of the horsemen bearing down on him at great speed. He scarce had time to aim and it was more by luck than skill that his arrow took the closest soldier through the throat. He hadn't even fallen from his horse before arrows from Scarlet and Stutely brought down the other two riders.

The remaining horsemen stayed on the road, clearly unsure what to do. They looked along the track as the last of the foot soldiers disappeared from view. Two of them drew out their swords and Robin prepared an arrow ready to meet another charge.

It never came.

John Little gave out a great shout. They turned to see his dagger playing around the throat of Sir Brian du Bois.

'Stay your hands!' John yelled. 'Throw down your swords or I'll cut du Bois's throat!'

The horsemen hesitated, looking all around for help that was never going to come. There were hurried words between them. And then one after another they threw down their weapons.

'Now get off your horses!' John ordered.

Some did but a pair of the men seemed reluctant to obey. They looked longingly down the road towards Newark, their minds obviously occupied with the possibility of escape.

'My hand's getting restless,' said John, his blade playing nearer to the throat of his prisoner.

'Do as he says!' du Bois almost screamed. 'Surrender! Now!'

The last of the soldiers dismounted.

The remaining outlaws sped towards them and within a few minutes du Bois and his men were tied like hogs ready for market.

Robin walked over to du Bois and grabbed him by his flaxen hair.

'You should have stayed in Newark, Sir Brian,' he said.

'I'll kill you for this, wolfshead!'

'You're hardly in a position to make threats, du Bois. This is Sherwood Forest. And you're now a guest in my domain. I'm contemplating whether to cut your throat.'

'So you intend to murder me?'

'I said I was contemplating it,' Robin replied. 'And I just have. No. You're going to live, du Bois. Do you remember the last time you chased me through this forest? You swore I'd be dead in a week. You said that you'd bring me back to Newark tied naked across a horse. You said you'd hang me naked from your castle walls.'

'You were fortunate, Loxley.'

'And this is going to be a fortunate day for you, du Bois. No one is going to cut you, or beat you, or hang you from the walls of Newark.'

'What then?'

'John, take off his clothes.'

'Eh?'

'Strip him of his clothes, John.'

'What? All of them?'

'All of them. Every last stitch. And then tie him to his horse. It's market day in Newark and he'll make a pretty picture as he canters into the town.'

'You bastard!' du Bois protested.

'And gag him, John.'

And stripped and gagged, du Bois was tied along his own horse, his face hanging down towards its rear.

'John, take Ralph and Much and escort my lord du Bois back to Newark. We'll keep his men tied here for the rest of the day before we release them. Then meet us back at our lurk.'

John nodded and led a furious du Bois's horse along the road.

'Yer'll have a goodly acquaintance with yer horse's arse before we've covered a mile,' said Much to du Bois, setting off yet more protesting moans from the prisoner.

'He won't forgive you for that humiliation,' said Stutely to Robin as the procession vanished into the trees. 'God preserve that you don't ever fall into his hands.'

'I wouldn't have died easy if I'd been his captive anyway,' said Robin. 'And the sight of their lord mortified will be a pleasure for the good townsfolk of Newark.'

~

From deep within the trees of Sherwood the archer had watched the battle, twice fitting an arrow into the bow, prepared to intervene. There was a certain frustration that there was to be no fighting that day. And a smile at the sight of du Bois being taken back naked to his own castle.

The archer slipped back into the forest.

There was just time to seek out Tuck with the news before the long trudge home.

Thirteen

Sir Guy of Gisborne rocked back in the chair, feet reaching across to the bed. He was almost choking with a bout of hysterical laughter. The girl looked across at him from the bed, where she lay naked on the covers. She was puzzled at his reaction.

'I don't understand?' she said. 'Robin got away with all of the tax money yet again. I thought you'd be livid?'

Gisborne laughed again.

'Worth every penny to see that oaf du Bois humiliated. Oh God! I wish I'd been in Newark when his horse brought him naked into the market place. They say the sight made even the meanest serf merry!'

'And my lord the Sheriff?'

'Ah, well he's not merry at all,' Gisborne added. There was another burst of laughter. 'My lord Sheriff almost wrecked the great hall in his rage. Threw over the long table that usually takes a dozen men to lift. And for once he couldn't put the blame on me.'

'He'll make life hard for Robin now?'

'Robin Hood will wish he'd stayed at Loxley. The Sheriff intends to take hundreds of men into Sherwood in a week's time. He's borrowing soldiers from du Bois and a half dozen other lords. They'll search every village and sweep the greenwood.'

'And will you go?'

'Oh, yes, though I don't believe it'll work. Robin Hood needs to be caught by guile, not force of arms.' He looked across at her. 'Unfortunately, the situation presents a dilemma here at the castle.'

'What kind of dilemma?'

He got up and walked to the table. He filled two flagons with wine and presented one to Clorinda, sitting down on the bed beside her.'

'You are the dilemma, Clorinda.'

'Me?'

He nodded.

'Yes, you,' he said. 'My lord the Sheriff is curious as to how Robin Hood found out about our expedition to Reynworth. Even the soldiery didn't know where we were going until we arrived there. That wretched bloody outlaw knew everything. Even that du Bois was intending to take the tax money to Newark. The Sheriff thinks you might have told him.'

'Me?'

'You're Loxley's cousin. Clorinda. It'd make a lot of sense.'

'I've not seen Robin for years!' she protested.

Gisborne noticed that the girl's face had reddened.

Ah, you're lying, he thought. She could never conceal her deceptions.

'The Sheriff is convinced that you betrayed his plans. And there's more than that, Clorinda. The Abbot of St Mary's nearly died from your potions. The Sheriff suspects that it was an attempt to kill him. He wonders how any poison might have been administered.'

'Well, you know how, Guy!'

He almost flinched at the familiarity.

'My lord!' he corrected her.

'Very well, *my lord*. You know how it was done and you know why.'

'Your potion didn't work!'

She considered for a moment.

'The poison was intended for the Sheriff. He's a thin man. If he'd taken it all he'd certainly have died. But the Abbot's fat. More room in his great gut to absorb the poison.'

'Anyway, du Bois's nasty little suspicions have been dripped into the Sheriff's ear. He knows that you served that meal. And your fame with potions goes before you. And he knows that you're my whore.'

Gisborne could see that the word hurt her.

'And the pain of this, Clorinda,' he continued, 'is that if you become suspected then I do too. Everyone in the castle knows that we share a bed.'

'I would never tell...'

'I know you wouldn't,' he replied. 'But there's more. And worse news at that. The Abbot dined with du Bois at Newark a few days ago. The bastard knight couldn't help but voice his thoughts over the venison. Now the Abbot believes he was poisoned... by you!'

'Oh God!'

'And the Abbot being the Abbot, well... he sees it not only as a personal attack on him, but an assault on the Church and the Body of Christ as well.'

'But it was never intended that we...'

He held up his hands in despair.

'And given that you used potions gathered in the countryside...'

'What's to become of me?'

'In the mind of the Abbot, anyone who gathers potions is a witch. He quoted Leviticus at du Bois: "Thou shalt not suffer a witch to live!" The Abbot muttered to du Bois that he wants you hanged for sorcery... or worse.'

Gisborne got a kind of joy from seeing the panic in her face. A realisation that she was nothing in the scheme of things, with as little protection under the law as a hunted animal. What a wretch she was. At times he found it hard to believe that he ever had these kinds of discussion with her, or took her so much into his confidence. He considered his feelings for Clorinda. Could it be affection? No, not affection. There was no future for her in his life. When the time came to dispose of her, well, she must be removed.

Perhaps this was the time?

And then he looked again at her long brown hair splayed over the pillow. The firm and generous young breasts. The pleasing shape of those naked legs.

Not yet. Not yet.

He had need of her. The need to possess. The need to conquer her brown flesh. A need for that dazzling feeling when he took her.

Not yet.

And besides, he had nobody else to talk to.

She was good at conspiracies.

Not yet.

'I think it would be wise if you left the castle, Clorinda.'

She looked horrified.

'You're sending me away?'

'From the castle, that's all,' he said. 'I'll find you a lodging in the town, for now. A place where I can still come to visit you. But out of the sight and mind of the Sheriff.'

'How long for?'

'Certainly while Robert de Lisle continues to hold that office,' he said. 'But soon I might be Sheriff and matters will be handled very differently in Nottingham. Who knows what might happen when de Lisle rides into Sherwood after your cousin? It's not impossible that he might fall to one of Robin Hood's arrows.'

'You promise you won't abandon me?'

His heart leapt at her pleading.

'You have my word,' he lied. 'And there's more...'

'More?'

'In twelve days, Count John of Mortain comes to the shire. He thinks well of me. Even if Lionheart doesn't. And Count John controls this shire. And I happen to know that he doesn't support de Lisle as Sheriff. De Lisle was King Richard's appointment before he left for Normandy. Nor does Count John favour that bag of dung, du Bois.'

Gisborne was talking to himself rather than the girl.

'If I'm clever,' he went on, 'really clever, well. I can see how I might not only become the next Sheriff of Nottingham, but gain the control of Newark as well. And with du Bois dead or disgraced, I can see that I might get my lands at Bowland returned to me.'

'I'll do anything I can to help, my lord.'

'That I take for granted,' he said.

~

Robin Hood was hunting for food a mile from Thripper's Drumble when he saw her treading one of the hidden paths deep in the greenwood. It was as though she was trying not to be seen. Every now and again she would draw into the shelter of a tree, look all around and listen for any noise that didn't belong

142

naturally to the forest. She was dressed in the rough clothes of a peasant woman, but there was no mistaking who she was.

Marian.

He watched as she wandered on along the path and thought it might be sport to trail her. Not an easy task when someone is trying to avoid being followed.

He walked the path with great care, making sure not to tread on any dry twigs that might crack and give him away. Very often he lost sight of her altogether, but he had no doubt that she was still ahead of him.

Occasionally, her position would be given away by the birds of the forest. Once a blackbird flew swiftly through the trees, giving out a rapid and noisy call of alarm. Then as she edged her way around a clearing, a flight of rooks overhead made a sudden diversion as they spotted the human figure looking up at them.

At the slightest indication that she had alarmed any creature Marian halted for a few moments, coming away from the path and into the trees.

Robin conceded that she was very good at evading recognition. Better than some of his own men. But just how good was she? He decided to put it to the test by getting nearer to the girl. And there she was again, heading into the thickest of the trees, just after the ending of a clearing.

He was now within a few yards, though she was out of sight again as he plunged into the cover himself. He pulled in against an oak and listened. No sounds at all but a breeze sweeping through the highest of the boughs. No sounds and no sighting. No...

The point of the dagger was against his throat, pressing into the thin band of flesh just enough to hurt.

'I could push it right in and claim the reward, wolfshead,' she said. 'Should I do that?'

'Gisborne would be pleased,' he croaked.

She withdrew the blade.

'Why are you following me?'

'Just for sport,' Robin replied. 'Just to see if I could...'

'Apparently you can't!'

'You're very good at this, Marian.'

'I grew up in Sherwood and had some excellent teachers.'

She took a pace backwards and looked him up and down, noticing the bow slung over one shoulder.

'Hunting?' she asked. 'For food or foresters?'

'On this occasion for food. Living in the forest gives my men a hearty appetite.'

'I'd heard you'd been busy,' she said. 'Your deeds at Reynworth are the talk of the shire. And my father was in Newark when Sir Brian du Bois came home. I'm sure du Bois is looking forward to encountering you again.'

'No doubt!'

She pointed to a fallen log and suggested that they sit.

'Do I call you Loxley?' she asked.

'Robin,' he said. 'I think it best to try and put Loxley out of my mind. My battlefield is Sherwood these days, not Loxley Chase.'

'Robin of Sherwood then, not Loxley.'

He nodded and they were silent for a while.

'Marian... why are you here?' he asked at last.

'Here? I live here. Edwinstowe isn't so far away on the broad track from Nottingham. I've just come for a country ramble in the forest.'

He looked her up and down.

'Dressed like that?'

'Well, you see, there are so many wolfsheads in Sherwood these days. It's best not to look as though I've anything worth stealing. And wearing these clothes makes me more likely to be accepted if I have to go into one of the villages.'

'Surely everyone recognises you as Marian of Edwinstowe?'

She smiled.

'They do but clothes create such an impression. If you wear the finest then there's always a distance placed between yourself and everyone else. Dressed like this they soon forget any differences.'

'I find that hard to believe...'

'Take away the finery and... well, look at du Bois. Riding naked through Newark. The townsfolk will never see him in the same light again.'

He turned to her.

'But it's not safe for a young woman to be alone in Sherwood. There are other wolfsheads in the forest who are desperate men. And dissolute gentry as well. They won't care if you're a lady or a villager.'

'You fear I might be ravished?'

She chuckled with amusement.

'There are men in this shire who love to despoil the innocent. Whether they be ladies or village maids.'

Marian looked sideways at him.

'And who says I'm so innocent?'

'Marian!'

'Why do you look so shocked? If my father had had sons nobody would have noticed if they'd sowed their wild oats. Why should I be any different?'

'Then you've...?'

'Well of course I have,' she said. 'When you're growing up you get curious about... certain matters. I've always been a great believer in the idea that curiosity should be satisfied.'

She was amused at just how shocked the outlaw looked.

'And does your father know about this?' he asked.

'He pretends not to. He turns a blind eye to a great deal of my doings. I'm sure I've other qualities that more than make up for my strayings in the forest.'

'Perhaps I should escort you back to Edwinstowe, anyway?'

Her dark eyes flashed dangerously.

'I think not,' she said. 'I'm on a journey to see a friend. It'll be evening before I return home. How are you finding Thripper's Drumble as a place to hide?'

Her humour returned at the look of astonishment on his face.

'How did you know we were there?'

'You needn't worry, I won't tell anyone,' she said. 'It isn't hard to work out. You needed a place of safety. Not far from the great roads through the forest, but somewhere where you couldn't easily be surprised. Where else but the Drumble?'

'You know the secret way in?'

'I've known it since I was a child. My father had an old servant called Bertram. He hid there during King Stephen's reign, when the Empress Maud's soldiers were attacking the villages in the shire. I'd heard the legends about a secret place in the forest, so I badgered him until he showed me.' She glanced sideways at him. 'I've had many a merry time bathing naked in the brook there.'

The vision filled Robin's mind.

'Of course,' she continued, 'I couldn't do it in front of all your men. But if they're ever away poaching and you're there alone... well?'

He looked at her, mouth open.

'You're shameless, Marian!' he said. 'You look as innocent as a nun, yet you admit to such doings.'

'It's a very good brook and a lovely deep pool at one end of the Drumble. Big enough for two, Robin.'

He didn't know what to say.

'You see now why I can't accept the Abbot's offer of a place in one of his nunneries?' she said. 'Though purity's the last thing on that old goat's mind when he looks at me. I'm sure he'd be thrilled to pin me down over the altar if he could.'

Robin tried to evict the blasphemous image from his mind.

'So who are you visiting in Sherwood?' he asked.

She was suddenly curt again.

'My business and not yours, wolfshead. And I'd better be on my way.' She stood and looked down at him. 'And if you try and follow me I'll have my dagger in your throat... all the way!'

She took out the weapon and drew the flat of the blade between two fingers, very slowly.

'So easy for me to do,' she added. 'You're outside the protection of the law, wolfshead. Any villein in the forest can slay you and be amply rewarded. Though Gisborne and du Bois would be frustrated at being thwarted. I'm sure they both have a very unpleasant death planned for you.'

She gave a quick nod of the head and strode away, her slender figure soon disappearing as the trees hid the bend in the track. Robin sat a few minutes longer on the log reliving the encounter and the conversation. He looked up into the great canopy of leaves and boughs, full of the colours of summer. But his mind could only see Marian's dark and dangerous eyes. Then his thoughts drifted to the deep pool in Thripper's Drumble. And then...

He stood, his mind invaded at thoughts of hungry men gathered around the Drumble's fires. He was, after all, supposed to be out hunting for food.

~

Sir Brian du Bois didn't like the look on her face.

She might be just a castle slattern but there was something impudent in her expression. She was new to Newark Castle. She had been laying out logs for the fire when he entered the great hall. She'd looked up and then bowed, her hand to her forehead. But not before he had seen her smirk.

They were all laughing at him.

He heard the jests wherever he went in the castle and in the town, though everyone jumped to serious attention when his gaze turned in their direction.

A ribald picture had appeared on a wall by the market place, a knight tied backwards to his horse, with unflattering additions.

Damned bloody wolfshead!

The girl was shuffling towards the door.

'You,' he cried out.

She paused and turned. He got some pleasure from seeing the fear writ large on her face.

'My lord?'

'What's your name?'

'Aelswith, my lord.'

A Saxon name.

Such names were still to be heard in the deeper parts of the forest. As though Senlac and the Conquest had never happened. You'd have thought, a century and more later, that the Saxons would be no more. They were a vanquished race but still they clung on. And he suddenly realised that he was talking to her in her own tongue. This foul English that seemed to be everywhere, used increasingly rather than the stately language of Normandy.

Du Bois's father had not understood one word of it. Now it was almost impossible to function as an overlord without some knowledge of this English.

He always found it rather difficult to actually pronounce the word.

English.

How splendid it would be to rule like the first conquerors who had no comprehension of this English. His forebears had heard these English gruntings with as little understanding as they might gain from the bleating of sheep or the panicked cries of a pig under the butcher's knife.

The spread of the language should never have been allowed. Lionheart could mutter but a few words. But the King's brother, Count John of Mortain, had a worrying understanding of what these English phrases meant.

Worse than that.

Du Bois had sat at table with Count John and listened to his conversation. The man was a positive traitor. John seemed to be almost embracing aspects of the English way of life. There had been times, when the wine and the ale flowed, when this scion of the Plantagenets had positively extolled the wonders of the realm.

Count John was a necessity to du Bois. Because, for all of his courage in battle, du Bois had received scant rewards from Lionheart. The stewardship of Newark had come from John. It had taken a great deal of effort.

Du Bois's father had gambled as badly as Gisborne, and lost much of the portion doled out by King William the Bastard after the Conquest. It had taken the younger du Bois a great deal of effort, both with the dice and even more unorthodox means, to get it back.

Indeed, he had done better than that. He'd cheated Gisborne of his properties at Bowland and gained a chase from the Earl of Huntingdon in much the same way.

He was...

Du Bois became aware that the girl Aelswith was still standing at attention by the doorway. He looked at her again. She was an ugly little thing. But there might be a novelty in that.

'Where do you come from, girl?' he asked.

'Maplebeck, my lord...'

One of du Bois's manors.

'Is your father a freeman or a villein?'

'He's dead, my lord. He was a ploughman. I was working the plough in his place 'til they brought me here.'

'Very well, you may go.'

He watched her leave.

An ugly little whore, but he'd plough her just the same. His steward could bring her to his bed that evening. He'd wipe that smirk off her face. She looked a virgin. Why should she not be? With a face like that who would have her?

And then his thoughts wondered again to his humiliation. He'd seen a similar smirk on Loxley's face. As he was bound backwards on his horse. As Loxley had slapped the animal's rump to send it on his way.

He'd drive that smirk right back into Loxley's skull.

~

A forester and three of the Sheriff's soldiers had cornered the boy in a glade just off the old north road through Sherwood. He had been poaching. No doubt about that. He had three rabbits strung by a cord over his shoulder and there were snares set nearby.

But it was his attitude that worried them.

There was none of the fear that they associated with captured miscreants. Just a bewilderment on the boy's face. He babbled away incoherently. Nothing he said made sense. He beamed a puzzled smile as he looked up the four men. And then he began to laugh hysterically. He stopped this crazed merriment as quickly as he had begun. Then he seemed to become obsessed with a twig lying on the path.

'He's moon mad, that's what he is? Bewitched maybe?' said the forester.

'Doesn't he realise what we're going to do to him?' asked one of the soldiers. 'Poaching in the forest and all...'

'We should leave him be,' said the forester. 'God's cursed him enough. Touch him and the madness might spread to us.'

Another of the soldiers had been standing a couple of yards away.

'I know him,' he said at last. 'He's the boy from Breevedon that Gisborne spared. Went half-witted when we strung up the villagers. His name's Matthew.'

The boy had started to hum a tune, all the notes askew, his hand tapping the ground in rhythm with the dirge.

'Matthew of Breevedon!' the soldier shouted.

But there was no reaction.

'I don't like this,' said the forester. 'Let's just leave him here and make no mention of ever seeing him.'

'That'd be for the best,' said a soldier.

'He was poaching in the forest,' said the first soldier. 'And he's mad. We can't just do nothin'. He has to be punished! Best to put the little cur out of his misery.'

He took out a dagger and pulling Matthew's head back by his hair, held the blade near to the boy's throat.

'Agreed?'

He looked at the faces of the other men.

They nodded.

He eased the dagger nearer.

Matthew of Breevedon seemed oblivious to any danger.

'He just don't care!' said the forester.

'Bewitched!'

'Get it over with,' said the forester. 'For Gawd's sake, he's giving me the creeps.'

'Here we go then...'

They were the soldier's last words.

An arrow thudded into his back, penetrating his spine. He barked with the shock of it as he fell sideways to the ground.

The other soldiers whirled round, drawing their swords as they moved.

Then two more arrows came out of the trees from opposite directions.

The first took a soldier in the chest, the arrowhead finding a rest in the man's heart.

The second plunged through its victim's left eye, piercing deep into his brain.

He was dead before he hit the path.

The forester threw down his own weapon and turned to run.

A pursuing arrow scored through a muscle on his right arm, severing a tendon and causing him to bellow with pain as he fled back towards Nottingham.

Matthew of Breevedon looked up with great curiosity as the archer stepped out of the trees. He clambered to his feet and walked across to his rescuer. He reached out and touched the face.

'Know you!' he said.

'That's right, Matthew,' the archer replied, 'you do know me.'

The boy seemed confused as he looked the archer up and down.

'Not like this though,' he said. 'Don't seem right...'

'That was good archery,' said Tuck as he walked up to them.

'You're good with a bow yourself, Brother Tuck,' said the archer, waving down at one of the soldiers. 'Hard to take a man through the head like that from such a distance.'

'A fluke,' the monk replied. 'I was aiming for his throat.'

'We were fortunate that we came along just now. They would have murdered poor Matthew.'

They looked across at the boy. He was collecting his rabbits and singing his tune up at the sky.

'What'll become of him?' asked the archer.

Tuck shook his head.

'Who knows?' He threw out his arms in despair. 'He may recover from seeing what happened at Breevedon in time. I'll take him back to Saint Withburga's shrine for a while and try and heal his mind. It's not safe to let him wander free in Sherwood.'

'I hope your saint heals him, Tuck.'

'Saint Withburga is well known for miracles. And I must pray for the souls of these poor men departed,' he added, looking at the three dead soldiers. 'Do you think I did right in letting the forester live?'

'He'll spread the word around the shire,' the archer said. 'Though I suspect that Robin Hood will get the blame for these deaths.'

'May God forgive us all for our sins,' said Tuck as he crossed himself.

~

'Gilbert.'

Robin took the blacksmith to one side as they strolled by the brook in Thripper's Drumble.

'I think it would be helpful if we rescued the tools of your trade from your old forge at Breevedon. You're the only smith we have and we may have need of arrowheads and other weapons.'

'I'll go over there tomorrow. I'll need some men and a cart.'

'Take Much, Ralph and Will Stutely. The sooner we have everything we need in the safety of the Drumble the better.'

He patted the man's great arm and walked on, following the brook to the great pool.

Marian was right.

There was enough room for two people to bathe.

The thought conjured up visions that quite entranced him.

Fourteen

'I've no soldiers to send, master clerk. You've had a wasted journey through Sherwood.'

Henry Fitzwalter looked up from his chair at this messenger from the Sheriff of Nottingham, pushing a parchment back up into the little man's hands.

'My lord de Lisle will be most displeased,' the clerk almost whimpered. 'He sees this as the best way to flush these wolfsheads from the forest. All the other lords in the shire have sent soldiers to Nottingham Castle. In preparation for the Sheriff's great expedition against these rebels.'

'Well I've no garrison here at Edwinstowe,' Fitzwalter replied. 'Just my servants and a few men retained to secure the safety of my home. And they're nearly as old as I am!'

The clerk shifted his weight from one foot to the other.

'I am to tell you... these words are my lord the Sheriff's... that he sees Edwinstowe as the very heart of the country where these outlaws run riot. Only last week three of the Sheriff's soldiers were murdered not very far from here. And a forester badly wounded. My lord de Lisle is quite convinced that this Robin Hood was responsible.'

Marian turned away from the fire.

'There are other outlaws in Sherwood,' she said. 'What makes you believe that Robin Hood was to blame?'

'The forester who escaped believes they were ambushed by this Robin Hood. They'd apprehended a half-wit boy who was poaching rabbits. They were about to exert summary justice...'

'For poaching rabbits?' said Fitzwalter. 'What business are a few rabbits to a King's forester? They are not game. No doubt this boy, half-witted or not, has to eat. What harm is done by taking a few rabbits?'

The clerk shuffled uncomfortably.

'My lord Gisborne has decreed it to be poaching,' he said. 'And this boy was a survivor of Breevedon. My lord Gisborne warned the lad against poaching after justice had been applied there...'

'Justice!' Fitzwalter interrupted. 'Bloody murder!'

'I would respectfully suggest that you don't use such terms in the presence of my lord Gisborne. He might adjudge such comments as treason.'

Fitzwalter regarded the messenger for a moment.

'Master clerk,' he said at last. 'I've spent all my life in Sherwood. I would suggest that I know much more about forest law than that oaf Gisborne. And you may tell him and the Sheriff that I'm concerned at the way the King's law is being administered in this shire. It is perhaps a matter that I might have to discuss with Count John when he comes here next week. His mother, Queen Eleanor, is an old friend of mine.'

And he gave a wave of his hand to dismiss the man.

For a moment the clerk hesitated. His mouth opened to continue the conversation. But the look in Fitzwalter's eyes made him quickly turn away and leave the hall.

Marian walked over to him, resting her hands on his shoulders.

'You know that that odious little sycophant will report all your words to de Lisle and Gisborne?' she said.

'I hope he does, Marian. Bloody Norman upstarts!' He looked up at her. 'Our family were administering laws in Sherwood, and fair justice too, when Offa ruled Mercia. Nay, even further back than that, when Penda was king. Our forebears fought alongside Alfred of Wessex, and then his bold daughter against the Danes. And with Athelstan when England was made. They heard the screams of the vanquished at the great battle at Brunanburgh...'

'And yet we're Norman too,' she said. 'Your father was a Norman knight. We share the blood of Saxon and Norman. Most of us have mixed blood these days.'

'Ay, Normans. You see the way they ravish the land? Their Viking past still stirs their souls.' He took her hand and sighed. 'And our souls as well, maybe? I can sometimes see the wild spirit of the Northmen in you, Marian...'

She said, almost to herself. 'It'll be a bloody day when the Sheriff's men come to Sherwood.'

The old man nodded.

'All the more reason why I wish you to stay around Edwinstowe. Some of these soldiers are the sweepings of the shire. Far too dangerous for you to be out on one of your country roamings.'

~

He had entered the gates of Nottingham disguised as a pedlar, his wares carried in a great pack on his back. His hair was long and beard untrimmed. The guards scarcely gave him a second glance, for it was market day and the streets were filled with the stalls of traders and the bustle of customers.

A few people looked twice, as though they might know him. But he had lost weight during his time in the forest and there were streaks of grey in his hair. His face was filthy, smeared with the marks of travel, and he seemed to lean on his wooden staff as though it was the only thing holding him up.

He unhitched his pack and set out his goods, trinkets worth almost nothing, on the top of the wall surrounding the market place. A few bystanders examined his offerings but speedily moved on.

Only the woman across the street seemed interested in the pedlar, watching him as he sipped water from a calfskin drinking flask. The pedlar caught her eye and then looked away.

A great procession of soldiers marched along the street and then through the main gateway of the castle. All carrying swords and shields, accompanied by a dozen crossbowmen. They were the troops of Sir Brian du Bois, for their shields bore his symbol of three hunting hawks.

The pedlar took a great interest in their passing. Gathering such information was the real reason he was in Nottingham at all. There was another motive, though none of the outlaws in Sherwood could have gathered what that was. Had they anticipated this other purpose then they might have sent someone else.

When the last of the marching men had gone by, Ralph Gammon leaned more easily against the wall and looked across the street once more. The woman had gone and several tumblers had taken her place; crazily somersaulting up and down the road, walking on their hands, and standing one atop another until their living column was as high as the roofs of the town houses.

And then she was at his side.

The woman he had seen earlier and hardly recognised.

'You didn't ought to have come, Ralph,' she said. 'It's not safe for you. Nottingham's not safe for anyone.'

His wife had aged ten years since she had been taken away to slave in the castle. The hair that used to be so dark was now entirely grey. Her face, once so smooth, broken by deep lines.

'I was sent here by the men I'm with,' he said. 'We heard rumours of a great gathering of soldiers in Nottingham.'

Joan Gammon choked back a tear.

'They're here to hunt all the outlaws in Sherwood,' she said. 'You, Ralph. Men like you. Anyone who fights with Robin Hood. Are you with him, Ralph?'

He nodded.

'Then you should run from Sherwood today. Get out of the shire,' she said. 'There's no safety for anyone. They say Robin Hood is the devil. We heard what happened in Loxley. There's only death if you stay with him in the forest.'

He noticed a soldier eyeing them from the opposite side of the market.

'Best look at my wares, Joan,' Ralph said. 'Don't want the castle guards to take too great an interest.'

She pretended to examine the goods he had lined up on the wall.

'And what's this Robin Hood to you?' she asked.

'He's a good man at heart...' he replied. 'He fights for the poor and against injustice.'

She wiped away a tear.

'Oh, but Ralph, what's the point of it all? He won't change anything. Lots of people'll die but nothing will ever change. It's the way God's ordered things. The many have to serve the few. We've no power ever to change it. The lords obey King Richard and we have to obey the lords. It's the way it is.'

He looked at her anxiously.

'How do they treat you in the castle?'

She was quiet for a long time.

'Well enough,' she said at last. 'It were hard at first, but now I'm trusted. That's why I'm let out into the town. The younger and prettier girls have a harder time.'

'But why don't you escape, Joan? Run away?'

'Where's there to run to? I can't live like a wolfshead in the forest. It'd only be days before I was hunted down. You know that.'

'Come with me, Joan. Follow me out of the gate. We're safe in Sherwood. We've a grand hiding place. Somewhere we could be safe together.'

She let out a deep breath.

'I'd never get through the town gates,' she said. 'The guards are on the lookout for anyone escaping from their bondage. Do you like this Robin Hood?'

It was a question he'd often asked himself.

'It's not that I like him,' he replied. 'But I do respect him. And the others are my friends.'

'He'll have you killed.'

'Robin saved my life once. When I was taken by Gisborne. Got me clean away.'

'I heard,' she said. 'And how William a' Trent died. Him that was the Sheriff's favourite. My lord de Lisle wants a vengeance for that deed. He wants your Robin Hood's head.'

'He might not find that as easy as he thinks...'

She put down a band of ribbon that was part of the pedlar's wares. Ralph Gammon noticed that she was deep in thought.

'There's a way we could be together, Ralph...' she said.

'What way?'

'The Sheriff's put it about that if anyone helps him capture this Robin Hood, well, there'll be freedom in it and a bag of gold to help them on their way.'

'He said that?' Ralph muttered in an appalled voice.

'He knows those of us who slave for him can get word out to the villages in Sherwood. And that Robin Hood's men can hear tell of it from the villagers.'

He looked around the market place to make sure than nobody was taking too great an interest in their conversation.

'Think of it, Ralph,' she said. 'We could be free and we could be together. And with money and the Sheriff's warrant we could make a new life miles from here.'

For a long time he didn't know what to say. A dozen thoughts and possibilities played around his mind. But all of them came back to an image of his friends dancing at the end of ropes from the walls of Nottingham Castle.

Joan felt fear at the way he looked at her.

'You can't want me to betray my friends?' he protested. 'No, I'd never do it!'

Tears ran down her cheek.

'Listen to me, Ralph,' she said. 'I don't know how long I can stand being held in that castle up there. They don't bother me like they plague the pretty women. But they're working me to death. I can't take much more, my sweet...'

'I can't betray them. Can't you see that?'

'You're a fool, Ralph! They're all going to die anyway and sooner than you think. But you don't have to die with 'em. We can have that new life. Don't you see how it is?'

He began to stuff the wares in his pedlar's pack.

'I'll not do it Joan,' he said. 'I probably will die in Sherwood, but I'm as free there as I've ever been. And I'd rather die with an easy mind than peach on my friends.'

She turned and walked away, wiping the tears from her face with a dirty hand.

'Joan!' he called after her but she didn't turn.

Ralph fell back against the wall, overcome with a great tiredness. He closed his eyes and listened to the sounds of the market all around. The sun came out again for he noticed the day brightening through his eyelids. What he would give, he thought, for peace of mind.

'You've packed up early, pedlar?'

He stared into the glare of the sun.

It took him a moment to focus on the man who was talking to him.

He was looking straight into the face of Sir Guy of Gisborne.

~

The arrow missed the knot in the oak tree.

A clumsy shot.

Robin Hood had been thinking of something else.

Someone else and somewhere else.

And a long time ago.

When he had been learning how to fire a bow his teacher had drummed into his head the most important rule of all. The one essential that made a man a great archer.

You always have to concentrate on the target and believe with absolute certainty that that's where the fired arrow will finish its journey.

Not that it was always easy to accept that belief. In the early days of practising with the bow there had always been a lot of moments of self-doubt. Trying almost too hard to line up the shot. And then lapses of concentration as other thoughts came unexpectedly into the mind. All of those failings led to missed shots and lost arrows.

But if you only believed that you would hit the target, well, you inevitably would.

It isn't the bow that fires the arrow home. It's the mind of the archer.

And that was why he'd missed the knot in the oak tree.

A memory of his father had come into his mind as he loosed the bowstring.

The remembrance had sent the arrow wide.

'You have to be a lot bolder than that,' the father said to the boy. 'Firing a bow isn't a game, Robin. Arrows are there for one purpose. To kill. Stop playing games with that bow, boy! Recognise it for what it is. Killing. Because if you forget that then you might be the rotting corpse.'

His father, Robert of Loxley, had been a free man. A learned individual, too. Educated by monks in the hope that he might go into a monastery. But Robert of Loxley had been a wild brigand. No monastery cell would ever have confined him. He loved the wild glades of Loxley Chase too much. He was always out there under the trees, poaching and living an untamed life. Tupping many a village maid. He'd never been outlawed, never been branded wolfshead, but that was only because of his woodcraft and cunning.

'Once they know your deeds and you're branded wolfshead, then death is already waiting for you on a forest path,' he'd said. 'We all walk with death, but don't you make it easy for them.'

They were words that had always haunted the boy.

Death waiting for him on a forest path. As a child he'd had nightmares at the thought. In those dreams he'd seen death often as a black-cloaked figure with rotting skin like a leper. Waiting. Just waiting. He might be there – in the nightmares he often was – just beyond the turn of the track.

Even now, in the quiet peace of this lonely corner of Sherwood Forest, he could shudder at the prospect of meeting Death. The horror of finding Death's putrid face before him.

It had to come.

But not yet.

Not yet.

Instinctively, he fitted another arrow into the bow. If Death approached then he'd be ready to try and fight him off. He might succumb but he would battle hard trying to defeat the inevitable enemy.

'I love my bow,' he'd said to his father, who had made it for him.

One of the many gifts the old man had given. That bow, made of beautiful yew, and with a pull that was hard for the boy to manage, had been the best he'd ever had.

But he had never dared to use it in the fight at Loxley. Nor did Robin Hood use it now. He could never risk losing his father's fine bow to some enemy.

But it *was* in Sherwood Forest and that was important to him. Hidden in a secret compartment in the wall of the shrine of Saint Withburga. Guarded by Brother Tuck. And the thought that it was near seemed to empower every other bow he carried in combat. As though those few feet of yew had a spirit that was transmuted through the hands that had once held it and into each new weapon of war.

'Being able to fire an arrow isn't enough,' his father had said. 'You need to be taught just why you must fire it. Shown what is

wrong with England. You must be taught to read and to write and to know the word of God. I've sent for a monk to instruct you.'

Robin had protested. He saw no need for such an education. He had even run off into the Chase and lived wild for several days. But his father had hunted him down, cuffed his ears, and dragged him home.

'If you didn't need instruction, then I'd never have tracked you down, you fool!' his father had said. 'And the good Brother is awaiting you...'

Robin had expected some ancient monk. Some wizened scholar from the abbey, whose brand of learning would be as dry as a summer drought.

But Tuck was not much older than himself.

So Robin had reluctantly embraced the world of letters. A whole month passed. Tuck and Robin sat at a form from dawn until dusk perusing the same grubby sheets of parchment. Outside, so clearly visible through the window, were the swaying trees of Loxley Chase.

And at last the temptation became too much.

One morning Tuck had come down to find Robin of Loxley preparing himself for a hunting expedition.

'Where are you going?' Tuck asked.

'Hunting!' the boy grunted.

'No you're not,' Tuck had said.

'Oh yes I am!' he had replied.

'No you're bloody not!'

Robin had moved to push the monk to one side. He scarcely remembered what happened next. Just a feeling of flight that seemed to last for hours, and then the pain of crashing down on to the stone floor. He'd been winded by the fall but soon clambered to his feet.

Dagger in hand he came back at Tuck, though not intending to do him serious harm. The monk reached sideways, grabbed a quarter staff and brought it smashing on to the boy's wrist. Robin yelped with pain and fell to his knees under the force of the blow.

Tuck sighed. *'More work! I shall need to instruct you in wrestling as well. There are scrappers in the villages who fight better than you!'*

And that brought about a new structure to their days. When, and only when, the scholarly tasks had been completed, Tuck had taken Robin outside and taught him to wrestle and to fist-fight. The boy accepted defeat after defeat. It was several months before he could hold his own against Brother Tuck.

'Did you learn all this in the abbey?' Robin had asked.

'Not altogether,' Tuck had replied. 'These are the reasons why I had to leave the abbey!'

Once hand fighting had been mastered, Tuck had shown the boy the best ways to fight with a quarter staff and then a dagger.

'Once you've mastered the staff and the dagger I'll give you some instruction with the sword. Though I know a bonnier fighter with that weapon!'

He had meant Robin's father.

Robert of Loxley had spent a few years as a soldier and had campaigned with the army of King Henry, the father of Lionheart and Count John of Mortain.

His father had held out the long blade of the fighting sword.

'I've killed many a foe with this sword,' the old man had said reflectively. 'In Normandy and France and in England too. It's a good job your mother isn't alive to see me showing you these evil ways of death.'

Robin had eyed the sword almost greedily, desperate to know its vicious ways of killing.

He wondered who he would kill with a sword, little knowing that the first slaughter was very near. He held the weapon, feeling its weight and balance. Strange to think how this solid, very physical instrument could extinguish a life. The blade bore the dark stains of ancient blood, its edges the marks and scratches of combat.

'I need to learn,' he had said. 'You told me so yourself.'

The old man nodded, a look of great sadness on his face.

'Very well. But remember this, Robin. There'll always be a man more skilled with the sword and the dagger than you are. One day you'll encounter the archer who can fire the arrow with

greater ability. And then it'll be your guts spilling out on to the ground. Your blood draining down the stones of a castle wall. And your soul tumbling to hell. Think of your own death every single time you wield any weapon.'

~

Robert de Lisle, Sheriff of Nottingham, sat at the great table in the castle hall, elbows on table and resting his chin on his folded fists. He looked up at Gisborne with an expression of boredom.

'And this creature is?' he yawned.

'My lord Sheriff, this is Ralph Gammon, a captured wolfshead.'

'Another one!' said de Lisle. He glanced at Gisborne. 'You bring me every wolfshead but the one I really want.'

'But my lord, this Gammon... he's one of Robin Hood's men.'

The Sheriff looked again, with more of an interest this time.

'And in which rat hole did you find him?'

'In the market place, my lord. In this ridiculous disguise of a pedlar. And I've seen him here before. He's been often, but I was never sure until today.'

De Lisle tapped his fingers on the table.

'And what made you so certain this time?' he asked.

'His woman, my lord. He has a wife working in the castle. A woman called Joan. One of the bitches I brought out of Sherwood when you needed more servants.'

'I'll kill you for that, you bastard!' Ralph muttered. 'She's a good woman.'

Gisborne brought a leather-gauntleted hand crashing against Ralph's face.

'Don't threaten me wolfshead!'

He turned back to de Lisle.

'Many a market day he's come looking for her, my lord,' he said. 'I've noticed him before, but never been quite certain. So I arranged to have his woman sent down there on an errand. There's no doubt. And I've seen him before. On the day I was ambushed by Robin Hood.'

The Sheriff looked up at Ralph Gammon.

'You are who my lord Gisborne says you are?'

Gammon remained silent, looking longingly past de Lisle at the open window in the furthest wall. De Lisle followed his gaze.

'Ah, how near freedom is,' he purred. 'Out there you can see the blue of the sky and the green leaves of the Sherwood trees. What a lovely thing it is to have freedom.' He looked again at the outlaw. 'Something you'll probably never enjoy again. And you'd break your neck if you did try and jump through that window.'

'Shall I take him to the dungeon, my lord?' asked Gisborne.

De Lisle gave Gammon a cold smile.

'You'll have heard about the dungeon, Gammon?' he said. 'A dark and stinking hole. A withdrawing place on the road to hell. Yet for all its misery some men prefer to spend their lives there... knowing the alternative. We've had men down there for years. Somehow they become used to the banks of shit that line the dripping walls. Better than what's outside. Better than what happens in the room above.'

'Go to hell!' said Gammon.

'A man of spirit, Gisborne!' declared the Sheriff. 'I always prefer a man of spirit. So much more fun in the breaking than a tamer beast. I could leave you in the dungeon all your life, Gammon. In the end disease would take you. But in the meantime you might make an amusing pet...'

'I'm not telling you anything...'

De Lisle held up his hands in despair.

'Listen to him, Gisborne?' he said. 'He talks to us as though he has a choice? Do you know what's in the room above, Gammon? The rack, the hot coals, a hundred ways of flaying you to a slow death. Ways of torture beyond your imagination.'

The Sheriff noticed the look of fear that crossed the outlaw's face. He gave him a few moments for consideration. The arrogance had gone from Gammon's face. There was only terror there now.

'Gisborne, I'm inclined to let this man go,' said de Lisle.

'Go?'

'Back to the greenwood, Gisborne. Back into the company of Robin Hood. And then, eventually, free to take his precious wife and find a home in another part of England.'

'My lord?'

Sir Guy looked puzzled.

'Yes, Gisborne. I believe I shall give this Ralph Gammon his freedom.' He waved a hand dismissively. 'I don't need him. I don't want him. My only interest is in Robin Hood. And I think this wolfshead will come to our assistance there. And without any need to send him into my dungeon. Or the room above.'

'I'll not betray Robin Hood!' said Gammon.

The Sheriff looked almost pained.

'I think you will, Gammon. After all, what's he to you? You know how he brought death and destruction to Loxley? Already the people of Sherwood are suffering because of his antics.' He smiled at the outlaw. 'You've been led astray, Gammon. And I'm inclined to forgive you for that. So I believe that you and I can come to an agreement.'

'What agreement?'

'It's really simple,' said de Lisle. 'The day after tomorrow I shall ride into Sherwood. I'll meet you in the forest. You'll be there alone. No doubt you can think of some excuse to get away from your fellows. You'll tell me exactly where I can go to find and trap this Robin Hood. I'm not that bothered about the others. They can freeze in the forest ditches next winter for all I care. I just want Loxley.'

'And you expect me to tell you?' said Gammon.

'Oh, I believe you will. And just think, Gammon. You'll be a wolfshead no more. There'll be a big bag of gold to send you on your way. In the company of your beloved wife. What could be better?' He raised the palm of his hand as though another thought had occurred to him. 'And something more... my cousin is Sheriff at Gloucester. I'll send him a request to provide you with a farm there. You'll be a free man Gammon. Gold in your pouch and nothing else to worry about.'

'It's still a betrayal...' Gammon whispered.

De Lisle looked up into the outlaw's eyes.

'I really do believe I'm being most generous,' he said. 'I've explained to you about the alternative. I can send you right now to the dungeon or the room above. You can be experiencing both in minutes. If you so wish. Or you can be freed into Sherwood. The choice is yours.'

De Lisle's eyes widened and his mouth came open as though another idea had struck him. He looked across at Gisborne and slapped the palm of his hand across his forehead.

'A better alternative even than that, Gisborne,' he said. 'What's the name of this man's wife?'

'I believe she's called Joan, my lord,' Gisborne responded.

'Joan,' the Sheriff ran his tongue over the word. 'Joan. A pretty name, Joan. A lovely wench too, I have no doubt.' He looked up again at Gisborne. 'Perhaps you could convey this Joan to my room above the dungeon?'

'Yes, my lord!'

Gisborne spoke with some enthusiasm.

'This Ralph Gammon can go too, Gisborne,' de Lisle continued, 'in chains. He can be made to watch... you do understand what I'm suggesting, don't you, wolfshead?'

Gammon knew all right. Robert de Lisle could see the look of horror in the man's face. He could see sweat on the man's brow.

'Well?' asked de Lisle.

'What am I to do?' asked Ralph Gammon.

'Hear my instructions,' said the Sheriff.

Fifteen

Brian du Bois had served as a page at the court of King Henry, the disputatious father of Lionheart and Count John. He had followed Henry on his long and often ferocious progresses around England, Normandy and Gascony. It was at court that he had decided to take up the profession of arms. Du Bois had been blooded in Henry's arguments against the French, when he was still very young. And then there had been a long period when King Henry's own sons were rebelling against their father.

Du Bois had found it all quite fascinating.

These family quarrels had plunged the nobility into something like a betting game. Which side to take in the argument? Whether to sit on the fence and not get involved at all? But the latter was not a very good prospect. Loyalty was asked for, no, demanded, by all of the warring camps.

It was heady stuff for a young man.

Make the wrong decision and ambitions would be quashed. Fortunes would be taken away. The shadow of death would linger over the keenest young warrior.

One day King Henry's party had sought rest at the castle of Chinon, one of his grace the King's favourite lairs. The old man had been exhausted and in a foul temper for much of that week. For the sake of their own safety, many of his nobles had sought tasks elsewhere in the countryside. At last only young Brian du Bois was left.

And King Henry, the wine dribbling down his beard, had noticed.

'Is it du Bois?' he said. 'By God it is!'

The King looked around the room.

'All the rest have gone! Yet you're still here, lad? Why did you not flee with the others?'

'My place is here with you, lord King.' Brian had said, giving a slight bow. 'Your grace shouldn't have to be alone...'

'You're a good lad, Brian. Aye, and a brave soldier. I saw you in the fight the other day. When you had that knight on the ground. The speed and zeal with which you cut his throat. His pleas for mercy lost to the wind.'

'He was a traitor, lord King!'

'He was your own cousin, du Bois. Didn't you grow up together?'

'He took up arms against you, your grace. That was enough for me.'

King Henry smiled and beckoned him closer.

'I'll give you advice, lad. You may not heed it, but you would do well to listen. That cousin of yours, Roland of Fontevrault was it? Yes, that's it... Roland. His father's a very rich man and a favourite of my son Richard. If you'd spared your cousin you might have gained a tidy ransom. And if Richard's claim to my throne succeeds then you might have won his favour as well.'

Brian looked humbled.

'Oh, don't take that as a criticism, du Bois,' King Henry continued, 'I know how matters play out in the heat of a fight. God knows I should.' He rested a hand on Brian's shoulder. 'You're a most valiant warrior, Brian. But you still have a way to go if you wish to prosper in these martial times.'

'I've learned a great deal from my service with you, lord King.'

Henry let out a guffaw of mirth.

'Hah! I look into your eyes, boy, and I'd expect to see flattery there. But, no, I really do think those words are uttered from your heart... I'm an unfortunate king but a grand teacher.'

'My lord...'

'Ah, don't spoil your record by being disingenuous, lad.'

'I meant to say that I welcome your advice, lord King.'

Henry nodded his head and smiled.

'Then you shall have it, du Bois!'

'My father is a poor man, my lord King. He lost much of the portion that my ancestor won at Senlac. I've had to fight just to be here. I know very little but combat. What more is there?'

A sad expression crossed the King's face. He was silent for a while.

'I wonder whether I should utter these words of learning to you at all...' he said. 'For once you hear them... if you should decide to heed them, well, then, your life will be enslaved to a vile philosophy.'

'My lord...'

'Ah, I see an eagerness in you du Bois, a thirst for secret knowledge?'

'You've always been my guide, lord King.'

King Henry sighed.

'Then I shall tell you, boy. The two words that will take you to the highest reaches of the court. And those words are cunning and cruelty. For without cunning and cruelty you'll almost certainly be kept down. Vanquished. The cunning you must use all of the time. The cruelty, well, just occasionally when it serves a purpose. Oh, and some other advice that might serve you by the way. Keep away from priests and women. God knows those two species have caused me much distress!'

'My lord King?'

'Ah, never mind, du Bois. I fear that you'll learn about those the hard way. But what really matters is the way you are cunning. Use people, du Bois. Treat every man as an enemy, even as you smile warmth at him. But bear in mind you don't always need to cut their throats. Exploit them, du Bois. And always put yourself first. As for the cruelty, well, your instinct will tell you when that is necessary.'

'I'm grateful for your interest, lord King.'

'Don't be, du Bois, for I fear I'm sending you on the swift road to hell with my thoughts. But then you see, du Bois, I'm near to feeling the devil's grip myself. I'm dying, lad. Did you know that? And soon my bastards may scrap over all I've ever owned.'

His thoughts seemed to stray.

'And who'll it be? Richard or John, or my dead son Geoff's boy? I quite favour John, you know. That'd take the smirk off Richard's face!' He laughed. 'And God knows it needs removing. I should have strangled him when he was a puking brat!'

Du Bois gave the King a sympathetic smile. Henry stood and strolled across to the window, his arm around the shoulder of Brian du Bois. He could smell the wine on King Henry's breath.

'You'll have a difficult decision to make, Brian. Whose part to take when the worms are at my flesh? Remember the words. Cunning and cruelty. Let them run through your mind when you're awake and haunt your dreams in the dark hours of the night.'

'Thank you, lord King.'

'And tomorrow, Brian, I'll do you a bloody and dangerous turn in front of the whole court...'

'My lord?'

'I'll get out my sword and make you a knight. Yes, and I'll give you a chest of gold to aid you on your way. And all I ask is that you mutter a prayer for me on each occasion when you cut a man's throat.'

'My lord...' Brian du Bois said, looking in wonder at the King.

'Ah, now no flattery or crawling or I'll renege on my promise...'

'My lord!' Du Bois smiled.

The next day, in the great hall of Chinon, King Henry tapped the sword down on the shoulders of du Bois, patting him on the hair when the deed was done.

And at the end of the week Sir Brian du Bois rode away from Chinon and the old dying man.

Days after that he threw in his lot with Lionheart and took up arms against King Henry.

And within a few months Henry Plantagenet was dead and food for worms.

~

'Where's Ralph?' asked Robin.

He'd been hunting in Sherwood and hadn't long returned to Thripper's Drumble. He'd seen the anxious look on Scarlet's face. Perceived the lack of conversation around the campfire. Quietness usually meant trouble.

'Not back from Nottingham,' Scarlet replied. 'But not too late to worry. Pedlars are best not seen being in too much of a rush. Will Stutely's taken the town road in hope of meeting him on the way back.'

'If nobody's worried why take the precaution of sending someone out to look for him?'

Scarlet raised his arms in a questioning gesture.

'Better safe than sorry,' he said.

Robin considered for a moment.

'I think it best that we send someone else as a spy to Nottingham market. Ralph's been there several times. He must have been noticed, and the traders of the town aren't as reliable in support of us as the villagers of Sherwood. It's only gossip we need to hear. We still have Alan inside the castle....'

'But he's not,' Scarlet replied. 'Alan's having a sleep inside the cave. He spent last night with Brother Tuck and came on here this morning...'

And at that moment Alan emerged from the cave, hiding a yawn with the back of his hand.

'Robin,' he said, 'I was hoping to see you before I returned. The rumours we've been hearing are true. Nottingham's become an armed camp. Most of the lords of the shire have sent soldiers. The Sheriff intends to sweep Sherwood for us. Tomorrow, perhaps. Maybe the day after that.'

'Do they intend to attack the villages?' Robin asked.

'Not this time,' said Alan. 'The Sheriff has a sly plan. Every patrol is to be sent out with a bag of gold. Every villager, every trader on the road, each lonely farmer in his cot is to be offered a wonderful reward if they're prepared to sell you. Every villein is to be offered freedom and a handsome new life. The price of their liberty is your head.'

'I'm pleased to know that de Lisle values me so highly!'

'We have an advantage,' said Scarlet. 'Only a trusted few know the secret of Thripper's Drumble. And this forest's a big place. If we lie low the Sheriff's army won't catch a glimpse of us.'

'So we skulk like foxes in our den while de Lisle makes free with Sherwood?'

'Better than the alternative, Robin,' said Alan. 'I've seen de Lisle's preparations. This isn't just a ragbag of foresters and unwilling pressed men being sent out. Many of these soldiers have fought in the Holy Land and Normandy. They're not to be played with. And the men who capture you are promised rewards, titles, land and gold.'

Robin sat down on the fallen tree trunk by the camp fire, throwing a log on to the flames. The others gathered around and there was a long period of silence. The outlaws had seen the grim look on Robin's face. Nobody wanted to be the first to make a suggestion.

At last he looked up.

'Well, skulk we must then,' he said. 'No fires after today, no smoke to betray us. God knows, I think Sherwood will be hot enough. It stands to reason we can't take on so many men in open battle. I learned that lesson in Loxley.'

'We're to do nothing?' asked John Little. 'They're soldiers after all and soldiers sometimes get carried away, whatever their orders. It seems strange to leave the people of Sherwood without any protection.'

Robin gave a bitter smile.

'John's right, of course. We must prepare for trouble. I'll take a few of you out with me. To the great glade by the Nottingham road. That's the way de Lisle's army will march. Just to try and gauge the mood. A couple of you can watch the other roads. The rest stay here.'

He pointed to the high escarpment that hid one side of the Drumble.

'We'll have a look-out up there. The view covers much of Sherwood. If we need aid we'll light signal fires and devise a series of messages of smoke. But hopefully my lord de Lisle and his carrion crows will have a wasted journey. They'll march up and down and find nothing.'

'I'll return to Nottingham then,' said Alan.

Robin walked with him to the entrance rocks of the Drumble. He rested a hand on the minstrel's shoulders.

'You're sure they don't suspect you?' he asked.

Alan shrugged.

'Who knows?' he replied. 'De Lisle's a clever man. I take nothing for granted where he's concerned. My forays into the forest must have been noticed by now. I did suggest to a captain of the guard that I went hither for inspiration... to come up with new words and tunes. But how long they'll believe that... well?'

'Take care, Alan. You're one of my oldest friends. I'd hate to lose you.'

'I'd hate to lose my head, Robin,' the minstrel replied with a chuckle, as he rolled back the sliding boulder and vanished from the dingle.

~

'If I didn't hold your father in such regard I'd call you a little bastard, Robin of Loxley!'

The young monk Tuck was in a bad mood. He had told his pupil that he couldn't rise from the wooden form until he had got the Latin text from the Bible quite correct.

Robin remembered, even all those years later on the edge of Thripper's Drumble, with what longing he had looked out towards the trees of Loxley Chase. As if to torment him further in his captivity, Tuck had propped the longbow, the quiver of arrows and the sword in one corner of the room.

'I see you gazing at them, Robin. I watch your fingers curl as though you were already gripping the yew wood of that bow or the hilt of that noble sword. And you know the answer to your impatience, boy? Hard work and study!'

Robin had protested.

'There's no Christian charity in you, Tuck. You should be excom... excom...'

'Excommunicated? Is that the word you seek? I already have been. Many times. My lord Abbot consigned me to the fires of hell on a daily basis. But he recanted, for he was in bad need of a wandering preacher in these heathen parts.'

'Just an hour, Tuck? A hour's archery practice? Where's the harm in that?'

Tuck folded his arms and looked down at the boy.

'Do you imagine I enjoy sitting here listening to your bad Latin?' he demanded. 'Do you think I've nothing better to do? And all the while I can smell meat roasting in the kitchen over there? And my stomach feels like a rat is gnawing at it in its emptiness?'

'Then let's rest from these awful labours,' Robin said. 'Just an hour, Tuck. Then I'll return to this...' he waved a dismissive

hand over the parchment. 'I can spend the time with my bow and you can eat...'

He could see from the expression on Tuck's face that he was wavering.

'Satan has your soul, Loxley,' he said. *'Very well and then... my God! What is that caterwauling?'*

The sound was coming nearer, along the track that led from the village. A high pitched singing accompanied by a violent strumming on the strings of a lute. They went outside and watched as the youth came nearer.

'Who the bloody hell are you?' Tuck asked.

The minstrel halted his tune and looked across at them.

'I'm Alan of the Dale,' he said *in a tone that suggested they might have heard of him. 'Sometime minstrel of the castle at Brough.'*

'Minstrel!' Tuck spluttered. 'You've a long way to go before you might call yourself a minstrel, boy. I've heard a dying moorhen sing sweeter!'

'I've been much praised....'

'Your last master was deaf was he?' said Tuck.

But the minstrel had lingered at Loxley and the two youths had struck up a friendship. At first it had been competitive, for Alan had proved to be no mean archer. And Robin had found it useful to have someone other than Tuck to practise with at the sword and the longbow. Alan was a skilled wrestler, though he had a weakness in that he always fought defending his hands, lest he damage the fingers that plucked the lute.

It was the beginning of a companionship that lasted. Robin and Alan and Tuck. Three of the oddest comrades in arms that could possibly be imagined.

Three wild souls that trouble found.

Robin Hood wandered back along the narrow path into the Drumble, his memory recalling the adventures they had shared, the dungeons they had escaped from, the lurks in the forest where they had sought shelter as they had been hunted, and the enemies they had killed along the way.

'God speed, minstrel!' he said looking upwards at the green on the boughs and at the blue of the sky.

~

'How long he's been like that?' asked the archer.

In the gloom of the shrine of Saint Withburga they watched as Matthew of Breevedon sat in a corner fingering his dagger and staring at the old stone wall.

'Too long,' Tuck whispered. 'It can go but two ways, as I see it. Either this long period of staring and silence will bring him to a cure, or...'

'His mind's lost for ever?'

'I fear so,' the monk replied. 'I've sat in front of him, hiding away the wall that so absorbs his fascination. But he looks through me as though I'm not there. He says nothing and his eyes are dead of all expression. He mumbles sometimes, but sounds that have no meaning. And he'll not yield up the dagger to me. Sometimes he clutches it with all the love a pining boy might give his mother.'

'Then we'd best leave him and talk outside.'

They strolled down to the little river that half-circled the shrine.

'You've heard about the preparations Robert de Lisle is making to invade Sherwood?' asked the archer.

'I hear of nothing else.'

'Does Robin Hood know?'

'He will by now. Alan a' Dale spent last night here on his way to Thripper's Drumble, full of the Sheriff's plans. I think it likely that Robin and his men will conceal themselves and not try to bring de Lisle's vast army to battle.'

'That would be the wisest policy.'

Tuck looked serious.

'And the wisest policy for you as well. I appreciate the fact that you enjoy danger and the thrill of the chase, but I ask you... no, beg you to stay out of Sherwood while these soldiers are roaming through it.'

The archer laughed.

'I admit it would be amusing to play games with them.'

Tuck turned to face the archer, shaking his head.

'Not amusing at all! Think of the consequences if you were to be captured. You wouldn't be spared because of who you are. Your rank would only make them more malicious. And others would pay the price in pain and death.'

The archer looked serious.

'I know, Tuck. I care little for myself but I won't bring that danger upon others. But it's hard to stand by and do nothing.'

'With the likes of de Lisle and Gisborne and du Bois, Sherwood is the most dangerous place in England. The one great area where the lords and masters have never quite managed to subjugate the people.'

'Well, de Lisle can't keep this army of his in Sherwood for very long,' said the archer. 'And the lords he's drawn to his side will soon want to take their men back to their own castles. Then we continue the fight-back against their tyranny.'

Tuck took the archer by the shoulders.

'I wish you would cease these games. I really do,' he said. 'I discovered what you were up to with no great difficulty, just by coming upon you accidentally. It wouldn't be hard for anyone else to find you in the same way. Sherwood seems vast and empty, but it's full with villagers and wolfsheads and travellers.' He looked the archer up and down. 'And that's not much of a disguise. One glimpse of your face and you and yours will be made wolfshead and hunted down and slain.'

'You think I should leave the fight to Robin Hood?'

Tuck nodded.

'He failed at Loxley,' said the archer.

'He may well fail in Sherwood. But he's the best hope we have. Already they talk of him in the forest villages and the taverns. Even now the minstrels sing his deeds in the back rooms of the castles and the market squares. His fame has already spread across these Midland shires. One day all England will thrill to his story...'

'It doesn't mean he'll succeed...'

'No,' said Tuck. 'No, it doesn't, but his legend might yet light a fire that'll spread and burn away all tyranny from this cursed realm.' He smiled at the archer. 'It would be enough for Robin Hood to know that he has your support. You could serve him in other ways than this. It would be safer. Won't you let me tell him about you?'

The archer looked angry.

'You made a vow, Tuck. A promise to me. You said that my secret is safe with you. I hold you to that vow.'

'Then I must keep it. But if anything happens to you, well, I'll never forgive myself.'

He looked up at the shrine.

'We'd better see how the poor lad is,' he said. 'He's not eaten for days.'

But Matthew of Breevedon was not in the chapel. Nor anywhere else where they could find him. They called and searched the woods around, but there was not a trace.

'He may well return,' said Tuck. 'He's gone off like this before. The lad'll probably be back before dark.'

'I must go,' said the archer. 'Before the vanguard of de Lisle's army blocks my route home.'

'Then take care, my bold friend, and in the name of sweet Jesus heed my words.'

The archer smiled and then walked at speed into the forest. Tuck went back into the chapel.

And from some yards away, Alan a' Dale, returning to Nottingham and seeking a drink at the shrine, questioned his own eyes and gave a low whistle to himself at the sight of the archer and the monk.

'Well, now I've seen everything!' he muttered to himself.

~

'What is it, Ralph?' asked Will Stutely, as the two men walked back to Thripper's Drumble. 'Did you face danger in Nottingham?'

Ralph Gammon didn't reply.

'You should let me go next time,' Stutely continued. 'You don't always have to be the one who takes all the risks. I can't imagine what it's like for you knowing that Joan is somewhere within those castle walls.'

'At least she's alive, not like your poor Meg...'

'In a way that must be worse for you. Never knowing if you'll ever be reunited. I know I'll never see my Meg again. In a way I died when she did. I just mark the days until I might join her. Death holds no fears for me.'

'Is that why you're so bold in battle?' Ralph asked.

'It's an odd thing,' Stutely replied. 'I never used to like fighting. I was frightened of getting hurt even when I was a boy. The lads in my village thought me quite the coward. Scarlet was always the hero, the scrapper...' He chuckled. 'And when I married his sister, well, I think he held me in scorn because I always ducked a fight...'

'But you don't now?'

'When they murdered Meg, I made up my mind to die. There seemed little point in living. I just wanted to seek oblivion. And I still do. So I took the risks that I thought might lead to death. I was at the front of any fight. The first to seek the enemy in every battle. Chance says that I should have been killed a hundred times. But somehow I never found that fate. It's as though God himself is laughing at me and thwarting my ambition.'

'Most people want to live!'

'Not I,' said Stutely. 'I want to die. But I want to go down fighting. I want to perish avenging the sort of men who murdered my Meg. And one day it'll happen. I've had a poor life. I want to die. But I want to end my life with a purpose.'

'I think Robin Hood will get everyone killed.'

'I take that for gospel.'

'Do you like him?'

'Not much. You see I don't understand him. When he talks about overthrowing kings and lords. That's the order of things, kings and lords. I know there are some that relish the free life in the forest. Those who are thrilled that they're freed from toil by being made wolfshead. But I'm not one of them. I'd give everything to be back at the plough and sitting by the fireside with my Meg.'

'And that's how I feel about my Joan,' said Ralph. 'I just want things to be back the way they were. I'd do anything for that to happen. You understand?'

Stutely nodded.

'I'm glad you understand, Will,' Ralph said to him.

Sixteen

Sir Brian du Bois walked through the great hall of Newark Castle clad in his best fighting clothes. Outside he could hear the impatient whinnying of the horses and the grunting of his men. It was time to set out for Sherwood Forest. Time to find Robin Hood and pay him back for the recent humiliation.

Time to get pleasure from the infliction of pain.

The little serving wench, Aelswith, stood in a dark corner. She'd been clearing the table when he arrived, hurriedly brushing away the remnants of last night's feast. On his entrance she had desperately tried to conceal herself in the shadows. Trying to evade his notice.

But it was too late. The great hall was not big enough for that. And the sunlight illuminated even the blackest of its corners. Du Bois turned and walked across to her.

'Look at me, girl!'

But she only half-raised her face.

He grabbed her hair and dragged her head upwards. God, she was an ugly little bitch. But he had enjoyed ploughing her just the same. Thrilled at her screams as he took her in the most violent of ways. And not just the first time. Every night since.

'You really must look at me when I talk to you, Aelswith. You really must. I'll be away for just a few days, and then it'll all begin again. You must be ready for me.'

He noted with joy the tears running down her cheeks. He knew how much she dreaded every moment of being in his bed. And the knowledge that there was no escape for her. For he was her lord and there was no possibility of her evading his desires.

He bent down and forced his tongue into her mouth. He thrust a hand up between her legs.

'Just a reminder of what it'll be like when I return, Aelswith. Say "yes"...'

'Yes,' she said.

'Yes, my lord,' he insisted.

'Yes, my lord.'

'That's better. Now get out!'

He felt the laughter in his soul as she ran from the hall, no longer even troubling to hide the tears. How wonderful it was to have absolute control over these peasants. To know they couldn't resist and must bend to his will.

Not that all the women came unwillingly. There were a better class of women that welcomed an opportunity to yield to him. Women with ambition. Women who could see that Sir Brian du Bois was going somewhere. Who could see that he was enjoying preferment at court. Woman whose company might prove to be an advantage to him. And these he tupped very gently.

But the rest, the servant girls in Newark and Nottingham, the young virgins in the forest. Well, he took them violently. For half the pleasure of the act was hearing them scream for mercy.

Not like that fool Gisborne, who had been tupping the same serving wench for months now. Where was the pleasure in that? Not that the girl wasn't attractive. She was better than most. Indeed, du Bois had lusted after her himself, but thought it wise not to invade that territory until Guy of Gisborne was safely out of the way. Not that he didn't think he could defeat Gisborne in combat. He took the possibility of such a victory as given. But accidents could happen. Even the best warriors had a day when a fight might go wrong.

No. He would wait until some forest wolfshead plunged an arrow into Gisborne's back. And then take this Clorinda. He didn't anticipate any great difficulty. She wasn't some shy virgin. She looked the sort who might be happy being poked by the entire garrison of Nottingham Castle.

Perhaps that day would come soon?

This expedition into Sherwood could be dangerous. Gisborne might well fall. It might even be engineered that a stray arrow, or a quarrel from a crossbow, might send Gisborne tumbling from his horse. An arrow or bolt that didn't quite come from the outlaws' side in any forest affray.

Du Bois grinned.

What a brilliant idea!

Gisborne would be no loss to the shire. And the wretched man had already gambled away the best of his lands. There was simply nothing to exploit any more, where Gisborne as concerned. Better to despatch him now, lest he find favour with Count John or crawl back to Lionheart.

And there was always the danger that Gisborne might work his way into the affections of Marian Fitzwalter. And, as far as du Bois was concerned, she was forbidden territory.

Marian was to be the Lady du Bois.

Not that he held her in any great regard. He didn't understand what love was all about. He never had. But he did like the thought of gaining all that land at Edwinstowe. And the girl herself was no shrinking violet. She had repulsed his previous advances with some spirit. A wild creature that he needed to tame... and he would. If he could subdue her resistance, but keep that spirit, well... how amusing she might be in his bed.

'The men are ready to march, my lord.'

The captain of the guard interrupted these fantasies.

'Very well,' he replied. 'Have my horse brought to the castle steps.'

The soldier bowed.

'To Nottingham then, my lord.'

Du Bois thought for a moment.

'No,' he said. 'Not to Nottingham...'

'My lord?'

'We march to Edwinstowe.'

~

Robert de Lisle was hunched up in front of the fire in the great hall of Nottingham Castle. It was the height of summer, but the evening was chilly. He could hear the men and the horses down in the courtyard. His soldiers were in a good mood and morale was high. For once they were not being sent in dribs and drabs into Sherwood Forest to fall under the arrows of this Robin Hood. This armed force was overwhelming in numbers and many a warrior was to be heard muttering that the outlaws and rebels would hide away. There was boldness and there was folly. Robin Hood would be a madman if he attempted to bring such a vast army to battle.

Such a possibility was a real concern to de Lisle.

The Sheriff had thought of little else but the idea that they would all march in and out of the trees and achieve nothing. Having summoned men at arms from so many of the lords of the shire he would look stupid if the whole expedition proved to be a failure. His very office of sheriff depended on their being some success. If Robin Hood was not taken he must at least be driven from Sherwood. The lords of the shire would accept nothing less.

It really all depended on how much the man Gammon loved his wife. That would determine how close de Lisle would come to taking Robin Hood.

He looked up to find Gisborne standing nearby.

'The men will be ready to march by tomorrow morn,' he said. 'We're to take the Edwinstowe road?'

The Sheriff nodded.

'Our friend du Bois is already on his way there,' he said. 'A message came from him just now. He suggests that we sweep the forest from the south and he from the north.'

'What damned impertinence to give us orders!'

'A feather in his cap if he takes Loxley before we do,' said the Sheriff. 'Du Bois knows Count John is coming into the shire. He wants something to brag about. Du Bois is a man seeking preferment, Gisborne.'

'It'd be good fortune if Robin Hood cuts his throat!'

'Indeed, it would,' said de Lisle, 'someone should. Du Bois is a man of ambition, Gisborne. We can't have too many of those in the shire. Men of ambition are a danger to the order of society. I believe it would be of great benefit to us if Sir Brian du Bois fails to return safely to Newark... you understand my meaning?'

Gisborne grinned.

'Only too well, lord Sheriff.'

'And for Loxley, well... we have this man Gammon in our power.'

Gisborne looked doubtful.

'But do we? He may have returned to Sherwood and told all to Robin Hood. We could well be marching into an ambush.'

The Sheriff shook his head.

'He loves his wife, Gisborne. The fear of what we might do to her was evident in his eyes. He'll be there. I'll wager on it. You understand the plan?'

'I do, my lord.'

'I'll take just thirty men into the forest at first light. To the place where I said we'd meet Gammon. If he's there and tells us what we want to know, well, I'll wait for you and our main force and we'll seek out this Loxley. If he's not, then we'll scour the forest until we do find him. Somehow we have to bring this rebellion to an end.'

'And Gammon's wife?'

'Put her in the dungeon for now, Gisborne. I don't want to risk her slipping out of the castle. If we've nothing to bargain with then all's lost.'

Gisborne bowed and began to walk away. De Lisle called him back.

'And Gisborne. Don't forget what I said about Brian du Bois.'

Gisborne laughed.

'No. My lord. That thought will be in my head until the deed is done.'

~

'Do you ever have a bad feeling, Robin?' asked John Little as the two men stood on the high escarpment overlooking Thripper's Drumble. 'A sense that your world's going to change for the worse?'

Robin gave a mirthless laugh.

'Every day of my life,' he said. 'How can there be peace of mind for us? We've no protection under the law. It's not as if we just skulk in the forest like other wolfsheads. We seek out trouble.'

'That's what I mean,' said John. 'There's no place we can go to in this realm where we're free from danger. We're hunted animals. The chase hasn't caught up with us yet, but it will. We're doomed to die.'

'We're *all* doomed to die.'

'Aye, but we're outlaws, so sooner than most.'

'The people of Breevedon weren't outlaws and they all died before their time. I don't mind the thought of death. It's the enemy we all have to face. But I don't dwell on it. When it comes it comes.'

'But why should people have to live like this?' said John. 'Always in fear? Who gave de Lisle and Gisborne such power over people's lives? And the worst of it is we outnumber them. We are many and they are few. Yet they rule our lives.'

'It was ever so,' said Robin. 'And that's why we must fight to overthrow them. Bring their world of privilege down to destruction. Halt their tyranny. Even if we have to die to make this a better world for all who come after. A world where there are no lords and all are equal.'

'We'll not see it.'

'No, we'll not see it. But perhaps people will remember that we fought the fight. That we lit a flame of freedom in Sherwood that men will talk about for hundreds of years to come. And perhaps those very people will remember why we fought and they'll take up arms against other tyrants and injustices.'

'I hope so.'

Robin Hood looked across at the setting sun.

'Hide though we must, I've a feeling that tomorrow will be an eventful day. There's blood in that sun.'

~

Matthew of Breevedon watched the sinking of the sun.

In the depths of the forest, under the dense foliage of the trees, it was already dark. Far down the hillside lay the main track from Nottingham to Edwinstowe. He had watched as a farmer drove an ox-cart back home from the market in the town. He knew him from somewhere but couldn't remember his name. Matthew couldn't remember very much about anything, just a vision of burning farmsteads and bodies swinging in the breeze.

Only one face seemed clear in his mind. One face that was never absent from his thoughts. And a name. A name Matthew had heard so often. A name he had spoken aloud, even as he cringed with fear.

Gisborne.

The name that seemed to be the only real word in his memory, a word that echoed back and forth. The sound of it bursting through his head like a bell in a church tower. Backwards and forwards. Backwards and forwards. Until he felt that his mind could take no more of the noise.

Gisborne.

The very sound seemed to block out all the cries of nature. A vixen yelped nearby, startling the greenwood. But he heard it not. He hardly saw the badger that took its own distinctive path up the steepest portion of the hillside. In the far distance was the last hammering of a woodpecker, but its toil went unnoticed. And then the bird was silent.

Matthew of Breevedon walked to the spreading roots of a great oak tree and ran his hands along the bark with such ferocity that the flesh was broken and blood spattered the wood. Almost without noticing what he was doing, he licked the damaged skin.

And then he lay down and curled up against the bole of the tree. Sleep came at last, but so did the nightmares. His body shivered with the terrors that beset him. He stirred a little, looking for a dawn which was a long way away. A breaking of day that might take away the pressuring pain of that face that was always in his mind. The name that seemed to invade his ears and cut into his brain.

Gisborne.

Seventeen

Henry Fitzwalter heard someone coming up the stone stairs to his hall, where he had busied himself for the morning examining estate documents.

He'd heard the horses in the courtyard and voices a few minutes before. That wasn't unusual. As a lord he had a great many visitors on all manner of business. But normally they waited in an antechamber close to the main gate until they were summoned. Only men of great rank presumed to climb the stairs unannounced.

Thomas, his steward, scarce had time to come into the hall to announce who it was before the visitor was at the door. Fitzwalter looked up into the man's nervous face.

'It's... it's Count John,' the words spilled out from the little man's toothless mouth, 'Count John of Mortain...'

And in a moment the King's brother swept into the room. He looked tired and dusty from a long ride. But there was the usual beaming smile, though few ever saw it but Henry Fitzwalter.

'My God, Fitzwalter, the journey I've had!'

Count John took off his cloak and hat and threw them on to a chair. He was a round-faced man of around thirty, hair cut short and with a particularly wispy beard that looked as though it might be better removed altogether.

'Your forest seemed to go on for ever,' John continued, 'and scarce a village to be seen on the road we travelled. We slept one night under the trees, drinking from a spring. And before that the hills of the peak land. Hard to believe there's so much bog in England!'

He held out both arms and embraced Fitzwalter.

'But there's nothing of you, man! You should eat more,' John said. 'Mind you, so should we all. I've had nothing but scraps of bread for three days. For the love of Jesus tell me you've some meat to roast over a fire?'

'Tell the kitchen to prepare a meal for Count John and his men,' Fitzwalter ordered Thomas. 'And swiftly...'

The little steward ran out at a pace he probably hadn't matched since his long-distant boyhood.

John took off his sword and flung himself backwards into a chair, stretching his legs before him.

'I always liked this hall, Fitzwalter,' he said, looking round. 'It's of a size you can actually heat, unlike the draughty barns I'm usually consigned to in all those dreadful castles.'

'My lord, you should have let me know you were coming...'

'No fuss, Fitzwalter, no fuss. I have but simple wants, though a strong desire for food at the moment. And I scarcely knew my own plans until a few days ago. I was at Worcester when I heard the news...'

'News, my lord?'

'I heard that a vast army is being gathered in Sherwood. Almost as many men as my brother Richard has serving him in Normandy. So I was told.'

'I think not quite that many...'

'Is the shire in revolt, Fitzwalter? Should I have brought an army to suppress a rebellion? I'm told that Hubert Walter was most concerned when *he* heard the news.'

'How is Hubert?'

John raised his eyes to the roof and threw out his arms in despair.

'I'll tell you the truth,' he said. 'Hubert Walter is a great trial to me. The idea that King Richard should have appointed that upstart as the virtual ruler of England, and when I was still in the realm... it's an insult, Fitzwalter. And I take personal offence that Hubert Walter is the same man who twisted me out of my lands not so long ago. These bishops shouldn't be allowed to meddle in politics.'

'Perhaps not...'

'Definitely not! I'll send him back to Salisbury as a beggar, not as bishop, when I become king.' He groaned. 'But then I'll have the Pope on my back again! I suppose I was fortunate to get a handful of shires out of the deal. And then the troublous ones like this Nottinghamshire.'

'I never find it quite that troublesome, my lord,' Fitzwalter countered. 'But it is badly administered. If Robert de Lisle took an easier hand with the Sherwood villagers then there would be no trouble at all. He seems to relish bother.'

'He always was an odious little man. And I hear that Gisborne's with him now? Now there's a chap I wouldn't want for an enemy. Still ambitious is he? He's come crawling to my court more than once since brother Richard threw him out of France.'

'I try not to have any truck with any of them,' said Fitzwalter.

John drew his fingers through his beard.

'I envy you, Fitzwalter. I really do. Sometimes I think you have the best life of all, living quietly in your manor. I've never met a man with as little ambition as you...'

Fitzwalter smiled.

'Oh, I had ambition once,' he said. 'A long time ago. Now I'm content just to sit by my fire.'

'And that's why I can talk to you and know that you'll always give me an honest answer. And I value your discretion' He leaned forward. 'But, you see, I *have* to have truck with them. I intend to be the next King of England and I can't rule without the support of bastards like them. An unpleasant prospect I know, but there you are. If my brother should die – and, from what I hear, Richard campaigns in France as though no arrow or sword could touch him – then I need the nobility to back my claim to the crown.'

'It's a dilemma.'

'It is indeed. So tell me why are the lords of my shire amassing an army?'

'To chase the wolfsheads through the forest...'

John chuckled.

'Ah, so that's it. Robin Hood.'

'You've heard, my lord?'

'They were singing ballads of his deeds on the streets of Worcester. When I heard the tale of how he sent Brian du Bois naked back to his own castle I was quite amused.'

'I thought du Bois was a supporter of your cause?'

'He is, but he's out of the same mould as Gisborne. He might smile to your face, but watch for the daggers he'll be plunging into your back.'

'Brian du Bois wishes to court my Marian...'

Count John looked solemn.

'Better that she die young than have to share a bedchamber with him.' He looked across at Fitzwalter. 'As overlord of the shire I shall forbid any such match.'

'You have my gratitude, my lord.'

'The least I can do for an old friend,' John replied. 'But this Robin Hood? Does he enjoy support?'

'The hero of the forest dwellers. And I'm something of an admirer myself.'

'Nevertheless, he will have to die. We can't have wolfsheads who threaten the very order of society. And I mind that this particular outlaw first found notoriety as Robin of Loxley. The rebellion at Loxley Chase was nearly successful. We always have to remember that there are more peasants than there are nobles.'

Thomas the steward hurried back into the room.

'Your pardon, my lords, but there are armed men approaching from the direction of Newark,' he said. 'Their shields bear the three hunting hawks of Sir Brian du Bois.'

Count John and Fitzwalter crossed to the window.

'Look at them all! He must have left Newark quite unguarded. What a fool that man is!' said Count John. 'He betrayed my father, you know? And only days after King Henry dubbed him a knight.'

'I've heard the tale,' said Fitzwalter.

'He came grovelling to Richard who took him as a pet. I said at the time that anyone as loose with his loyalties as that man should never be trusted. I'll use him, Fitzwalter, but I'll never let him get close. Remember what I said about daggers?'

'Indeed...'

Count John turned to Thomas.

'My guts are aching with hunger, steward. Is the food ready?'

Thomas gave a nervous bow.

'Venison, my lord. And mutton. They're bringing the food up right away.'

'Excellent.'

'Should we invite du Bois to dine with us, my lord?' asked Fitzwalter.

John thought for a moment and then laughed.

'I fear that the appalling little sycophant might turn my stomach, Fitzwalter!' He turned back to Thomas. 'Steward, tell Sir Brian I'll grant him an audience in an hour, and that I'm not to be disturbed before that hour is up.'

Thomas started to walk to the door.

'Oh, and steward...'

'My lord?'

'Do give Sir Brian some scraps from the kitchen,' said John. 'He must be hungry after such a long journey.'

~

Even in the darkness it was hard to evade the soldiers of Sir Brian du Bois.

They were everywhere. Clustered in the courtyard of the Fitzwalter manor at Edwinstowe; bending over fires in the grounds beyond, and settling down to sleep wherever they could find a dry spot of earth.

Fearing a pre-emptive attack, du Bois had stationed a ring of sentries all around the house. And then a further series of patrols where the fields met the first trees of the forest.

The archer was having great difficulty in negotiating a route between so many threatening enemies. Even knowing the ground well, the archer had to plot a very indirect route. The thought occurred that it might be possible to overpower a sentry and put on his clothes and light armour. But this was as quickly dismissed from the mind. Although skilled with the bow, the archer had little experience of close killing. One cry from the victim and there would be a situation that could never be explained.

From the high window came a burst of laughter. Count John of Mortain. And then the quieter tones of someone else. Something amusing must have been said, for Count John laughed even more heartily.

The archer crept into a hollow made by two converging walls. The shadows gave a temporary haven from discovery while matters were considered. From this point it was but a hundred yards to the nearest trees of the forest. But there were five fires lit in scattered order between the walls and the beginnings of

Sherwood. And in their glow the archer could see the foot patrols walking the forest edge every few minutes.

But it was the only possibility. There was even now raucous laughter and chatter from the direction of the courtyard. It would be impossible to gain entrance back to the house that way.

The archer looked across the open ground.

Another fire had been lit. Almost a bonfire, its red blaze eclipsing the smaller pyres of the hungry soldiers. But with it came a better fortune. One soldier had engaged in some game with dice a yard from its flames. And the sound of men in wager drew the attention of many of the others who wandered across to see what was happening.

There was now almost a clear avenue of escape between the house and the forest, even if there was no cover.

Without waiting the archer walked boldly towards the trees. Always better to walk as though the place belonged to you. As if there was nothing to hide. Then you might be adjudged to be about legitimate business. Out of the corner of an eye, the archer noticed a man near the great fire, looking across. But as the archer was making no attempt to hide, and in the dim light of the smaller fires, no suspicion was aroused.

The archer waved a hand in greeting. The soldier gave a salute in return.

Now the trees were just feet away and the residual light of the fires and the stars revealed the narrow path into the forest. A familiar route into the heart of Sherwood.

And it was then that it all went wrong.

The forest patrol of three men, hearing the babble of excited voices around the bonfire, turned early to see what was happening. At the same moment the full moon of a summer month came clear of a cloud.

There was a shout. A shout of challenge.

One of the men cried out for the guard and the other two ran towards the archer, drawing swords as they charged. Some of the men at the great fire turned to see what was happening, unsure whether to abandon their sport or get involved in the alarm.

The archer muttered a prayer of thanks that the bow had been strung. The two arrows were sent flying within a few seconds of each other. The nearest soldier dropped almost instantly as the arrow penetrated his heart. The second gave a great cry of agony as a metal arrowhead and wooden shaft lodged in his gut. The third soldier dived to the ground for cover, still shouting for the guard.

The archer fled, risking a glance at the other soldiers. They were running from the bonfire towards the trees, spreading out in a line as they came. Crashing into the undergrowth in pursuit of the fugitive, running at great speed.

The archer jinked to the left along a side path before pausing for a moment and looking back. The soldiers couldn't be seen but the noises suggested they weren't far behind. And they were circling round to left and right in an attempt to encircle their prey.

Too near for an escape on such a winding path.

And then the archer jumped at the familiar bole of an oak tree. A friend known from past times, its high and thick boughs spread out over many of its smaller neighbours. The density of its leaves at the height of summer hiding away the ground beneath and the sky above. The archer scampered to nearly the highest branch and clung closely to its rough bark. There were few better places for sanctuary in all Sherwood. It was not the first time that the archer had hidden there.

And in the darkness of the forest the ploy worked. The archer heard the soldiers pass beneath, swearing as they were caught up in brambles or as the branches of tinier trees, forced forwards by their comrades, whipped back into their faces.

Within a very few minutes the line of searchers swept back again, returning past the massive oak tree to the open ground by the manor house. The archer heard the sounds of the victims of those fired arrows being carried away, one still screaming with pain and praying loudly for death.

An hour later, the archer came down from the tree and slipped deeper into Sherwood Forest.

~

'Where do you see your future, du Bois?'

Count John sprawled back in the great wooden chair. The two men were alone in the hall, for Henry Fitzwalter had gone down to arrange wine for his many guests.

'My future, my lord?'

'Well, yes, du Bois, your future? You are one of the most accomplished soldiers in the realm. It seems wrong that a man of so many talents should be hiding away in a quiet corner like Newark.'

'Hardly hiding away, my lord. I undertake many acts of governance and, well, this is a most lawless shire. There's always a spirit of revolt simmering in these Sherwood villages. The place needs a firm hand.'

Du Bois wondered just where this conversation was going.

'I see,' said John.

'Not that I'm opposed to the idea of moving elsewhere should the need arise,' du Bois went on. 'My sword and my heart are always at your disposal, my lord....'

'Pretty words, du Bois, pretty words. You seek advancement?'

'I wish to serve you in the best possible way...'

Count John stood and warmed his hands by the fire.

'My brother Richard has taken great losses recently in France and Normandy. I'm sure he'd be grateful to have such a fearless captain by his side.'

Du Bois tapped his fingers on the long stone lintel over the fireplace, considering quite how to respond. Count John was a puzzlement to him. Past experience of the man had always led to confusion. John could often joke about the most serious matters. But then again he could seem serious and really be indulging in some strange bout of humour. Count John was a hard man to keep on the right side of.

'I'm to return to Normandy myself and very soon,' John continued. 'I would enjoy having you at my side, du Bois. What great battles we might fight together.' He gave a great bellow of laughter. 'Why, we might even eclipse the shining glories of a Lionheart!'

Du Bois stayed silent, not being sure whether he dared be derogatory about the martial deeds of King Richard, which at that moment seemed to be endlessly bloody but not progressing very fast.

John threw out his hands in a questioning gesture.

'But as you say, du Bois, this land of ours does need a firm hand. And not that of Hubert Walter. His days as my brother's administrator are numbered. Bishops should remain within their cloisters, do you think?'

'I couldn't agree more, my lord...' du Bois gushed.

'Ah, so you oppose the church and its influence?'

There was more than a hint of challenge in Count John's voice.

'I didn't say that, my lord,' du Bois said. 'I only meant that the King of England has been appointed by God to rule over this dreadful country. And that the church should better know its place in the order of things.'

'Dreadful country, du Bois?'

'England, my lord...'

'You don't *like* England?'

'To be honest with you, my lord, I prefer Normandy.'

'Huh! You've not been there lately, have you? My brother has turned Normandy into a cock pit. All blood and bodies. We need the Duchy, of course. Normandy and Gascony and all the rest. Just so that we might dominate France. But they're nowhere near as precious to me as England.'

Count John went quiet and thoughtful. Du Bois thought that safety and preferment might better lie in changing the subject back to himself.

'The Abbot of St. Mary's is concerned about the rebellious nature of the people of Nottinghamshire, my lord. He gave a blessing on our forthcoming expedition into the forest. He believes that Robert de Lisle and Gisborne have failed to bring order to Sherwood. I'll endeavour to do my best to remedy their mistakes.'

'I'm sure you will, du Bois. And when you return tomorrow night, we'll have a further discussion about your future. As I've said you're too good a soldier to waste on menial matters.' He looked up at du Bois as though he'd had a sudden inspiration.

He wagged a finger at the knight. 'I know just the place for you, du Bois!'

'Normandy, my lord?'

'Wales.'

'Wales?' du Bois spluttered.

Count John took him by the shoulder, leading him to the window. He pointed to the west.

'Wales, du Bois. The Welsh have been uppity of late. And their Prince would just love to plunge a dagger into our backs while we're occupied elsewhere. There'd be a castle in it for you, du Bois. And some land... though that would have to be in Wales itself. I doubt that Hubert Walter would sanction English manors.' He waved an arm. 'Still, land is land, as they say. And you wouldn't have to actually live in the wretched country. You could command the Marches along the Welsh border. Though you might have to make regular forays into the mountains.'

Du Bois sank down on to the window seat, but noting that this disrespect had been observed, sprang up again almost immediately.

'Your pardon, my lord,' he said, 'I must have been overcome by the heat of the fire.'

He looked at Count John and noted the humour in those eyes. The damned man was laughing at him! Lionheart should really have had that mocking head removed the last time John had tried to seize power. But now the two brothers seemed to be back in the most amenable of relationships.

Damn these Angevins, these bastard Plantagenets. They really were the spawn of the devil. How wonderful it would be to knock the crown from their heads. And then take the heads as well. But no use dreaming. You had to work within the intrigues of the court.

'I had, my lord... hoped to fight at your side in France...'

'And so you shall, du Bois... so you shall. I'd wish for nothing better. But not just yet, eh? I'm not sending you to Wales for life. A year or two, no more than that. Just to contain a perilous situation, eh? And then who knows? An earldom, perhaps? A castle in Normandy? What could be better than that?'

'Two years?'

'No more than that, I promise.'

'Then I would ask one boon?'

John smiled.

'Whatever I can give, I shall give.'

Du Bois took in a great breath before speaking again.

'I would like the hand of Marian Fitzwalter in marriage.'

Count John returned to his chair. He looked up at the roof, thoughtfully, for a minute or two. He waved a hand at du Bois. A gesture of despair.

'My dear friend, it cannot be. The Lady Marian is a royal ward... I cannot allow such a match. Only the King may do so. And I know that he will not.'

'Why not?' du Bois almost shouted.

'I appreciate the heat of your passion, du Bois. But you must cool your temper. I have to say I'm surprised that you'd want to take Marian to your bed. She has little land to come, just these few acres in Sherwood and this old ruin. I'm sure that you can do better than that. I met Marian on my arrival here. She's a sweet little thing. But for you, du Bois?'

'I want the girl!'

'Is it a love match? How touching! Does the Lady Marian feel the same?'

Brian du Bois looked embarrassed.

'She's refused me, though God knows why?'

'Then shouldn't that settle the matter?'

'But if you were to order it, my lord. Say that such a match to a soldier of my calibre was in the best interests of England...'

'She is a royal ward...'

'Only on the death of her father. She's free to wed while Fitzwalter lives.'

'I simply cannot permit it, du Bois, and in your own interests. You're a man of ambition. You must at some point make a dynastic marriage... and then...'

They were interrupted by a great cry from outside, and then the shout of a hundred men. Someone yelled the alarm. A moment later the captain of the guard rushed into the room and gave a hasty bow to Count John.

'We may be under attack, my lords. Two of my soldiers have been taken down with arrows. The killer has fled into the forest. I've sent men...'

Count John waved a dismissal and du Bois ran from the room. John rose from the room and looked out at the forest, now illuminated only by firelight and the moon.

What a strange country was England. Always there was trouble. Always dissent. His brother Richard cared nothing for it. He'd said to John that he'd sell the whole bloody place if he could find a rich enough buyer.

And John wished he had sufficient gold to buy it from the ungrateful bastard. But then, maybe, one day it would all be his anyway, for Richard showed no signs of breeding, and the other claimants were... well, disposable.

Count John loved England so much that he'd kill anyone who kept it out of his grasp. It was the greatest of prizes. And he was determined that it would all be his. And sooner rather than later.

He thought back over his talk with Sir Brian du Bois and gave a great explosion of laughter. What a merry English evening it had been.

Eighteen

They were about so early that they almost fell over the deer grazing in the forest glades. The grass and the leaves on the trees were wet with dew. It was a beautiful morning, the woodland canopy a deep green against the vivid blue of the sky.

'A fine day to die!' muttered John Little.

'Let's hope it doesn't come to that,' said Robin. He turned to the others. 'Remember, we're not here to seek a fight. Only to protect the villagers of Sherwood if de Lisle and his soldiers turn on them.'

Robin Hood had left men to guard Thripper's Drumble, bringing only Scarlet, Ralph Gammon and John Little with him, all armed with longbows, swords and daggers.

'Just as well,' said Scarlet.

He looked around at the others.

'They'll outnumber us a hundred to one. There aren't enough arrows in all our quivers to do more than mark them.'

'Not even that,' said Robin. 'We're dormice today, not wolves. We'll retreat rather than ravage. These lords have enough soldiers out to put everyone in Sherwood to the sword.'

'You've learned from what happened at Loxley then?' said Scarlet.

Robin turned in his direction in anger.

'What happened in Loxley was completely...'

He began and then paused.

'No, Scarlet, your words are just. A great many mistakes were made at Loxley and I take responsibility for all of them. The revolt failed because we were impatient, because we didn't know when to hold back. The faults were all mine. Good men and women died because of me. And their faces will haunt me till the day I die.'

They were all silent.

'Ah, well,' John Little said, 'we can all die but once. Better to die fighting than under the lash of the lords or worn out at the plough. And as a wrestler I've always loved a good brawl.'

They had come to a clearing in the forest, dominated by one great and ancient oak tree standing solitary in the midst of the grass, its huge branches sweeping low towards the ground. An oak that had been old when Offa ruled these Mercian lands; its hollow trunk a shelter for fugitives when the first Norman King, William the Bastard ravished the shire. A tree that would live for centuries more, until the weight of its wood would finally bring it crashing to the ground, or a flash of lightning fire its bark and innards, burning away a living link with the history of England.

It was a tree well known in a forest of immense oaks, a lonely tree set so far apart from others that it was always noted. A dozen legends had sprung out of its sprawling roots; a score of ghosts haunted its glade. The people of Sherwood almost worshipped this primeval oak as a god.

'They say this tree grew massive on the blood of the outlaws who've died in Sherwood,' said Ralph Gammon. 'There's a spring over yonder whose waters come from its roots, and which often runs red.'

'A tale for old wives!' said Scarlet. 'Like the old stones in the circle near Boughton, which they say dance on a midsummer sabbath. I've roamed Sherwood most of my life. I've not seen a phantom yet. Nor the blood running from the water at the edge of the glade.'

'Will's right,' said John Little. 'There's little to fear in Sherwood except the bastards who are hunting us down. They're enough to shiver about.'

Ralph looked around the clearing.

'I've never been happy in this place. I'm glad to go..'

On the journey from the Drumble he had volunteered to be the sentry on the old road from Nottingham, near a mile away.

'You're still happy to guard the road, Ralph?' Robin asked. 'There could be peril in it if they see you. Keep well hidden. When the soldiers have passed, come here and tell us who they're serving and how many there are.'

Ralph was silent.

He walked a few paces on his journey and then turned.

'Robin...' he said.

'What is it, Ralph?'

'Lost your courage, Ralph?' said Scarlet. 'Rather stay here with us and the ghosts of the oak?'

'Damn you, Will!' Ralph replied, turning and striding off across the clearing and on to a path leading into the thick of the trees.

He didn't look back again.

~

Alan a' Dale ran as if all the devils in hell were chasing him. Ran for the clearing in Sherwood with the famed oak. Already the summer dawn had broken. And he knew that Robert de Lisle, Sheriff of Nottingham, was way ahead of him. Marching covertly into the forest with just thirty men. Ahead of the greater force being led along the same road by Sir Guy of Gisborne.

Alan hadn't been back at Nottingham Castle for many hours when he'd heard the rumour. He had verified its truth in a discussion with a serving wench with whom he was on particularly friendly terms. She'd heard the news from one of the soldiers who'd been picked to march out through the castle gates before first light. In the wake of Robert de Lisle.

'A secret mission,' the wench had whispered, as she licked Alan's ear. 'That's what he told me, a secret mission. There's gold in it. Gold for treachery. The Sheriff goes early to the forest. To fetch back Robin Hood.'

Alan had brushed her aside.

'To fetch back Robin Hood? How?'

'In the tavern last night, the tavern carved into the rocks beneath the castle. The soldier was called Edmund. Drunk and boasting he was. Trying to make out he was important. Not that I wasn't interested. I minded your words about gathering gossip. And I'm ever so fond of you, you know, Alan?'

She eased him back on to the bed. Her tongue exploring the exposed skin at the top of his chest.

'Why don't we take our clothes off, Alan?' she said. 'We'd be so much more... comfortable.'

'What did the soldier say?'

'Well, even with the drink he didn't want to say nothing. Said he was the soul of discretion. And much favoured by the Sheriff...'

Alan took her by the chin and forced her head back.

'Ow! That hurts!' she protested.

'What did the soldier say?'

'Well, nothing. Least not till I let him put his hand up my thigh. Silent as the grave he was till then. But then he just had to boast. All men are the same when they're in their lusts. Think it might sway a girl...'

'Tell me what he said!'

'Just coming to it, my sweetheart. The soldier said that the Sheriff and thirty men were going out before Gisborne and his army. Out into Sherwood. Where they had a meeting with... hold on, let me get this right... with one of his men...'

'Whose men?...'

'Robin Hood's, of course! Stupid! Haven't I just said that?'

'The Sheriff's going into Sherwood to meet one of Robin Hood's men?'

'That's what I just said, isn't it?'

'Why?'

The girl thought for a moment.

'One of Robin Hood's men's going to betray him. For gold and a pardon. The Sheriff's riding into Sherwood before dawn to meet him and find where that Robin Hood's hidden.'

'Which one of Robin Hood's men?'

'I don't mind his name...'

'The soldier must have said something?'

'Well, only that the man's wife slaves in the kitchens here in the castle. She did, anyroad. They've pushed her into the dungeon now. That's men for you!'

Alan a' Dale leapt off the bed.

'Where you going?' the girl protested. 'We haven't started yet!'

Alan was tearing his way along the path. Fast. Fast and furious. Deep into the heart of Sherwood. To the glade with the great oak tree. The dawn had broken. The sun was already hot in the sky. Alan was running and sweating. Running and sweating for the sake of a friend's life.

And running out of time.

Sir Brian du Bois waved an arm to signal the start of the march into Sherwood Forest. He looked back. Not the best body of men he'd ever led into battle, but enough to deal with a bunch of rebellious Sherwood peasants.

Some of the soldiers had had real experience of fighting; in Normandy, France and on the road to Jerusalem, but the majority were garrison troops who had never been out of England. No matter. They would serve the present purpose.

He looked up at the window of the manor house. There was Count John, standing next to Henry Fitzwalter. John waved an arm in salute as du Bois passed out through the gate.

Du Bois thought back over the conversation they had had. Conversation? No, more a humiliation. The nerve of the man, giving out orders as though he were Lionheart. Count John was no soldier, that was for certain. He didn't know how to value a trained warrior.

And Wales? A backwater for such a seasoned soldier. Many years before, du Bois had taken part in a punitive raid into the Welsh mountains. Two hundred men, half of them mounted, had gone out for two weeks in pursuit of a band of Welsh bandits who'd ravaged land close to Shrewsbury. Hot pursuit at that, for the Welshmen had no more than half a day's start on them.

And all they found was endless rain and sleet, mud and snow-drifts, deserted villages and abandoned farms. The word had spread very quickly that an English army was on the prowl.

They had returned to Shrewsbury without a single captive. Not one Welshman had paid with his life.

And now Count John expected him to march into Wales and repeat that dreadful experience, not once but many times.

He would turn down the offer.

But could he turn it down?

It had been an order, not a request. Count John had made it sound like an offer. But it wasn't. It was a command. But how to counter it, that was the dilemma? It might be different if Lionheart was in England. For all his sins, and they were many,

Lionheart was a real soldier. He would understand where the best men should be posted.

Could he get a message to King Richard? Probably not. Might it be possible to desert England right now for Normandy?

Lionheart would forgive such a move; probably think it a handsome prank. But Count John would never forget such treachery. The name of Sir Brian du Bois, the soldier who had deserted his duty in Wales, would always be lodged in the most malevolent corner of John's cunning brain.

And given the risks Richard was taking in his battles with the French, it might not be long before John of Mortain was King of England.

No, there was no future in desertion.

The best prospect was to return to Edwinstowe with the head of Robin Hood. Only that would convince Count John that Sir Brian du Bois was fitted for greater duties than harrying Welsh savages. It might at least buy him more time at Newark, so that he could see the way the wind was blowing in regard to the succession to the throne.

But would it get him Marian Fitzwalter?

Count John had seemed adamant on that matter.

Whatever he did it seemed unlikely that he would gain the lands at Edwinstowe. And Marian in his bed. But then again, she was an awkward woman at the best of times. Would the novelty of having her fade once he had bedded her a few times?

It probably would.

And there was some truth in Count John's suggestion that he should make a dynastic match. Some wealthy beauty that would bring forth lands and position.

But then the thought of Marian came back into his head. Those daring brown eyes, the dark hair brushing the pale skin of her shoulders, the fiery spirit.

Perhaps it might be possible to enjoy her anyway, without the burden of marriage? Just once or twice, in her bed or out in the forest.

Why not?

And then abandon her.

Soiled goods for some idiot like Gisborne to take on. Perhaps with a du Bois already growing inside her to be the heir to someone else's lands.

This vision of the future caused him much amusement.

The men riding alongside du Bois wondered why he was laughing.

~

The archer had spent much of the night walking deeper into Sherwood Forest. Evading du Bois's troops had not been difficult. His soldiers had a great reluctance to wander amongst the trees in the dark. Dreading the thud of the arrow or feeling the sharp blade of a knife at the throat. And always the danger that you might, in the confusion, be brought down by one of your fellows.

Taking secret and narrow paths through the woodland, the archer struck the track that led from Edwinstowe to Nottingham. This was the way that the Sheriff and Gisborne would travel as they began their expedition into Sherwood. The place where a friend of the folk of Sherwood needed to be.

Where to go?

It was likely that Robin Hood might just hide in the caves at Thripper's Drumble. That would be the safest thing to do, given that the outlaws were completely outnumbered. If so they were relatively safe. For if they did happen to be out in the forest they would stand little chance of survival if they encountered the massed soldiers of de Lisle, Gisborne and du Bois.

Perhaps Tuck would know what to do?

The archer journeyed to the shrine of Saint Withburga, reaching there in the early hours of the morning. It all seemed very peaceful, though the donkey, grazing in his little meadow, brayed as the archer approached.

But there was no sign of Tuck in his tiny cell beside the chapel. The archer checked the secret compartment where Tuck kept his bow, dagger and sword. All of the weapons were gone. And there was no food store in the monk's larder. A sure sign that Tuck had not spent the previous night there.

The archer considered making the longer journey to the Drumble, but there would be no chance of getting there until long after daybreak. Enough hours for the Sheriff and his men to wreak havoc in the villages along the old road to Nottingham.

That was the place to be.

Even if it meant death.

Somewhere where the arrows in the archer's quiver might be put to good use.

~

Alan a' Dale almost fell with exhaustion when he reached the edge of the clearing. His unexpected appearance caused the outlaws to arm themselves and rush away from the great oak to the edge of the denser undergrowth. Robin held out a hide flask of water to the minstrel. It took Alan a good minute to get back his breath.

'You're... betrayed, Robin,' he gasped out the words. 'One of your own. Meeting the Sheriff in the forest...'

'Who?' Robin asked.

'Only one man... it can be.' Alan took a deeper breath. 'They hold the wife of this outlaw captive as a servant in Nottingham Castle. As far as I'm aware there's only one of your men that...'

'Ralph? You're barmy,' said Scarlet. 'There's not a truer man in Sherwood than Ralph Gammon. You've been misled, friend.'

Alan shook his head.

'The word comes from a soldier called Edmund. In the Sheriff's own guard. And it wasn't said to me, but to a wench he was trying to impress. I've had information from this Edmund before. He may be a drunk and a braggart but he's always been truthful with what he's told to me.'

'But why would Ralph betray us?' asked John Little.

'They have his wife,' Robin said very quietly. 'Isn't that enough?'

'And who knows what else de Lisle's offered him,' said John.

Scarlet looked bemused.

'But Ralph? I've known him for many a year. I would never have...'

'I would,' said John. 'I've seen how the capture of Joan Gammon has been tearing him apart. Watched him trying to amuse Much and the others. The jokes and the capers. All forced. And have you noticed how quiet he's been afterwards? As though he's felt guilty at not thinking only of her, every minute of the day.'

'And the Sheriff's now holding her in the castle dungeon,' said Alan. 'Who knows what threats de Lisle's made against her?'

'Thinking of it, Ralph's hardly muttered a word to me since he came back from Nottingham the other day. That must be when the deal was done,' said Robin.

He looked at the path leading out of the clearing, the winding track that led to the Nottingham road.

'Well, if it's true it'll be now,' he said to Alan. 'Ralph offered to go alone to the old road from Nottingham to Edwinstowe. He's completely alone. And we know that's the way the Sheriff will march. We'd better go and find out. One way or the other. There's no point in waiting here for de Lisle and his men to arrive. And if Ralph's betrayed the location of Thripper's Drumble as well...'

He marched off at a great pace into the forest. It took the still breathless Alan a while to catch up with him.

'And there's something else, Robin. The mysterious archer who saved your neck and whose arrow dropped William a' Trent...'

'What of him?'

Despite their predicament Alan smiled.

'You don't know who the archer is?' he asked.

Robin gave a shake of his head.

'A fine bowman by all accounts,' he said. 'If he's a wolfshead then I wish he'd throw in his lot with us...' He glanced at Alan. 'You know who he is?'

'I saw that archer the other day. In the dim of evening. At Saint Withburga's shrine. In conversation with Tuck...'

'Tuck? What's Tuck got to do with this? How many secrets are there in this forest?'

'This is the biggest secret of all, Robin. Your archer is...'

He whispered the name, careful that the others should not hear.

Despite his hurry, Robin stopped dead, his mouth open with shock. He shook his head.

'It can't be... it just can't...' he said.

Nineteen

Robert de Lisle, Sheriff of Nottingham, held up an arm and brought his thirty men to a halt at a point where the old track from Nottingham to Edwinstowe passed through a grassy meadow, the wide lea broken only by a few scattered trees.

The men seemed relieved at the prospect of a break, for they had marched at breakneck speed all the way from the castle. It was turning into a hot day, though the grass was still very wet with dew. A stag and a pair of hinds broke the stillness as they wandered into the shelter of the forest.

For a moment he thought the outlaw Ralph Gammon had broken their agreement, for no one seemed to be about in the open space between the trees.

The captain of the guard rode up alongside him.

'He's not turned up, my lord,' the soldier said. 'There's nobody here.'

The Sheriff looked at him and gave a nod.

'He'll be here,' he said. 'I know he will. I've broken men like him before.'

Was that said with hope or with conviction?

The Sheriff wasn't quite sure himself.

And then the captain of the guard touched his arm and pointed.

'There, my lord Sheriff.'

A figure emerged from behind one of the trees in the meadow. A broken man, de Lisle thought, a hunted wolf backed into a corner. Glaring at the hunter with terror in its eyes, knowing that the long chase was at an end.

'Give me the bag of gold,' said the Sheriff.

The captain reached into a pouch on his saddle and handed the bag over to de Lisle. The Sheriff climbed down from his horse and handed the reins to a nearby foot-soldier.

He looked up at the captain.

'You know what you have to do?' he asked.

The captain gave a curt nod. 'Yes, my lord.'

'Very well.'

The Sheriff unbuckled his sword and dagger and handed them to a soldier. And then he walked across the dewy grass towards Ralph Gammon.

'You see, Gammon, I keep my word.'

Ralph Gammon looked all around the clearing.

'Where's my wife?'

'She's safe enough,' the Sheriff replied. 'She's in Nottingham town waiting to meet you, Gammon. And here's the bag of gold I promised you. I've sent a message to my cousin who's the sheriff at Gloucester. There'll be a farm awaiting you there. For you and your wife. And you'll be a free man at last...'

He walked over to Gammon and handed over the bag of gold.

'There's enough gold in there to last a lifetime, Gammon. What a prosperous farmer you'll be...'

Ralph looked across at him, searching the Sheriff's eyes for any hint of betrayal. But all he could see was good humour. The Sheriff gave him a broad smile.

'Rest assured, I always take care of anyone who demonstrates loyalty to me. And I've asked so little in return...'

'Just Robin Hood?' said Gammon.

The Sheriff held up his arms in a gesture of agreement.

'All I ask for is Robin Hood,' he said. 'I'll set free any of his men. They're of no interest to me today.'

'I have your word on that?'

'You have my word.'

The Sheriff beamed at the outlaw, his head held to one side in a sympathetic gesture.

'I know how difficult this has been for you, Gammon. But you're doing the right thing for the people of Sherwood. You really are...'

'Then... I'll tell you. He... Loxley... Robin Hood. They're just a mile from here. In the clearing of the great oak. Loxley and two of his men. They're good men with him. You'll let them go?'

The Sheriff smiled again and nodded.

'I wish you well on your journey, Ralph Gammon,' he said, walking a few yards to one side of the outlaw and the tree.

As he moved he gave a slight nod of his head.

The first quarrel from a crossbow caught Ralph Gammon in the left shoulder, just as the Sheriff turned to face him. He looked across at de Lisle with a sudden expression of understanding.

The second bolt tore into his stomach, passing right through his body and burying itself into the trunk of the tree beyond.

The third and fourth thudded into Ralph Gammon's chest, sending the outlaw into a crazed dance, his arms flinging outwards and his legs moving somehow beyond his control.

The fifth quarrel took off the right side of his head, whipping away the bone of the skull and splattering fragments of the man's brain across the wet and dewy grass.

His body shivered with a great convulsion as it hit the ground, the hips and thighs raised as if Ralph Gammon was trying to get back to his feet. And then he lay still, a horrible rattle of death coming from deep within his throat.

The Sheriff glanced across at his men, waving an arm, ordering the crossbowmen to put up their weapons. He strolled casually across to where the corpse lay and picked up the bag of gold. Looked down at the dead eyes reflecting the blue of the summer sun.

After a moment's thought he reached into the bag and took out a solitary piece of gold and threw it down on to Gammon's body.

'There's your gold, wolfshead,' he said. 'Let nobody say that I don't pay my debts.'

~

Henry Fitzwalter stood at his gate looking out towards Sherwood Forest. The army of Sir Brian du Bois had long since departed and the dust from the road had settled. Summer was advancing. The green on the leaves had long cast off that first freshness that was always such a delight to him. And, as with the snows of winter, he wondered how many more times he might see the changing seasons.

'You have a fine view of the forest, Fitzwalter.'

He turned his head to find Count John standing beside him.

'Sometimes, my lord, I do wonder what will become of it after I'm gone? I fear there's no place for my Marian here. I really needed a son to safeguard all of this.'

'We make a folly of the importance of possessions. We're born without them and we die without them,' Count John replied. 'It's a pity that our nature makes us enjoy them so much while we walk this earth.'

Fitzwalter nodded.

'I cherish Edwinstowe. I really do. I've had happy days in this manor. But now I'm an old man. I fear I've little time left. All my thoughts now are on doing the best for Marian.'

John smiled. 'Ah, but she's a spirited maid. She'll do well. And when I do become King I'll always watch out for her.'

'Thank you, my lord.'

'Where is she? I would like to see her before I think of leaving?'

Fitzwalter nodded in the direction of Sherwood Forest.

'Out there somewhere, my lord. She wanders the greenwood from dawn to dusk. I never know where. It's in her nature to roam. But I wish she wasn't out there now. There'll be bloodshed in Sherwood today. I feel it. I know it.'

'You've met this Loxley... this Robin Hood?'

'An impudent devil, no doubt, but he has a certain charm. Not that I approve of his methods. If there's to be change in the ordered scheme of things then it should be done gradually. But I have to say I do think de Lisle has mishandled the running of the shire. And I sometimes think Gisborne is quite mad with his lust for blood. As for du Bois, well...'

He threw up his arms in despair.

'And on the subject of du Bois...' Count John said. 'I've made it quite clear to him that the Lady Marian is not... available.'

'I'm grateful, my lord.'

'I'm doing my best to send him to Wales...'

Fitzwalter laughed.

'I thought that would amuse you,' John continued. 'I have to confess a certain selfishness in that decision. Not all to do with keeping him out of sight of your Marian...'

'My lord?'

'Du Bois is, as I'm sure you'll agree, a most able soldier. My brother the King has an occasional fondness for him. And Lionheart has too many allies left in England. All of them dripping poison about me in Richard's ear, if they get the chance. Better that there's one less.'

'But Wales?'

'He'll probably do very well there. And I suppose the thought is always in my mind that such an admirer of Lionheart might end up with a Welsh arrow in his back. Du Bois is well connected. If he wasn't I'd have him removed myself...'

'My lord!'

There was more than a hint of protest in Fitzwalter's voice.

'Oh, you know how things are done at court, Fitzwalter? We live in a bloody age. It would be lovely to settle down to quiet days in forests, like your Marian. But we all know the threats faced by England.'

He turned to look Fitzwalter in the eye.

'I really do believe that I have a destiny with England,' he said. 'That only someone with a love for England should rule. I'm convinced that's me. My father believed it. Towards the end of his life he was heard to say that I should succeed rather than Richard or Geoff's boy. He knew, in his heart, that I have a feeling for England that is quite lacking in Richard.'

'King Richard would be uncomfortable with your words, my lord...'

Count John smiled.

'He would indeed, Fitzwalter, but he knows how I think. And in his heart, the sensible portion of his heart that isn't *Coeur de Lion,* he knows I'm right. Richard loathes England. He has no time for it. Normandy will have his bones, as I hope to God England shall have mine.'

'But I hope not for a while, my lord...'

Count John rested a hand on the old man's shoulder.

'What I like about you, Fitzwalter, is that you're always perfectly honest with me. All the others squirm and smarm, but not you. And we've opposed each other in the past. Been on conflicting sides. And still I think of you as a friend. Because you never let the matters we've disagreed upon cloud your judgement.'

'My only loyalty is to do what is best for England...'

'And mine! And mine! I love my brother Richard. I really do. And this past year we've been closer than we've ever been. I go now to fight at his side against France. But the question of England will not go away. Nor who comes after Richard.'

'And Robin Hood?'

'I suppose I shall have to see him hanged,' said John. 'Or cut down in the forest. I was given governance of this shire. I simply can't have Richard hearing tales of rebellion. It's such a nuisance to me. It might imperil the future of England. I can't have that. Not at all. Best if Robin Hood were to vanish from the face of this realm. We must restore order to Sherwood. We really must.'

~

They found Ralph Gammon lying on the damp grass, a few yards from a solitary tree. His dead eyes had lost their brightness and flies buzzed above the open mouth, feasting on the goblets of blood.

John Little knelt and picked up a gold coin lying just by the red pool soaking the dead outlaw's chest. He held it up for the others to see.

'He must have betrayed us,' he said, 'or else why the coin?'

'A jest of de Lisle's I suppose,' said Alan. 'He's known as a man who always pays his debts – one way or another.'

Robin Hood looked at the broken down grass leading out of the clearing. Heading out towards the main track leading to the clearing with the great oak. They had come to find Ralph along a series of more covert, circuitous and narrow paths.

'I fear he did,' he said, pointing to the trail of de Lisle and his men. 'Or else why would they be journeying that way?'

John closed the dead man's eyes.

'If he told the Sheriff about the clearing, he might have betrayed the location of Thripper's Drumble.'

'We'll never know,' said Scarlet.

'We certainly can't take a chance on it being safe,' said Robin. 'Scarlet, you go and light the signal fire. We'll rally at the lightning oak near to Rufford. You wait then and meet the others on their journey. Send Much back to keep an eye on the Drumble. I'd like to discover if the Sheriff knows of it.'

Will Scarlet nodded at the body of Ralph Gammon.

'We should bury him...'

Robin shook his head.

'There isn't time. De Lisle could come back this way at any moment. You'll be passing Crocker's Farm on the way to the lightning tree.' He tossed the gold coin up to Scarlet. 'Give the farmer this coin and ask him to bring his ox-cart and take the body to Tuck's chapel. We'll have Ralph buried near there. And with the proper blessings.'

He looked around the faces of the others. 'We all know what the Sheriff must have threatened to get Ralph to do this. It wasn't just gold. It was the safety of Ralph's wife.'

'What can we do about her?' asked Alan. 'She's already in de Lisle's dungeon.'

'I don't think there's anything we can do,' said Robin. 'Is it safe for you to return to Nottingham, Alan?'

'For now, though I doubt I can remain there for very much longer.'

'You'd better go. And take the secret paths. If you were to meet with the Sheriff or Gisborne they might ask just why a minstrel is wandering in the greenwood?'

Alan nodded and went off.

'I'll kill de Lisle for this...' said Scarlet, looking again at the corpse of Ralph Gammon. 'And I'll make his ending so painful that he'll scream for his own death.'

'Whatever he did, Ralph was one of my men,' said Robin. 'And those who murdered him will pay a price for this day's work. Off you go, Will. There's much to be done before anyone's safe in Sherwood.'

Twenty

Robert de Lisle looked around the clearing. A slight breeze arrived and stirred the green grass and the leaves on the trees and departed as suddenly as it had come. A flock of birds hovered around the massive oak tree, all warily watching the Sheriff's men.

'There are the only birds that haven't flown,' he remarked to Gisborne, who had just ridden up with six of his men. 'No sign of Loxley here. You got my message, Gisborne?'

'I did, my lord. I've left the rest of my men out on the road to Edwinstowe. So the wolfshead betrayed you?'

'It seems so.'

'These peasants are not to be trusted. Did you kill him?'

The Sheriff gave a nod.

'He was fortunate to die such a quick death,' he said. 'If I'd known he was lying I'd have wrung the truth out of him with a much slower ending.'

'And his woman?'

De Lisle shrugged.

'As far as I'm concerned she can rot in the dungeon. Perhaps the other prisoners might find some amusement there. But I'll have her told that her man is dead. She might as well suffer with grief. There's little else I can do.'

Gisborne looked around the edge of the trees.

'Of course Loxley might still be here,' he said. 'Hiding in the thick of the undergrowth. We should have brought dogs to find the trail of his stench.'

'You may be right. I'll send out some men to look at the skirts of the forest.'

Gisborne considered the clearing.

'What is this place?' he asked. 'It gives me an uneasy feeling.'

'Ah, that is *the* great oak of Sherwood. A place where men would rally to form an army for the Saxon kings. A tree that's as much legend as wood. Haunted by spirits. A refuge for the people of Sherwood when the Danes marched this way.'

'I'd have it chopped down!'

'Steal a piece of its bark and you're cursed.'

'A tale of old women!'

'I'm not so sure, Gisborne. If men believe in something, well, there's potent magic in that. No, we'll leave the old tree alone to bewitch the men who ride after us. However...'

The Sheriff looked again at the mighty oak.

'My lord?'

'They say that when the Conqueror was ravishing the shire, men and women hid in that tree.'

'Hid in it?'

'It's hollow, Gisborne. I looked once. You could probably conceal twenty men in its great trunk. I wonder...'

Gisborne turned to the six men he'd brought with him.

'Come with me!' he ordered, dismounting from his horse and drawing his sword.

The Sheriff watched as they crossed the clearing to the great oak.

'A strange land...' Gisborne yelled back at him.

A strange land, indeed, he thought as he walked across to the tree. But at the end of the day it was *just* a tree. He never ceased to be amazed at de Lisle's occasional dabbling with Sherwood superstition. The Sheriff had been around Sherwood Forest for far too long.

And yet there was something about this oak. Gisborne had never seen any tree quite so large. Or with such rough bark that seemed to present faces and weird patterns as he approached. Or any tree that seemed to exude such a feeling of malevolence.

He reached out and touched the tree.

And he felt almost overwhelmed with a feeling of darkness and hopelessness. As though all the bloody history of England was somehow stored in its huge trunk. A thick branch swept the ground so low that he was obliged to step over it. The breeze came again and died away, causing the great giant of the forest to sway and groan. A flurry of green leaves showered down upon him.

And there was the hollow. Dark and twisting, its sides a deep and unpleasant yellow. The sap, that once covered the softer wood inside, now dried and marked with curious rings and whorls of black. A man of superstition would see a dozen faces in those patterns. A man of superstition would...

And there was a face. Looking back at him. Bearing an expression as grim as death. As malicious as anything Gisborne had ever seen.

He shuddered.

Even as he raised his sword, he shuddered.

For the face was human, ghastly with the hate it bore. A face that he'd seen before. Though it seemed to have aged a century since then.

'Come out of there...' he ordered, astonished at the fear he could hear in his own voice.

He saw a mouth crease into a horrible smile.

Matthew of Breevedon stepped out into the clearing.

Still smiling.

Still smiling.

'You know who I am, boy?'

He could do no more than whisper the words, as though the power of speech was deserting him.

'*My lord Gisborne... Gisborne... Gisborne...*'

'What are you doing...' he began to ask.

He watched, almost as though he was detached from his own body.

The boy walked across to him. He watched as the boy rested his left hand on his own shoulder.

Heard the boy's voice say once again.

'*Gisborne...*'

Watched as Matthew swept his right hand from behind his back.

Saw the dagger, its blade rough and covered in rust and ancient blood, sweep upwards towards his own chest.

At first Gisborne thought that the boy was only making a dramatic gesture. He felt no pain, just a slight touch as though a heavy hand had swept across his ribs.

He looked down and almost felt surprise at the sight of the dagger's blade being revealed as it was pulled free of his own body. Surprised at the gushing fountain of blood which followed.

He looked at the boy with a sense of astonishment.

Matthew put his mouth against his ear and whispered the word once again.

'*Gisborne...*'

And then Gisborne's mind seem to drift. Away from his wound and towards the ragged old bark of the tree. He heard shouts and cries nearby.

And suddenly Gisborne's eyes were near to the ground.

The grass of the clearing seemed to be growing into his face.

And then he knew no more. ~

Tuck had spent long hours chasing the youth through the forest. But Matthew of Breevedon was, for all his madness, fleet of foot. Just occasionally Tuck had glimpsed him, ahead and at some distance. Matthew had looked and smiled. Sometimes he'd waved an arm and a burst of laughter had shot back at the monk across the forest glades.

And onwards.

And onwards.

It would have been easier if the youth had stuck to the tracks and paths. But every now and again, Matthew had torn off into the undergrowth, forcing a way through what seemed to be impenetrable brambles. Even with the aid of his quarter staff, bashing and crashing the vegetation away or to one side, Tuck found it hard to follow. The brambles were piercing his skin and pushing him away from where he wanted to be. And yet the boy seemed to find no obstruction in his journey.

At last exhaustion overtook the monk. In order to get his breath back he was obliged to lean back against the smooth bark of a beech tree and gasp for breath.

There he was in the distance, holding up both arms as if in triumph.

'*Gisborne!*'

The great shout echoed through the forest, so loud that Tuck thought it must carry all the way back to the gates of Nottingham.

He wiped the sweat from his eyes and looked again.

Matthew was lost from sight.

Having regained his breath, Tuck wandered on. The trees were thinning now, but it still took him an hour to reach the clearing of the great oak.

He saw the mounted men and the soldiers on foot.

Saw the Sheriff at one end of the glade, looking towards the oak.

And there was the youth by the tree, almost embracing Sir Guy of Gisborne. Tuck watched as the knight fell to the ground, with Matthew of Breevedon standing over him.

Looked in horror at the expression of evil delight on the boy's face.

It was as though he was seeing the smile of Satan himself.

~

'My lord Gisborne is dead!'

One of Gisborne's own men was bending over the body, his hand wet with the blood that dripped out of Gisborne's mouth. The front of the knight's jerkin was red. Somehow the dagger had found a way through the chain mail and right into Gisborne's chest.

'He's dead, my lord Sheriff!' the soldier cried out again.

Two of the other men had grabbed Matthew of Breevedon by both arms. The bloody dagger lay down on the grass at the boy's feet. Matthew looked at the approaching Sheriff with a look of bemusement upon his face.

Robert de Lisle got down from his horse and walked over to the youth. Matthew smiled at him, his eyes dancing with delight.

'Why?'

But the youth didn't answer. His head dipped to one side and a little laugh came from somewhere deep within.

'Tell me why?'

Matthew laughed again.

'He's mad, my lord!' declared one of the soldiers.

'He's dead,' the Sheriff said. 'I'll bring his madness to an end.' He turned to the soldiers. 'No trial. No hanging. I want his throat cut with his own dagger.'

The two soldiers forced Matthew down on to his knees. Another grabbed the youth's hair and dragged back his head, exposing the white flesh beneath. A vein in the youth's throat seemed to be pulsating blue with fast-flowing blood, as though it was desperate to escape the living body.

The soldier who had been the first to reach Gisborne picked up the knife from the grass. He walked over to the youth.

'Stop!'

The Sheriff looked askance to see Tuck tearing across the clearing towards him. Tuck knelt down at Gisborne's side, reaching out and opening an eyelid with two fingers.

'Don't waste your time, monk,' said the Sheriff. 'He's murdered. Slain by this half-wit.'

'I think not,' Tuck replied. 'He breathes...'

The Sheriff walked over to Gisborne.

'Are you sure?'

'I'm certain of it,' said Tuck. 'This man is not dead. But he'll bleed to death if the wound is not wrapped.'

'See to it!' The Sheriff gestured towards Gisborne's men. Two came forward, one removing and tearing his own jerkin to use as a bandage. As they tended to the wound the fallen man was heard to groan.

'Will he live?' the Sheriff asked.

'He might yet die,' said Tuck. 'He needs care. He'll not survive the journey back to Nottingham.'

De Lisle thought for a moment.

'The hunting lodge of Castle Malvoisin is but a mile away. There'll be shelter there. Take him.' He ordered a dozen men who were clustered nearby. 'Cut some wood from the trees and bind them together. Carry him on that to the hunting lodge. I want him well guarded. Robin Hood could be anywhere in these trees.'

'And the youth?' asked Tuck.

The Sheriff shrugged.

'He has to die,' he said. 'You saw what he did? Whether he took Gisborne's life or not is irrelevant. He attacked him and the penalty is death.'

Tuck stepped forward.

'But can't you see that this lad has lost his wits? His own parents and neighbours were murdered by Gisborne...'

'Murdered!'

The Sheriff's roar filled the glade.

'Hanged for no reason,' Tuck continued. 'His parents and most of the rest of the villagers of Breevedon. All but one man. And for no good cause. Was that not murder?'

De Lisle regarded the monk for a while.

'Nobody at Breevedon was murdered,' he said very quietly. 'Sir Guy found that village in a state of rebellion. Guilty of disobeying the forest laws. He had every right to exact a punishment.'

'They killed a few rabbits, and for your own table. There was no rebellion there. It was not even poaching. Gisborne killed them because he enjoys killing. You know that.'

'I know nothing of the sort. Order has to be kept in this shire. King Richard has demanded that it be so. Does your Holy Order not say that you should obey the wishes of God's anointed deputy on this earth?'

'God also decreed that thou shalt not kill. And that is the highest law of all.'

'Except at the requirement of God's deputy,' the Sheriff persisted.

'Holy law does not say that!'

'Holy law was made up not by God but by the old women who take holy orders. I have to govern this land. And govern it I will. And who are you to initiate such a debate on the meaning of God's word? Are you an abbot? I know you not! A bishop maybe?'

'I have charge of the Shrine of Saint Withburga...'

'Ah, yes, I've heard of you. A beggar monk, always touting for alms and offerings. A mendicant. No doubt despatched from your order because of an unsuitability for community life...'

'All that is true,' said Tuck. 'But I guard the bones of a holy saint. A most blessed person whose creed was forgiveness...'

'Forgiveness?' the Sheriff said. 'How can a youth who stabs a noble ask for forgiveness under the laws of England? Whether or not Gisborne dies? And I don't see I should debate these laws with you, monk.'

Tuck held out his arms.

'Let me take the boy,' he said. 'Back to the shrine. Let me try and heal a mind that's become so damaged. He's a good lad. Worthy of a second chance. He doesn't deserve to have his throat cut in an act of vengeance.'

'It is not vengeance,' said the Sheriff slowly and deliberately, like a child reciting a catechism. 'It is the law of our land. You can't expect me to turn a blind eye to what he's done?'

'Nor do I,' said Tuck. 'But he has at least a right to a trial?'

'Why prolong the agony?' asked de Lisle. 'Even if I were to take him to Nottingham and put him on trial, would the verdict be any different? My way is more merciful. A quick cut to the throat is surely better than long minutes dancing at the end of a rope.'

'It would be an act of barbarity...'

Robert de Lisle looked across at the boy and then back at Tuck. He gave the monk a thin smile.

'So, you think that cutting the throat of a murdering rebel is an act of barbarity?'

'I do.'

The Sheriff smiled.

'On reflection perhaps a cut throat is too sudden a death,' he said. 'Faster than hanging, certainly. Some might even view such a manner of execution as merciful.'

He considered for a moment longer.

And then he turned to the soldiers holding the youth.

'We will not cut his throat,' he ordered. 'You are to gut him!'

'My lord?' said the soldier holding the knife, a look of horror on his face.

'Gut him!' said de Lisle. 'Disembowel him like the forest swine he is.'

'Lord Sheriff!'

Tuck stepped forward.

De Lisle waved a hand at his men.

'Seize the monk,' he said. 'Make sure he doesn't interfere.'

Four men stepped forward and held Tuck.

'My lord...' said the soldier with the knife.

'Do as I say or you'll be gutted as well.'

De Lisle watched as three of the men pulled Matthew on to his back on the ground. He saw the soldier with the knife muttering words. A prayer, perhaps, or asking forgiveness of the boy.

It didn't matter, really.

And then, grasping the dagger with both hands and raising it high into the air, the soldier plunged it down into the youth's stomach, just below the lowest of his ribs. And then he dragged the long blade down across Matthew's stomach. There was a great expulsion of air, and blood spattered over the youth's chest and the soldier himself. The guts of the boy spilled outwards and down towards his crotch.

And Matthew of Breevedon watched as all of this was done to him. But there was no cry. No scream. Not a tear on his face, nor a groan from his mouth. Just something like a smile. And a kind of look of relief.

And then he died.

Tuck flung off the soldiers who were holding him.

He crossed the few yards of the clearing to the boy's corpse. He made the sign of the cross. And then brought his head forward and spoke the holiest of words into the dead boy's ear.

And at last he turned to the Sheriff.

'May God forgive you for this day's work, de Lisle!'

'This rebel got what he deserved. And if you ever address me again without the words, my lord, I'll gut your fat and disrespectful carcass as well!'

And then he climbed back on to his horse and rode away, signalling to his men to follow.

The soldier who had done the deed dropped the dagger to the ground. He looked at Tuck, tears in his eyes and his face deathly pale. Almost with a look of pleading.

'Brother...' he began.

'And may God forgive you,' said Tuck, glancing up at him. 'But I fear you'll spend an eternity burning in the fires of hell. And that bastard de Lisle alongside you.'

Twenty-one

'Who were they?'

Sir Brian du Bois called out to his captain as the man came galloping up.

'Just traders on their way to Nottingham market,' the captain replied. 'Eight men with an ox-cart. We searched it thoroughly, my lord. Just the goods they expect to sell.'

Du Bois looked around him. He had scarcely thirty men left. All the rest had somehow got themselves lost in the forest. Scattered, like autumn leaves in the breeze.

It had started well. After leaving Edwinstowe they had searched three villages for wolfsheads. Villages where not a villein was to be seen harvesting crops or out with the plough. All work had been abandoned because word had spread that soldiers were searching Sherwood for Robin Hood and his men. A few brave souls clustered out on village greens, watching with surly disapproval, the passage of du Bois and his men. But mostly the doors of the little homesteads were shut and barred.

'You have a duty to be out at work,' he'd said to the headman of one village. 'Not laying abed all day. If your lord hears of this he'll have you whipped.'

The headman bowed.

'With respect, my lord, there are wolfsheads in the forest.'

'You've seen them?'

He leant forward on his horse, a thrill exulting his body. The excitement of the first hint of the prey in a long hunt.

'All the world knows they must be there, my lord. For it's the talk of Sherwood that it's wolfsheads you've come to hunt. And you're armed men. We've nothing but staffs and cudgels to protect us. It's not safe...'

'Have-you-seen-them?'

'Not as such, my lord. But then we haven't left the village.'

Du Bois couldn't be sure whether or not the man was being particularly stupid or plain cunning.

'Are you mocking me?'

'No, my lord. Just trying to give you an honest answer.'

And at first that had been the reaction at many of the villages and farmsteads his men had come across. But later in the day it seemed as though the people of Sherwood had recovered their courage. Men, women and children were seen out working in the fields, or gathering firewood in the forest.

But were they all villeins?

He couldn't be sure.

Soldiers had been sent in dozens of directions to interrogate anyone he caught a glimpse of. Particularly those men who were fleetingly glimpsed, vanishing into the greenwood. Peasants who didn't appear to be accomplishing any of the usual tasks.

And not wishing to halt his advance while inquiries were being made, Sir Brian du Bois had moved his column onwards, determined to scour most of Sherwood before Robert de Lisle and Gisborne could be the first to bring the quarry to bay.

And so, by the middle of the day, he'd found himself with a depleted force in the very heart of the forest.

And it was there that he came across the men carrying Sir Guy of Gisborne to Castle Malvoisin.

He dismounted and walked over to the wooden stretcher. He raised the cloak that had been thrown over Gisborne and looked down at the face of his rival.

'Is he dead?' he asked.

'No, my lord,' said one of the soldiers, 'though I fear he soon will be. He was stabbed. Right in the chest. By a peasant who'd been hiding in the great oak of Sherwood.'

'A wolfshead?'

Du Bois felt a tremor of excitement.

Prey at last.

'Just a villein, my lord. A youth from Breevedon. The boy my lord Gisborne spared when he hanged the rest of the villagers.'

'And what happened to this youth?'

'My lord the Sheriff had him gutted.'

Sir Brian du Bois felt a kind of sadness that he'd missed such a colourful execution.

'And where are you taking Sir Guy now?' he asked, climbing back on to his horse.

'To Castle Malvoisin, my lord.'

Gisborne not dead and already on his way to hell, thought du Bois. Even hearing the very name of that hunting lodge made him shudder. He'd heard the tales surrounding the most sinister place in the shire. Perhaps in the kingdom. He'd been there only once. It had been a short visit. Du Bois had been glad to mount his horse and resume his journey that day.

'I understand that Sir Hubert Malvoisin isn't at home?'

'Word is he's in Lincoln, my lord.'

Aye that would be the way of it. Gone to Lincoln. Always work there for a man like Malvoisin. Meeting with the Templars to plan mischief, mayhap. Or the Jews. There were always Jews to kill in Lincoln. Though of late Lionheart, and Count John – who had some influence in that town – had frowned upon their slaughter. Everyone needed money from the Jews these days.

'Where is the Sheriff now?' he asked.

'Coming behind us, my lord. A mile or two back. With perhaps thirty men.'

'So few?'

'My lord the Sheriff arranged to meet a man in the forest. An outlaw who betrayed Robin Hood. He thought he might not be noticed if he entered Sherwood with a smaller force...'

Du Bois nodded.

'And this treacherous outlaw?'

'Dead, my lord. Cut down with crossbow bolts as soon as he'd given his information.'

How like Robert de Lisle, thought du Bois. Never a man to keep a bargain if he could wriggle his way out of it.

'But no sign of Robin Hood?'

'It seems the traitor lied,' said the soldier. 'Or got the story wrong.'

A great smile crossed du Bois's face. Gisborne mortally wounded and Robin Hood still out there to be hunted down.

What a day for the chase!

He watched as the sorry little procession set off in the direction of Castle Malvoisin. Much as he loathed Gisborne he still crossed himself at the thought of any knight ending up there.

Castle Malvoisin.

Better that Gisborne died than enter its gates.

Du Bois breathed in very deeply.

Castle Malvoisin.

To hear the very name felt like being cursed.

He turned to the few men he had left. They looked exhausted, worn out by the long day in the forest and the many miles they had tramped. Soldiers always needed bucking up when their spirits were low.

'Let's go and cut down these wolfsheads,' Sir Brian du Bois yelled, spurring forward his horse. 'Gold to any man who slashes one of their rebellious throats!'

~

'Who did this?'

Tuck was praying over the corpse of Matthew of Breevedon.

He looked up into a familiar face.

'Who did this?'

The archer looked shocked, face pale and eyes showing a deadly anger.

Tuck stood and raged at the sky.

'I don't know where God was this day? Not in Sherwood that's certain sure,' he shouted. 'When boys are held down and butchered like the beasts of the field... I ask again, where was God today?'

The archer rested a hand on his shoulder.

'Who?'

'That murderous bastard Robert de Lisle... he did this. Well, a soldier at his instruction. It makes no odds. The Sheriff is responsible. The man who held the dagger is just his creature.'

'What had the boy done?'

'Done? He stabbed Sir Guy of Gisborne. And why not, I ask you, why not? Hadn't Gisborne murdered Matthew's family and his neighbours? All in his village, bar Gilbert of the White Hand. Vengeance is mine, sayeth the Lord, I will repay... and perhaps he chose Matthew as his instrument. Who is to say?'

'Is Gisborne dead and in hell?'

'He lived when they carried his body away. He may yet die. He may not. Who knows?'

'Where did they take him?'

'To Castle Malvoisin.'

The archer gave a look of satisfaction.

'Well, alive or dead, he'll be in hell there. And de Lisle?'

'He and his men were riding in the direction of Edwinstowe.'

'Then that's where I must go,' said the archer, 'to the Edwinstowe road. I'll make de Lisle suffer torments for this day's work. Where is Robin Hood?'

'Either at the Drumble or somewhere out in the forest. The idea was that the outlaws should lie low. I hope they have. There's been enough blood spilt in Sherwood today.'

'There'll be more before the dark.'

Tuck grabbed the archer by the arm.

'You can't do this,' he said. 'Not alone anyway. I'll light a signal fire to bring Robin Hood to this place. At least let me do that...'

'There's no time to wait,' the archer replied. 'I must strike at de Lisle while he's still in Sherwood. If he reaches Edwinstowe or Nottingham it'll be so much harder.'

'I can't allow this... you mustn't put yourself in such peril.'

'We live in a word of peril, Tuck. While men like de Lisle exist and prosper then we always will.'

The archer gave Tuck a quick smile and ran off along the track.

~

The lightning tree on the road to Rufford had been struck seven years before, during a great storm that was still the talk of the villagers in Sherwood Forest. The blast of the lightning had cleaved the tree nearly in two, throwing off its branches in all directions. The heat of the bolt had started a fire in the heart of the trunk and scorched its bark black.

But somehow the ruin of a once proud giant of the forest remained standing. A meeting place for journeymen, pilgrims, and peasants who came along the various Sherwood paths. Folk who wished to journey together to the market in Nottingham or seek shelter in company at the tavern in Edwinstowe.

It was a favoured rendezvous for the wolfsheads of Sherwood. A place near to a busy road along which someone who might be robbed might be found and profited by.

In a country of many trees it was a useful point of recognition. Everyone in Sherwood Forest knew where everyone else meant by the simple utterance of the words lightning tree.

The outlaws who had remained in Thripper's Drumble had sped there after seeing the smoke from the signal fire lit by Will Scarlet. And it was at the tree that they met up with Robin Hood and were told of the fate of Ralph Gammon.

'I knew there was something amiss with him,' said Stutely. 'The last I saw him, when we walked together. He wanted to tell me something. Confess to what he'd done, maybe?' He turned to Robin Hood. 'I know what it's like to lose a wife. But how much worse for him, knowing that his Joan was alive and suffering God knows what torments in Nottingham Castle. You mustn't think too hard of him...'

'I don't,' said Robin. 'The blame rests on the shoulders of de Lisle. Ralph's great mistake was in trusting that viper. Well, I intend that the Sheriff and Gisborne and du Bois pay a heavy price for what they've done this day.'

'You can spare Gisborne. He may be dead already.'

Robin turned to see Tuck walking up to them.

He told them of the attack on Gisborne at the great oak and the slaying of Matthew of Breevedon.

'So they've taken Gisborne to Castle Malvoisin?'

'They have, Robin, though he was more dead than alive.'

'We should make sure,' said Scarlet. 'One of us should go there and cut Gisborne's throat.'

'Not me,' said Much. 'I'll not go near that cursed place. You know what they say about Castle Malvoisin?'

'Ah, they're just tales!' said Scarlet. 'Fireside fables to frighten children to sleep. Sir Hubert Malvoisin is no better or worse than any of the lords of the shire. Just as vicious. Just as grasping. Just as cruel.'

'That's not what I've heard,' said Much. 'They say he's in league with the Devil. Some say he's the Devil himself.'

'Aren't they all devils?' said Scarlet. 'Every last bastard one of them. From Lionheart down. I'm not scared of shadows, Robin. Let me go there now and make sure of Gisborne.'

'I think perhaps we should,' said Robin. 'But not yet. If Gisborne is as badly wounded as Tuck says, then we have days before we need act. Better to wait until the Sheriff and his men are out of the forest.'

'And that's the other matter,' said Tuck. 'The Sheriff rides this way. Count John of Mortain is at Edwinstowe. De Lisle goes to report to him and no doubt seeks favours.'

'If he's coming by way of Rufford then let's ambush him here and now,' said Stutely. 'I'd be happy to put an arrow through his black heart.'

'He's mine!' said Scarlet.

'He has too many men for an open attack,' said Robin. 'We can't bring them all to battle. Perhaps an arrow just for him. A shaft coming out from the densest bushes of the greenwood.'

'Aye, that's the way of it,' said Scarlet. 'One man alone, silent and deadly. A quick pull of the bow and then away. Safer for one killer to take to his heels and lose himself in Sherwood. Or go to ground after the slaughter's done.'

'He doesn't have as many men with him as you think,' said Tuck. 'He came into the forest with about thirty. I have word of it. Most of the Sheriff's men are combing the southern reaches of Sherwood. But you have a rival who is as anxious as you are to bring down de Lisle.'

'A rival?'

'A certain archer. Someone used to killing alone. I think I'd better tell you who...'

'I know who the archer is,' said Robin. 'Alan a' Dale witnessed the meeting at your chapel. He couldn't believe his eyes. I find it hard to believe myself.'

'It's true enough,' Tuck replied. 'And the archer lies in wait, even now, for the Sheriff. Determined to take that shot of an arrow you talk about.'

'The fool!'

'We must get there, Robin,' said Tuck. 'Lest our friend is overwhelmed.'

231

Robin turned to the outlaws.

'We may yet have to bring the Sheriff and his men to battle. Are you with me?'

'If we're to die then better we perish taking out de Lisle,' said Scarlet. 'At least we'll have cleared some of the vermin from the forest.'

John Little looked up at the clear blue sky.

'A beautiful day if it's to be our last!' he said.

~

Clorinda walked the old road to Edwinstowe that Gisborne had taken earlier in the day. She hadn't meant to leave Nottingham. She really hadn't. Guy of Gisborne had said to her that the forest would be a dangerous place that day. But wasn't it always? Perilous on every day of every year.

She had watched Gisborne and his men ride out of the castle gate. Walked up on to the battlements and saw the column of men weave their way through the busy streets of the town. Looked on as they took the dusty road through the meadows. Gazed after Gisborne until he and his soldiers disappeared into Sherwood.

And all with a feeling of utter doom.

Somewhere out there, under the green mantle of the forest, was her cousin Robin. Her first real love. A man who could still make her ache with longing for him. But there was another man now. Someone who treated her like the peasant she was. Hardly a lover, just another lord claiming what he thought was his right. And yet he hadn't looked at another woman since he first took her to his bed.

Except Marian Fitzwalter.

There was always her. But Clorinda knew as well as Gisborne that that was a yearning that would never be reciprocated. When all was said and done it was Clorinda's arms he fell asleep in every night.

And that was enough love for her.

She had passed a great many soldiers on her journey into the forest; men tired and dusty, some walking or riding singly, others in small groups. Making their way home. Some had looked at her lustfully but, recognising her as Gisborne's whore, had left her alone. None had seen Gisborne since he had departed in search of de Lisle. Nor had any of them encountered Robin Hood.

She was three quarters of the way to Edwinstowe when the blow fell.

A small party of soldiers came out of a side track. They looked utterly worn out and dispirited. She recognised one of them, a fat soldier at arms from Bowland. A man who had long served Gisborne's family. She noticed the look of agitation he gave her as he walked over.

'Sir Guy's dead isn't he?' she said.

'Not... dead.'

'Then dying?'

'I think so,' the soldier replied. 'Badly wounded, with much of his blood gone.'

'Wounded by an arrow?'

'A dagger.'

'Who delivered the blow? Was it Robin Hood?'

'You'd think so, wouldn't you? More understandable if it was a wolfshead. But it wasn't. It was a half-wit boy from Breevedon. The one Sir Guy spared when he wiped out that village. Nothing to do with outlaws at all.'

'Does the boy live?'

'The Sheriff had him gutted.'

Well, that was something. Very often a wounded man might live if the person who struck the blow died first. That was the superstition. Clorinda had often known it to be so.

'Where is Sir Guy?'

'The Sheriff has had him taken to the castle in the woods, the old hunting lodge. Malvoisin? Yes, that's the name of it. Malvoisin. But it's no use you going there...'

He yelled after her as she ran off along the track. 'They won't let you in...'

~

233

The old road to Edwinstowe made a great bend not far from the new abbey at Rufford. Once this had been impenetrable forest, but over the years, and certainly since the coming of the monks a half-century earlier, it had been gradually won back by the hands of men, determined to create rough pasture for their beasts. The nearest trees were now a good three hundred yards from the road itself.

Too far for the flight of a killing arrow.

Too open for an ambush.

The archer considered all of the possibilities. There would be just one chance to take out de Lisle if this was to be the place of killing. Time only for one arrow aimed at the man who would be riding at the head of his men.

Then only seconds of realisation after the Sheriff fell from his horse. Before the mounted men to his rear came charging down this road, blood-hot with the desire for retribution.

It would mean stepping out in full view of the Sheriff and his men. Being observed while the arrow was being nocked and the bowstring pulled back. Plenty of time for a countering action to be taken. A great deal of time for the beginnings of a charge.

And yet, the lack of cover for the archer meant also a lack of cover for the archer's prey. If the Sheriff himself rode forwards in a charge he might still be brought down. If he attempted to flee for the trees he could be taken with a clever arrow long before he found shelter. Only if he hid behind his men would he be protected. And he would have very little time to do that. And de Lisle was not known for his cowardice.

The arrow would strike home first.

But for the archer the consequences would be severe. Just halting long enough to shoot the arrow would mean inevitable capture.

Well, that was the way of things.

Playing a dangerous game had such consequences.

The archer stepped out on to the road and practised taking the shot.

~

'How far to Rufford Abbey?'

Robert de Lisle turned to his captain.

'We should be there within the hour, my lord Sheriff. The road comes out of the forest just beyond the next bend. Then it's open country all the way to Rufford.'

Thank God for that anyway, thought de Lisle. The track to Edwinstowe had narrowed considerably and the green trees of Sherwood Forest pressed outwards, brushing the shoulders of the marching men. A fine place for an ambush. An outlaw could almost reach out and cut a throat without emerging from the undergrowth. At least there was room to manoeuvre on open ground.

'Very well,' he said. 'The men can rest for a while at the abbey before we march on to Edwinstowe. We'll see if we can prise some wine out of the avaricious old shrew the abbot.'

'My lord,' the captain grinned.

The Abbot of Rufford was renowned equally for his wine cellar and his complete lack of hospitality to travellers.

'The men must make the most of it,' the Sheriff said. 'There'll be little in the way of refreshment at Edwinstowe if Count John is there with his entourage.'

The trees began to thin as they approached the clearing. The darkness of the track diminishing as the light of the summer day broke through the overgrowth. The track widened again as it circled around the heath in a huge bend. In the far distance de Lisle could see the smoke from the fires of Rufford.

He felt a weariness from all the long riding of the day. And what to show for it? A peasant boy butchered, and Gisborne down - dead or dying. The whole day had been wasted. He really should have kept the wolfshead Ralph Gammon alive and a prisoner until Robin Hood was taken. And only then put him to death, painfully and slowly in the room above the dungeon in Nottingham Castle.

'We'll spend the night at Edwinstowe in the hall of that old fool Fitzwalter,' he said to the captain. 'I dare say Count John will find some amusement in our failure to capture a single wolfshead.'

The captain tapped his shoulder and pointed.

'He might have to laugh on the other side of his face, my lord. Look along the track...'

The Sheriff raised his head and focussed his eyes against the glare of the sun. At first he thought that it must be a deer or some other brown animal fixed in terror at their approach. But as his eyes got used to the light he could see it was an archer clad in brown and green, a hood up over the back of the head. An arrow already nocked on the bowstring.

'What the devil?'

'Not a forester, my lord,' said the captain. 'Not dressed like that. And nobody else is allowed a bow in Sherwood. It might be Robin Hood himself?'

The Sheriff put up his hand once more to subdue the glare of the light.

'I'd expected a taller man from Gisborne's description.'

'Another wolfshead then,' said the captain. 'One of Robin Hood's men. But standing there so boldly. And alone?'

Both of them looked around the distant edges of the woodland.

'It's a ruse,' said the Sheriff. 'It must be. It must. No wolfshead would position himself like that unless he intended to draw us into an ambush.'

He turned and waved his men into a line.

'Don't aim at the archer,' he shouted at the soldiers carrying crossbows. 'Hold your bolts until you see wolfsheads come out of the trees.'

But still the archer hadn't moved. The man was just standing there. The arrow nocked but the bowstring still not pulled. Out there, in the middle of the track, with no route of escape.

'It's a ruse,' the Sheriff said. 'It has to be. It would be madness for one man to challenge us alone and out of cover like that.'

The captain thought of the actions of the youth, Matthew of Breevedon, who only hours before had thrown away his life in order to attack Sir Guy of Gisborne. Maybe all the outlaws of Sherwood were prepared to sacrifice their lives in the same manner if it meant bringing down the lords of the shire. Could it be that Robin Hood and his wolfsheads might believe that the death of one of them would be worthwhile if it meant bringing about the destruction of the Sheriff of Nottingham?

'Stay with the men and watch for the outlaws,' de Lisle ordered. 'I can be on that archer before he has time to draw his bow.'

'My lord?'

'Do it!' the Sheriff yelled. 'Better not to see Count John empty handed. I'll take him the head of that outlaw!'

He drew his sword and spurred the horse forwards in a fast charge.

Twenty-two

Gisborne's head rolled from side to side as the men carried him along the rough forest track. He fell in and out of consciousness and when he was awake he felt light-headed, as though his mind was somewhere very distant from his broken body.

Dappled sunlight coming down through the canopy of the trees dazzled his eyes with an almost painful intensity. And then for a long while there was only darkness as the little expedition penetrated deeper into the forest.

He was more alert on his next waking. The track was wider now and was entering a glade amidst the trees. Gisborne raised his head a little to take in a building just ahead of him.

A castle.

A fortification of the olden style, a round tower on top of an earthen mound, a low wall enclosing a small bailey. One of the swiftly-built defences Norman soldiers had erected soon after the Conquest, when they had first ridden into Sherwood to subdue the shire.

He dragged his head round and noticed how close the trees were growing to the curtain wall with its rough crenellations. When the little castle was first constructed the trees would have been cut way back to prevent the covert approach of opposing warriors. Now it seemed that defence was not a high priority. The whole building gave off an air of neglect, almost abandonment. And yet, as he passed through them, Gisborne could see that the wooden gates were new and of a formidable thickness. A more recent building had been erected on one side of the bailey, not very big but no doubt offering more comfort for the occupants.

The procession came to a halt.

His eyes scanned the ramparts for defending soldiers.

But the place seemed deserted. A gate leading into the stables creaked open and shut and open and shut in the slight breeze that came from the forest.

The castle seemed familiar and he fought with his memory to bring its name to mind.

Trying to speak to the men who had carried him, as they laid him down, produced only a groan. And even that sent a sharp pain rolling through his chest.

One of the soldiers crouched down and put his head near to Gisborne's.

At last he managed to utter the word.

'Where...?'

'Hunting lodge, my lord Gisborne,' the man said. 'Close to where you was attacked. Couldn't get you back to Nottingham. That wound's too raw.'

Gisborne struggled to rise. He seized the man's arm, pinching the flesh beneath the jerkin. The movement sent a great wave of pain through his chest.

'I know this place...'

'Hunting lodge, my lord.'

'Whose?'

'Sir Hubert Malvoisin's, my lord Gisborne. The ancient castle in the forest as was. The one that used to guard the old road to Edwinstowe.'

'Mal...?'

'That's right, my lord. Castle Malvoisin.'

It took a while for the memories to fight their way to the surface, through the dark confusion in his brain.

'Is... Sir Hubert here?'

'Seems empty, my lord. I did hear as how he was in Lincoln.'

Gisborne raised his head very close to the soldier's face.

'You have... to get me away... from here.' Every word brought a spasm of pain. 'Back to... Nottingham...'

'My lord Gisborne, if we move you any further you'll bleed to death.'

Gisborne struggle to breathe and speak at the same time.

'How many men have... you got here?'

'A bare half-dozen, my lord. All that the Sheriff could spare.'

'Listen to me, man,' said Gisborne. 'I... want you to close the gates. There could be outlaws... out there. Place a man on the tower... look out.'

'Yes, my lord.'

239

The soldier began to stand but Gisborne held on to his arm, bringing him back down.

'Wait...' Gisborne ordered.

'My lord?'

'Send some men to search... search this castle. Make sure nobody is concealed here. Tell them... tell them to be sure...'

'My lord.'

The soldier waved at three of the men and they headed towards the buildings, swords drawn.

'Come here...'

Gisborne pulled the man closer.

'I want you... I want you to stay with me, do you understand? You... or one of the others. Don't leave me alone... not for a moment. Not in this place...'

~

Halfway through the charge, Robert de Lisle pulled back his sword ready to cut down the archer. He gave a great yell to spur the horse into a hurrying fury.

But still the archer stood there, hardly moving, just raising the head a trifle, as though fascinated by the sight of the man coming at him with such great despatch. Otherwise doing nothing to counter the attack.

The Sheriff was puzzled. The man's arrow was still nocked on the bow, but he seemed to be making no attempt to draw back the bowstring. It was as though the archer was just waiting to die.

Ambush, it must be an ambush. And the archer the bait, he thought. Was he charging to his own destruction? De Lisle risked a glance from side to side, but he could see only the trees at the distant sides of the meadow. And his own men were protecting his rear.

He was close to the archer now.

It was as though the villain was paralysed with terror.

Though the arrow was nocked, the bowstring was still not drawn.

De Lisle gave a shout of triumph.

He was so close he could almost feel his weapon slicing through the man's throat. He raised his sword arm a few inches higher. Pulled it a small distance further back.

Then...

A tiny gust of wind caught the archer's hood, easing the material back from the head.

To reveal more of a face.

A face the Sheriff knew only too well.

The jolt of surprise caused him, almost subconsciously, to ease back on the reins. The horse half sensing the gesture slowed, breaking the momentum of the charge. The yell of triumph died in the Sheriff's throat. His lips formed a word.

A word that was a question.

A question that was a name.

In that tiny portion of a second, he saw the bowstring pulled back. Caught the briefest yellow flash as the sunlight caught the shaft of the flying arrow.

There was a deadly span of silence.

It seemed that some force had lifted him from his horse.

And then he was on the ground, the breath dashed from his lungs.

He could see nothing but the blue of the sky.

But he knew that the arrow had struck home.

~

Robin Hood came along the track and out on to the edge of the meadow just in time to see the Sheriff fly from his horse. In a heartbeat he summed up the whole situation.

Robert de Lisle hitting the ground.

The soldiers, drawn out in a line with their backs to the track, walking hesitatingly forward as the archer nocked another arrow into the bow.

As the rest of the outlaws joined him, he watched the captain, careless of his own safety, rushing across to the Sheriff, waving and shouting an instruction to the men with crossbows even as he made the dash.

And in that heartbeat, the archer seemed to waver, as though not sure whether to fire the arrow or run backwards towards the far-away trees. It was a hesitation that could lead to the archer's destruction. It was an act of indecision that could see a body torn apart by the heavy thuds of six crossbow bolts.

But even before the fastest soldier could aim his crossbow, Robin's arrow cut into his back and severed his spine. Oblivious to what had happened to their comrade, five more men were still raising their weapons. But as they tried to get a sight on the archer Robin heard the whisper of arrows pass him on either side as the other outlaws opened fire.

Two soldiers fell with arrows in their backs. A third with an arrow through his neck. One screaming, wounded, as the shaft took him through the shoulder. The fifth soldier turned as an arrow skimmed across the top of his helmet, knocking it from his head.

He raised his crossbow, letting loose the quarrel, but almost without aim. Robin felt its draught pass somewhere close to his throat. As he watched the soldier struggling to wind back the crossbow to reload, Robin took a quick aim with his longbow and saw his arrow drill into the man's face, midway between the eyes.

'Take them! Take them!' he heard the captain shout. The man was bent over de Lisle, head moving continuously as he tried both to tend to the Sheriff and watch the attack of the outlaws. All the while conscious of the peril that might come from the solitary archer at his back.

There were some twenty soldiers left. All turning and drawing swords. Then running fast towards the outlaws.

A flight of arrows brought down five more, dead and wounded.

But the charge came on.

The archer sent an arrow over the head of the captain, dropping a soldier, stone dead. And then a second arrow, halting the run of another man as the shaft caught him in the top of the thigh.

As the archer nocked a third arrow it seemed that the ground shook all around. A quick turn. Horsemen, and only yards away.

The nearest whirling a sword. The archer stepped to one side to dodge, hardly seeing a second mounted soldier and then a third. The horse of a fourth delivered a glancing blow, sending the archer crashing to the ground, the bow and arrow flying yards across the grass of the meadow.

The archer was stunned for some moments.

And then she came round with the tip of a sword blade pressing against her throat.

Looking up at a familiar face under the shadow of a helmet.

The face of Sir Brian du Bois.

Open-mouthed. Gasping for the words in his astonishment.

The words were her name.

'Marian Fitzwalter.'

She read her name on his lips, for he could barely utter more than a whisper.

'Marian Fitzwalter.'

~

Sir Brian du Bois and his men had come from Rufford Abbey, where they had bullied the monks into giving them refreshment.

Du Bois had decided to have one last sweep of the edge of the forest before returning to Edwinstowe.

As they entered the meadow they had come across the fight.

Watched as the Sheriff went down. Then saw the struggle between the soldiers and the outlaws.

He didn't need the pointing finger of his own captain to see the solitary archer close to the track and not so far away.

'Robin Hood?' asked his captain.

'I don't care who it is. We're having him!' Du Bois cried, waving his men into the attack.

His horsemen had charged alongside him.

The foot soldiers, invigorated by the Abbot of Rufford's ale, rushing in his wake so that they might be in at the kill.

~

The soldier screamed as Robin plunged the sword deep into his chest, his eyes rolling with fear of pain and the inevitability of death. Blood poured from the man's mouth. He staggered and fell. Robin put his foot on the man's body to force back the blade that had somehow got snagged among a broken ribcage. A horrible dry rattle of death carried across the glade from deep in the soldier's throat. The accusing eyes looked up at the outlaw. And then all light went from them.

Robin Hood had scarce a moment to regard his victim before another of the Sheriff's men came charging at him, bare-headed and angry. Sword in one hand and dagger in another. He seemed more determined than most, a look of hatred and vengeance on a narrow brown face. His mouth held open in a determined grimace of rotting brown teeth. And from the way he held the two weapons, undoubtedly a warrior of some skill.

Even as the man's sword came towards him, Robin could see the waving of the dagger. First visible, to intimidate. Then backwards, half behind his foe's back, as though to put thoughts of it out of sight and out of mind.

Then the man's sword was thrust forwards, inviting a parrying blow from Robin's own weapon. But Robin could see from the soldier's eyes what was intended. How his defending blade might be twisted and held towards the ground while that deadly dagger was pushed forward into his own unprotected body.

Instead, he took a half step backwards causing the soldier to lurch a step towards him. The man was forced to lower his sword as he fought to regain his balance, bringing the dagger sweeping forwards in defence as he realised the danger he was in.

Robin swung his own blade now, not aiming at the dagger itself but the vulnerable hand behind it. His blade caught the soldier's narrow wrist, severing the hand from the rest of the man's arm. The soldier screeched with agony and shock, his eyes blood-red with anger. The dagger fell to the ground, the severed hand still holding it. A gushing fountain of blood from the soldier's arm coloured the grass red. The brown face of the soldier turned white.

With one last grunt of energy the wounded man swung his sword in a great arc towards Robin's head. But there was not enough strength behind the attack to carry it home.

Robin stepped backwards to evade the blade and then forward again, sword grasped in both hands bringing the weapon crashing down on the man's head. Down through the lank hair, biting into the skull and then the brain. Tearing through the soldier's face, splitting the nostrils and the mouth and the rotting teeth.

The man fell like a damp rag from a line.

Robin looked up to see two more soldiers advancing towards him, swords raised, yelling something he couldn't make out. He turned to face them, his sword wavering first at one and then at the other. Both men pulled daggers from their belts and came nearer, double-armed.

Which of them would come in first. Which one would...

An arrow tore into the throat of one of the soldiers. Robin watched, almost as though he was seeing it in a dream. The man dropped both his weapons and clutched at the bloody shaft. The other soldier hesitated, unsure what to do, looking quickly at his wounded comrade, then back again at Robin, and then back at the dying man. He lowered both his sword and his dagger. Two arrows bore into his chest, both above where his heart must be. He crumpled forward with a terrible groan.

Robin glanced over his shoulder. John Little and Scarlet stood at the edge of the trees, fresh arrows already nocked in their longbows. Raising the weapons at the remaining soldiers.

But the slaughter had been enough for the soldiers of the Sheriff. For a moment they wavered, shouting to each other.

And then they broke.

And then they ran.

~

'Over there, my lord du Bois,' shouted the captain. 'It's Robin Hood!'

Sir Brian du Bois looked down at Marian Fitzwalter, and then across at the prostrate body of the Sheriff. And then back at the fight. Robert de Lisle's soldiers were retreating. Being forced backwards by the outlaws, who were now grouped at the fringe of the forest.

Loxley and his men raised their longbows and loosed a volley of arrows. But not at the Sheriff's men. The arrows were being fired to one side of those fleeing soldiers. Du Bois heard screams and saw four of his foot soldiers fall to the ground.

'We have no crossbows, my lord,' yelled his captain. 'We daren't close with those wolfsheads. They'll have us before we get halfway across the clearing.'

Du Bois knew the truth of the man's words. He didn't have enough men left to succeed in a charge. They'd all be cut down before they'd taken a dozen paces.

The outlaws loosed more arrows in his direction. Two more of his soldiers, who had been guarding Marian Fitzwalter, died. The rest of his men cowered on the ground as the remaining arrows flew low above their heads.

His mind was made up.

He ran across to Marian Fitzwalter and dragged the still dazed woman to her feet, his dagger at her throat. He looked up at the approaching outlaws and shouted his terms.

'One step more and I'll cut the throat of this treacherous little bitch!'

It was a gamble.

It could well be that Robin Hood didn't give a toss about the woman.

But his words hit home.

He saw Robin Hood raise an arm. The outlaws halted in their steps.

'Let her go, du Bois!' Robin said. 'Let her go and you and your men can leave here unharmed.'

'I don't deal with traitors, Loxley. I'm going and she's coming with me.' He turned to the captain. 'Is de Lisle alive?'

'Yes, my lord.'

'Mount him on a horse and get him out of here.'

'To Nottingham, my lord?'

'Don't be a bloody fool! Do you think they'd let us live on such a journey through the forest? Back to Edwinstowe. I want Count John to see this prize. And I want that old bastard Fitzwalter dead and his head hung over the gate.'

'My men are going from here, Loxley,' he said, 'and we're taking the woman.'

Robin Hood made a pace forwards.

Du Bois pulled back Marian's head, exposing more of the pale white skin of her throat.

'I mean it, Loxley! I'll kill her if I have to.'

Robin halted.

Brian du Bois clambered up on to his horse, dragging Marian up in front of him.

'If you kill one more of my men as we leave here I'll slit her throat,' he shouted across the meadow.

He laughed.

'Remember that, Loxley. I never care who lives or dies.'

Much ran back across the meadow from the direction of Rufford Abbey, his face dripping with sweat. For all his size and round body he was the speediest runner.

'You were right, Robin,' he gasped. 'That scum du Bois and his men have taken the fork in the road. They're not going to the abbey. They're riding to Edwinstowe.'

Robin thought for a moment.

'If we take the old track through Clipstone and ride hard we might be able to get ahead of them,' he said. 'The new road winds a long way to the north. It'll take them longer to get there that way.'

They looked at the five horses happily chomping the grass nearby. Their former riders dead on the ground nearby.

'Five of us could go now.'

He looked at the outlaws.

'Who knows how to ride?' he asked.

Will Scarlet, John Little, William Stutely and Gilbert of the White Hand all nodded.

'All right,' he said. 'We five can go at once. Much, you make your way as fast as you're able to the fringes of Sherwood. Position yourself outside the castle at Edwinstowe. We may need a man with a bow to help us get away...'

'You're not going to the castle?' asked Tuck.

The monk had been concealed amidst the trees, firing arrows at the soldiers. In the absence of enemies he had walked across to join them. His face was red in the heat.

'They'll expect an ambush in the forest,' Robin replied. 'They'd never suppose us to give them a greeting from inside the castle.'

'Are you mad?' asked Scarlet. 'We've killed a lot of them but they still outnumber us. And don't forget the rumour that Count John's at Edwinstowe. He'll have troops of his own.'

'It's a deadly business, Robin,' said John Little.

'A fatal business,' said Tuck. 'Far better to let me go alone. They didn't see me here today. I might be able to negotiate for Marian's life.'

'They'll not spare her, whatever you say, Tuck,' said Gilbert. 'Her arrow brought down de Lisle. And they know she's killed others these past weeks. What in hell could have possessed the girl to play such a dangerous game?'

The monk shrugged.

'It was always in her nature to be wild,' he said. 'Marian's like us. She can't bear the cruelty of this world. She can't bear sitting quietly at some fireside.'

'And they'll hang her for it.' said Scarlet. 'Or maybe a slower and more painful death.' He looked Robin in the face. 'We just have to accept she's lost to them.'

'I won't do that,' said Robin. 'I won't. Do you remember the first time we saw her as an archer? How she loosed her arrows and saved our necks? We owe her, Scarlet.'

'Aye, there is that,' said John.

Robin grabbed the reins of one of the horses.

'I'll go alone if I have to...' he said.

'No, we'll go with you,' said John.

'I'm coming too,' said Tuck.

'No, Tuck. They didn't see you here. And the people of Sherwood need a priest.'

'I'll go with Much then,' said Tuck, 'and loose my arrows from the trees. Supposing you get a chance to escape that bear's den.'

Scarlet was the last to mount a horse.

He rode over to Robin.

'If this stupidity costs the life of one of these fools, I'll kill you myself Loxley.'

He spurred the horse along the old road to Edwinstowe.

~

Gisborne looked up into blackness.

This is death then, he thought. And death is nothing. Just going out into the dark and oblivion.

And then he felt rather than saw a light and tried to raise himself.

The pain was almost more than he could stand. A feeling of hot irons penetrating his chest. The darkness before his eyes turned red, and someone was screaming, and then cursing very loudly into his ears.

He realised, with some surprise, that the shattering voice was his own.

He gasped and shuddered and then lay still.

Something brushed across his forehead. First one way and then the other. And whatever it was came to rest. Gently, very gently. As soft as a feather.

It was a hand.

A hand.

He wanted to cry out, so fearful was he of anyone touching him in this place. Faces filled his mind. One face in particular. A man whose features had become disfigured with evil. Eyes glaring red like the fires of hell. A mouth twisted with the damned words it had uttered. Better to look into the eyes of the devil himself than that face.

'Say my name. Say my name. Say my name...'

Over and over again, the mouth in the face uttered the challenge.

Say my name.

No. More an invitation than a challenge.

And whoever spoke the word was lost. Gisborne fought hard to not even think the name.

And then the agony came again. And to try and abate the pain he felt he had no choice but to scream out the word.

Better the surrender than the torture.

'Malvoisin!' he yelled into the darkness.

And then the pain seemed to ease. The darkness became light. The gentle touch of the hand rested again on his forehead. The fingers stroked his cheek. His eyes opened properly and his head rolled to one side. And *she* was there.

'You must rest, Guy,' Clorinda whispered. 'The injury is very bad. I've dressed your wound with plants from the forest. The bleeding's stopped but you're very weak.'

'You... here?'

'I walked into Sherwood to find you. The soldiers told me you'd been brought here. They let me in to try and heal you.'

'Am I going to die?'

'I fear you might,' she said. 'And you certainly will if you don't rest.'

Gisborne fought for more breath.

'You know this place?' he said.

She nodded.

'It is Castle Malvoisin?'

She nodded again.

'I thought... thought it might... just be a nightmare.'

'You would have died if they'd tried to carry you further.'

He looked across at a black wall and a great oaken door.

'Better to die...'

'I won't let you die,' she said very firmly.

He took several deep breaths.

'You have to... get me away from here...'

The girl sighed.

'I will, Guy, but not today. Today you must rest. Tomorrow perhaps...'

'Is... he... here...?'

'Sir Hubert Malvoisin's in Lincoln,' she said. 'Your men found the creature who serves him. In a hut not far from the castle walls. Sir Hubert won't return for a week.'

Gisborne breathed a little easier.

'And we'll... we'll be gone before then... won't we?' he pleaded.

Clorinda leaned forward

Her lips brushed against his own bloodstained lips.

'A long time before the week is out,' she said.

~

Sir Brian du Bois rode fast alongside the few horsemen he had left, not bothering to wait for the foot soldiers who limped along in his wake. The girl Marian, slung in front of him across the horse, seemed barely conscious.

They had halted just south of the village of Ollerton, to pull the arrow from de Lisle's shoulder and dress his wound. The Sheriff's chain mail had checked the velocity of the shaft and the injury looked to be clean and not too deep. But he had lost a lot of blood and rested forward on his horse, only just managing to grasp the reins.

But du Bois's thoughts were all of the girl. Even now he could scarcely believe that the deadly archer of Sherwood, always seen at an arrow's distance, was Marian Fitzwalter.

And he considered how he might play the game to come.

At first he had been inclined to plunge his sword into her throat. The very thought of doing that had excited him. Had he not had to contend with the rebel Loxley he might have done so.

But now?

As the horse jogged forwards on the rough track her limp body rubbed against him, stirring all those longings he had had for her over the years. Had he been alone he would have ridden into the greenwood and taken the girl there and then, perhaps strangling her as he writhed in ecstasy.

His men would have turned blind eyes at such a diversion. They often did. But de Lisle would have resisted. The Sheriff of Nottingham had a morality that du Bois found baffling, given that official's behaviour on so many bloody occasions. Sir Brian du Bois played with the idea that the Sheriff should succumb to his wound. His own men would connive at such an outcome if he rewarded them enough.

Du Bois nearly yielded to the thought of a double murder. But as they neared Edwinstowe, du Bois knew he would have to face the searching eyes of Count John of Mortain. And that would be as challenging as trying to explain the sequence of events to Lionheart himself.

And there was the land, the acres of forest and farm that Fitzwalter held from the King. The manor and pleasances that might be his if his played the game... politically.

Perhaps.

Capturing the mysterious archer of Sherwood and suggesting that her actions were part of a rebellious plot against the throne. Implicating the girl's father. Rescuing the Sheriff of Nottingham from certain death at the hands of Robin Hood. Positing the notion that there was a threatening conspiracy to murder Count John while he was under the roof of Fitzwalter...

Now there was a thought.

And what better proof than the Lady Marian trying to kill the Sheriff before he could ride to reinforce Count John's men at Edwinstowe?

Better all of that than a dismal destiny of endless patrols through the rain-soaked valleys of Wales.

~

'Not really a castle at all,' said Scarlet. 'Not much of a challenge here. A child could take the place in a straight fight.'

The outlaws had left the horses tethered a little way back in Sherwood and crept to the edge of the trees. The manor house of Edwinstowe with its crumbling Norman tower stood before them, lights burning brightly in many of the windows.

'They say it fell three times in King Stephen's reign. And without much of a siege,' said Robin. 'I've heard the tales. How the family had to flee into the forest.'

'I know the place well,' said Gilbert. 'There's many a time I've been within its walls to carry out my work as a blacksmith. The house was never meant for defence. It's little more than a farm.'

'And the tower?' asked Robin.

'I doubt they've used the tower since Stephen's time. The last occasion I was here it was a ruin without a roof. They kept the pigs within when the weather was poor.'

'So what is there?' asked Robin.

Gilbert of the White Hand knelt down and drew a plan in the forest dust.

'There's the long stretch of the house we can see,' he said. 'All of the grander rooms are on this side. There are two wings at the back where the servants live. With the stables beyond they form a courtyard. A gate at the side gives entrance. You can see the windows of the great hall at the upper level. Where the lights burn brightest of all.'

'There...'

They looked in the direction of John Little's pointing figure just in time to see two sentries turning the corner to where the gate would be.

'We don't know how many men are in there, Robin,' said Stutely. 'I know Fitzwalter has only a handful, but Count John won't have come alone. I suspect those sentries are his.'

'This is madness!' said Scarlet. 'It won't be hard to scale the walls and break into the hall. But what then? How many soldiers are on call? If we get in we'll probably never get out.'

'We can't leave Marian to die...' said Robin.

'And who's to say she isn't dead already? I know du Bois. He's probably cut her throat back there in the forest. Why bother to carry her back here alive?'

'I just have a feeling,' said Robin. 'I've fought du Bois before. He'll want a prize to flourish in front of Count John. And I fear he'll try and bring old Fitzwalter down as well.' He looked again at the house. 'You don't have to come, Scarlet. You can stay here and use your bow to give us cover if we manage to get out again. I'll go alone if I have to...'

'I'm coming,' said John. 'She fought for us, so I'll fight for her.'

'And I,' said Gilbert.

'I'm with you, Robin,' said Stutely.

'You're all bloody mad!' said Scarlet. 'But then I'm bloody mad too!'

'I've been watching the place,' said John. 'There've been no more sentries. The front wall's unguarded. If we're going to do this then now's as good a time as any. Likely as not those guards are at supper.'

They were about to cross the open ground to the house when they heard the hooves of a horse just back in the forest. They drew their swords and waited. Someone was coming towards then, breathing deeply. A moment later Tuck emerged from the undergrowth.

'Much and I borrowed a horse...' he began. 'We had to share...'

'Borrowed?' said John.

'A lone soldier riding home through the dusk. Tired after a long day in Sherwood. He'll have a bruise from my staff when he's conscious again. Much is tying up the horse next to yours.'

He looked across at the house.

'Do you want us to come in with you?'

'No,' said Robin. 'I want you and Much to stay out here and bring down anyone who tries to stop us getting away.' He turned to Stutely. 'I want you here too. We need as many good archers as we can get to cover our retreat.'

Will Stutely gave a nod and began to string his bow.

~

'It sounds like du Bois has returned.'

Count John of Mortain looked through the little window in the great hall that looked down on to the courtyard. He and Fitzwalter had heard the cries of men and the sounds of horses.

'I suppose he'll want something to eat,' said Fitzwalter, standing at his side. 'Does he have Robin Hood with him, my lord?'

He noticed Count John's puzzled expression.

'Our friend du Bois has very few men with him,' said Count John. 'He must have lost the rest in Sherwood. But there's something wrong... wait, let me see...'

Count John held up a hand to block out the fire and candlelight in the hall so that he might observe better.

'They seem to be helping the Sheriff from his horse.' He half-turned towards Fitzwalter before looking back. 'My God, I think de Lisle is wounded. They're bringing him to the steps up here. And...'

He almost leaned over the sill. And then turned again with a look of excitement.

'Well, they've taken at least one prisoner. Sir Brian has someone captived over his horse...'

'A wolfshead?'

'Maybe, but someone very slight. Not Robin Hood, I think.'

'Probably some peasant who was having an innocent walk in the forest.'

Count John grinned.

'Mayhap, but they have the rogue's hands tied behind his back. I do hope it's not really a wolfshead. We'll never hear the end of it. And du Bois will be seeking better lodgings than the dreary hills of Wales.'

'He really is an odious man, my lord.'

'I've heard the tales, Fitzwalter. I'd rather not have him in my neck of the woods. But my brother Richard has some respect for him. Du Bois has many faults but he's an effective soldier.'

'All the better that he goes to fight in Wales then. Sherwood will be a cleaner place without him. I don't rest easy with du Bois as a neighbour.'

'I'll do my best, old friend,' said Count John. 'I'll do my best. I really will. Ah, he's bringing the prisoner up here.' He noticed the look of anxiety on the old man's face. 'Fear not, Fitzwalter. I'll not soil your home by hanging the villain at Edwinstowe. Better that these matters are attended to in Nottingham, where the crowds might see the man swinging in the wind.'

~

It was not a difficult wall to climb, for it had never been meant for defence. Its stones were uneven in size, the sandstone very pitted with the effects of the weather, giving Robin Hood a good grasp as he climbed. A broad ledge ran along the entire front of the house and it was here that he waited until John Little, Scarlet and Gilbert joined him. They could hear voices coming through the large and open windows of the hall. And then the sound of a large door being thrown open and a triumphant shout.

Twenty-four

'What in God's name is this, du Bois? Some sort of jest?'

Count John sat back in the chair before the fireside, as du Bois and his captain entered the hall with four soldiers, two aiding the wounded de Lisle. The other pair held Marian Fitzwalter, her hands tied securely behind her back.

'Marian?'

Fitzwalter looked bewildered at the sight of his daughter dressed as a man, hood halfway back from the locks of dark hair. She looked at him with the wildest of expressions. More like a captured animal than a woman.

'Du Bois?'

Count John leant forward in the chair.

'My lord Count, this woman is the traitor archer who's been aiding Robin Hood. She's killed any number of soldiers over the past weeks and, today, in front of my own eyes, wounded my lord the Sheriff.'

Fitzwalter stepped across to his daughter, reaching out a hand to wipe a speck of blood from her face.

'What is all this, my love?' he asked, very gently.

Du Bois turned to the soldiers who had helped the Sheriff to a bench.

'Seize that man,' he ordered. 'He's in this up to his neck with his treacherous daughter...'

Count John got to his feet.

'Up to what exactly?'

Du Bois gave a curt bow.

'It's my belief, my lord, that there's a calculated plot to kill you tonight. Fitzwalter and his murdering bitch of a daughter are in league with the rebel Loxley. They're seeking to inspire a great rebellion against you and his grace the King. Your death, my lord Count, is merely the start of the proceedings.'

'That's a lie!' shouted Fitzwalter. 'I will not have my honour and reputation tainted by this rascal, my lord Count. If he has any accusations that might be tested I demand the right of trial by combat.'

'And you shall have it!' said du Bois, drawing his sword. 'I'll cut him down now, my lord, and spare him a hanging.'

'Put up your sword, du Bois,' Count John said. 'I'll decide who goes to trial. Not you.' He turned to the Sheriff. 'What is the truth of this, de Lisle?'

'I don't know for sure, my lord,' the Sheriff replied. 'But it's certainly true that Marian Fitzwalter fired the arrow that wounded me. I know nothing of any wider plot.'

Count John walked across to Marian and pushed her chin up with the palm of his hand.

'I'll have to hang you if this is right, Marian...'

She looked up into eyes that were as green as hers were brown and dark.

'Then I'll have to dance at a rope's end, my lord Count. It's true I fired the arrow that wounded the Sheriff. I was aiming to kill him but a breeze took my arrow away from his throat. He was charging at me at the time. He would have killed me with as little regret.'

'My daughter fired the arrow to defend herself...' said Fitzwalter.

'Don't be absurd!' thundered de Lisle. 'She took the shot quite deliberately. She's killed many of my soldiers in just such a fashion. And she turned my men to give a chance for Robin Hood and his men to shoot them in the back.'

'Liar!' said Marian.

'It's not a lie,' said du Bois, 'that's exactly what happened.'

'I didn't know Robin Hood was even there. I was seeking vengeance on the Sheriff for murdering a boy in the forest. Gutting him like a pig.'

'You killed a boy?' said Count John.

'A villein who'd stabbed Gisborne.'

'Is Gisborne dead?'

'He may well be, my lord.'

'Then you had good reason to slay his killer.'

'The boy had lost his mind,' said Marian. 'He didn't know what he was doing.'

'He knew enough to stab Gisborne,' the Sheriff retorted.

'I tell you, it's a conspiracy, my lord,' du Bois persisted. 'I demand that Henry Fitzwalter be arrested.'

'My father knew nothing of this,' said Marian.

'Fitzwalter?'

Count John looked searchingly at the old man.

'I will not have my loyalty questioned by *that*...' Fitzwalter pointed at du Bois. 'I demand my right of trial by combat. Let God decide who's the liar here.'

Count John put an arm around Fitzwalter's shoulder and led him into a corner of the hall. He spoke to him in a whisper.

'If I let you fight you'll be slain,' he said. 'Du Bois's one of the finest swordsmen in England. And you have years on him. It'd be madness to take him on. And whatever the outcome it won't save Marian.'

'There is no conspiracy,' Fitzwalter insisted.

'I never thought there was,' said Count John. 'I'm no stranger to cunning and plots. And I know that such deeds are not in your nature.'

'Well, are we to fight or are we not to fight?' cried out du Bois.

Fitzwalter turned.

'If I fight you and win then Marian goes free?'

'How can she?' said the Sheriff. 'Her father may be innocent but she's a proven traitor.'

Sir Brian du Bois gave a ghastly smile.

'My lord Count, I'm prepared to accept these terms,' he said. 'If by some miracle I'm killed in this trial by combat then I have no objection to Marian going free, as well as her father.'

'I will not allow this...' Count John began. 'It is...'

'My lord Count, every knight has a right, under the law, to demand a trial by combat. Fitzwalter called for it first. I agreed. Now *I* demand trial by combat. Such a request can only be denied by Lionheart himself.'

Grasping his injured shoulder de Lisle struggled to his feet.

'But the girl has conspired with Robin Hood,' he said. 'And her arrow wounded me. And I'm Lionheart's representative in this shire. Marian Fitzwalter is one of Robin Hood's followers.'

'She is not one of my followers,' said Robin, as he stepped across the broad stone window ledge and into the room. 'That's a charge that can't be laid.'

'It's Robin Hood,' the Sheriff yelled at the two soldiers by his side. 'Kill him!'

The soldiers dashed forward, drawing their swords as they ran across the hall. They were not halfway to the outlaw before arrows in their chests took them to the ground.

The Sheriff looked to the other windows. John Little, Scarlet and Gilbert had already nocked fresh arrows into their bows and were covering the room, bowstrings drawn.

'My next arrow goes through Count John's throat,' growled Scarlet. 'And my friends here'll kill you other two bastards,' he added looking at the Sheriff and du Bois.

'Now this is treason,' said Count John.

'It certainly is,' said Robin. 'But you leave me with little choice. I'll not stand by and see du Bois murder that old man for my sins.'

'Not murder,' du Bois replied 'trial by combat.'

'Not a fair trial though,' said Robin. 'The old man has years on you and you're a practised warrior.'

'It's the way of these things,' said du Bois.

'Very well, I appoint myself the champion of Henry Fitzwalter,' said Robin. 'You want a trial by combat. I'll fight it on his behalf.'

'That's absurd,' said du Bois. 'You're not even a knight.'

Count John came between them.

'Sir Henry Fitzwalter *is* a knight,' he said, 'and he's at perfect liberty to appoint a champion in a trial by combat.'

'My lord Count!' du Bois protested.

'If I fight du Bois then I fight for Marian as well as her father. I want your pledge that she'll be spared death?' said Robin.

'This is ridiculous!' said the Sheriff. 'She tried to kill me!'

'I cannot spare Marian Fitzwalter,' said Count John. 'The Sheriff is right. She's committed capital crimes. Only a king may pardon those. And I'm not the King of England. Not yet.'

'Exactly,' said the Sheriff, 'the girl must die.'

'But I do have the right to delay the penalty of death.'

Count John turned to the girl.

'Marian Fitzwalter. If this rebel triumphs in a trial by combat against Sir Brian du Bois, I'll give you an hour to get out of my sight. After that you'll be declared wolfshead and put outside the protection of the law. Any man may kill you without consequence. And if you come before me again I'll have you hanged.'

'And does Fitzwalter agree to having this rebel fight for him?' demanded the Sheriff.

The old man looked at Count John, deep in thought. It was several moments before he replied.

'My lord Count,' he said very slowly. 'As a knight and a gentleman I wouldn't ever appoint a champion in this way. But if there's a glimmer of hope for my daughter then I've no choice but to agree. I'm happy to die in combat if that's the will of God. But I'll not stand on principles while Marian is threatened.'

'I shall complain to his grace the King about these matters...' said the Sheriff.

'Be silent!' roared Count John, giving de Lisle a withering look. 'Remember whose presence you are in! I am the overlord of this shire and it's my *pleasure* to settle this dispute in any way I choose.'

'If this is your final word, my lord Count?' said du Bois.

Count John nodded and sat back down in the chair. He turned to Robin Hood. 'And I expect a vow from you, wolfshead? If du Bois kills you in fair combat, I want your word that your men will do no harm here. I want your promise that they'll leave this place as they came, with no more blood being spilt? I'll give them a hour's law.'

Robin turned to his men.

'So be it,' he said to them. 'If I die here today, you're to leave at once. And no more killing.'

His men gave him a grudging look.

'I mean it, Scarlet,' Robin said.

Will Scarlet gave a nod.

'This fight should really take place at a tournament,' said the Sheriff 'so that all might see justice being done.'

'Don't be an idiot, de Lisle. Here and now. These are my terms,' said Count John. He looked across at du Bois. 'In the name of God get on with it...'

Sir Brian du Bois gave a bow and drew his sword. Walking up and down he waved it in front of him to loosen his wrist and get familiar with its weight. Robin Hood took out his own sword and waited patiently by the window. Fitzwalter came across to his daughter and eased her away from the two soldiers, bringing her close to where Count John was sitting.

Du Bois was walking back across the hall, still apparently testing the sword and breathing deeply. Then he suddenly gave a great yell and charged at Robin, swinging the sword in a great level cut towards the outlaw's neck.

Robin took a quick step backwards and brought his own weapon across, sending du Bois' blade up towards the roof, and almost loosening his grip. But before he could counter, du Bois took several paces backwards.

'I see no point in fighting if you intend to run away,' said Robin.

Du Bois stood in the middle of the hall and sneered back at him.

'As a peasant you obviously don't understand how a gentleman fights.'

'No, but I know how a coward flees...'

'I'll cut out your tongue and ram it up your arse for that!'

He came forward again very slowly, his sword waving from side to side, almost inviting Robin to come forward and engage.

But the outlaw remained standing where he was.

'So, you want to force me into battle, wolfshead?' said du Bois. 'You want me to bring the fight to you? Be careful what you wish for.'

Then du Bois took a step backwards and then to one side, the tip of his sword almost touching the ground.

And then he was coming forward, fast. So fast that it was hard to see quite how he covered the distance in so brief a moment of time. In all the many fights he'd been in Robin had never had an adversary move so swiftly.

Du Bois's blade seem to be swirring towards him from a score of different directions at once. First a blow towards his head. Then a thrust towards the gut. Repeated again and again. Then du Bois gripped his sword with both hands, creating a great vertical descent that would have cleaved off Robin's shoulder and sword arm if it had connected.

But even as Robin parried that blow, du Bois's sword was sweeping in towards his face, its steel reflecting the fire and candles and sending slivers of light all around the hall.

There was a loud clash after clash as blows were exchanged and parried, the noise deafening in the speechless quiet around them.

After another parry, Robin swung his blade around and over in a circular motion, sending du Bois's blade flying upwards, forcing his opponent off balance. To save himself du Bois was forced to disengage and pull backwards towards the middle of the hall.

'Not as easy as raping women, is it du Bois?' Robin shouted after him.

'I've not even started with you, wolfshead. I'll make you scream for death before I finish you.'

'Don't gloat over the wolf's corpse until you've hunted it!' said Robin.

He moved forward very slowly, sword raised high, all the time looking not at du Bois's sword but at his face. And he saw something there that was unexpected. He saw *doubt*. It wasn't unfamiliar to Robin. Time and again he'd fought men like du Bois. Time and again they had imagined an easy victory against some villein who couldn't possibly know how to use a sword.

Sir Brian du Bois's face gave a signal to his opponent. The knight was re-calculating how to continue the combat. How to bring down an enemy who was so much better at arms than he had anticipated. It wasn't an unusual procedure for a soldier who had fought and killed so many skilled warriors.

Every moment of every fight was just such a constant re-evaluation. This was not some practice feat of arms. In a fight for life a swordsman who had always been both skilled and lucky knew that his foe had been capable and fortunate too.

Never defeated. Never fought to a standstill. Never brought to death.

And that out there on a battlefield or in single-combat was the man who might be better than you. Or luckier. Or who had God on his side on some bloody day.

As he watched du Bois's face, he saw the doubt vanish and a fresh confidence take its place. Saw the glow in the eyes and the smirk on the lips. Watched as the knight took in a deeper breath. Something he had done before when he had come in with his sudden attack, his sword flailing in all directions.

And this time Robin was ready for him, moving quickly out of the way of that flashing blade as it swirled and cut the air and fire-smoke of the hall.

To du Bois's horror he found the outlaw not in front of him but to one side, Robin Hood's sword coming at his face in a sweeping circular cut.

So great was the danger that du Bois was forced to fall to his knees to avoid the blade, his own weapon scraping the ground in front of him. He glanced up and saw the outlaw's sword halt in its swing. Watched as it rose and came flying down towards his face.

Sheer instinct made du Bois roll across the floor to evade the blow. But in an instant he was back on his feet, his back to the windows, facing the wolfshead and gasping for breath.

And in that second Robin Hood saw another expression on du Bois's face. He vaguely wondered if it had ever been there before in all the knight's distinguished career as a swordsman. So fleeting was the look that Robin thought he might have imagined it. Maybe it was only in the man's eyes that he detected it at all. A brief glimpse into his soul.

A momentary betrayal of fear.

But then it was gone, a look of anger and challenge taking its place, as though du Bois wanted to expunge the shame of that moment.

He came in slowly now, sword not whirling from position to position as before, but held out in challenge. Not wanting to commit. Almost demanding that Robin make the next attack.

The outlaw stepped forward towards du Bois, the tip of his sword reaching towards the other man's weapon, but not quite touching. Forcing du Bois to come closer and closer.

'I'm tired of these games, wolfshead!'

'Sherwood is tired of you, du Bois!'

'Then I'll see you in hell, villein!'

Robin saw the blade coming towards his face, though he never could understand how du Bois was able to make the move with so little preparation.

One moment du Bois's sword was down towards the ground, matching the position of his own. And the next the heavy steel of its blade was dashing towards his eyes as the knight charged forward to give weight to its deadly delivery.

Alarm rather than conscious thought caused Robin to drop to his knees, even as the sword caught the dark locks of his hair.

Du Bois was not finished. He stood almost over Robin, twisting the blade so that it might come down onto the outlaw's head.

But in that second Robin's own sword came upwards, thrust with the power of both hands.

Into the body of Sir Brian du Bois, just above the groin. Up through the gut, gashing the heart, the tip of the blade tearing open the man's shoulder as it found its release from his flesh.

Du Bois's head jerked backwards, his face red with the blood that sprayed the hall in that brief snatch of time before he died. His sword fell on to Robin's shoulder and then clattered to the ground, coming to stillness even as the knight fell close by.

There was a great silence in the hall as the spectators at the fight regarded the corpse. It was as though the moment had been preserved in a tableau at a country fair, the people manikins in some crazed display.

Robin had taken Marian's arm and led her to the window before anyone else recovered from the shock of the battle.

The Sheriff was the first to move, clutching his shoulder and getting up from the bench by the high table.

'Seize him!' he yelled to the two soldiers.

John Little's arrow vibrated as it struck the wood of the table inches from de Lisle's hand. The soldiers, who had been on the point of moving forward, jerked into life by the sudden command, halted. Will Scarlet and Gilbert had pulled back their bowstrings, the deadly arrows pointing at the soldiers' hearts.

'The next one of you bastards who moves is dead!' shouted Scarlet. He aimed his bow away from the soldiers and at Count John. 'You gave your word... *my lord.*'

'And I'll keep it,' said Count John. 'So don't you dare aim your arrow at me. Don't you dare! But the next time you're all before me I won't be so merciful. I promised you an hour's law. I give you that. But the candle is already burning, wolfshead.'

Robin pushed Marian out through the window. And in a moment the outlaws had gone.

'Raise the alarm!' the Sheriff yelled at the soldiers.

'Stay!' countermanded Count John.

He turned to de Lisle. 'I will not have my oath broken by you.'

'They're wolfsheads! No oath made to them is binding.'

'It's binding to me. I have to ride through Sherwood tomorrow. Do you think I want an arrow in my back?'

The Sheriff walked across to him and Fitzwalter.

'Well, there's one here who can pay the price. Sir Henry Fitzwalter, I arrest you on a charge of high treason and...'

'Don't be a bloody fool, de Lisle!' Count John thundered. 'There was a trial by combat. Fitzwalter's champion brought down his accuser. God has declared this man innocent.'

'But my lord Count...'

'That is my final word, de Lisle. Unless of course you want to find yourself fighting in Normandy? This man is loyal and under my personal protection. Do you understand?'

'As my lord wishes...'

Count John looked at the Sheriff with a malignant glare.

'Exactly,' he said. 'As your lord wishes.'

~

The summer was coming to an end and all the fresh green had vanished from the trees of Sherwood. Already the first of the fallen leaves were beginning to hide the broad dusty tracks and narrow winding paths of the forest. A cold wind stirred the woodland canopy, bringing shivers from the east.

'So what do we do now?' asked Much, stirring the fire back into life.

'Prepare for winter, I suppose,' said Stutely. 'They searched Sherwood and didn't find us. We're safe for a while. Time to go to ground like all hunted animals.'

Robin looked across at the girl. In the month that had passed since the killing of du Bois, she had been very quiet. They had scarcely talked at all. He had once tried to raise the subject of her role as the solitary archer of Sherwood. But she had simply turned and walked away. In those first days she had vanished from the Drumble for three days. He had found her at last at the fringes of the trees looking over the fields to the castle at Edwinstowe.

He had put his hand on her shoulder to lead her back into the greenwood, but she had brushed him away. There had been a terrible and haunted expression on her face and tears in those dark brown eyes. They had journeyed home without a word.

'Robin?' John Little looked up from the fireside.

'What?'

'Should we store in food for the winter?'

He nodded.

'And hide out here?' asked Gilbert.

He didn't reply for a long moment.

And then...

'The old men of Sherwood can huddle by their firesides. We've got work to do.'

'By God, Loxley, is there to be no end to it? Do you want us all dead?' demanded Scarlet. 'Is this how it's going to be? One fight after another until we're slain or taken? No rest and no peace?'

'You're a born fighter, Will. Well, I'm giving you something to fight for. I hear that Sir Hubert Malvoisin rides from Nottingham to his castle on Friday. With gold given him by the Templers in Lincoln. Enough gold to see the villagers of Sherwood through the winter. It's my intention to go and rob him, Will. Are you with me?'

'How many men has he got?' asked John Little.

'About fifty.'

'Fifty?' said Scarlet. 'Is that all?'

'It's enough,' said Gilbert.

'Who's with me?' Robin asked.

He looked across at Marian.

She was loading her quiver with arrows.

THE END

Watch out for The Second Chronicle of Robin Hood

Historical Note

So did Robin Hood actually exist? And if so where and when?

In a way it doesn't matter if there was an historical Robin or not. He exists in the minds of billions of people around the world. He is, to employ an over-used phrase, a cultural icon. The outlaw in the forest. A fugitive from injustice. The rebel who fights the wealthy and powerful. Robs from the rich and gives to the poor. In Britain today we even have a "Robin Hood Tax Campaign" which seeks to even up the balance between the haves and the have-nots.

Just say the words "Robin Hood" to virtually anyone in the world and they'll know who you mean. An image of the outlaw will have appeared in their mind. Not bad for someone who - if he lived at all - probably started out as an English (and very localised English) rural bandit!

And go to many parts of Britain and you'll find quite a supply of Robin Hood's graves, wells, caves, larders, and so forth. Yorkshire has a village named after him, Robin Hood's Bay. There's even a Robin Hood International Airport near to Doncaster! And it's not just the outlaw chief. The last resting place of Little John may be seen near to his old home town of Hathersage. Friar Tuck and several of the other merry (or, often, not so merry) men can boast local connections.

Much of the tourism industry in Nottinghamshire depends on Robin Hood. He has a statue outside Nottingham Castle. He's well featured in the Sherwood Forest Visitors' Centre. You can even glimpse men dressed up as him in Sherwood Forest.

Robin Hood is an attractive figure even in our own troublous times, when the wealthy and powerful seem to have scant regard for the struggles of the less fortunate. He is the most potent symbol in our culture of the idea of Right fighting Might. If that sounds very political it is. Can there be any grander political ideal than upsetting the *status quo* and battling for equality?

Alongside the legend of King Arthur, Robin Hood is one of the two essential English myths. Someone we've all grown up with, in novels, television series and numerous films. If there was an actual individual who inspired these yarns he'd probably be amazed at his legacy.

So what do we know about the beginnings of the Robin Hood legend? The answer is precious little. There are a small number of old ballads relating the deeds of the outlaw. Just five of them of reasonable vintage, and a tiny portion of an old play. The oldest extant ballad probably appeared only in the fourteenth-century. There is a mention of the wolfshead in Langland's *Piers Plowman*, probably from around 1377 – the earliest mention of Robin in literature. Troubling for those of us who love the outlaw, the Robin Hood in these ballads is not quite the freedom-fighter of our imagination. He and his men are portrayed as rather less generous and rather more as bloodthirsty villains. Killing and mutilation are their stock-in-trade.

Furthermore, the setting is not usually Sherwood Forest, and the king of the time is named Edward rather than the Richard the Lionheart of so many books and films. The suggestion is that the Edward in question is perhaps Edward II.

Some of the popular characters of the Robin Hood story only get a mention in the later ballads. Maid Marian doesn't make an appearance in the story until the late fifteenth century. She was almost certainly put in for romantic purposes by some wily author or printer who knew his market. He pinched her from French literature in a thieving gesture of which Robin himself would have been proud. I have put Marian in my story because I think she's an essential part of the mythology of Sherwood. In some recent accounts she's been portrayed as a simpering drip. I've tried to do something different with her. Marian is living through some very tough times.

For some years there has been an historical fight over the body of Robin Hood. Should he be in Sherwood Forest during the reign of Richard the Lionheart, sometime in the 1190s? Or elsewhere, perhaps in Barnsdale near to Doncaster, during Edward II's reign in the early 1300s?

Anyone who writes stories of Robin Hood has to make a personal choice. If you've read this far you will see that I have chosen Sherwood in the days of Richard the Lionheart. I have two motivations for picking this period and location. The first is purely sentimental. I grew up with the idea of Robin in Sherwood, fighting the Sheriff of Nottingham and Guy of Gisborne in what was then the wild forest around Edwinstowe. The dominant culture of all those films and television programmes has sunk into my mind so deeply that I can't imagine the outlaws being anywhere else.

And I do believe that there is an argument for Robin existing long before the reign of Edward II, even if a Robert Hood gets a mention in the records of his time. J.C. Holt, in his definitive and quite excellent book *Robin Hood* (read the revised edition of 2011 if you are seeking it out) presents us with a number of outlaws bearing the names or rather nicknames Robinhood, or Robehod, in the 1200s, well before Edward came to the throne. Even a Robert Hod, fugitive, tried at York assizes in 1225. I'll not delve deeper into Professor Holt's quite superb account here. Everyone who loves the legend should read it for themselves. Holt, provably, puts the figure and legend of Robin Hood back through written sources to at least 1261-2.

The argument may be made that people were so familiar with the legend or concept of Robin Hood by that time, that outlaws and highway robbers generally were being branded with his name in the court records. And such myths take a time to grow in the public imagination, decades at least, perhaps a century. Therefore, someone, somewhere, must have been the first Robin Hood. The individual whose name was then adopted by the outlaws that followed, becoming almost a title passed on down the line.

As these ballads began life as oral tales, long before they were written down or the advent of printing, who is to say how they might have been altered? It is quite likely that local versions existed, promoted by a population with a good ear and memory for such ballads. And they were probably updated as they went. The King's name of Edward in the printed versions might well have originally been Richard or John or Henry in the oral ballads. We will never know. And the versions that promote Barnsdale over Sherwood are just the survivors. People living in a very insular fashion in remote parts of England, where very few people strayed far from home, would insert their own local forest. The original ballads could as well have referred to Sherwood as much as anywhere else.

And if the *terminus ante quem* of the Robin Hood who is mentioned in historical documents *is* as early as 1261-2, then it is good common sense to suggest that that individual and the other Robinhoods, Robehods, Hods, and so on, are taking these tribute names from an earlier and factual individual, who might well have been a contemporary of King John.

And talking of John, Prince John is usually portrayed as an outright villain. One of the trio of baddies, with Gisborne and the Sheriff of Nottingham, who are the arch-enemies of Robin Hood. There is no doubt that John (count, in reality, not prince) could be petty, ruthless, autocratic and occasionally vicious. But he has suffered a bad press, particularly given that the histories of his time were written by churchmen who couldn't stand him.

Historically, he was no worse and often much better than many other medieval kings. I've tried to do him some justice. He certainly was, as I have suggested, much fonder of England than his brother Richard the Lionheart, who plundered the country to pay for his foreign ventures. John deserves an historical revision.

My character of Sir Brian du Bois is new. I created him, though he is based on several knights and lords of that time. His standards of behaviour were not exceptional in medieval England. In fact there are still more than a few like him in public life today. His name is suggested by the anti-hero of Sir Walter Scott's *Ivanhoe*, the troubled and far more noble Sir Brian du Bois Guilbert.

Readers who wish to know more about archery and the weapons used in Sherwood Forest are in for a treat if they seek out the quite excellent book *Longbow*, by the actor and historian Robert Hardy. Like Holt's book on Robin Hood this is absolutely essential reading for enthusiasts.

I have taken some liberties with the geography of Sherwood Forest, which was a vast and wild place in the 1190s. Mostly so that I might keep the action moving. Very little of ancient Sherwood remains, though there are traces and all of them worth exploring. There is no secret dingle called Thripper's Drumble, (well there is, but it's a long way from Sherwood – see if you can find out where?) and the home of the Fitzwalters bears no resemblance to any actual castle.

Nor is there a sinister hunting lodge called Castle Malvoisin – a place that will feature much in the next novel.

For this outlaw has not ended his adventures just yet. He's still a mysterious figure that we need to know a lot more about. So there will be a lot more to come in the Second Chronicle of Robin Hood. Watch out for it.

And do I think there was an original Robin Hood, one character who lived and created a legend?

The answer is yes!

John Bainbridge

If you have enjoyed Loxley, then please do leave a review on its page on the site of any online bookseller you might have used, and tell your friends about the book. It would be much appreciated.

More John Bainbridge books are featured on the following pages.

Do keep up to date with the adventures of Robin Hood and our other novels at the following blogs:

www.johnbainbridgewriter.wordpress.com

Our mystery and crime novels can be found at:

www.gaslightcrime.wordpress.com

John Bainbridge also has a country walking blog at:

www.thefreedomtoroam.com

You can contact John Bainbridge at:

johnbainbridgenovels@yahoo.co.uk

By the same author –

THE SHADOW OF WILLIAM QUEST

London in 1853. In the capital of Queen Victoria's empire, the grand houses of the idle rich lie a stone's throw from the stench of poverty, crime and despair. Life for the poor, condemned to exist in vile slums and rookeries, is brutal and short.

A mysterious stranger stalks the night houses and elegant squares where society gentlemen seek their pleasure.

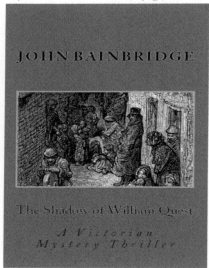

A man with a swordstick, compelled to fight for justice.

Who is the elusive William Quest?

Inspector Anders of Scotland Yard is determined to uncover the truth.

With as many twists and turns as a sinister, gaslit alley, the trail leads through the teeming streets of London to a deadly denouement on the lonely coast of Norfolk.

This exciting Victorian thriller is the first in a series recounting the adventures of William Quest.

In paperback and on most eBooks

A SEASIDE MOURNING

Devonshire, autumn 1873. The peaceful seaside town of Seaborough, half-forgotten on the eastern border of the county, seems an unlikely setting for murder.

When a leading resident dies, the cause of death is uncertain. Troubled Inspector Abbs and eager, young Sergeant Reeve are sent to determine whether the elderly spinster was poisoned.

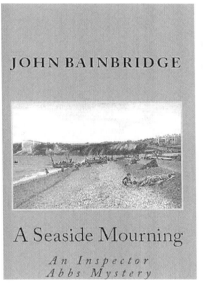

JOHN BAINBRIDGE

A Seaside Mourning

An Inspector
Abbs Mystery

Behind the Nottingham lace curtains and over the bone china tea cups, trouble has been brewing.

Seaborough is changing, new houses are going up and some prominent inhabitants are ambitious for the town to become a popular resort.

When a second death follows, the detectives need to work fast to unravel the truth. Behind the elaborate rituals, is anyone truly mourning?

As the leaves fall and secrets are laid bare, unmasking a murderer may have terrible consequences...

Now in paperback and on most eBooks

A CHRISTMAS MALICE

Inspector Abbs is spending Christmas with his sister in a lonely village on the edge of the Norfolk Fens. He is hoping for a quiet week while he thinks through a decision about his future.

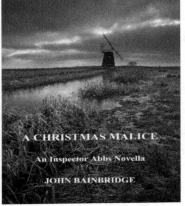

However all is not well in Aylmer.

Someone has been playing malicious tricks on the inhabitants. With time on his hands and concerned for his sister, Abbs feels compelled to investigate...

This complete tale is a novella of around 33,000 words.

The events take place one month after the conclusion of Inspector Abbs's first case, *A Seaside Mourning*.

Now in paperback and on most eBooks

BALMORAL KILL

In 1936 the British royal family were rocked by their greatest scandal as Edward VIII gave up the throne in order to marry an American divorcee.

John Bainbridge

Many ordinary people regretted the loss of their popular king. In the dark corridors of power, not everyone was sorry...

A year later the Abdication Crisis seems forgotten and all eyes are on the Coronation that summer. In August the new King George VI will retreat to Balmoral, his remote holiday home in the Highlands of Scotland. As the shadow of war falls across Europe, a sinister conspiracy lies deep within the British establishment.

A man lies dead in a woodland glade. An unfortunate accident or has the first shot been fired in a secret war?

Sean Miller is recalled home to take on his deadliest challenge – but where do his loyalties really lie? In a frantic chase, from the slums and sinister alleys of London to the lonely glens of the Scottish Highlands, Miller must hunt and bring down his most dangerous opponent.

His mission - to foil the final shot that will plunge Europe into the abyss of a new Dark Age.

Now available in paperback and on most eBooks

Non-Fiction by John Bainbridge

THE COMPLEAT TRESPASSER

In 1932, five ramblers in England were imprisoned for daring to walk in their own countryside. The Mass Trespass on to Kinder Scout, which led to their arrests, has since become an iconic

symbol of the campaign for the freedom to roam in the British countryside.

The Compleat Trespasser – Journeys Into The Heart Of Forbidden Britain looks at just why the British were - and still are – denied responsible access to much of their own land. This ground-breaking book examines how events through history led to the countryside being the preserve of the few rather than the many.

It examines the landscapes to which access is still denied, from stretches of moorland and downland to many of our beautiful forests and woodlands. It poses the question: should we walk and trespass through these areas regardless of restrictions?

An inveterate trespasser, John Bainbridge gives an account of some of his own journeys into Britain's forbidden lands, as he walks in the steps of poachers, literary figures and pioneer ramblers. The book concludes with a helpful chapter of "Notes for Prospective Trespassers", giving a practical feel to this handbook on the art of trespass.

Now in paperback and on most eBooks

31601537R00162

Printed in Great Britain
by Amazon